Grifters & Gingerbread

~ Moorehaven Mysteries: Book 3 ~

MORGAN C. TALBOT

Grifters & Gingerbread

Red Adept Publishing, LLC

104 Bugenfield Court

Garner, NC 27529

https://RedAdeptPublishing.com/

---

1.   http://StreetlightGraphics.com

This book is dedicated to Dr. Marilyn Glaim, who taught some of my favorite English classes at college. She let me write an eight-page *Uncle Tom's Cabin* fanfic instead of a four-page essay, and she listened sympathetically when I lost a job offer because I showed my prospective boss my poetry. (Know your audience, guys.)

1

"Raymond is my middle name, and it suits me down to the ground. And no, I'm not tellin' you what the *A* stands for."
A. Raymond Moore, 1936

"RUFUS IS DEAD, AND you killed him in cold blood, Tyleen. Admit it!" I thrust an accusing finger across the table.

My fiftyish neighbor flinched, her wide blue eyes darting beneath her pale Gay Nineties wig. "I did no such thing!" she protested, clutching at her starched lace collar.

"Hey, I thought lying wasn't allowed." Jordan Harper, my BFF, lowered her penciled eyebrows in obvious confusion. Unlike the rest of us, she'd procured a genuine antique outfit for the evening's festivities, a navy-blue tulip bell walking skirt and a white puffed-sleeve blouse with generous front pleats and braided trim. And she looked absolutely dazzling in it. But she also had a point: Tyleen had been very specific about the game's rules regarding official accusations of guilt. "And shouldn't you use her character name?"

"Right. Sorry. Joy Lesse, I think you killed Rufus," I told Tyleen.

"I'm not lying, you guys," Tyleen insisted. Her gaze darted to her sandy-haired son, Sebastian, who nodded encouragingly, then all around the large table that filled the dining room. Outside the sliding glass door behind her, I could barely see her peaches-and-cream Victorian house through the fog.

"But the clue," my sister, Trudie, pressed. She reread her own clue card, showed it to her boyfriend, Gabe, then gestured at mine with it. We'd each been issued cards specific to our characters, and they listed what we could share during the game's three rounds and what we should do our best to keep secret unless specifically asked. "My esteemed sister in the lovely plum gown—she *has* got the clue right, hasn't she? Tyleen's character, Joy Lesse, really did know who the 'unknown recipient' of Rufus's flower bouquet was."

Tyleen frowned and examined her own card. "Yes, my character did know who got flowers from the man she loved, but..."

Ruslan, the only mystery-writer guest currently staying at my bed-and-breakfast, chimed in as well. "Ah, yes, that must be because Joy doesn't get blinded by cobra venom until evening—hours after teatime—because the last thing she remembered before the cobra attacked was the loon calling at dusk."

Ruslan Penley was eighty years old if he was a day, of middling height and weight, with a white halo of hair around his balding head. The prolific Turkish-American writer hadn't brought any costume pieces for his stay at Moorehaven, since Tyleen hadn't persuaded us all to participate in beta testing her murder-mystery game until two o'clock that afternoon, but he'd been thrilled to join in. He'd turned his anorak inside out and tucked a frilly white doily into his shirt collar, effecting a poor-man's cravat. A minute's work had combined an eyeglass cleaning cloth with a shoestring to create a dashing eyepatch for his character, a crusty sea captain with a checkered past.

"Did I get that right, Wren?" His face creased with happiness as he offered his usual broad smile to one of my last-minute guests, Wren Lundin.

"Er, yes, I think that's right." Wren adjusted a large hand-crocheted doily she'd good-naturedly tied with a wide white ribbon around her shoulder-length blond hair to approximate an evening cap. She checked her clue card. "Yes, I found Joy blinded at dusk. Or rather, Vienna Street found her. She had just received the bouquet from Rufus and was heading home to put them in a vase. 'Vienna Street.' *Tsk.*

"Tyleen, did you ask Geneva Laine if you could parody her name for a character in this game? I'm not sure she'd approve of you suggesting she's gone blind."

Morton Roark, Wren's long-time neighbor, friend, and business associate, chuckled appreciatively. "Geneva wouldn't mind at all. Not if this game of yours brings more good publicity to Seacrest." He gazed in a friendly fashion at Tyleen. "We all know Geneva would commit actual murder if it served this town."

Everyone chuckled, and I joined in. Despite Mort's words, I couldn't actually picture the grand old dame of Seacrest, with her constant poise and savvy business sense, murdering anyone. Her disapproving looks were pretty sharp, but she was somewhat north of ninety.

"This is way more fun than Clue. And I love Clue," Sebastian said. "Being a pet psychic doesn't have any game-playing perks, but I love sneaking through the secret passageways!"

My boyfriend, Lake, brushed my hand with his. "We still need to figure out who killed Rufus, though. The clues seem pretty straightforward. Joy saw Rufus giving a bouquet to Vienna, so she killed Rufus for betraying her. Right? I mean, are we missing something?"

I drank in the sight of him. He was all dolled up for Tyleen's historical murder dinner with his gelled black hair plumped into Byronian curls, a high-collared jacket and fancy cravat courtesy of Tru's dab sewing hand, and a high forehead, a straight nose, and full lips courtesy of Mother Nature. Lake was intelligent, funny, and practical, but he'd also been blessed with looks that would rival the most sought-after aristocratic French poets. *Even Tom Hiddleston wishes he were Lake Ivens. I am a lucky woman.*

I nodded at him and turned to Tyleen. "So we really did get the killer wrong? It's really not Joy Lesse?"

Tyleen pursed her thin bright-red lips. "Do you really think I'd go to all the trouble of making a murder-mystery game based on some of Seacrest's actual residents, past and present, then arrange it so the killer is a really obvious parody of Felicity Moore herself? God forbid! I'm trying to *promote* the town, not get myself run out of it on a rail."

Jordan chuckled. "Aren't we all?"

Beside Tyleen, Sebastian fingered a buttonhole in his black frock. "Then, Mom, we need to make sure your clues actually connect. That's what this whole dinner is for, isn't it? You're beta testing your game."

Tyleen sat up straight, and her wig wobbled. "Well, and the food, of course. But yes, I am."

Great-Uncle Hilt swept into the dining room from the kitchen, looking dapper in his black tails and bowtie. My assistant, Chloe, followed in his wake, wearing a black dress with a white apron and carrying a large tray.

"We all knew this dinner wasn't about your recipes, Tyleen," Hilt said, his gravelly voice warm. "You're the best cook in the county, if not the state." He started picking up our plates and stacking them on Chloe's tray.

Chloe, who had been twenty for almost a month, nodded at me with a half grin. "The dessert we've been plating in the kitchen is definitely top-notch. I should know—I ate two slices." Tyleen shot my goth-ish assistant a suspicious side-eye, but Chloe shrugged it off with the ease of youth. "What? You gave us two extra loaves of gingerbread, Tyleen. And didn't, like, rich people have food tasters back then anyway? Just doing my part for historical accuracy."

"You're really not," Lake teased.

"Whatever. The gingerbread is to die for." Chloe dropped the morbid compliment with the ease of a longtime Seacrestan. "Rufus got murdered, so his ghost is already eating a slice. He says it was totally worth it."

Tyleen flushed prettily.

Gabe handed his plate to Hilt, who put it on the stack. "Sounds like the real mystery tonight isn't who killed Rufus but where Tyleen's clues went offtrack." He leaned his elbows on the edge of the table and grinned around at us. "If anyone can solve it, it's us."

"This is Moorehaven, home of world-famous mystery author A. Raymond Moore," Mort added.

Tru giggled. "You knew what you were doing when you asked to test your dinner here, didn't you, Tyleen?"

"She certainly did." Wren's wry tone suggested she had spotted Tyleen's tactic but didn't disapprove.

Tyleen had been working on her game for months, and she'd asked me for permission to test it at Moorehaven nearly as soon as she started. I readily agreed, but she had trouble getting twelve guests to participate. Or rather, she had trouble getting *only* twelve guests to participate. Everyone and their spouse, brother, neighbor, long-lost uncle, and dog wanted in on a free meal in one of the most exclusive B-and-Bs on the Oregon Coast, especially since it formed the cultural heart of Seacrest. Tyleen also had her sights set on a solid marketing plan. She'd asked the other members of our cozy social group, Glaze & Gossip—Jordan and me included—for ideas to lure in a couple of Seacrest's wealthiest and most influential members.

Enter Naoma, editor of Seacrest's weekly newspaper, social climber, and breezy friend to all. "I know just the people you need, Tyleen," she'd said, and she'd delivered: Wren Lundin owned a nursery empire, supplying everything from fall bulbs to sod to entire orchards for customers up and down the coast. Nearly every speck of green on Moorehaven's property had come from one of her top-notch nurseries. And Morton Roark was a powerhouse of a real estate developer, specializing in building a full range of summer homes and rental properties along the entire length of the Oregon Coast. He often said that climate change was good for his business. "So why fight it when you can make money off it?" With their support and backing, Tyleen's project had a much better chance of becoming a reality.

Provided the game actually worked, that was. Knowing what an airhead Tyleen could be, I hoped our plot hole would be small and easily filled in.

"All right, brass tacks, it is," Mort said. He rubbed his hands together. "Who's the real killer?"

"No," I called, "don't give it away. Let's work through the clues over dessert." I waved a hand at Chloe and Hilt as they departed with the supper plates. "See if we can't figure out who really dunnit."

A minute later, Chloe returned, bearing ten plates of thickly sliced gingerbread topped with whipped cream and a sweet drizzle sauce on her platter. She handed them out, and I immediately freed a giant bite of gingerbread with my fork and lifted the moist morsel to my mouth. *Mmm, sweet heaven.*

"So I decided to use Seacrest as the location for my mystery," Tyleen was saying. "It's common knowledge that Seacrest was founded by three great families who built three great houses. And not to discount the contributions of the other two, but Seacrest has been known around the world as Raymond Moore's hometown for decades. I do live just across the fence, so it seemed like the easiest choice to use his great-aunt and the founder of Moorehaven, Felicity Moore, as inspiration for the central character.

"At first, I was only going to base my characters on historical ones, but then I realized that Seacrest had only a handful of residents in the 1890s, and some of them weren't complex enough to borrow from. Besides, mystery writers—like Ruslan here—make characters up all the time." She smiled winningly at the octogenarian author.

"So I decided to do the same thing. I borrowed from a few historical characters and made up the rest."

Tru giggled. "First, you say Geneva Laine is blind. Now, you're calling her historical?"

Tyleen gave her a moue of mock exasperation.

Ruslan hesitantly wagged a finger in the air, as if asking for permission to speak. "I can guess that Vienna Street is based on Geneva Laine and that Joy Lesse is based on Felicity Moore. Were any of the other characters based on real people?"

Tyleen nodded at Gabe. "Only Rubicon Planktown, the wealthy recluse."

Gabe sat up straighter and grasped his lapels proudly. "That's Mr. Planktown to you."

Wren made a small noise of amusement. "Where do you get these quirky fictional names from, Tyleen?"

Tyleen shot an uncertain glance at Ruslan, and he gave her a conspiratorial wink. To Wren, she said, "I use a secret method that I like to call 'thesaurus and Google.' Rubicon Planktown is based on Tiberius Woodville. He built that haunted house up toward the hills. Though I expect it wasn't haunted at the time, since no one had died in it yet."

Lake set his fork down and leaned back. "With all these historical characters you used, Tyleen, I'm getting the feeling that maybe the reason we picked the wrong killer is because we missed a historical detail."

I glanced at my boyfriend with admiration. I had simply been assuming that Tyleen had made a mistake and given the wrong clues to the wrong characters. But she nodded and looked down as if embarrassed.

"I wanted to give players that old-timey feel, so I asked Wallis for some ideas on clues, and she told me all about the Victorian language of flowers. I thought it was perfect!" She leaned on the table with her elbows. "Back then, people could send flowers to each other as messages. It was basically Victorian Twitter. Different flowers meant different things, and even the colors of the flowers mattered. They could be combined into bouquets that said many things at once. And I thought, how perfect would this be for my game?" Her shoulders slumped. "I've only just now realized that a florist like Wallis is the only person who would catch that clue nowadays."

Mort frowned and tapped his fingers on the tabletop. "So that bouquet Rufus sent to Vienna... that wasn't just flowers of admiration. He was sending her a message. Yeah, that clue makes all the difference."

Chloe, empty tray in hand, paused before leaving the dining room. "Wait, Joy saw that bouquet before she got blinded by the venom. She must have known what it said too."

Tyleen pointed at her. "Exactly."

"Aha," I said. "Joy didn't kill Rufus. The message in the flowers, that he chose Joy over Vienna, didn't make her angry. Which means it must have made Vienna angry, since they were rivals for his affections. Vienna's the real killer, right, Tyleen?"

Tyleen smiled. "Well done, Pippa. I need to figure out how to replace that clue so it's not quite so obscure. Once I do that, I'd be happy to make dinner for a new batch of guests at Moorehaven."

Everyone groaned in disappointment. "We can't come back and play the same characters?" Jordan wheedled teasingly.

"But, Tyleen, you make the best food," Gabe added. "No offense, Pippa."

I laughed. "None taken."

Mort polished off his last bite. "Mighty fine vittles, indeed."

Tyleen flushed, pleased.

Sebastian wore a small proud smile as he looked at his mother. "In case some of you didn't know, you can get all you can eat of her cooking out at the Fork and Dagger. Best diner on the coast. Two of those Food Network diner shows have shot episodes there."

Oohs and *aahs* went around the table, and Wren nodded, clearly impressed.

Everyone had finished their dessert, so I put my hands on the table and stood. "Moorehaven's charter only allows mystery authors to book rooms, but it doesn't say anything about guided tours during special events. And as often as some of you have been here, you haven't heard half of Moorehaven's secrets yet. Would anyone be interested in taking a closer look at this fine Victorian mansion? Since we're all in costume, it seems like a lovely way to finish off our evening. Who would like to join me?"

Several of my dinner companions voiced interest, so I said, "Let's meet at the base of the stairs in ten minutes. Feel free to explore the first floor until then, and don't forget to check out the Raymond Moore Memorial Library."

My guests all excused themselves, and Chloe and Hilt returned with large platters to collect the dessert dishes. As I gathered plates and cutlery, my neighbor slipped something out of her pocket, but she held on to it as Trudie hurried to her side.

"I tried it, Tyleen. The top-down cleaning method! It worked so well on the rental's kitchen, like a professional maid service has been in there. And those glam gloves you gave me to wear really made the difference. I felt like a movie star."

Tyleen nodded encouragingly. "Good for you, Trudie."

My little sister gushed, "And I'm trying to remember all the sensory checks you've taught me for cleaning things like windows, counters, and dishes. Does it look clean? Does it feel sticky or gritty? Does it smell dirty? Is something rattling or squeaking inside? And, um, does it taste clean?"

Tyleen put a hand on Tru's arm. "You know what? Let's just skip that last one. If you have reason to think it won't taste clean, just wash it again, okay?"

Trudie nodded enthusiastically. "Good idea. Thank you so much for all these guidelines. Our startup vacation-rental cleaning service is really helping me get out and about while still giving me enough time to work on my art. I'm really hopeful that Gabe and I will get better feedback from the owners this time."

Tyleen gave her arm a squeeze. "I hope so too." As my sister moved off, Tyleen added under her breath, "Hard to get any worse."

"I hope you have ethical plans for that recipe I lent you," I murmured to her. "The mini quiche one. It's a Felicity Moore original."

"Don't worry, Pippa. I promise you, no one will say a bad word about it. Not one. It'll be such a hit."

"I wish you'd tell me what you're going to use it for, but I trust you." *Mostly.*

Tyleen smiled angelically. "Your trust in me will never be misplaced." She let go of whatever she was holding, and as it softly plopped onto the floor, I heard the pitter-patter of little feet. My two cats, Rex and Svetlana, were clearly hoping for something tasty.

I shifted around the table to pick up the plates on that side and spotted pure-white Svetlana and gray-tabby Rex lolling lethargically next to her shoes, rubbing their cheeks against what looked like a fabric mouse. I squinted. "Tyleen, is that mouse filled with catnip?"

Her eyes, far too wide to be innocent, met mine. "What mouse? I don't see any mouse."

She tried unsuccessfully to nudge the toy under the table with her foot, but the cats were wriggling all over it.

I handed Hilt another plate. "Tyleen."

She gave me a mischievous pixie grin. "Merry Christmas?"

I couldn't help but chuckle. "Christmas isn't until next week."

Tyleen slyly shrugged one shoulder. "True, but the cats don't know that."

Behind her, Sebastian couldn't muffle his chuckles anymore. I turned to him with a mock-accusing look. "Was this your idea, Sebastian?"

He held out his wrists, ready to be handcuffed for his crime. "I confess everything. Shall I serve my sentence in the kitchen, cleaning up?"

Tyleen pushed his arms down. "No, I'll serve it for you. You go on the tour." To me, she added, "This boy. Always getting me in so much trouble."

"Hey, I'm not the one in our household who knows how to infuse certain *herbs* into certain foods like brownies," Sebastian protested.

From across the room, Tru perked up. "Hey, Tyleen, when can I come over for some snacks, some more personal instruction, and some snacks?"

Nearly everyone giggled but not my most distinguished guests. I pressed my lips together to keep from making my usual exasperated face at Trudie's social goofiness.

I made my way around the entire table and ended up next to Trudie and Gabe, who had slipped into a quiet conversation, holding each other's hands.

"I want what you want," Gabe murmured. "You say you want a white picket fence. Well, I can build it for you."

Trudie squeezed his hands and replied just as quietly, "Just as soon as we have a house to build it around. We'll be so happy." She gave him a kiss and excused herself to the ladies' room, but once she was out of his sight, she leaned against the hallway and took a deep, shaky breath. I knew that pose well. Tru had a habit of saying whatever she thought others wanted to hear, even at her own expense, but it took a lot out of her. Clearly, there was some kind of trouble in my sister's romantic seaside paradise.

I began to follow Tru down the hallway, but Jordan stopped me with a friendly hand on my arm. "I've got this," she said. "You have a tour to give." Without waiting for my reply, she headed after my sister.

Gratitude warmed my chest. Jordan was like the second sister I'd never had—the cool, competent, sassy sister I wished I could be for Tru.

I gently herded everyone else toward the base of the stairs, catching snippets of their conversation. Sebastian and Lake discussed the virtues of Christmas carols barked by dogs, while Mort pointed at a small scar on his nose and told Ruslan to avoid interacting with trust-fund babies who'd just graduated from Harvard and taken up hard drinking. Wren shot Gabe a glance out of the corner of her eye and offered him a friendly smile but declined to speak to him. I wondered whether she was thrown off by the scar visible through his short hair or by the sexy mermaid tattoo on his arm. Or perhaps she was simply tired after a long day.

With everyone at the base of the stairs, I made my way to the lowest step. Svetlana trailed after me with a languid strut, but Rex was too far gone in catnip heaven to abandon Tyleen's early Christmas present. I smiled in anticipation of showing off my favorite building and spilling just a few of its delightful secrets.

Lake picked up on my eagerness and gave me a lascivious wink.

I raised my chin, pretending to ignore him. "Moorehaven was built in 1891, as one of the founding trio of mansions that literally put Seacrest on the map. Since then, it has seen generations of Moores and mystery authors walk its halls." I lovingly rested a hand on the gleaming wooden banister. "Every room, every wall, every window in Moorehaven has a hundred stories to tell you, if you listen. Some of them will make you laugh, many will chill you to the bone, and a precious few will move you to tears.

"Now then, ladies and gentlemen, if you'll follow me, let's explore the house that Felicity Moore built."

2

"Which room do I sleep in? Well, if I have company for the evening, I like to give her a tour and let her choose. Otherwise, it's whichever bed is closest to my glass of scotch."

Raymond Moore, 1947

I LED THE WAY UP THE staircase and gestured toward the foyer. "Felicity Moore personally selected most of the I for Moorehaven, and we are privileged to still have much of it with us today, including such masterpieces as the chandelier in the foyer, which contains one hundred eight glass panes painted to resemble peacock feathers in the art nouveau style."

Last in the line behind me, Mort asked, "How long did it take her to build this place?"

I reached the top of the stairs and hung a right toward the front of the house. "The main structure was begun and finished in 1891, but like any great lady, Felicity wanted just the right feel to the place. It took her another few years to finish decorating every room exactly the way she wanted it."

Interested murmurs reached my ears as my guests took in the view from the upper level of the open foyer.

"Down here on the left, we have the Silver Room. No relation to the Silver River two blocks away, it was named after Raymond Moore's seventh book, *The Silver Serpent*. All of Moorehaven's rooms are named after various books written by Raymond Moore. Felicity Moore's own room is directly above this one. We call hers the

Diamond Room." I opened the door to the empty guest room that occupied the middle floor of the southwest turret, just above Hilt's bedroom, and we all filed inside.

"Oh, this is lovely," Wren blurted in an admiring tone laced with surprise.

I tried not to begrudge the tone in her voice. Each Moorehaven room was precious to me, and I spent a dedicated portion of my free time maintaining and updating each room's unique looks so that my guests could find rooms with the best atmosphere for their writing.

Svetlana eased past my ankle and into the room, gauging who would give her the most attention, while I stood near the door and enjoyed the sight of everyone soaking up the room's ambiance. The bed's metal head- and footboards gleamed in the foggy light, their rails like burnished pillars. Over the years, I had gathered a decent collection of small silver hand mirrors, and they hung on the wall in an artistic arrangement, adding more light and size to the room. Opposite them in the octagonal room, next to the rightmost of the three windows, hung a much larger silver-framed mirror. A small silver chandelier with flame-shaped bulbs drew the eye to the center of the ceiling and bestowed a classy antique ambience.

A small wooden desk and a chair upholstered in pale gray sat under the center window, and Svetlana hopped into the chair, accepting some love from Gabe. To my left, a small chest of drawers sat topped with a collection of silver picture frames I had found at secondhand stores. Dark-gray carpet helped to set off the two-tone silver-stripe wallpaper, and just to the right of the door, I had artfully hung a variety of silver necklaces that held everything from brooches to lockets to clunky silver flowers inset with bright petal-shaped stones. The variety of gleaming throw pillows that covered half the bed made it look like a floating cloud.

"The Silver Room is requested the most by historical-mystery writers," I said. "They tell me that this pale backdrop helps them see through the mists of time more clearly."

Lake chuckled and pointed. "Most days, they can get that by looking out the window."

Gabe abandoned Svetlana, who glowered after him, and fingered a necklace on the wall, a heavy silver pendant with a swirl of inlaid deep-red stones that formed a rose. "Do you know any stories about this piece? Trudie likes fractals."

I recalled what I knew about the necklace. "If I remember right, that actually belonged to Felicity herself. It's from the art nouveau period, which she seemed to prefer. I haven't found any pictures of her wearing it, but I believe it was found in one of her jewelry box-es after she passed. Raymond Moore simply left those things in stor-age, but Hilt suggested that I spread her personality around the place when I started redecorating the rooms."

Wren and Sebastian had gathered at the chest of drawers and were studying the pictures on top. She looked up from a matching pair of frames she was holding, showing a prim maid in 1920s attire opposite a young boy and a shaggy dog that was taller than he was—Felicity's maid, Tilly, and Raymond Moore before he moved out west. "Well, you've done an absolutely fantastic job, Pippa. This room is a delight, and I'd love to see the rest of them. Except for the room Mr. Penley is staying in, of course."

"Then follow me, please, and we'll do just that."

As we filed out, Wren stayed behind and touched Sebastian on the shoulder. "I wonder if I might call you later to make an appoint-ment," she murmured. "Do you make house calls?"

I led my group around the rest of the second floor, showcasing the Jade Room, the Cobalt Suite, and the Cardinal Room. We paused for drinks in the second-floor sunroom, with some sitting on the padded barstools at the back of the room to chat, while others clustered at the large windows facing the sea. It wasn't visible through the fog, but in quiet moments, we could hear its faint crash against the thirty-foot cliff across the street.

Once finished, we headed for the stairs to the third floor. "Felicity really built this many rooms originally, huh? No add-ons later?" Gabe asked.

"That's right."

"Did she plan for a large family back then?" Wren asked. "She never married, did she?"

"She didn't, no."

Mort chuckled and interjected, "Good thing Raymond came along, then. Every castle needs its king."

For the sake of my other guests, I pretended I hadn't heard his outdated comment. "Her life before Seacrest is mostly a mystery, but once she moved out here, she dedicated her life to this town and its future. She never spoke about her past, preferring to focus on the present."

We left Ruslan's room, the Emerald Room, unexplored, but I took my guests—with Svetlana companionably at our heels—on a tour of the meditative Amber Room and the soothing Lilac Room before ending with Felicity's own bedroom, which occupied the top of Moorehaven's front turret. "Welcome to the Diamond Room."

"Do you think there are secrets in here about Felicity?" Sebastian asked.

I chuckled. "No doubt there are, but it's hard to know what to look for when you don't have enough of the story." I'd pored over her letters often enough up in the gallery, hoping to uncover new tidbits, but all I ever ended up with were new and unprovable theories.

"What are these grates? I meant to ask earlier. Heating?" Mort asked, indicating a large metal facing of curving, lacquered metal that covered a large square hole in the wall just above the floorboard.

Svetlana approached it, sniffing inquisitively.

"It's a laundry chute, actually. Each room has a chute that deposits linens directly in the basement's laundry room. I still have to carry the clean linens back upstairs myself, but it's pretty handy to be able to toss them in a chute and keep working."

Mort frowned thoughtfully. "Seems like a lot of work for a single lady to go to. Did Ms. Moore run this place as a boarding house before Raymond moved west? Or anything else?" His expression shifted, hinting at steamier options.

He wasn't the first to wonder why Felicity Moore had such a full-service mansion, and I wasn't offended. "Not that we've discovered, no."

"Ha, but would you tell us if you did?" Mort's chuckle was full of insinuation.

Wren's sharp glance made me feel better—I wasn't imagining his smarmy tone.

"Who can say?" I said lightly. "Reputation is so important these days, isn't it? One little slip, and everyone knows everything."

Sebastian and Gabe glanced from me to Mort, clearly uncertain whether I was calling him out. Lake pressed his lips together, trying not to smile, because he knew that I was. But I let Mort off the hook after holding his gaze just a second too long—he was my guest, after all. "I imagine Felicity had the same difficulties back then—small towns are small towns, right?"

Mort studied me for a second as if trying to decide whether my opinion actually mattered. "Sure are. Nothing really changes around here."

"Even if it should," Wren added with a smile.

"And on that note, our tour concludes. Thank you for exploring Moorehaven with me. I hope you enjoyed yourselves this evening." Lake took my hand as I followed everyone else downstairs, and I squeezed his.

"Pretty cool when other people like what you like, isn't it?" he murmured.

"Makes me feel like I have impeccable taste," I replied.

Svetlana meowed enthusiastically, as if confirming my evaluation.

"Nice to see even people like Mort can appreciate Felicity's mystery," he continued in the same low tone.

I nodded.

"You know," he continued, "the more I get to know you ladies, the more I think you have in common."

Surprised and flattered, I glanced up into his sea-blue eyes. "Felicity and me? Really? Like what?"

A smile peeked out from the corner of his mouth. "No one really knows what either of you is up to."

I tucked my arm through his and let him properly escort me downstairs. "Just the way I like it."

3

"I love newspapers. Some of my best novel ideas have come from reading the advice columns. My publisher cuts Dear Abby a royalty check every month."

Raymond Moore, 1958

AT BREAKFAST THE NEXT morning, I forwent my usual character quiz for Ruslan, opting for a chat over our bacon egg cups and mini gingerbread scones with cherry-citrus glaze.

"Why don't you tell Chloe about your plot, Ruslan? Hilt and I know your style from your visits of Christmases past, but this is Chloe's first Christmas at Moorehaven."

Ruslan reluctantly set down the mini scone he was about to inhale whole. "Oh, ah, yes. Well. This one's an international thriller, with a merry band of ne'er-do-wells, some of whom have never met, gathering to hunt down a master assassin—or at least, that's what they claim."

Chloe stabbed a bacon egg cup and grinned at Ruslan. "Sounds cool. Where do they start?"

"In England, where I was born. And they chase the killer across all of Europe then end up in Turkey, where my father was born."

Chloe glanced uncertainly between Hilt and me. "I mean, if I wrote a book about chasing a killer from my birthplace to my dad's, it would stretch about what? Forty miles? Not exactly international. Dude, Ruslan. That's a cool idea. So, how many people are chasing your killer?"

Ruslan ran a big hand over his smooth-shaven chin. "I think I'm up to seven, by the end. No, I tell a lie. Nine. The victim's daughter, her handsome but mysterious neighbor, and a pair of local fences get together when the retired lady who runs the local smoke shop finds the body and tells them what she saw. She has a past of her own and a stake in catching the killer because she has a connection to the victim that even his daughter doesn't know. So off they go, and in various countries along the way, they pick up a bounty hunter, his fake apprentice, and a pair of sisters whose antique-collecting father has designs on a vital clue the killer left behind."

Chloe's fork paused halfway to her mouth. "Dude. You've got to finish that so I can read it. What's your writing style like?"

Ruslan shifted and delicately lifted another glazed scone from the serving plate. "Well, you've heard of the Bourne series?" When Chloe nodded eagerly, he added, "It's not like that in the slightest."

"More like *Murder on the Orient Express* meets *Mission: Impossible*," I suggested. "It's not the crossover you expect, but it's the crossover you deserve."

Chloe hummed appreciatively around her bite of food.

Knowing Ruslan's habit of using his own dearly departed family members to inspire his characters, I asked him, "Who are you basing these characters on?"

The author's warm brown eyes softened. "Well, I have a fine collection of family folks for this book, some new and some as familiar as a comfortable pair of well-worn gloves. Farina, the victim's daughter, is based on my daughter, Susan. She died in a skiing accident when she was twenty-eight. She was quite the firebrand, my Susan. Easily able to carry the whole book by herself if need be. I've used her as inspiration in every single one of my novels. And I've decided, at long last, to use my uncle Talha for Gregor, the bounty hunter. I've never used Talha before. He was a complicated man, and his story was left unfinished with his death. I suppose I never felt I was worthy of trying to complete it before. But it seems like the right time."

"How did he die?" I asked gently.

"In the Blitz, with the rest of my family." Ruslan's tone was matter-of-fact. "It was he who smuggled me to America, to live with his wife's half sister and her husband. How does one repay a giant of a man to whom one owes one's entire life past the age of six? I could never find a role large enough for him. But now I'm giving him—through Gregor—the impossible task of catching a killer with seemingly endless resources and a biker gang of murderous minions. When I figure out how he catches the sly Sylvester in the end, I'll know how to thank my uncle for saving me."

My heart melted at Ruslan's soft expression, and my eyes found Hilt's. I knew about being saved by a beloved uncle. He acknowledged my smile with a simple nod.

"But you have some family to celebrate with, right?" Chloe asked.

"Not in the traditional sense," Ruslan replied. His fork stilled. "More than a hundred members of my extended family, across three countries, have passed away in the past century. My father escaped the Assyrian genocide as a child, in the midst of WWI. He settled in London and started a family—me, my sisters—then the Blitz came. My children, my cousins—the world has taken them home, leaving me to soldier on alone." His smile was broad, and his too-large hand covered his heart. "I carry my family here, my dear. My parents, aunts and uncles, my siblings, my dear wife, and even my children have all gone on ahead. But they remain here with me, at their best and most beloved, and I remember them by writing them into my tales."

Chloe hesitated, obviously overwhelmed by his loss. She glanced at me, and I opened my mouth to reassure her that Ruslan was content with his memories of his family.

Hilt spoke first. "'They are the timeless, lost in time.' That's what Moore says 'bout the departed."

Ruslan's face creased with a smile of recognition. "Yes." He nodded at Hilt. "Yes, that's it exactly."

Chloe raised her hand like a child in school. "Sorry, young whippersnapper not following."

Hilt cleared his throat. "When someone dies, time has no more hold on them. They become timeless. That's why we remember the dead as they were in life."

"But how are they lost in time, then?" Chloe asked.

Ruslan fielded that one. "Time is memory. Those who have passed are free to roam the halls of our memories—now in this doorway, now at that window—and we relive our moments with them as they come to us, like autumn leaves on the wind."

"Sudden and colorful, here and gone." A memory of my college roommate flashed before my eyes—laughing as she chased me with a hose across the yard of the house we shared with a few other students. My heart twanged hard.

Ruslan lifted his chin. "Like Christmas." His eyes gleamed with nostalgic fervor, and I used it as my cue to return us all to a more felicitous state of mind.

We lingered over scones and coffee and listened to Ruslan spin tales that were part truth and part imagination. He took people he had known well—and some he'd only heard stories about as a young boy—and embellished their personalities before dropping them into his plot and letting them run amok. By the time the coffee was gone, I felt like I was a part of Ruslan's extended family myself—or part of his plot, at least.

After breakfast, I located the last box of Christmas decorations in my attic so Moorehaven would be as festive as humanly possible. I brushed away a thin layer of dust and read the note I'd written in Sharpie the previous year: *Overkill Box. Open in Case of Ruslan.*

Then my phone rang. It was Naoma. "Pippa, morning. You've heard about the storm?"

"What storm?"

"Big winter blow headed our way in about three days. I'm gonna be out taking pictures of the giant waves for a new calendar. Make sure your hatches are battened."

"Will do."

"The main reason I called is that there's something I need you to see. I'm putting the final touches on the Christmas edition of the *Register* right now, but can you meet me in about half an hour?"

Naoma's serious tone piqued my interest. "Sure, Naoma. Where do you want to meet?"

"You know which one of my duplexes is empty?"

I recalled the pair of duplexes Naoma owned, old holdouts from the ground floor of a boarding house built soon after Moorehaven. "The one opposite Mallory." I'd never been to Mallory's place, but I took a tiny, perverse bit of pleasure in everyone being scared to share a wall with Seacrest's strict police chief. I knew I would be, and the month before, I'd spoken in favor of the word "acting" being dropped from her title of acting chief of police.

A thread of excitement stitched its way through Naoma's voice as she murmured, "I've found something inside a secret space. You are the first person I called, Pippa. I haven't even told the Glaze & Gossip girls yet."

"What is it, Naoma?"

Her tone was urgent and foreboding. "It has to do with Felicity Moore herself. I'll see you in half an hour."

Tingles shot down my spine, and a sense of doom made my tummy cramp. I carried the box of decorations down the ladder, but as I turned toward the staircase, I nearly ran straight into Ruslan, who seemed to be on a mission. Svetlana trailed him by several feet while staring toward the staircase, but I didn't buy her disinterested act.

The spry old author insisted on carrying the lightweight box downstairs for me, and my cat followed us down, bounding several steps at a time before sitting to lick her paw.

"I hope you don't mind helping me get in the proper mood for writing the Christmas chapters in my novel," he said.

"Not at all," I reassured him. "Moorehaven is going to be amazingly festive, thanks to you. Are you finding enough time to write when you're not hanging decorations?"

Ruslan chuckled amiably. "Oh, yes, yes. You and your staff are most kind. I'll have to thank them each individually and effusively in my author notes in this book for the extra attention this time around."

"You really don't have to do that in every book you write here, but I do appreciate the free publicity."

"You deserve it, my dear girl. You take such good care of this old man."

My heart filled, and I wanted to kiss him on his bald head, as if he were one of the Seven Dwarfs, but I managed to refrain.

We reached the large front parlor, where Hilt and Chloe stood on stepladders in opposite corners, holding a measuring tape between them that spanned the diagonal length of the room.

Ruslan set the box on the coffee table in front of my big red couch and began to pry open the cardboard lid. Svetlana watched eagerly from one of the chairs. When no treats were forthcoming, she took matters into her own paws and hopped right into the box, claiming it as her personal nest.

For the next twenty minutes, I gingerly eased decorations from under my cat, helped to hang garlands that crisscrossed the ceiling, and dangled glass icicles that glinted gorgeously in the light from the Tiffany lamps. But my heart wasn't in it. I couldn't stop thinking about what Naoma wanted to show me. Every now and again, someone brought me an item attributed to Felicity Moore, and I loved putting them on display in the gallery. But something about Naoma's foreboding tone told me I might not be in for such a treat. Finally, I made my excuses to Hilt and Ruslan and left Chloe in charge, knowing she would get a kick out of giving orders to a couple of old guys. They'd get a kick out of following them too.

I bundled up against the chilly fog that blanketed the town before I unlocked my bicycle from the covered rack outside, not wanting to bother getting my car out of the garage for such a short drive. With my scarf tight and my ear flaps down, I pedaled my way up the slight slope that led away from the sea and hung a left at the second bridge, crossing the Silver River. A couple of blocks past the main tourist drag, I made one final turn and pulled my bike onto the sidewalk, right across the curved letters stamped into its old concrete: 3rd Street.

Two identical duplexes took up most of one side of the street. The one farther down the block was a sunny yellow, with cars in both of its driveways. But the sea-blue building right in front of me only had one occupant—Mallory Tavish, Seacrest's chief of police. For some reason, she hadn't even picked the side of the building on the corner. The best view from any of the duplexes—a broad slice of the endless Pacific horizon—went unappreciated.

Naoma hadn't arrived yet. I walked my bike up to the small porch and leaned it against one of the posts. Like any self-respecting Peeping Tom, I took a quick look through the window. On the outside, the duplex had updated storm windows, appealing flower beds, and a fresh coat of paint. Inside, the space looked like the set of a 1940s sitcom, minus the furniture. The front room was small, the ceiling low. Unable to resist the urge to peek through Mallory's windows while she was away, I slipped around to the back of the house.

To my shock, someone was already standing behind Mallory's half of the house. I froze, no excuses coming to mind. After half a second of mutual surprised staring, I belatedly took in the other's details.

A woman about my height wore a ball cap and navy-blue coveralls. Her dark hair was pulled into a ponytail, and she wore thick black-framed glasses. In one hand, she held an old white plastic jug with a hose attached, and in the other, she held its sprayer.

Pippa, you got busted peeping by an exterminator. I frowned. "What are you spraying for this time of year?" I asked.

She used her wand to gesture at her jug of poison. "Ants. They like to come inside when it's cold."

"Oh, yeah, obviously. I'm just waiting for my friend. She owns this property. She must've hired you, right?"

Before the exterminator could answer, Naoma's car pulled up along the curb twenty feet behind me.

"Well, good luck. With the ants, I mean. Yeah." *Mouth, you are so annoying when you get tongue-tied like that. She's just doing her job.*

I hurried over to greet Naoma as she stepped out of her car. "What did you want to show me?" I asked. Then I took a good look at her. The corners of her eyes and mouth carried fine wrinkles, a sure sign that she was stressed. She'd left a pen tucked behind her right ear, and it disrupted the clean line of her jaw-length bob. Even her bright-fuchsia suit and matching pumps didn't seem to cheer her up. I put a hand on her arm. "Naoma, how bad is this? You look terrible."

Her gaze flicked to the exterminator in the distance behind me then back to my face. "Oh, Christmas shopping woes." She waved my worries away with her fuchsia manicure. "I've been online shopping for three weeks, trying to find the perfect present for my sister-in-law. The woman is impossible to please, I tell you." She led me to the front door as she searched through her key ring. "She's obsessed with everything coffee, and I've already bought her more coffee-related items in the last twenty years than I ever knew existed. It's becoming a real struggle."

She unlocked the door, and we stepped inside the empty unit. As she let out a big sigh, her shoulders slumped. "That, and I just can't get the layout of this week's newspaper the way I want. I swear, I just need to print it already so I can't keep fiddling with it. No one else notices my layouts one way or the other." She straightened her shoulders and popped her keychain back into her suit pocket. Then she met my eyes with a look that told me to brace myself.

I swallowed. No doubt Naoma really was fussing over the newspaper layout—she had a spot for everything and was happiest when everything was in its place. But that was just a cover story for the real issue. "No offense, Naoma, but why would a secret about Felicity Moore be hiding in a place like this?"

Naoma finally smiled and wagged a finger at me. "That's a surprisingly germane question. You know these duplexes used to be the lower floor of Seacrest's first boarding house?"

I nodded. "They saved these parts when the structure became too unsafe, right?"

Naoma's bright fingernails glowed like runway lights as she waved an invitation to follow her down the hallway. "With a lot of remodeling, yes, these bits of the much larger structure were salvaged. But some of these walls are more than a hundred years old. And one of them holds a secret I never expected to see."

I made a face. "Please don't tell me that's going to be your clickbait headline when this hits your next edition."

Abruptly, Naoma turned back to me and clasped my wrist. "When you see what I've found, you won't want me to publish it. And you see, that's not the first time this problem has come up."

Tantalized and worried, I followed Naoma down the hallway to the back bedroom, which shared one wall with Mallory's side. Near the center of the building, a small closet door sat open, and inside, a bare bulb shone over plain walls covered in old white paint. Naoma stepped right into the empty closet and began tugging on part of the back wall. I peered over her shoulder as she wiggled a panel of wood free and set it aside. "This panel has always been a problem. It never lay flat against the studs. Now, I know why." She dusted off her hands and reached into the hole behind the wood.

I held my breath in anticipation.

Naoma brought out a package wrapped in old brown paper and twine. It bent as she lifted it, like a ream of printer paper. "I opened it, but once I saw what was inside, I tied it back up. You go ahead and open it now." She offered me the package.

It was heavier than it looked. With a puzzled glance at Naoma, I set it down on the tan Berber carpet in the middle of the empty bedroom, crouched beside it, and untied the twine. I folded back the crinkly brown paper, nervously eager to see what it had hidden for so long.

A straight, even stack of old newspapers met my eyes. The top page sported narrow rows of articles in tiny print. Their all-capped headlines weren't much easier to read. I frowned and picked up the top copy. Then I noticed that the issue below it was identical. I thumbed through the stack in surprise. "Hey, these are all the same. Are they all from the same print run?"

Naoma nodded. "Read it. You'll know the article when you see it."

I crossed my legs and brought the tiny print close enough to read. The paper was dated April 7, 1912. Advertisements for medicinal cures lined the bottom of the page, and an announcement for a spring festival headlined the middle-right side. But the far-left side bore a headline that nearly stopped my heart: *Felicity Moore, Grifter and Madam, Shame of Seacrest.*

I double-checked the other copies again. They all carried the same headline. Naoma stood quietly, her hands folded tightly, while I clasped the paper with both hands and read every tiny word. In my shock, much of the article fled my mind like water through a sieve as soon as I read it, but certain details and phrases jammed them-selves into place, unshakable. *Moorehaven is a house of ill repute... Miss Moore, who has never married, hides her evil intentions behind a façade of upper-class decency... Over the years, young women have been seen entering Moorehaven in the dark of night and are never heard from again. This author must wonder whether the poor young ladies have been made into pies or bricked up within the cellar! Whatever their fate, surely, no one is up to any good within those fine ivory-tower walls. These young hussies are believed to steal jewelry for Miss Moore, who no doubt sells them to further her appearance of gentility. To bor-row a newly coined term, Miss Felicity Moore is nothing more than a grifter.*

I stared at the paper, unseeing. Finally, I managed to murmur, "Why did this get printed, and why did it get hidden?"

Naoma, ever the journalist, responded with a question of her own. "Is there any truth at all in what this article says?"

I shook my head, still stunned. "I can't imagine there is. I've lived in Moorehaven for seven years now. I've read all of Moore's journals, all his notes, every scrap of paper in the Raymond Moore Gallery—some of which have never seen the light of day. I know all the stories, including which ones are true and which are just legends. And I've never heard this story before."

Naoma sat beside me on the old carpet, tucking her legs to one side. She rested a hand on my shoulder. "That doesn't mean there's nothing to it. Think about this: Raymond Moore remodeled Moore-haven after his great-aunt died. And Hilt remodeled it after Moore died." She waved her fingers at the hole in the back of her duplex's closet. "Things that were already secret can get completely hidden when that happens."

"You think that Hilt and Raymond Moore hid away an entire whorehouse in my walls? That's not who Felicity Moore was!" I protested. "This smacks of rumormongering—someone taking a potshot at a successful woman because she doesn't fit the mold." But I felt a worm of doubt wriggle uncomfortably. *You don't know who Felicity Moore really was,* I told myself. *No one does. It's not a crime to want a private life.* I sighed, caught in the misery of uncertainty. Sure, some people might find the checkered past of a historical figure intriguing. But plenty of others might look at me as an incompetent business owner—or worse, a liar—for withholding an unpleasant truth from the public. My business could suffer. No matter how much Hilt adored Felicity, he wouldn't want that, and neither did I.

Naoma gave my shoulder a squeeze. "You know, my book club is reading *The Diamond Charm* right now," she said encouragingly. "You've heard the rumors about that book, just like I have."

I squeezed her hand, grateful for the distraction from my darkening thoughts but unsure where she was going with it. "That's the book Moore wrote that was supposedly based on Felicity's life. If that's true, he knew a lot more about her than anyone else ever did. Hilt says that too many details from that book had never been corroborated, like the main character's pregnancy. But I haven't read it in a couple of years."

"Read it again. See if you can figure out any details one way or the other. I want to work *with* you on this, not against you."

I blinked. "Work with me on what, Naoma?"

Naoma picked at the skin near her index fingernail with her opposing thumb. "I'm a journalist, and I've found a mystery on my own property. I can't *not* investigate it." Her penciled eyebrows dipped apologetically. "But at the same time, you are a dear friend, and I don't want rumors or even a partial truth to hurt your reputation and your place in Seacrest. I would love to be able to say that I found these salacious old rumors behind the wall of an old closet and that there is absolutely no proof whatsoever to support them. We can all have a good laugh at how silly the whole thing is. But I need to know for sure before I report on it, and you're the best person to help me with that."

My tummy twisted. I couldn't in good conscience ask her not to look into it—and it would do me no good anyway. Naoma was a bloodhound. "But what if the rumors aren't false?"

Naoma pressed her bright lips together. "The actual truth is usually somewhere between both sides of the story. Somewhere between this article and what you've heard at Moorehaven. And as always, I must consider the source." She tapped a fuchsia fingernail on the byline of the offending article.

"Cecelia Front," I read. "Who was she?"

Naoma's smile was wry. "Well, that depends on who you ask. I've found references to her timely reporting and her ability to navigate the social waters, shall we say. I've also read complaint letters sent to the town council, accusing her of meddling and unfounded gossip."

I looked down at the stack of articles. "So the truth probably *is* somewhere in between."

"Exactly. The trick will be figuring out which she was using more of when she wrote this article."

I handed her the copy I had read. "You have access to all the historical articles the *Seacrest Register* has ever published. See what you can dig up on Cecelia Front and any missing persons cases that could connect to Felicity."

"I've already started. But there's more." She gave me a knowing smile. "If Cecelia Front wrote the article, and it clearly got published, why didn't everyone get one of these copies? Why wasn't this rumor spread all over town?"

I shifted until my seated position mirrored hers, with my legs tucked to one side. "You're grinning because you already know the answer to that."

Her smile fairly glowed. "Indeed, I do. Whether through intent, spite, or pure accident, Felicity Moore owes the quashing of this rumor to an Abigail Travers, one of Seacrest's most valuable librarians."

I grinned. "'Most valuable librarians'? Now, there's a phrase you should save for a headline."

"Noted." Naoma took a moment to jot her words down in a notebook she pulled from a pocket. "The library in Seacrest has always been called Diogenes's Lantern, in accordance with the town founders' habit of naming things after lanterns and Greek people."

I chuckled. "As one does."

"And," Naoma continued, "while Ms. Travers served as the town librarian, she lived..." Naoma waved a hand around the room.

My eyes widened. "In this room in the old boarding house."

She nodded. "Somehow, she got her hands on the entire print run of this edition of the paper. Perhaps they were distributed from the library itself, and she simply hid them. I'll look into that. But I can tell you this: once the following week's paper came out, Cecelia Front could have screamed all she wanted to about her lost article, and no one would have cared."

My brow drew together as I tried to figure out what great historical event had taken place the week after April 9, 1912. Then I gasped. "The *Titanic* sank! Without the article and with this new, big story to talk about, any rumors that Cecelia Front brought to life would have died. Now, that's something neither Cecelia nor Abigail could have predicted. What do you know about Abigail? Were she and Felicity friends?"

Naoma shook her head, and her glossy dark hair swayed. "I'll double-check, but they orbited in different social circles. I'm sure each knew of the other, but I can't think of any reason that Felicity would have more than a casual acquaintance with the town librarian. After all, she had her own library."

I had to nod at that. "It's definitely mysterious. Listen, Naoma, I know I can't ask you not to look into this story. That's not how Moore would handle this, nor Hilt. And I hope that's not what Felicity would want either. So let's do this together. I'll talk to Hilt, and I'll read *The Diamond Charm* again. You do research on Cecelia and Abigail and anything else you can think of. Tell me the minute you find anything, and I'll do the same." I started to get up then paused. "And please, until we know a little bit more..."

Naoma met my eyes with a reassuring look. "I won't tell anyone, not even the Glaze & Gossip girls. You have my firm word on that, Pippa."

A weight lifted from my shoulders, and I offered her a hand up. She wrapped the newspapers carefully and tucked them into a plastic shopping bag she pulled from her purse. On our way out, I poked my head around the corner to take a look at the kitchen. The sink and stovetop were minuscule, and the appliance over the stove was not a microwave but a toaster oven. The cupboards were small and white, and there wasn't any room for a dishwasher, but the unit had a nice new fridge. The linoleum was black-and-white tile, old but clean.

I must have been looking for too long. Naoma nudged me and said, "Yes, Mallory's side looks just like this one, except her floor has a little dip in it that runs all the way across, just past her fridge. I told her I'd get it fixed before she moved in, but she was in too much of a hurry."

I dropped my gaze, a little embarrassed by my nosiness regarding Lake's ex-wife, and made my way back out to the small porch. I had to admit, though, that it did make me feel better to know that the high-and-mighty Mallory was living in half of a tiny duplex, where no neighbors wanted to share a wall with her.

I adjusted my scarf and gloves and gazed into the thick fog. "Seems a little late to be spraying for ants, doesn't it?"

Naoma hugged the plastic-wrapped newspapers against herself and pulled her suit jacket close around her throat. "What?"

I nodded toward the back of the duplex. "The exterminator you hired. I ran into her today just as you arrived. You saw her."

But Naoma shook her head in confusion. "I didn't hire an exterminator. Maybe Mallory decided to take care of the problem herself, though I'd have paid for it, if she'd asked me to arrange it. She's not one to delegate when she can handle it herself."

"You're probably right. I'll see you later." I walked my bike down to the sidewalk, swung a leg over, then looked back at the duplex that Mallory shared with absolutely nobody except, apparently, way too many ants. With a grin, I pushed off and headed for home, reveling just a little in the knowledge that at least something was bugging Mallory.

4

"I came to Moorehaven thirty-three years ago last autumn. Nothing compares to the western view from my own widow walk on a clear, bright morning. But I still don't care for fog."
Raymond Moore, 1952

I HAD TO TELL HILT—AND only Hilt—what Naoma had found and was investigating. "Do you think there could be anything to the grifter thing?" I worried my lower lip.

Hilt waved a wrench at me from where he stood on the ladder in the laundry room. "You couldn't have waited until I got down to the floor before shockin' me like this?"

I blinked. "Sorry."

He clambered down, set his wrench in his toolbox, and gave me a thoughtful frown. "I don't think there's anything to it, no. Don't seem like her style, the way Ray talked about her. But I ain't exactly a walkin' encyclopedia of all things Felicity. Ray Moore, sure. But Felicity was before my time."

"You never uncovered anything... suspicious... during remodels or renovations?" I pressed.

He furrowed his brow. "Well, does a hundred-year-old hairbrush count?"

I snorted. "Doubtful. But I don't need to tell you what the Trust could do to this place if even part of that article is true. You know what Truitt's like when he gets antsy."

Hilt adopted the fussy manner of the Moorehaven trust officer who liaised with us and waggled an invisible pen at me—Truitt's nervous tic. "That's Officer Volavola to you."

I grimaced, remembering the trust officer's last visit. With his usual grating panache, he'd managed to knock one of my cooling cheesecakes onto the kitchen floor while suggesting that my *cats* were to blame for slack hygienic practice, threatened to shut us down over a dripping sink, and given Tyleen an anxiety attack over a slightly misaligned gate hinge in our shared fence. "He's not even here, and I've had enough of him. We should check the attic, sort through all those boxes of hers, and see if we can find any proof ourselves."

Hilt raised a smudged hand. "I'll do that soon as I can. I find anything, I'll let you know straight away."

Later that afternoon, the fog thickened to a soggy, forlorn spirit that pressed tiny wet fingers against the windows and wept upon the lawn. From the front parlor, I couldn't see the street, let alone the boardwalk or the ocean. I was grateful that Tyleen had whipped up a big Crock-Pot of clam chowder and brought it over to share with us for lunch. A belly full of warm, hearty food was a great defense against the foggy chill of the Oregon Coast.

Chloe and I stood side by side in the damp air that oozed in from the stained-glass window. She stared out the clear glass panel too. "I hate fog. Gives me claustrophobia sometimes."

I tipped my head toward the library. "Plenty of places to escape to, right in there."

She shrugged one shoulder and brushed her black hair from her left eye. "I know. It's not really the fog, though. Well, it is, but... the fog feels like it's inside my head recently, and seeing it outside, too, it's just..."

"Too real?" I guessed.

Her shoulders relaxed. "Yeah. Exactly."

"Did something happen? Maybe I can help."

Chloe flashed a grumpy frown as she traced one of the diagonal lead lines on the stained glass. "My mom called. She wants to spend Christmas with me."

"What about your dad? Is he invited?"

"No. But yesterday, he invited me back to the house for Christmas dinner." Chloe had moved out of her father's house at the end of summer, but both parents had begun playing tug-of-war with her feelings during the holidays, and she looked lost.

"Do you want to do either one?"

"Yes!" She bit her lip. "No. Maybe." She let her confusion show on her face—a sign of her trust in me. "I don't know, Pippa. Ever since my mom left Seacrest, I've gone overboard trying to please her whenever she blows through town. But last year, it finally sank in. I wasn't enough to keep her in town when I was little, so I'm never going to be enough to bring her back. And now, I'm not sure I want to. What should I do?"

I rubbed her shoulder. "Only you can decide that. But I'll be happy to listen. How do you feel about your parents right now?"

Chloe flung her hands in the air and gave a frustrated growl. "That's just the problem. I have no idea. Like, part of me is still their little girl, trying to please them and be good. I helped my mom pack up all her art supplies in the rain last month. And even though I'm not giving house tours for my dad anymore, he still asks me to help with little repair jobs, and I can't say no to that. He was big on getting on Santa's nice list, so it's even harder to think about this stuff now that it's Christmas."

"And the other part of you?"

Chloe's face drooped, and she idly ran a finger through a thin layer of pale dust on the windowsill. "I haven't figured out what the other part of me wants yet. That's the grown-up me, and I'm just starting to be her. I mean, I only moved out a few months ago." She raised her eyes to the foggy view. "I'm adrift. Like a ship caught between two currents. My uptight-lawyer dad is flowing one way, and my hippie-artist mom is flowing in a whole other direction. Whichever current I pick will pull me away from the other one. I kind of want to hate them both, but I can't. And I can't pick one over the other."

I hugged her with one arm and stared out the window with her. "That's a great metaphor, Chloe. I've felt adrift too. Lost, not knowing where I want to go."

She snorted. "You? You have it all together. How could you ever be lost?"

After seven years, my memories didn't hurt like they used to. "Once upon a time, I lived in a house with five roommates at college. One of them—my best friend—killed herself just before our graduation. I came home from college, lost. I didn't know who I was, and I couldn't figure out what to do with my future. Or why I should have one. Why me and not her? How could I be useful to anyone else when I couldn't even see how much my friend needed me?"

Chloe sucked in a breath. "Oh my God, Pippa. I didn't know."

"No, that's just the beginning of the story. All these currents were pulling me, spinning me. And I didn't know which one to follow. Just before Christmastime, Uncle Hilt invited me to stay with him at Moorehaven. Seven years ago yesterday, in fact. I hardly knew him back then, but for some reason I still don't fully understand, I said yes. It took me a few weeks to get my bearings out here, if you will, but you know what happened when I did?"

Chloe was breathless, rapt. "What?"

I stared into her green eyes, which were the color of kelp shallows. "I dropped anchor."

Her lower lip trembled, and she searched my face. "I can do that?"

My smile stretched a mile wide. "Of course you can. Just find the right spot—and that's not always easy. But once you find where you want to stay, then stay. Sometimes, we like to sail with the wind.

Sometimes, we need a port in the storm. And other times, we want to ride two currents at once. But that's your call to make. You can set rules for yourself, just like any other adult, even with your parents. You are the master of your fate."

"And the captain of my soul?"

"You said it, Captain Chloe."

She took a deep, slow breath while biting her lip then puckered up and let it back out. "Thanks. Thanks a lot. You always seem to know what to say." She held out an arm, hesitantly asking for a hug, and I gave her a big one.

Chloe let out a big sigh that told me she'd found her footing. "I think I'll visit my mom today, then, just to test the waters."

"Lake's water puns are really rubbing off on you. Let me know if you need to unwind afterward. I'm here for you, okay?"

"Okay. And happy Mooriversary."

"What?"

"You said it's been seven years since you moved out here. Yesterday was your Mooriversary."

"Mooriversary. I like that."

My phone rang. I glanced at the screen then turned to Chloe. "Is it okay if I take this?"

"Yeah. I'm good." Her lopsided smile assured me she meant it.

I smiled and stepped into the library. "Naoma. News already?"

"Yes and no, in that order." My friend's alto voice was taut. "I found information on Cecelia Front, our nosy reporter from 1912. She moved to Portland and got her own column when the *Daily News* became the *Portland News* later that year."

"Someone shuffled her out of town quickly."

"Yep. But Portland was a better fit for her style. She worked there all her life. I found Abigail Travers easily enough, too, your most valuable librarian. But she only seems to exist as far back as 1909."

"Maybe Travers is her married name."

"I thought of that, among half a dozen other ideas. The Seacrest courthouse has no record of a Mr. Travers marrying anyone that year. Whoever this Abigail is, she seems to have been birthed from the sea-foam like Aphrodite."

I frowned. It wasn't like Naoma to fail in tracking down a lead. "What did you learn about her here in Seacrest?"

"If I didn't know better, I'd say she was too perfect." Naoma's voice held a note of cautious respect.

"What does that mean?"

"You know when someone's trying so hard to blend in that they end up standing out? That's Abigail. She lived in the boarding house, worked at the library. Attended church faithfully like everyone else in town back then. Wrote little memos from the library on new books, meetings, and the like. She was the perfect citizen."

"But?" I prompted.

"But despite her lower-middle-class lifestyle, she aligned her attitude and her politics with Felicity Moore in every instance I could find. Some of them made sense for both women to agree on, like supporting a local school, but others... I can't see a humble librarian throwing her weight behind the notion of petitioning Salem to bring a state highway to town. Town issues, yes, but state issues? Seems a little above her pay grade."

I nodded thoughtfully. "You think they knew each other better than they let on?"

"It seems so, though I couldn't guess how."

I could guess all day. "Blackmail? Long-lost sister? Secret mind-control project? Government spy?"

"All right, showoff," Naoma said wryly. "I did find a picture of her. Want to see? Maybe she's standing in the background of one of the old Moorehaven photos."

I agreed, and Naoma texted me a black-and-white image showing a woman standing stiffly outside the old Seacrest library. She tilted her face down into shadow, making her features hard to see, but I did recognize one thing clearly: she was wearing the clunky rose necklace that currently hung on the wall of the Silver Room. My spine stiffened, and I got chills.

"Pippa?" Naoma prompted.

With a heaviness in my gut, I explained the necklace connection to her. "How did Felicity end up with Abigail's necklace?"

"We don't know which woman owned it first. Maybe Felicity gave it to her."

"And took it back at some point? I found it in an old trunk my first year here, when I was looking for antiques to decorate the rooms with."

Naoma's sigh was sympathetic. "Unfortunately, it's very possible that Felicity had some kind of hold over Abigail—or whatever her name was—whether through charm or threat. We don't have anything to dispel these rumors of grifting yet—in fact, it seems we're just gathering more evidence to support it. So I'll keep digging. I've got a discreet friend in Portland, Benji, who can help search through old records that have been scanned into his database. Something's bound to come up."

I felt shaken. "Thank you, Naoma. And thanks for keeping this under wraps until we know more."

"I hope we're still on friendly enough terms at the end of this that you'll give me a quote."

"Me too." I hung up and clutched my phone to my chest. Mystery writers might not mind the threat of scandal tainting Felicity's memory, but Moorehaven Trust Officer Truitt Volavola would. And he signed my checks.

"Excuse me? Pippa?" Ruslan's voice came from the doorway.

I turned and saw him standing with his hands folded, displaying wrinkled, swollen knuckles. After a moment's panic, I didn't think

I'd said anything terribly scandalous in the time he'd been standing there. "What can I do for you, Ruslan?"

"I've finished the chapter that shows off all the Christmas decorations you kindly put up in here, and it's got me thinking. What do you think about trying your hand at some classic English Christmas dishes?"

"Oh, that sounds like fun!" Before I could continue, someone knocked on the front door. "Excuse me."

My boyfriend stood on my porch, wearing jeans and a thick navy-blue peacoat that worked magic on his eyes. A chill, damp breeze tousled his black locks and pinked his cheeks. "Hi, sweetheart," he said.

"Well, I wasn't expecting an irresistibly handsome outerwear model today, but I will definitely buy whatever you're selling," I cooed.

Instead of his usual self-deprecating grin, he gave me a serious look and a cream envelope with gold-inked calligraphy on the front. "You may regret saying that."

I took the envelope. It read simply Miss Philippa Winterbourne, Moorehaven. "What's this? I didn't know you could do calligraphy."

"I can't. Well, I can but not this well. Anyway, it's not from me. I'd never call you Philippa." His bright-blue eyes were hooded in uncharacteristic uncertainty. His whole body was tense, in fact. I couldn't remember a time I'd seen him so out of sorts, and that alone made me worry. I slid a finger under the flap, opened it, then pulled out the card inside.

You are cordially invited to an intimate family dinner with the Ivenses, it read, followed by a date, time, and location. I read it again, confused. "The Ivenses? In Summerpoint? That's only half an hour up the coast. Do you have relatives there that you never told me about?"

Lake took a deep breath. "Not yet, but I will by Saturday night."

I took his cold hand in mine. "Lake, what's going on? You seem really stressed out."

He nodded distractedly. "My crazy wealthy family—and did I stress the word 'crazy' enough?—is spending Christmas on the Oregon Coast. And they want to meet you."

5

"My cure for writer's block is scotch and the *New York Times* crossword. I drink the scotch, I throw the half-finished crossword into the trash, and when I wake up from my rage nap, I've usually got a great idea for my book."
Raymond Moore, 1972

THE LOOK OF FOREBODING in Lake's eyes hadn't been enough to deter me from agreeing to attend his family's party with him. On party day, I had mixed feelings, but I'd poured plenty of optimism into my emotional blender.

I knew a little about them—his parents were one-percenters who dipped their fingers into politics to amuse themselves, and he had a younger sister named Bliss. But that was about all the information I'd been able to pick up in the eight months I'd known Lake Ivens. He'd walked away from his family—disowned himself, he called it—and never looked back. But it seemed like they weren't quite ready to cut that very last tie of spending Christmas together. Their gesture gave me hope that they could reach some kind of peace. And maybe I could help bring it about.

I'd kept busy the evening before, ordering last-minute gifts from local stores and switching up meals on my menus. By the time I had a free minute to start reading *The Diamond Charm*, I was curled up in my pajamas and bookended by a pair of warm, snuggly cats. I managed to stay awake for the first chapter or two before I drifted off to dreamland.

The morning of the party, I was deep in thought as I mixed dough for a huge batch of German pfeffernuesse, so when Hilt tapped me on the shoulder, I jumped a good foot in the air. I turned off my mixer, letting the stiff, spicy dough catch its breath, and blurted, "Good heavens, Uncle Hilt! Don't kill me before my time of death."

"Sorry about that, Pip. You didn't answer the four times I called your name from the doorway." He brushed a cobweb from his thick, wavy gray hair. "I poked around in the attic trunks for a couple of hours this morning. Didn't find anything obviously damning, o'course. But there is something you should see."

I wiped my hands on a towel. "What is it?"

"We found a Tiffany lamp clock. It has something inside that's not supposed to be there."

"Wait, 'we'? Who's we?"

Hilt shrugged apologetically. "Ruslan wanted to tag along. A couple of old fogies pokin' around in a Victorian attic for stuff that's older than we are? How could we resist? Don't worry," he added as I began to protest. "I didn't tell him why I was lookin'. Kept him on the trunks full of hats and figurines. Pop that dough into the fridge, and come have a look-see in the little parlor. Light's good in there. If we find something we don't want to share, we can always ask him to step out."

"Fair enough." I stretched a cover over my dough bowl, found some space for it in the fridge, and hurried down the hallway. In the little parlor, Ruslan and Hilt had pulled three green wingback chairs around a small table, upon which sat an unusual item. Ruslan studied the clock, while Hilt knelt and fiddled with the clock's cord. I took the empty chair and leaned forward to examine the antique item. Wherever it had been hiding in the past seven years, I had never seen it before.

The Tiffany clock sat about a foot high, with warm golden stained-glass paneling on all four sides. The front panel bore a glass inset of a clock face marked with Roman numerals and a pair of delicate brushed-steel clock hands as well. Patterns of art nouveau roses in pink and scarlet decorated the side panels and the arched top of the clock. The light inside was out, and I desperately wanted to see it lit up.

"That should do it," Hilt said. Something clicked, and his smile was lit from the lamp's golden glow.

I clapped my hands in sheer joy. "Oh my God, it works! It's beautiful."

He waved off my excitement. "I'm fluent in old wiring."

Enthralled by the rose-and-gold lamp, I stood and circled it, taking in its antique charm and glorious color. "Wait, what's that?" I pointed at a straight-line shadow inside the clock. "Is something broken inside?"

Hilt chuckled. "Toldja she'd spot it right away," he said to Ruslan.

The old writer grinned. "So you did." He stood and carefully lifted the top of the lamp. "See for yourself."

I looked inside, behind the clock workings and the light bulb. A small envelope lay within, its top edge resting against the outer glass. I snatched it out eagerly. "You think this is related to Felicity's secrets?"

"Doll, I think that *is* one of Felicity's secrets. Look at it."

I flipped the sealed envelope over. Deep-blue ink looped its way over the crisp old paper: *For Raymond.*

"This is Felicity's handwriting. I've seen it in some of her letters in the third-floor gallery. But..." I tugged on the flap. "Moore never found it. It's still sealed."

"I'm guessing he put it in the attic after Felicity passed without ever turning it on again, and he never knew she'd left it for him. God knows how long it's been in there."

Ruslan rubbed his chin with a big hand. "A message from beyond the grave. What do you think she said to Mr. Moore?"

The air around us crystallized, preserving our wonder in a single golden moment. The mystery of the letter seemed almost sacred, one final message from the woman who built the house I was standing in. I finally murmured, "It could be anyth—"

Hilt plucked the envelope from my fingers and unceremoniously ripped it open then pulled out a single small, folded page.

I gaped at him.

"Letters are made to be read, Pippa." He squinted and tried to find a good distance to hold the page from his face—near, far, near again—then gave up and handed it to me. "Here, Whip, you read it."

He only calls me Whip when he's feeling old. I told him to get reading glasses, but nooo.

I took the page delicately. Its ink was dark blue, penned by a strong, bold hand, unfaded by the passage of time. Felicity's spirit filled the parlor as if she were whispering in my ear.

Ruslan's face was wreathed in such transcendent reverence that I instinctively knew I could trust him with any of Felicity's secrets I might uncover. I read the note aloud.

"Raymond,
By now, you know I've
Reached my destination.
I don't want you to worry.
Crack the case, and
Keep writing your books.
F."

"That's all she wrote?" Hilt rubbed his index finger across his silvery stubble.

"Odd," Ruslan said. "Did she usually write such short letters?"

"All the letters I've read of hers were long and full of strong opinions," I said. "She'd doodle pictures in the margins sometimes. We have a few pieces of scratch paper where she and Moore played word games with each other, making it up as they went alo—holy ginger snaps, it's a puzzle!"

"What?" the old men chorused. They crowded around me, and I placed the letter flat on the table.

"Look. The first letter of each line." I pointed them out. "It spells *brick*."

Ruslan tipped his head in confusion. "Are you sure it's not just a coincidence?"

Hilt and I looked at him with equally confident smiles.

"We're sure," I said. "Felicity taught Raymond Moore all the tricks she knew. Puzzles, human nature, how to see the world, how to lie. Everything he is, he learned from her. This is no coincidence. She left this for Raymond for a reason. We need to find out what that reason is." I gave Hilt a sober look. "Even if it's nothing more than another one of their puzzle games."

Ruslan held up a large hand. "Wait just a moment. I'm sorry. Do I have this right? We're about to embark on a puzzle quest, left for the internationally famous mystery author Raymond Moore by his mysterious great-aunt Felicity, within the walls of Moorehaven it-self?" When I nodded, he placed his hand on his chest. "I'm so excit-ed, I'm not sure my heart can take it. Do I have time to make a will before we begin?"

Hilt sat again and stared blankly. He waved a hand around now and again as if flicking through mental notes.

"Are you doing your Sherlock impression again?" I asked. "You know you don't really have a mind palace."

My uncle shot me a brief, impatient look. "I have a mind Moore-haven. I remember all the repairs I've ever done to this place. I'm just trying to get a feel for how likely it is I've ripped out and replaced whatever brick Felicity's referring to."

"Aw, no, we haven't even gotten started yet. It can't end like that."

Hilt shook his head and smiled. "Not to fret, Pippa. Almost all the brick I can think of working on was deep inside the walls. Far as I can recollect, no major repairs or remodeling took place while Felicity still lived here. She wouldn't have had access to much brick at all."

What's your game, then, Felicity? I looked around the room. "What do you think about that, Hilt? Does that count as brick?" I pointed at the crown molding that ran around the room—and around all the rooms on the first floor. Unlike wood or plaster, Moorehaven's crown moldings were cast uniquely for the house out of hollow porcelain. The detail was exquisite, much finer than any wood molding. Throughout the house, the moldings showcased Felicity's roses and ribbons in the finest art nouveau style.

Hilt spoke over my shoulder as he gazed upward along my pointing arm. "By Jove, I think she's got it."

"But how do we know which brick is the right one?" Ruslan asked.

"Her initials, maybe," Hilt said.

I nodded. "Any symbol out of place could be a marker. And she'd want it obscured so not just anyone could spot it casually."

Hilt took a deep breath. "I'll get a ladder. Pippa, you get a flashlight."

"Me?" I looked from one old fellow to the other. They stared back at me, clearly impatient with my slow grasp of the rickety state of their knees. "Oh. Yes. Me. Absolutely."

Ruslan and Hilt held the ladder for me while I checked all the nooks and crannies of the moldings in the little parlor. The cats found my behavior fascinating. Svetlana watched my every move from atop the closest piece of furniture, while Rex insisted on resting on the ladder rung just below my feet, especially when I was ready to step down. I found some spiderwebs and a wacky pencil cartoon accompanied by the words "Kilroy was here," but nothing seemed to be a clue left by Felicity.

Hilt carried the ladder to the big parlor, and we started again, shifting furniture to make room for the ladder along the walls. The cats trailed us with the intense interest of authors taking research notes.

"I really hope there's a next clue or something," I said. "I'm all for cleaning the tops of these moldings, but I will definitely be disappointed if that's all I accomplish on this ladder today." I grumbled and went back to shining my flashlight on the corners of the molding. Roses, ribbons, a robin with spread wings. Just like the other pillar on the other side of the wide doorway.

I was climbing down the ladder as Chloe let herself in the front door. She looked tired and stressed.

"How did it go?" I asked gently.

She straightened her shoulders and lifted her chin. "Okay. Not as bad as I'd imagined it. I just need some time to process." She grinned at my pair of geriatric adventurers. "What are you guys up to? Did somebody break something again? Ruslan, are you trying to figure out if someone could survive jumping from the second-story railing?" She pointed at the open floor plan above.

"My dear, it's so much more exciting than that," Ruslan said urgently.

We took a break to fill Chloe in on our fun little quest, and that led to a quick supper of soup and sandwiches. Then we went back to work, checking the first-floor sunroom. I ascended my ladder once more, and Chloe got so impatient that she climbed up the bookshelves to feel around on the molding in the northeast corner of the room.

"Don't you break anything," I cautioned her.

"Don't worry. I drink my milk."

I grinned. "I meant don't break my bookcases."

Bookcases. I nearly dropped my flashlight. "Wait, everyone. Why did Felicity say 'crack the case'? Moore's not a detective. He's a writer. What case is he supposed to crack?"

Chloe pointed at me. "You think it's some kind of clue."

I backed down the ladder and shined my flashlight on the bookshelf Chloe had been climbing, even though the lights were on in the room. I could almost feel the epiphany zooming into my brain from wherever inspiration zoomed in from. "To the library!" I shouted, brandishing my light.

I jogged through the doorway into the Raymond Moore Memorial Library. I was gratified to see that everyone else had actually followed me, including the cats. Before us stood the shelves that held all of Moore's novels as well as his favorite books written by his contemporaries. He'd been particularly fond of Agatha Christie's works, and they'd become pen pals during World War II, so she had a substantial section of her own.

I gestured to the books. "Crack the case. What if she meant a bookcase? Her nephew was a writer, after all."

Chloe eyed all the bookshelves. We had a solid dozen, long and tall. "Where do we crack it?"

"I don't know," I had to admit.

"Maybe there's a book titled *Brick*," Ruslan suggested.

"Nope," I replied. I'd dusted the shelves often enough to become familiar with all the titles, and that one wasn't on the list.

"These books have been moved and reshelved," Hilt said. "It's unlikely that any one book in this room is where it was when Felicity lived here. Plus, openin' a book ain't exactly crackin' any cases."

"A secret container built into the wood!" Chloe blurted. "Like in that one movie with What's-His-Name."

"The which with who?" Hilt asked.

For once, I got the brain wave Chloe was sending out. "Yes, *National Treasure: Book of Secrets.* Could be. But there should be a marker of some kind." I began checking a bookcase no one was searching yet. "Some clue that marks the spot."

We each studied a different bookshelf, running our fingers over the panels and joints, shifting books to peer behind them.

"We still don't know what kind of mark we're looking for," Hilt grumped.

"How about a brick?" Chloe asked.

I laughed. "That would be nice, wouldn't it?"

"No, guys, there's a little brick carved into the shelf here." Her voice rose with excitement.

I hurried to the center of the room but was the last to arrive. Rex even sat atop the bookshelf, sniffing toward Chloe's pointing finger, while Svetlana perched on the big library table. I aimed my flashlight over Hilt's shoulder at the spot Chloe indicated. A small deformation rested in the horizontal plane of the wood.

"Well, batter my buns, fry me, and sprinkle me with sugar," Hilt blurted. "I always thought that was a flaw in the wood, but now that I know it's a brick, I'll never unsee it."

Chloe and Hilt gathered the books from the shelf and set them on the floor, exposing the gleaming old wood. They felt around all the edges of the shelf while I provided the light. After a few minutes of not finding anything, I began to feel disheartened. We hadn't located a button, a lever, a false wall, or even a "ha-ha, you suckers" note.

"Maybe this is just a wild goose chase after all," I murmured. "If this were an escape room, we'd never make it out."

"No, there's one thing we haven't tried yet," Hilt said. His voice was brash and strong, and before anyone could stop him, he grasped the empty shelf with both hands and ripped it straight out of its frame. Rex made a panicked, yowling leap for the table, startling Svetlana and bowling her over, and they both scampered for safety. "Consider this case cracked," he proclaimed.

Aghast at his destruction, I staggered back and nearly fell into the bookcase behind me. "Hilt!"

"Hilt, you genius," Ruslan said. He leaned down and pointed at the gap where the shelf had fit into the right side of its frame. "Pippa? Your light?"

I lunged forward, flashlight first, and lit up the hole. Inside the hollow edge of the bookcase was a brown paper package tied with old string. I fitted my hand into the hole and gingerly retrieved it, scraping my knuckles in the process. By its weight, I knew what was inside.

Taking a cue from Hilt's treatment of Felicity's letter, I untied it then and there. Inside lay a small journal with a pressed-linen cover sporting a dark-pink rose. *My favorite flower!* I opened the cover. Felicity had written *The Journal of Felicity Moore, January 1930* across the first page.

So excited that I was shaking, I looked at my uncle. "Hilt, you really did crack this case wide open."

6

"There are few things as terrifying as a dame with a smile as cold as it is beautiful."
Raymond Moore, 1940

"WHAT DOES IT SAY INSIDE?" Chloe's voice was breathy with eagerness.

Ruslan shook his head at her. "I don't think this is our secret," he said.

Chloe looked at us inquiringly, and I was too excited to keep from sharing. "Just one peek. We all deserve that." I turned to the first page of the journal. Felicity's fine handwriting began on the first line. I read, "Raymond, I believe someone is trying to poison me!" I whispered an epithet but broke off as a sudden heavy thump elsewhere on the first floor dragged my attention from our precious find. "What was that?"

Voices filtered through the doorways from the direction of the front parlor. I shared confused looks with Uncle Hilt. "Are we expecting more guests?"

He shook his head and lowered his gray eyebrows.

I closed Felicity's journal carefully and handed it to Hilt. "I'll see what's going on. Nobody read ahead without me."

As I followed the voices, I finally recognized one: my boyfriend, Lake. My heart felt light and warm, and I smiled broadly as I stepped into the parlor.

The sight that met my eyes melted my smile like a chocolate Santa. Two older gentlemen in expensive casual wear had pushed my long red couch from beneath the stained-glass window over to an angle in a corner on the other side of the room. Lake stood ramrod straight on the opposite side of the room, near the doorway to the hall, with an older woman and a girl who barely looked out of her teens. His face was too blank—a look I'd only seen a few times—as he tried to hide his feelings. A young woman who could have passed for a Norwegian model was standing right on the couch, and her high heels stabbed down into its soft suede. As I stared in shock and surprise, she reached up and lifted down one of Moore's favorite paintings. "This thing is hideous. What was she thinking?"

Across the room, Lake pinched the bridge of his nose. The older woman next to him clasped his wrist as if he were a misbehaving toddler and pulled his hand down, directing his attention away from me and back to her.

"Why don't you ask her yourself?" Another familiar voice: Mallory Tavish. The police chief lounged on one of my chairs with an air of smug ease, her chestnut hair and dark-blue uniform perfectly immaculate, as usual. The look I gave her was merely frosty—she was the devil I knew, after all.

What in God's name is going on in my parlor? I wanted to shout the words, but I barely managed to keep them trapped behind a shaky version of my hostess smile.

"What in God's name—" Hilt began copying my thought as he approached behind me. His tone indicated he hadn't actually clapped eyes on any particular part of the disaster yet.

"No, no, I've got it." I couldn't let Hilt see the parlor like that. He would blow a gasket. "You go on back. Leave this to me. Go ahead and read that journal without me. Someone should." My smile must've been mesmerizing in its anxious brilliance, because my uncle actually agreed and returned to the library.

Lake was still standing like a statue who didn't know he was a real boy, but I was too distracted by everyone else's chaotic movements to really focus on him yet. The blonde on the couch stepped down with exquisite grace. *If only she'd twisted her ankle.* Instead of handing me my own painting, she rested it against a small lamp table. Only then did she bother to meet my eyes. "Do yourself a favor, hon. Hire a good interior decorator. This place needs a makeover almost as badly as Kait." She shot an arrogant smirk at the young girl standing next to Lake.

Slender with fair coloring, Kait seemed unperturbed by the insult. "At least I have a *personality*, Bliss."

"Girls, girls. Let's not be rude during our visit," one of the older men said. He turned to me but didn't offer a hand. "I'm Devereaux Ivens, Lake's father." His tone heavily implied that I should be honored. Then he gestured to the others in turn. "My brother, Odie. My wife, Auda." He pronounced her name with a European "ow" sound. "My daughter, Bliss, and her friend Kait. And, of course, you know our good friend Mallory."

Mallory offered me a straight look and didn't even pretend to smile. I found her simple honesty refreshing.

Lake's family had just shown up in Moorehaven, without calling ahead. Lake's *family* had taken over my front parlor. *Lake's family* had decided they would redecorate my front parlor. And my *archnemesis* was their *good friend*. My smile slipped, and in my distress, I waited a second too long to paste it back in place. Frustration at Lake's lack of adequate warning flooded my chest, but I managed a toothy smile. "How lovely to meet you all. Welcome to Moorehaven."

The new arrivals barely glanced at me, so I took the opportunity to study them. Bliss pointedly ignored me as she studied the Tiffany lamp atop the table where she'd leaned the painting. In her three-inch royal blue Manolos, she towered half a foot above me. Her blond hair was perfect, and so was everything else about her, right down to her understated Christmas manicure. She embodied Californian perfection, and the smirk that lingered on her plump lips told me she knew it and had judged me wanting.

Across the room, her friend Kait seemed far more approachable, someone I might enjoy hanging out with. She looked to be barely over five feet tall, and she wore flats, making her appear diminutive next to Lake and everyone else, including me. Her caramel hair was pulled into a simple ponytail, and she nearly disappeared into the background with the neutral tones she wore.

"Morning, Lake." I gave my boyfriend an encouraging smile, but he slid those gorgeous blue eyes toward his mother after a bare nod, as if using some kind of subtle rich-people conversation-directing technique. I'd never seen him act that way before. His mother rested a hand on his arm and smiled at me in a distinctive *you-don't-deserve-him* sort of way. Her statuesque pose reminded me of Helen Mirren, and her titanium-blond hair would not have looked out of place on a queen. Auda Ivens clearly had a lifetime of practice at being looked at.

Lake's father gave me a gentlemanly nod, but there was no warmth in his blue eyes. He stood exactly the same height as his wife, several inches shorter than Lake, sporting Lake's black hair and straight nose. I felt chilled to see a face so like that of the man I loved staring me down with such cool judgment.

The other man, Lake's uncle Odie, had moved to stand near Mallory. He gave me a jaunty two-fingered salute, and I instantly liked him a little better than everyone else. He seemed a little shorter, wider, and more disheveled than his brother, Devereaux, and his dark hair, full of copper gleams, was swept into an old-fashioned pompadour, perhaps in an attempt to appear as tall as his brother. I gave him a friendly smile.

Then my eyes dropped to Mallory, who regarded me intently. *Wait, did Lake bring everyone here, or did Mallory? Does she think she can just drag these rich people into my place of business? What is she up to? I thought we were getting all along a little better, but this is not cool.*

Mallory must have read my face, because she walked over and pulled me toward an unoccupied corner. Over her shoulder, I could see Bliss pulling a few books off a bookshelf and rearranging them to suit whatever order she deemed best.

"This wasn't my idea, Winterbourne," Mallory began in a low voice. "They invited me along. As you see, I'm on duty." She flicked her gaze downward, indicating her dark-blue police uniform.

Feeling sour, I murmured, "You can't say no to them? Then maybe I should." I began to turn away, but Mallory grabbed my wrist.

"Not like that, Winterbourne. Play smart."

I raised my eyebrows and looked at her, awaiting an explanation.

She continued, "You have an invitation to their party, just like I do, but you don't want to go because you know you'll feel out of place. Lake will be there. But he may be... distracted. Isn't there someone you'd like to bring along to make you feel more at ease?" A half smile briefly graced her lips. "It's hard to ask favors from someone once they perceive that you don't like them."

Mallory's tone told me she was referring to more than just Lake's family—she was hinting at our own turbulent relationship.

She gets dragged away from work and plopped down in my parlor, and she still finds time to hint at an alliance with me? Maybe she really is warming up to me. Or maybe she needs allies to get her through this party. Either way, Mallory's better at this game than I am. "I'll keep that in mind, thank you. If you'd like to stay, I have some fresh gingerbread cookies and hot chocolate. But if you need to get back to patrolling the fog and battling ant invasions, I do understand."

Mallory squinted one eye at me. "Ant invasions?"

"Yeah, I saw your exterminator yesterday when I, uh, ran into Naoma. As your landlady, she was concerned that you hadn't told her you had an ant problem."

Mallory's gaze drifted toward Auda. Her voice took on a distant tone as she said, "I don't have an ant problem. But something is starting to bug me. If you'll excuse me, Winterbourne."

Mallory made her excuses to Lake's mother and headed for the front door. She must have still been in earshot when Auda loudly proclaimed, "Lakyn, I can't believe you let such a fine woman escape your clutches. And after twenty years of such close, pleasant association too! What were you thinking?"

Lake's reply was mild. "It's a lot easier to be pleasant with some people when you're *not* that close, Mom."

Her words stabbed me, and his didn't do much to patch up the wound. I'd forgotten that Mallory's family had grown up with Lake's. *They're all rich, and they all know one another. Of course his mother approves of Mallory. And she doesn't approve of me. But did she have to say that right in front of me? Ouch!*

I approached Odie in hopes of finding more neutral conversation. "So, is everything set for the party?"

Odie seemed mildly surprised that I had spoken to him, but he didn't seem offended. "Oh, ah, yes, I believe so. Dev's assistant, Cam, has made all the arrangements, with her usual draconian efficiency. We will see you there?"

I nodded determinedly. "I wouldn't miss it for the world. I'm looking forward to getting to know all of Lake's family better. I'm sure we'll be great friends."

"Do you have family locally?"

Odie's tone indicated an openness to including them at the party, so I considered my options. Uncle Hilt would enjoy sticking it to the Man, but there was no way I'd be able to wrangle him into formal wear. Trudie, though... My sister's delightful chaos would be perfect for a stuffy rich-people party. And she loved to doll up. "Yes, my sister lives here in town. She's an artist, very good with sea glass and jewelry." I looked at him expectantly.

His dark eyebrows seemed confused as to which direction they should go, drawing together then rising in an *is that so* formation. "I never possessed any talent for art, but my lack has given me a stronger appreciation for those who can create. Does she have a plus-one?" When I nodded, he reached into his suit pocket. "Please pass on these invitations to her and her friend. I'm sure I speak for everyone when I say that we would be delighted to meet them at the party."

Lake caught my eye briefly and gave me a nod and a smile, clearly pleased to see me mingling with his family, but he still stayed tightly within his mom's orbit. Bliss and Kait were apparently texting each other while standing together, though their attempt to hide derogatory comments aimed at my B and B failed because they kept reading them under their breath. Dev was on his phone, too, but in a serious-businessman way that automatically put a six-foot bubble of do not disturb around him.

I swung my attention back to Odie. He reminded me of a classy old British gentleman—either he was exactly what he seemed, or he was masking a twisted soul behind a façade of civility. For the moment, I was mostly sure that Odie was in earnest. After he learned that his favorite concierge at Seven Vistas was the same Jordan Harper who held the title of my best friend, I found myself in possession of a third invitation card.

"If I believed in psychics, I would swear up and down on a stack of Bibles that Ms. Harper is one of them," he proclaimed. "She knows my every whim before I even think it. I have never met a more intuitive concierge, here or abroad. I don't suppose she'd be interested in becoming my personal assistant? Dev has his, and I think I should find my own."

"I don't think there's enough money on the planet to convince Jordan to leave Seacrest. She has more ties to this community than you'd think. Money can't buy family."

"Well, that's not true." Bliss's laconic words surprised me as she suddenly appeared at my shoulder. "I bought Kait."

"What? You *own* her?" I sputtered.

Bliss raised one perfectly penciled eyebrow. "I mean, basically." She aimed a casual glance toward her short friend. "She lives in our house, and she does what I tell her. Isn't that how it goes when you own somebody?"

Caught off guard, I couldn't formulate a reply.

Kait heard her and came to her own defense, though, surprising me with her ramrod-stiff spunk. "I guess that means your father owns you, too, seeing how you dumped your one true love just because he told you to." She adopted a casual pose and brushed imaginary lint off her sleeve.

Bliss masked an expression of betrayal with a controlled lift of her chin. "Killian was just another plaything, and you know it." Her mouth was tight as she glanced at me, though, and without another word, she returned to texting her personal servant.

Odie waved the issue away with a hand that sported a couple of heavy gold rings. "Don't mind her, Pippa. Bliss believes that edgy is the new cool, but it's all millennial claptrap to me. What really happened, if you want to know"—his eyes sharpened as he glanced at his niece—"is that Kait's parents worked for Dev a dozen years ago. He sent them to Hong Kong for a great opportunity, and in return, they left Kait with our family. She and Bliss are the greatest of friends, but you know how difficult it can be when you're young, wide-eyed, and trying to find your place In the world."

I nodded. I did know that feeling, but I wasn't sure that Bliss had ever been wide-eyed or innocent in her life. Her body language screamed jaded, though she looked even younger than I was.

"I assume you've contracted with a caterer for the party tonight. I know an excellent cook whose food is to die for—almost literally. It's too bad Devereaux's assistant didn't inquire locally. You'd really be in for a treat with her dishes. Perhaps next time you're in town?" I added, trying my hand at some posh networking. *Speaking of one's place in the world...*

Odie's eyes twinkled. "How do you know we *didn't* hire her?"

"Don't be silly, Odeon." Auda pitched her voice to carry, though she stood only a dozen feet away. "Our party will not be a backyard potluck. We have *standards*."

Offended on Tyleen's behalf, I opened my mouth to retort, but Odie's chuckle distracted me. "Don't worry about her. I'm the foodie in this family, if you hadn't noticed." He patted his ample belly with both hands. "I made sure Cam hired the best caterer, and that's what's important."

"Yes, of course." My agreement was reluctant, and my eyes wandered until I spotted Lake near the doorway to the hall, deep in conversation with his father. I'd hoped to take refuge with him for a few minutes, but they looked serious enough that I dared not interrupt.

I focused on the foodie again. "Do you have time to stay for some gingerbread? It's a Moorehaven tradition to serve gingerbread at Christmastime. Some of the recipes for my favorite gingerbreads have been handed down from Felicity—"

"That won't be necessary," Auda interrupted. "We won't be staying."

Lake glanced back at her. "Mom, Pippa's a really good cook. You guys should really stay and have—"

Auda turned her icy blue eyes on him. "I believe I've made my position clear." Her voice was soft and cutting, like a dagger sheathed in velvet. "One can't expect Michelin-star dining from an old house in a wide spot on the road, after all. Come, Devereaux. We should be leaving. We have reservations."

Affronted, I could only marvel at her bald-faced rudeness. *Well, I have reservations, too, and they're all about you.*

Devereaux offered Lake and me a charming smile and took his wife's arm. "We'll see you tonight, then? Excellent." They swanned out into the hallway, and the others took that as their cue to follow.

Odie offered me another two-fingered salute. "Until tonight, my dear. I look forward to meeting your sister and Ms. Harper."

Given his recent attempts to stand up to them, it surprised me that Lake obediently trailed after his parents.

I strode after him and caught his wrist just before he followed everyone else onto the porch. In the quiet foyer, I said, "Lake, wait. Stay with me. I need a break after all this."

His brow furrowed for a moment. "Something's come up. I just need a little while to look into some options. Besides, whatever's come before, this is my family. They're not really any different from Hilt and Chloe and Trudie."

I couldn't keep a smidge of incredulity out of my laugh. "Are you serious right now? Moorehaven may let us live comfortably in the middle class, but there's as much of a difference between my life and the one-percent lifestyle your family enjoys as there is between a cloudy day and a full solar eclipse. And we just saw a solar eclipse together, so you know exactly what I mean. Your family and I have nothing in common except you. I need you to help me understand them. I don't know what to do around people like that."

"They're just people, Pippa. I really have to go now, but I'll see you later." Lake disentangled his hand from my grasp, kissed my fingers, then slipped away like water.

After his departure, Moorehaven was suddenly achingly empty. I felt more than a little betrayed.

7

"Always pay your staff well. They know all your secrets, and they know how you like your coffee."
Raymond Moore, 1933

I SIGHED AND PICKED up the painting Bliss had abandoned against a lamp table. Life in Seacrest made it hard to remember that Lake had grown up in a totally different social class from mine. I hadn't thought about how wealthy and privileged he used to be while he and I watched the local high school drama club perform *Romeo and Juliet* set in 1920s Chicago. I didn't care about his elite prep school or his first Lamborghini when we walked barefoot in the surf at sunset, looking for jellyfish and having kelp tag fights.

I did care, though, when his sister jabbed holes in my red couch with her blue Manolos, and he didn't say anything to her. *Does he think his sister deserves to walk on my couch? Or does he believe my couch is just so crappy that anyone can walk on it? And what does that say about me? I love that couch.*

I flipped the center cushion over to hide the holes until I could repair them. Then I jerked to a halt midstride. *Oh my God, the journal! Where is everyone?* I rushed back into the library, where I'd left Hilt, Chloe, Ruslan, and Felicity's hidden diary.

The three of them were crowded around the journal at a reading table, engrossed.

"Hey, can I get a quick hand in the front parlor? It's kind of a mess. Then you can tell me all about the journal."

Hilt immediately rose to help, but the moment he set foot in the parlor, he flinched. "What happened in here? It's been, what? Five minutes?"

"Ten, at least." My uncle still had some issues with Lake, and I didn't need him trying to kick Lake out of his first Christmas at Moorehaven. "Just a misunderstanding. Let's just get things back to where they were."

Chloe and Ruslan lent their help, and in just a couple of minutes, my parlor looked as neat and tidy as ever. *Like the Ivenses were never here. Seems bad that I've just met them, and I already prefer a world where they don't exist.*

A minute later, I leaned my elbows on the library table and stared down at Felicity's neat, loopy handwriting. "So, someone actually thought they could get away with poisoning Aunt Felicity?"

Hilt flipped back to the first page. "Don't worry, Pippa. Felicity wasn't really being poisoned. She said in the next paragraph that she thought Ray might like to use that line for a novel. Then she accused him of buying the wrong brand of tea and said that's where she got the idea—from inferior tea."

I chuckled, and my spirits lifted in relief. "She was such a character! I wonder if any of Moore's characters are based on her, aside from the pretty obvious Raquel in *The Diamond Charm.*"

Hilt frowned in thought. "I can think of half a dozen easily. But you gotta hear this one bit. I don't think this journal is the prize Felicity wanted Moore to find."

Ruslan hummed in excitement, and I grinned at him.

"What do you mean, Hilt?" I asked.

Chloe tapped a page. "The journal's just the next clue. At least, Hilt thinks so."

"Clue to what?" I tried to slide the journal in front of me, but Hilt rescued it and cradled it in his hands.

"Listen, and see what you think." He flipped a couple of pages and cleared his throat. "*Whatever you do, Raymond, leave the laundry system intact. I do not recommend you examine it too closely, however, as you are rather too large for comfortable accommodation. Perhaps Tilly can assist you, if you insist on being curious. You usually do. But for her sake, take precautions with the laundry basket. It would not do to break your maid for the sake of your own curiosity.*"

An electric moment captured the table, and we all stared at one another.

"Whaaat?" I murmured. "Is she saying the laundry chutes have another purpose? Has there been a giant secret in Moorehaven this whole time, right under my nose?"

Hilt harrumphed. "*You're* surprised? Imagine how *I* feel!"

Ruslan sat back, took a deep breath, then held it a moment before speaking. "I don't wish to deflate anyone's hopes, but isn't it possible that any secrets the laundry chutes might have led to could have been torn out by now? This journal was written before I was even born, and I'm *really old*."

Hilt's craggy face registered reluctant agreement. "Yeah. This place has had a few major overhauls. I was in on a few of them myself."

"We'll have to read the whole thing and sift it for clues," I said. A ripple of excitement shot up my spine at the prospect of pitting my intellect against Aunt Felicity's.

Hilt flicked his bright-blue gaze between Chloe and me. With reluctance, he slid the journal to me. "Knock yerself out. We skimmed ahead a bit without you, so you should catch up. But I wanna take a look at the laundry system right now."

"You're not much smaller than Moore," I protested. "You could get hurt clambering around inside those chutes."

He barked a laugh. "I ain't gonna clamber anywhere. I've already got that ladder set up in the laundry room to fix the whine in the fan.

Might take a gander around the bottom end of the chute while I'm up there. Chloe can hold it steady for me."

"I'll hold the flashlight," Ruslan offered.

The three of them headed for the basement stairs in a flutter of excitement, leaving me alone in the library with Felicity's journal. I pressed a hand to the inked page. "You clever old girl. Decades later, you're still making us jump and scurry."

I flipped back to the beginning and began to read. In her words to her great-nephew, Felicity Moore was smart, teasing, and affectionate in turn. She alternated between admiration for his international fame and chastisement for minor infractions, as if he were still a trickster youth.

Then I reached the portion where Felicity instructed Moore to leave the laundry system alone. I read it several times and ended up staring at her words, deep in thought. *Sounds like the maid, Tilly, can fit inside, but Moore can't. Maybe all that scotch had padded his middle by this time, and Felicity was teasing him. But she doesn't seem to mind if the chutes get examined. They angle through the house—none of the chutes fall straight down. Did Felicity always mean for them to be climbed through?* I sat bolt upright, remembering one of the black-and-white photos on the dresser in the Silver Room. *Tilly was about my size. If she can fit, I can fit.*

Wary of leaving the journal where Lake's nosy family could discover it, I hurried to my bedroom, behind the secret door in the pantry. I slid the dust cover off an Oregon Coast birding book on my bookshelf, wrapped it around the journal, then tucked it down on the bottom shelf. Knowing the diary was safe, I hurried back into the hallway and rushed upstairs.

Everyone else in the building was down in the laundry room. A thrill of glee tickled my spine as I imagined the looks on their faces when I slid into view. Then I had a more reasonable thought: *What if I get stuck?*

I skidded to a halt in the third-floor hallway, my arms outstretched like an action superhero in midfight, chest heaving. Then I darted to the linen closet, grinning like a madwoman.

Five minutes later, I sat on the bed in the third-floor Lilac Room, holding one end of a chain of bedsheets tied together. I'd anchored the other end to a heavy bedpost, just like in the old movies. *Eight sheets should be enough, right? I hope?* A heavy, lavender-hued flowerpot pressed the ornate laundry-chute grate all the way open and held it against the floor so that it wouldn't swing shut on me. Sure, I'd always known that Moorehaven's chutes were larger than they needed to be. I'd even worried about dropping my phone down one of them. But I'd never contemplated throwing myself into one on purpose.

I took a deep breath and padded in stocking feet to the opening near the floor, dragging my colorful bedsheet lifeline behind me, scooted into the hole, and stuck my feet into the angled metal chute. Still worried about damaging my phone, I took it out of my pocket at the last minute. Then I giggled and sent a quick text to Chloe.

Geronimo!

I set down my phone, slid forward, and leaned back, and gravity grabbed me by the ankles and pulled. I always screamed on roller coasters, and I couldn't help but shriek like an excited banshee as I zipped downward in the pitch blackness. The bedsheets unwound rapidly from my arms. I clung to the end with both hands. The chute jinked right then left, jostling my hips and shoulders, and my delighted howling suddenly turned the air blue.

The chute's angle abruptly lessened, and I saw a gleam of light ahead.

Then Chloe cried frantically, "Get the laundry cart! She's coming!"

I realized that the gap at the bottom of the chute could drop me onto a hard concrete floor if the basket wasn't in place. My heart rate skyrocketed, and I scrabbled to get a grip on the part of my sheet lifeline that was unspooling. I had way too much sheet, and in my confidence, I'd only grabbed the very bottom end of the last one. My hands thumped wildly against the chute's walls. I sounded like a panicked cat in a dumpster. *This is the dumbest thing I have ever done!*

Chaotic voices and a loud wooden clatter rose from the opening in the chute. Finally, my hands closed on the sheet that was actively zipping out of my arms, and I jerked myself to a stop. I lay on my back in the nearly horizontal chute. From the knees down, my legs dangled into empty space through the laundry drop. My heart thundered in my ears. An eerie silence blanketed the room below me.

Something narrow and hard tapped my ankle. "Pippa? You dead?" Chloe called.

"No. Uh, not until Hilt gets his hands on me, that is. I should've thought this through a little better. Sorry. Is everyone okay down there?" I raised my head, but I couldn't see down the drop hole very well. I did see that the chute didn't just dead-end past the drop, though.

"We're fine, but it's a good thing you didn't fall right out of there," Chloe replied. "Hilt fell off the ladder while we were scrambling to catch you, and Ruslan and I managed to catch *him*—in the laundry cart. He'd have been pretty annoyed if you'd landed on top of him."

Embarrassed, I waited patiently on my back in the chute for Hilt to get rescued from the laundry cart. He still hadn't said a word by the time Chloe guided my feet to the ladder she'd moved for me, so I knew I was in trouble. I eased my way onto it, climbed down, and looked for Hilt.

My uncle's lips were pressed into a firm line. His eyes were flat, his arms were crossed, and he hadn't bothered to smooth his mussed hair. He wanted me to see how disheveled he'd gotten during my antics.

I met his eyes for several apologetic moments. "I'm so sorry, Uncle Hilt. I should've been clearer about my intentions when I texted Chloe. But hold on—I saw something up there. What was it?" My gaze shot away from my uncle's sigh of forgiveness and back into the laundry chute, and I climbed back up a couple of steps. "Someone, give me a flashlight. I left my phone in the Lilac Room."

Ruslan's big-knuckled hand clapped a flashlight into my outstretched palm, and I aimed it at the far end of the laundry chute.

"Guys, you're gonna want to see this." A wooden panel had been hammered in place across the metal chute, clearly blocking the way. *But to what?* The chute itself angled upward, as if to prevent laundry from sliding too far. *And—*

"What do you see?" Chloe called.

"Handles. Handles in the sides of the chute." I squatted on the ladder. My grin must've been a mile wide. "There's a wooden panel blocking the way. Why would someone need handles up in here? Why is there more chute past the laundry room? Where does it go?"

Uncle Hilt cracked his neck to one side. "All right, I know when my comic-relief plotline's being abandoned. Let me get my tools and take a crack at that panel, and I'll forgive you for knocking me off the ladder."

Caught up in the thrill of the hunt, I leaped down and hugged him tightly. "You're the best!"

8

“It may be *du jour* to arrive late to a party, but you get your pick of the best hors d’oeuvres if you show early.”
Raymond Moore, 1961

EVENING ARRIVED WITH early-winter punctuality. The weak sunlight that had filtered through the clouds all afternoon died with a tiny burnt-pink gasp on the horizon, leaving the world enveloped in a monochromatic tomb that let us explore its edges all we liked but would never let us escape. My cats each sat in a different window in the front parlor and stared outside, eternal guardians against the pressing void. Fog rolled in as Chloe zipped me into my dress, chosen by committee from a small selection Jordan called “Pippa chic,” and I headed out to pick up my date at his lighthouse.

“Good luck,” Chloe said. The wry arch in her eyebrow told me she had way too much cynicism for one so young, but she wasn’t wrong to have doubts about mingling with Lake’s über-rich family. I had plenty myself. But I marched out to the garage and fired up Sadie’s engine, ready to take on the evening. *I can do this. I’m not going to be alone anyway. I’ve got backup. Lake, Jordan... even Tru counts as backup in these desperate times.*

Lake hopped in and offered me a warm kiss and several admiring comments on my look, which I returned eagerly—how often did one get to see their boyfriend in a tux, anyway?—and we were off. With both hands on the wheel, I guided Sadie—Hilt’s affectionate name for the car—through the thick fog.

"

I dared to shoot a quick glance at my handsome passenger, whose hands rested easily in his lap. "I'll take it as a compliment that you aren't grabbing the oh-crap handle in this crazy fog."

Lake gave me a fond look. "I trust you. How can I not, with the number of times you have literally saved my life?"

I smiled and turned my attention back to the road. "Well, there is that." Another glance, that time at his bow tie. "Did you really just have that tuxedo lying around? Because I don't think that's a thing."

He shifted, and I felt him look at me more directly. "You don't think ordinary people own tuxedos?"

A silent chuckle tipped my head forward. "One, you are far from ordinary. And two, I've seen your closet. Unless you have a secret vault in the back wall like Bruce Wayne or James Bond, I'm pretty sure you didn't own a tuxedo last week."

He raised his chin and adjusted his bow tie with a smile. "Ivens. Lakyn Ivens."

I turned Sadie's wheel as the road slowly ambled to the right. "As long as the Ivens girls don't have the same terrible fate as the Bond girls do, I'm in."

"You'll be just fine. I promise there won't be any gunfights or explosions tonight. Just some hors d'oeuvres, some small talk, and I hope a quiet corner where I can get you alone for a few minutes. I'm not the only one who looks absolutely stunning in this car."

Without thinking, I gave the front of my cream-and-gold dress a tug. My double Ds were way more exposed than usual, and it made me nervous. "You're sure this is okay? It's not too cheap? In either sense?"

Lake shook his head. "You'll fit in just fine. Your gossip girls did a great job of helping you pick out a dress. Trust me. Everyone else is going to think I'm a random piece of furniture you happen to be standing next to."

I flushed at his compliment. "Hey, there are pieces of furniture out there that are worth more than my life. Now, before we get there, are there any unspoken rules I should know? I don't want to embarrass you."

Lake squeezed my thigh. "You could never embarrass me, Pippa. Just be yourself, and don't talk to Uncle Odie about cars like Sadie here, unless you have two hours to kill."

"Duly noted." We drove the rest of the way to Summerpoint in companionable conversation. Half an hour later, I turned onto a long, curving drive. An enormous stately house emerged from the fog. As we drew closer, short white pillars materialized, marching rank and file along the edge of the drive. They got taller as I drove up to the main doors. I felt like I'd taken a wrong turn and ended up in Greece by accident.

A valet in a red velvet jacket opened my door for me. I took his gloved hand and stepped into a foggy wonderland lit by warm, flickering torchlight. My long skirt brushed my ankles, and I adjusted the retro golden-rabbit-fur shrug Jordan had insisted I borrow. I tucked my clutch under one arm then dropped my keys into his hand, and he wished me a good evening. Then he offered Sadie's ticket to Lake.

Just be myself? I can do that. "Hey, dude. Which one of us just got out of the driver's seat?" I held out my palm expectantly.

The young valet hesitated, an uncertain look in his wide brown eyes. "But this is Mr. *Ivens.*"

I shot Lake an exasperated look, but he only seemed amused. He raised an eyebrow at me as if to tell me to do my thing.

I took a breath and did just that. *I am the assassin Sylvester, and I will happily subvert the rules you play by so that they work for me.* I plucked the ticket from the valet's fingers and tucked it into my cleavage. "Yes, it is, darling. I *do* know who I'm sleeping with."

Lake's eyebrows nearly reached his hairline, but he was grinning as he held his arm out for me. I really wanted to look back and see the expression on the young man's face as I took my boyfriend's arm and strolled toward the front door, but I didn't think Sylvester would, so I didn't either. *Ugh, I'm channeling Sylvester, but I feel more like Auda.*

A doorman in a cap and a long coat opened the door ahead of us, and we strolled into an enormous foyer that was made of pale marble and heavily decorated with gold and evergreen floral arrangements. A double staircase curved up to the second floor, the marble steps overlaid with a scarlet runner that trickled down from above like a dripping bloodstain.

I shivered. "Silly me, assuming it would be warmer inside than it is outside." I spotted a coat-check window and sighed. "Looks like I'll have to turn on my internal oven." I turned my back to Lake, and he slid my shrug off my shoulders and checked it for me.

When he returned, he rubbed my arms and pulled me into an embrace. "Any time you get cold, just ring for your personal warmth distributor, and I'll come running."

I squeezed him tightly and gave him a careful peck on the lips, careful not to smear my lipstick. "Let's go find out if anyone else is here yet. I can't wait to see what Trudie shows up in. It really was sweet of your uncle to invite her and Gabe."

"After you pressured him into it, you mean?" he murmured through a smile.

"Yes," I said brightly. "So generous of him. He's my favorite now, and you can't change my mind."

"Oh, he's my favorite too." Lake chuckled as he took my arm and led the way down the broad parquet hallway. Elegant mirrors and rich paintings stood witness to our passage. "After what Jordan wore to Tyleen's dinner, you know she's going to stride in here like she owns the place. I bet there's at least one guy who asks her for a personal tour."

"Knowing Jordan, I'm sure she could probably fake an actual tour just fine."

A broad archway opened on our left, and through it, an enormous ballroom gleamed in readiness for guests. The floor bore warm golden paneling, and the open space was punctuated by the occasional tall cocktail table overburdened with enormous decorations in gold and evergreen. A string quartet played snippets of a classic theme as if they were just warming up.

The room was huge and echoingly empty. In a panic, I checked my watch. "Is this really what counts for a 'small' party? Are we too early? Are we the first ones here?" I looked at Lake. "Is it rude to be the first ones here? Why didn't you tell me to come later?"

Lake chuckled helplessly at my discomfiture. "Relax. Nobody cares who comes first."

I held his gaze with a wicked grin. "That's what *he* said," I said saucily.

"Whoa, I surrender," Lake said through his laughter. He took my hands and interlaced his fingers with mine.

A woman's firm voice interrupted us from deep within the ballroom. "No, the truffle canapés circulate, and the mini quiches stay put."

My eyes widened with surprise. "That sounds like Tyleen."

Lake's surprise lasted only a moment. "My uncle did tell you he hired the best. Go on in. I'm going to find my sister. I assume she's barricaded herself in one of the bathroom suites upstairs because the hand-soap scent clashes with her perfume or something, and she's sent Kait to steal her some more. Back soon, promise." He dropped a kiss on my knuckles and headed back to the stairs.

I turned, nearly tripped over my long skirt, hastily gathered it, then clicked my way across the bright wooden ballroom floor in search of Tyleen.

To my right, a gentle arc of serving tables curved out from the kitchen's double doors. Strings of white lights emanated from a central spot on the high ceiling, forming a Christmas tree shape behind the tables. The lights were also festooned with enormous golden Christmas ornaments twice the size of my head. Their mirrored edges beautifully reflected the strings of lights.

Three members of the waitstaff, dressed in black pants and white button-down shirts, busily arranged stacks of plates, decorations, and towers of stacked platters under the direction of a woman in white over black with her back to me. Her bright-gold hair was pulled back into a tight chignon.

"And make sure there's enough gold leaf in each champagne glass. It's supposed to peel off when we pour and float like snowflakes." The woman must have heard me approach because she turned, bearing a bright, professional smile. "Welcome! *Pippa?* Whatcha doin' here? *Ohh.* Lake's family. Right. Glad to see they let you in."

The head caterer was indeed my neighbor Tyleen, but my appearance seemed to have cracked her concentration. I was thrilled to see her, but I didn't want to throw her off her game.

"Good evening," I said formally then slipped her a wink, as if I'd walked out of an old noir film. "It smells heavenly in here. What's on the menu for tonight? I bet it's to die for."

Tyleen pressed her dark-red lips together in amusement. "You're probably smelling the peppermint-peach pasticcio for our main course this evening. Dinner will be served in the Expedition Hall, which offers a lovely view of the sea while you dine." She gave me an exaggerated wink in return. We both knew the entire coast was socked in by fog.

I struggled not to giggle. "But what if I'm hungry now? I see a lot of yummies right here."

Tyleen gestured to a stack of small crystal plates. "Tonight is a low-key affair, just an informal gathering with friends and family. Feel free to eat as much as you like while the other guests are still arriving. I highly recommend these mini quiches." She led me toward a table where a large tower offered dozens of little quiches on a series of crystal platters, fetched one with a pair of tongs, and handed it to me on a plate. "This recipe is an old favorite, kindly lent to me by a good friend with excellent taste." She gave me another giant wink.

"Felicity's quiche recipe! This is what you wanted it for! You really were sworn to secrecy, weren't you?"

"Mr. Ivens's assistant was very clear that the Ivenses were to be the ones who told people they were in town, not me. So yeah, I think that counts as being sworn to secrecy." She giggled. "But I have my ways of including people. You didn't know who I was making it for, and they didn't know where I got it. I figure that balances everything out." Tyleen shrugged breezily.

Probably for the best, considering. I glanced at the quiche tower. All the food was arranged perfectly, and mine was the only one missing. I picked up the quiche and inhaled deeply of its cheesy, spinachy goodness. As the hostess of a bed-and-breakfast, I never ate first. By the deep satisfaction hovering in the corners of Tyleen's smile, she was taking advantage of my guest status to treat me like an honored dignitary.

"Felicity would be so proud right now," I murmured just before I stuffed the quiche into my face.

A laugh like the tinkling of bells carried across the ballroom. I shot Tyleen an elated grin. "Jordan's here!"

She shooed me toward my BFF like a mother hen. "Go. Have fun. You deserve to enjoy yourself."

Jordan, Trudie, and Gabe entered together, followed by a dozen people I didn't know. My friends beelined for the food tables, but Trudie detoured toward a platter that Tyleen picked up and offered:

champagne glittering with gold flakes. I was disappointed not to see Lake with them.

Trudie offered me an exaggerated curtsy and raised her glass. "Now we can get this party started!"

9

"I'm too old to party. I was born too old to party. Give me a quiet chair, a book, and something to drink, and leave me in peace. No, I mean right now. Skedaddle."
Raymond Moore, 1977

I TUGGED UP MY BODICE, lifted my skirts, and joined my friends.

Jordan wore another antique gown—courtesy of her consignment friend, no doubt—in midnight blue with a gathered skirt and gently puffed sleeves. Her pomegranate hair was upswept into a style that was positively Anne Shirley, and she totally rocked it. Trudie wore a slinky copper dress under a matching drape that set off the highlights in her loose curls, and Gabe wore black jeans and a retro leather jacket with copper undertones. *Oh my goodness, Tru...*

"I told you guys that I needed social backup tonight, and you just asked me where. I appreciate you so much. Jordan is just in from Prince Edward Island, I see, but you two," I said to my sister and her date, "look more like a 1940s mobster and his moll."

Trudie snaked an arm around Gabe's neck and shot me a coy look. "See, sugar? I told you she'd pick up on our vibe."

Gabe shook his head and wrapped his arms around her waist. "You're both so smart. If I had your brains or even a pile of money like the Ivenses do, I'd feel more at home. But I don't. What am I even doing here?"

Jordan pointed a midnight fingernail toward the buffet table.

His eyes lit up. "I'll be right back."

Other guests began to trickle in, dressed to the nines with compound interest. It didn't really surprise me that the Ivenses could pull a few dozen wealthy folks out of the rustic coastal woodwork. The newcomers offered polite nods and smiles, though they didn't mingle with us. I didn't mind one bit, since I had some of my favorite people in the world to talk to.

Wren walked in on Mort's arm, looking regal in powder blue and carrying a blue-and-gold clutch under her arm. Mort tipped his black cowboy hat at us, and its silver buckle winked in the light. Fallon Vanderveer arrived a couple of minutes later, spotted us, and made a beeline.

"My favorite sisters," the Seven Vistas hotelier said. He gave us both air kisses, bowed over Jordan's hand, and gave Gabe a hearty handshake. "What have I missed?"

Trudie showed him her mostly empty plate. "About a dozen mini quiches. And I'm not stopping there."

Fallon's laugh echoed around the room, turning heads. He snagged a glass of champagne from a passing tray.

"How do you know the Ivenses?" I asked.

He took a sip and shook his head. "My father was a good friend of theirs. I understand they had a bit of a friendly rivalry over luxury hotel properties in Las Vegas and San Diego, but they worked through it, as businessmen do."

More than two dozen guests had arrived by then—none of them members of the Ivens family—when Mallory Tavish walked through the door. I had to do a double take because at first glance, I didn't recognize her. A cream sheath dress set off her olive skin, and she'd taken down her perma-bun and tucked her dark hair into a loose, romantic knot just behind her left ear. Simple gold jewelry was all she needed to set off her lean beauty.

"Is that Mallory?" Jordan stage-whispered.

I nodded, still staring.

Fallon said what we were all thinking. "Wow."

Wow, indeed.

But Mallory didn't stride into the room with her standard-issue towering confidence. She lingered hesitantly in the doorway, one hand clasping her other elbow.

I waited for someone from her old life to rush over and greet her, but no one did. Seconds ticked by, and I finally realized what was going on.

No one knows what to do with Mallory Tavish now that she isn't an Ivens. Lake and Mallory both left their world of wealth, but Lake is here as part of his family. Mallory has no such protection.

I took a bracing breath and stepped over to greet her, aware that I probably wasn't helping her cause. "Hey, Mallory. You look great."

Mallory's dark eyes scanned me like a facial recognition system. "You're not so bad yourself, Winterbourne." Her gaze flicked past me and took in the people I'd been chatting with. "No one from the Ivens crew is coming over to talk with you, either, huh?"

I took umbrage on Fallon's behalf, but I knew Mallory had a better handle on the social situation than I did. *She probably wouldn't accept any help from me, but it goes against my nature not to offer it.* "Listen, Mallory, do you want to come—"

She shifted her weight and looked me right in the eyes. "A piece of advice, Winterbourne. Don't talk about Lake here."

My offer of help had just been co-opted and inverted, and I felt a little attacked.

My indignation must have shown on my face, because Mallory continued, "I mean it. Lake turned his back on everything these people represent. They've worked hard to get where they are, to maintain and increase their influence. Lake threw that away, so don't bring him up first. Everyone here knows he's slumming it in Seacrest with you."

"I—how—" I did a great impression of a largemouth bass gasping with outrage.

Mallory cast an eye across the room and spoke again without looking at me. "I'm serious, Winterbourne. You're a goldfish someone chucked into the ocean. You have no idea of the depths you're getting into here." A calculating look slowly came over her face, and her eyes shifted back to mine. "Although... Pippa is short for what? Philippa?"

Irritated by her frenetic topic jumping, I replied coolly, "It is."

The corner of her mouth shifted partway in the direction of a smile, and she shot a glance toward a cluster of wealthy gentlemen across the room. "Where's your family from?"

I told her, and she offered me a rare grin of camaraderie. "Come with me. I don't get to do this often, and I want to see if I've still got it."

I guessed I had to go along with it, just to ease my desperate curiosity about what Mallory had in mind. With one reassuring glance back at my disbelieving sister, I strode after Mallory and did my best to copy her social mannerisms. *I can always bail if Mallory's tactics set me on fire or something. But where the heck is Lake?*

But I didn't need to bail. Ten minutes later, Mallory had introduced me to a third cluster of wealthy guests as "Philippa Winterbourne, of the Albany Winterbournes." The men always nodded and smiled knowingly, and the women offered both of us congratulations on catching an Ivens man. Mallory laughed off the surreal awkwardness of those comments, and I did my best to follow suit.

Many of the wealthy enjoyed discussing politics as if they were chatting about their favorite pets, and Mallory could play just as well on that level as any other. With half a dozen other guests gathered around us in a self-satisfied coterie, she said, "Prop 8? No, that was me."

I recalled the controversial California bill. "You wrote it?" I blurted.

The others chuckled politely at my gaffe, but Mallory simply replied, "No, I killed it. Believe what you like about personal choices, but no one comes into my state, throwing money left and right, and gets what they want. My state, my rules. And don't get me started on Russia!"

Guffaws all around.

I laughed, too, but had to wonder. *Is she serious, or is this how the rich talk to impress one another?*

After detaching herself from the latest cluster of guests, Mallory snagged a glass of gold-flecked champagne and downed it in one gulp. She wiped a small piece of gold leaf from the corner of her mouth with her ring finger then scraped it back onto the rim of her glass. "By the way, Winterbourne, which Albany is your family actually from?"

After cramming during Mallory's crash course in how to sound richer than God, I simply looked at her with a smug smile and said, "Exactly."

She swapped a second glass of champagne for her empty one and lifted it in a subtle toast. "Smarter than you look, Winterbourne."

I picked up my own glass and clinked it against hers. "Generally preferable to the opposite." Halfway through my chug, the Ivenses finally graced us with their presence, and I nearly choked on my champagne.

Devereaux Ivens entered first, looking svelte in a dark suit with a white shirt and no tie. On his arm, Lake's mom, Auda, exuded more regal grace than the queen of England, sporting a gown of gold and green. Beside her, wearing an emerald party frock, Bliss was texting, looking bored. On Bliss's other side, her friend Kait wore a similar frock in mocha and cream. Her anticipatory grin hinted at a clever joke only she knew.

Lake wasn't with them. He'd said he would be back soon, but his sister had shown up without him. I started to wonder if I should wander through the unfamiliar mansion, on a quest to retrieve him, but then the woman on Devereaux's near side captured my attention and nearly made me do a spit take. She was my height, with dark hair upswept and tendrils framing her excellent cheekbones. Her navy-blue dress was simple, more practical than the others'. Her gray eyes lent a dramatic flair to the Asian influence in her features.

The last time I'd seen her, she'd been dressed as an exterminator outside Mallory's house.

"Who is that?" I murmured to Mallory, nodding toward the mystery woman.

"No idea. Must be new. Probably Devereaux's assistant. He never goes anywhere without at least one."

Cam. She set up the party, hired Tyleen... and spied on Mallory's house? Lake's dad has some nerve. I need to be extra careful with Aunt Felicity's secret. God knows what a man like that would do to my business if it amused him.

A server in a tux smoothly approached and served the Ivenses champagne. As he stepped toward me, I belatedly realized it was Sebastian. I flicked my eyebrows up when he and I made eye contact, and he pursed his lips to avoid grinning, though his eyes twinkled.

He paused near me and murmured, "Mom has something in the kitchen for you when you get a chance."

"Have you seen Lake yet?"

He shook his head. "I'll keep an eye out, though, okay?" I nodded, and he swanned off with his tray.

Devereaux Ivens stepped forward and raised his glass. "Welcome, family, friends, and honored guests. We're so pleased that all of you could join us this year for our little holiday celebration. Some of you have come a long way, and we thank you for deciding to spend the evening with us. As you know, our prodigal son, Lake, is taking a sabbatical in the charming town of Seacrest. And from his own introduction up here, I see—where is that boy?"

"He'll be along," Auda murmured brightly.

"Always did have an obsession with getting his hair just right," Devereaux told the room with a grin. "Bit windy and damp here for that sort of fashion. He's probably forgotten how it goes."

Quiet chuckles rang in the room, and I clenched my teeth as I realized that Devereux and some of his rich friends were mocking my boyfriend and my town. Mallory slipped her cool fingers around my wrist and gave me a sharp squeeze, though her attention seemed fixed on Devereaux.

He continued, "So we have decided to come and see what this small corner of the world could possibly possess to ensnare our son so thoroughly." To my surprise, he raised his champagne glass and looked directly at me. "And now that I've met the lovely Ms. Winterbourne and seen her abundant charms"—his eyes danced up and down my figure in a distant, objectifying manner—"all has become clear." More subtle laughter, this time at the expense of my double Ds.

A hot flush of anger and embarrassment crept up my neck, and I started to reach for my bodice again to give it another upward tug. But Mallory's grip turned into a manacle. She casually turned and lifted her champagne glass toward me, ignoring the viselike hold she maintained on me as if her other hand belonged to someone else. Through her glazed-peach smile, she murmured, "Not now, Winterbourne."

I couldn't do much but stare at her face, not sure whose side she was on. My nostrils flared so hard that I felt like an alarmed cow.

"So please, everyone, enjoy yourselves. I know I will," Devereaux finished.

He and his family began to mingle with their guests.

Sebastian swooped back in and offered us fresh champagne, his jade-green eyes hooded with concern. "Are you okay? That comment was uncalled for."

I straightened my spine and tossed off Devereaux's words. "I'll be fine. Thanks, Sebastian. Better keep moving, though. Lake's mom is watching us."

"Okay, but I got your back." Sebastian lifted his tray and swanned off into the crowd.

Before I could ask Mallory to help me learn more about the fake exterminator, Bliss sauntered over to us. She gave me a prejudiced once-over then turned her attention to Mallory, as if I didn't exist. "Hey, Mals. Haven't seen you in forever. Did you drag that dress from under the same rock where you've been hiding or a different rock? There's so many around here to choose from."

Mallory turned to face Bliss directly and adjusted her body language in a display of power, shoulders back, chin up, eyes unblinking. "Not all of us can shop all day every day, Bliss. Some of us actually have enough skills to get a job."

Obviously unoffended, Bliss merely shrugged one shoulder. "Hey, I have my charities. I help tons of people."

"No one ever has to buy you organic, locally sourced hand soap for Christmas, do they?" Mallory asked in the same arch tone. "Because you never actually get your hands dirty from helping."

Bliss's smile brimmed with daggers. "At least I don't use hand sanitizer as perfume."

Impatient, I said, "I hate to interrupt this love fest of a reunion, but who's the woman who was standing next to your father when you came in?" *And where the hell is Lake?*

Bliss and Mallory both stared at me as if I had appeared out of thin air.

"Don't talk to her," Bliss said, referring to Cam. "She's just an employee, anyway. My father's favorite fetcher. Mals, there's someone I want you to meet." Without further ado, Bliss took Mallory by the hand and led her into the crowd, leaving me alone. I tried not to feel betrayed by Mallory reconnecting with her wealthy frenemy. We'd only been allies for about half an hour, anyway. But I was frustrated that Bliss had taken off before I could ask her about Lake.

I was alone for about six seconds before Jordan swooped in, dragging Gabe and Tru with her. "Did he *just*?" Jordan began, referring to Devereaux's uncalled-for comment.

"We can lure him into a dark alley for you," Tru offered in a conspiratorial whisper.

"He may or may not come out again," Gabe added. The serious gleam in his eye belied his light tone, and his criminal record—he'd done time for defending his grandmother—jumped to the front of my mind.

I raised my chin. "I'm a big girl." I glanced down at my cleavage and giggled at my own double entendre. "The girls and I can handle ourselves. Please, no alley dragging. Now, I need to slip off and meet Tyleen in the kitchen. But thank you, guys. Your support means a lot. I'll be right back, okay?"

I found Sebastian in the crowd and nodded toward the kitchen. He gave me a nod that said he would join me as soon as he served the last champagne glass on his tray. I tried to act like I belonged as I pushed through the swinging kitchen doors, but I'd stepped into a realm of ordered chaos, and I stopped short so I wouldn't get run over. Half a dozen waitstaff dashed around, preparing salads, sauces, and meats for dinner.

Tyleen spotted me right away and waved me toward a steaming pot the size of a sea mine. "Welcome to the kitchen! I want you to try this butternut-mushroom reduction." She picked up a clean spoon and scooped some straight from the pot, cupped a hand beneath it, and held it up for me to taste.

I blew gently then sipped the thick, savory golden liquid. "Oh my God, that is the best squash soup I've ever tasted."

"I knew you'd like it. You've been serving squash this and squash that at Moorehaven all autumn long. You want the recipe?" Her blue eyes sparkled.

I folded my hands as if in prayer. "Please?"

A server hurried by with a tart pan laden with piping-hot quiches, and Tyleen aimed a thumb at the food. "It's only fair."

Sebastian slid past his mom and dropped a kiss on her bright-golden hair. "I need to get that special order ready." He retrieved a Ziploc bag full of greens from inside the walk-in refrigerator and took up a station by a cutting board.

"All this food, and you do special orders too?" I asked.

"Sure do." He separated the greenery into piles of kale, avocado, apple, spinach, and more. "By the way, you look amazing. It must be nice to come to a party where you don't have to hang out in the kitchen all the time and cook, right?" He selected a knife and began chopping the apple slices into fine pieces.

I took a deep breath and glanced at Tyleen. "I don't know yet. I'm really out of my element here, and Lake's taking his sweet time showing up to help me out. Everyone's so focused on getting everything perfect, with gold leaf and giant decorations and all this food. I mean, shouldn't that door be covered in green baize?"

Tyleen chuckled at my reference to the pre-WWI habit of marking the servants' doors in mansions with green baize cloth. "It's not quite Downton Abbey in here. Wealthy folk are a lot more like you and me than you might think. The big difference is that they have enough money to protect themselves from the unfortunate surprises of life. The rest of us just make do."

I squinted at her, not quite following. "Rich people don't like surprises?"

She shrugged amiably. "You've lived in Seacrest for a while now. Not all the surprises here are what I'd call life-affirming. Wouldn't you pay to avoid those if you could?"

The past year had been plagued with more than the usual number of murders—it was true. "I see your point. But hey," I added, side-stepping the morbid thought, "I'm so excited that you guys are catering this party. I could take a picture of you with your phone if it's handy."

Tyleen handed it over. I did my best to frame them artistically and get some good lighting, using the side wall of the kitchen as a backdrop. I studied my handiwork. *Naoma's so much better at this than I am. She'd know better than to stick a blender just behind Sebastian's elbow. Oh well.* I texted myself a copy of the photo because I'd just gotten a fun little idea.

"Thanks, dear. Better get back out there," Tyleen told me.

I took a deep breath. "Once more unto the breach."

"Henry V captured Harfleur after that speech," Sebastian said as he finished chopping the apples. "You've got this."

I nodded at him, impressed. "Look who knows his Shakespeare. I'll see you out there. And thanks for all this amazing food." I faced the kitchen door, squared my shoulders, then headed back out.

I paused by the hors d'oeuvres table, snatched a little tartlet laden with pecan crumbles and gold-leaf sprinkles, and studied the room. Trudie was pulling Gabe by the hand while pointing ahead at Fallon.

She called out to the hotelier, "Yeah, well, you sprained an ankle the last time we went kite surfing!"

Several guests near Fallon looked concerned for a moment, but then Fallon burst out laughing and launched into an animated story of how he'd injured himself while trying to copy Trudie.

Lake had finally returned to the ballroom, and he and his mom were talking to another cluster of mostly young, attractive women. As I happened to glance at them, she glanced at me too. Our eyes met, but she didn't stop talking or acknowledge me. One of her hands lifted to rest on Lake's shoulder, turning his back more fully to me, and she smiled broadly and continued talking to all the pretty girls surrounding her son.

Could she be more obvious? Geez.

Then a rush of a familiar perfume enveloped me, and a little golden plate laden with an assortment of hors d'oeuvres veered into my line of sight. Jordan deliberately blocked my view with food, grinning like a maniac. "Nibbles, darling?" she asked, affecting a posh accent.

"Oh my God, I love you so much right now." I took the plate and stuffed the first three things I could reach into my mouth. "Mmm, what kind of cheese is this?"

Jordan picked up a similar cheese wedge on a golden toothpick and gave it a sniff. "Something Italian, maybe?" She ate it. "Not bad, but if I eat any more food covered in gold flakes, I'm going to end up with a rapper's grill." She snapped at me toothily. "So, what's going on? Why did everyone abandon you, and how many of them do I get to kill in your defense?" I opened my mouth to reply, but Jordan wasn't finished. "And did I mention yet that Lake's dad is a complete jerk? Because I feel like I forgot to mention that *he's a complete jerk*."

I tried to tell her that yes, she had mentioned it, but my best friend was on a roll.

"I mean, who does that? Your son's girlfriend may look absolutely stunning in the dress she wears to your party, but that's no reason to make euphemisms about her boobs to the whole crowd, is it? No. No, it is not." Jordan aggressively chomped on a cracker stacked with bits of colorful food.

Exasperated, I popped a stuffed mushroom into my mouth and said around it, "That was, like, six questions. Do you actually want me to answer any of them?"

Jordan blinked twice in quick succession. "Of course, sweetie. What do you—"

"Never mind." I'd just spotted the mystery woman Bliss had told me not to talk to. "Come with me." I steered her by the elbow in the woman's direction. As we approached her, I murmured to Jordan, explaining where I had seen her before.

I parked myself in front of the woman in the navy-blue dress and met her gray eyes. I was planning to pretend I didn't know who she was, but the glint in her eye and a hint of a smile in the corner of her mouth made me change tactics. "Hello again," I said.

Her smile broadened, and she tipped her head in a subtle gesture of approval. She stuck out her hand to shake mine. "Cam. Cam Cooper. It's nice to finally meet you, Pippa."

I reached out slowly and shook her hand, maintaining eye contact. I gave Jordan a side nod. "This is my best friend, Jordan Harper."

Cam shook her hand as well.

"So, when you were pretending to spray for ants at Mallory's house... You don't actually know Mallory at all, do you?"

Cam's face adjusted subtly as she absorbed my deduction, and her expression landed somewhere in the region of pleasantly impressed. "Only by reputation. I was actually following you."

My eyebrows shot up. "Well, that's refreshing." I turned to Jordan. "Stalkers don't usually confess straight out like that. Do you think this might become a trend?"

Jordan gave a judicious nod. "With such a shining example, I certainly hope so." She offered her plate to Cam. "Gold-flecked chocolate strawberry?"

Cam gave us a tolerant blink and waved away Jordan's offer. "Following someone isn't a crime. I was under orders from Mr. Ivens. Mr. *Devereaux* Ivens," she clarified.

As if Lake would hire someone to follow me. But now I'm more concerned about protecting Aunt Felicity's secret. "From his comment earlier, I assume he asked you to get close enough to guess my measurements. Or have you also broken into my panty drawer?"

Jordan added, "Bliss called you his fetcher. Maybe you took a few things too. Pippa, are you missing any unmentionables?"

I raised an eyebrow. "I'll check when I get home. So, does being a personal assistant mean you get off scot-free for cute little burglary charges, on account of your boss being so important and all?"

Cam's grin was cocky, at odds with her conservative dress. "Look at the two of you. So feisty and in sync and everything! I like it." Her smile faded. "I do whatever Mr. Ivens instructs me to do, but he hasn't asked me about your personal details or your measurements. I just kept an eye on your known associates and waited for one of them to contact you."

I offered her a mildly suspicious squint. "You were at Naoma's rental before I got there."

She grinned again, unabashed. "I knew you were coming."

"You listened in on Naoma's phone call to me?"

"Force-pairing cell phones does tend to have that effect. Don't worry," she added as I was preparing to splutter indignantly about phone tapping. "I'm not listening in on anything anymore. Mr. Ivens has already judged you and doesn't feel the need to inquire further. It's not a bad gig, making yourself indispensable to the wealthy. You think Mr. Ivens would be able to arrange a trip to visit his long-lost estranged son without my assistance?"

I frowned at her implication. "Are you saying Lake's dad didn't even know where Lake lives?"

Cam's grin was downright mischievous, putting me in mind of a smug, almost impudent fairy. "Like I said, indispensable." She reached over to Jordan's plate and nabbed a golden toothpick with two cheese cubes bookending a slice of apple. With a smile, she trapped the food behind her teeth and pulled the toothpick free. She chewed then swallowed. "Enjoy the party, ladies. I'm sure I'll see you around."

She tucked the toothpick into her cheek, hayseed-style, and meandered off through the crowd. Something about her casual insouciance struck a chord deep inside me, but I couldn't place it.

Beside me, Jordan pouted, staring after Cam.

"What?" I asked.

"There's no neutral with that one. But I can't decide if I love her or hate her yet."

I glanced at Devereaux's assistant and felt an odd crackle in the air. "You ever feel like you should've been hitting the gym for weeks already because something wild and woolly is about to go down, and you're about to run for your life?"

"When I'm around you? Pretty much constantly."

"Tell me, darling," I said, affecting a posh accent, "how many calories does that sass burn per hour?"

Jordan clamped her laughter into a smile. "Let's just say I could power the town if I ever let them plug me into the grid."

"A whole new meaning to 'girl power.'" I took a deep breath and glanced around the ballroom again. Forty people in elegant clothing chatted and snacked while the string quartet played at the far end of the room. Gigantic Christmas decorations winked and glittered overhead. "Well, if she is half the facilitator she claims to be, she's really good at her job."

We picked up a few more delectable nibbles and began a slow orbit of the ballroom, casting about for familiar faces.

Mort Roark was trying to hold Sebastian captive with a conversation while he drank from one of the champagne flutes on Sebastian's tray. "I'll give you a great deal, kid. You don't really want to live with your mom forever, do you?"

Bafflement flickered over Sebastian's freckled face. "But if I moved out, who would cook my favorite meals? Or clean my room?"

Mort froze and studied Sebastian's face. "Aren't you, like, twenty-five years old?"

Sebastian smiled apologetically. "Thirty-two."

"Sounds like your mom doesn't know how to raise a man right. Don't let someone like that keep you from reaching your full potential, kid. She's just holding you back."

Ignoring Mort and his sly insults, I leaned against Sebastian's shoulder and said, "Hey, Sebastian, thank your mom for that homemade furniture polish she gave me last week. I don't know how she got that stuff to shine up so brightly, but it's done wonders for my poor, abused staircase banister. She must have tried a dozen different recipes over at your house before she hit on something so perfect."

Sebastian's gentle smile held a gallon of gratitude. "I'll let her know. Mom's always happiest when she's helping others."

Mort managed a disapproving frown and a quick bow before drifting off into the crowd. Sebastian whispered his thanks and returned to his duties. Jordan and I lifted a mini quiche apiece and tapped them together like champagne glasses.

Trudie and Fallon formed the center of a large group that listened, rapt, as my sister spun a tale of her latest outdoor adventure with her hotel-owner friend—one that involved BASE jumping.

Lake's uncle, Odie, nodded along as if he, too, would like a young, athletic friend to throw himself off a cliff with. I couldn't help but feel sorry for Gabe, having his girlfriend swept up into some rich guy's outdoor activities all the time, but Gabe didn't seem fazed one bit—and he didn't have a very good poker face. I'd won enough Oreos off him to know.

Lake's mother had finally let him wander off, though I couldn't see him. Auda held court over three other ladies and didn't seem to care about the volume of her comments or their content. "I can't believe my sweet little boy washed up in such a dirty little backwater.

He told me he's living in the basement of a condemned lighthouse. Can you believe such a thing?"

A strident voice replied at equal volume but not from Auda's coterie of adherents. "No, my dear, I cannot. Perhaps because it isn't true."

Startled, I glanced behind and to my right, where the redoubtable Geneva Laine was striding forward, seemingly enjoying her disruption of Auda's little rant, dragging a silvery cape on the floor behind a conservative black-and-silver gown. She thumped her ivory-headed cane on the ballroom floor with every other step. Each thump made Auda wince and Geneva's smile widen until the grand old lady paused right in front of Lake's mother. The long stares they shared were so intense they could have triggered a nine-pointer earthquake in the Cascadia Subduction Zone just offshore.

But when they spoke, their voices were perfectly civil, their expressions neutral. "Geneva, how lovely to see you again."

"Auda, darling."

"How are you this evening? I wasn't sure you would accept my invitation," Auda said, indicating Geneva's cane, "considering your extreme age and infirmity."

Geneva rapped the foot of her cane against the wooden floor twice. "As fit as a fiddle. All this sea air. Good for what ails you. Though I don't think it can cure the failing standards of California's finishing schools. Alas."

Jordan clutched my shoulder in delighted shock. Auda's eyes bugged for just a second, as if Geneva had slammed her cane's ivory head into Auda's stomach. I had to stifle a chuckle at the image of the nonagenarian jauntily taking on a woman thirty years her junior.

"For instance," Geneva continued serenely, "I wouldn't be caught dead without a snappy reply to such an insult, but it seems that *you* have been. Good evening, my dear." She swanned onward, her silver cape gently billowing behind her.

Jordan and I waited a moment to give Geneva her due distance after such a dramatic feat. I caught Wren's eye a few feet away, and she offered me a collaborative grin at Geneva's sauciness. Behind the luminous pale blue of Wren's Christmas gown, Mort stood impatiently, as if Wren had abandoned him in order to observe Geneva's takedown. Mort murmured something to her, and a tired expression crossed her face.

She turned her head and addressed him over her shoulder. "No, go get it yourself, Mort. I don't work for you."

I couldn't hear his reply, but his body language shuffled through a few responses before settling on amiable agreement.

To me, Wren said, "I had no idea Tyleen was such an expert caterer. The meal at Moorehaven was definitely scrumptious, but look at this!" She held up her hors d'oeuvres plate and pointed at the stuffed mushrooms and mini quiches. "And this is just the snacks. I can't wait to see what she's cooked up for dinner."

"Everything okay with Mort?" I asked tentatively. "You seemed on better terms at Moorehaven."

She waved a hand. "Oh, no, don't worry. We bicker like an old married couple. Sometimes I feel like I should apologize to my dearly departed husband for how Mort and I get along."

"Oh, I'm sorry. Did he pass recently?"

"Not at all. We'd only been married a year when I lost him. A sudden brain aneurysm, no way to predict it. I'm just glad he gave me Monsieur, our first corgi. All my precious fur babies have been descended from him. They've truly been my life's joy. When I'm with them, it's as if Theo is still with me too."

"Oh, that's beautiful," I said. "Who do you have now?"

"I've got Parsnip and her two grown kids, Pacifica and Legolas. Leggy is so good with people and other animals that I'm considering training him to be a therapy dog."

"That sounds great. Is that what you wanted to talk to Sebastian about after the Moorehaven tour?"

"Oh, of course. He gave me good counsel. Sebastian is so in tune with animals that it's no wonder he makes such a good pet psychic. I swear my dogs talk to him more than they talk to me. I trust him with their happiness more than anyone." She smiled and disappeared into the crowd, and Jordan and I continued wending our way around the room.

I hadn't seen Lake in way too long. Several minutes later, I came across Mallory again, in conversation with Odie, Bliss, and others I didn't recognize. Kait hovered at Bliss's elbow, and it struck me that I hadn't seen her for a while either. She'd been dressed to blend into the background and let Bliss shine, though. Mallory saw me coming, and something in the way she quickly turned her head told me that I wasn't invited to that particular discussion. I steered Jordan toward a nearby cocktail table, and we set our plates down and pretended to chat while we eavesdropped on her.

"And how do you like it, out here in the middle of nowhere?" a woman in a strapless black dress asked Mallory.

"I don't mind the small-town look at all, because it's usually hidden in all this fog," Mallory said, eliciting a round of laughter.

"And you managed to find a nice place, of course?" the woman pressed.

Mallory paused, clearly caught off guard, before replying, "Absolutely. I'm embracing the retro-chic trend right now. It wasn't easy to find a place I could live with, but I managed to make good friends with one of the area's best landladies and finagle my way into the perfect cozy little house."

A worm of discomfort turned in my tummy amid Mallory's admiring murmurs. Her comment was ninety percent fabrication on top of ten percent truth, and I didn't like what that truth was: Mallory was embarrassed to tell her rich friends where she actually lived.

She was ashamed of her cobbled-together duplex and probably of Seacrest too. The worm twisted harder as I wondered whether Lake harbored similar judgments down deep.

A man with a California tan and an expert dye job said, "Tell these guys how you got this gig in the first place. I thought you were pretty clever, pushing out that Podunk policeman so you could take his place."

Out of the corner of my eye, I saw Mallory roll her shoulders. "I didn't really push Officer Harris out so much as pull him somewhere else. His sister and her kids were struggling financially up near Portland, so I simply made a few calls and arranged for him to get a job offer from the chief of police in her town. He was gone so quickly that I think it made Chief Craig's head spin. I just stepped into the gap."

"The gap that you created," the fake-blond man commented.

Mallory shrugged. "Nature, vacuum. You know how it goes."

I clenched the edge of the table until my thumb turned white. Any sympathy I had ever had for Mallory Tavish evaporated in furious heat. Not only had she come to Seacrest with designs on getting her ex-husband back, but she had manipulated her way into Officer Harris's job too.

Jordan jabbed my thumb with one of her used golden toothpicks.

"Ow!" I yelped before sucking on the injury. "What?"

Jordan made a moue at me. "You weren't responding to me hissing your name or kicking you under the table, so I had to resort to drastic measures. I know what you're thinking, and I'm kind of there with you, but hear me out."

I raised a hand to jab in Mallory's direction. "But did you hear—"

"Hear. Me. Out," Jordan said as she caught my hand and pressed it firmly to the tabletop. When I finally nodded, she continued,

"Mallory has power we don't. Let's just accept that now. But she could have used that power to do something horrible to Officer Harris to force him out of Seacrest. Instead, she looked into his personal life and found a way to help his family. Yeah, she helped herself at the same time. And it wasn't to your benefit—we both know she tracked Lake to Seacrest. But I'm just saying she could have been mean, and she wasn't. Keep that in mind."

Sebastian tapped me on the shoulder before I could decide whether or not I could bring myself to agree with Jordan's perspective.

"What?" I snapped at him. Immediately, I reached toward him in apology. "I'm so sorry, Sebastian. That was rude of me. I just had some disconcerting news. Please, forgive me. What can I do for you?"

Sebastian gave me his usual gentle smile. "That's okay, Pippa. I'm just passing on a message. Devereaux Ivens wants to meet with you and Lake up on the dais at the far end of the ballroom. I believe Lake's already there."

I rested a hand on his arm. "Thanks, Sebastian. Again, I'm so sorry. I was just out of sorts for a minute. I didn't mean to take that out on you."

He grinned beatifically, and his cinnamon freckles glowed. "It's okay, really. Good luck up there." He headed back across the room with his tray.

I turned to Jordan. "If I don't come back down in twenty minutes, send in the cavalry. I mean it. I want actual horses and handsome officers wearing shoulder braids."

Jordan gave me a jaunty salute. "Sir, yes, sir!"

I squared my shoulders and headed for the dais, where the Ivenses posed like a movie-perfect tableau of rich people with rich friends. Even Lake fit in. Every step I took seemed to ring out a knell of doom. I hadn't spoken to Devereaux or Lake since the party began, yet they wanted to meet with me. I nibbled the inside of my lip and seriously considered calling Lake's dad out on sending his fetcher to spy on me. I took another deep breath and let it out slowly, trying to calm my nerves. But I couldn't deny that I had a bad feeling about the situation.

10

"Time is the one commodity that's impossible to hoard, no matter how wealthy or influential you are. Five bucks is easy. Five minutes, though? Once you spend them, they're gone forever."
Raymond Moore, 1949

I SWANNED UP THE STAIRS to the dais, making extra sure not to trip over the hem of my dress in front of Lake's family—they were all up there, chatting idly among themselves and casting cool, judgy glances across the room as if three steps' worth of height above the crowd somehow made them better people. Cam hovered in the background, wearing a thoughtful expression that nonetheless told me I was going to be on my own. But I was relieved to see Lake, my port of familiarity in that wealthy storm.

Lake kissed me on the temple—a little distractedly, it seemed. "There you are."

"You would not believe the antics we've been getting up to," I began, giving an animated wave.

But Lake tossed me an impersonal smile and a half nod of disinterest. "I'll bet." Then he turned back to his father.

A flash of hot frustration zinged across my vision. Lake had disowned himself from his family, but they had sucked him back in too quickly, and he was acting affected. I wasn't a fan of the whole situation.

Devereaux launched back into a conversation they'd clearly been in the middle of. Since he'd summoned me, I feigned interest in

Hong Kong capital gains for several minutes, waiting for him to include me. But he never looked away from Lake, never directed any welcoming asides toward me, never even paused in his monologue. *Am I jealous that Lake can keep up or just grumpy that he's so focused on his dad?*

Oh, I can definitely be both.

Am I supposed to be eye candy, pretty but silent? Or is he doing some kind of power play, summoning me then making me wait? I fumed behind my polite smile. *What if I just interrupt him? What if I just bail and walk back to my friends?*

I was saved from attempting a social prison break by a peremptory tap on my arm. "She'll know," Kait said to Bliss.

Not much of an improvement on manners, but at least they're talking to me. I turned to face the pair of younger women. Up close, Kait was exceptionally pretty, with her cream-and-caramel color scheme extending from her skin and eyes to her lovely neutral-tone dress. Bliss dazzled in that glitzy emerald dress, but her face appeared statuesque and not in a good way.

"I'll know what?" I asked.

A spark of genuine interest lit Kait's light brown eyes. "You hang out with... *you* know... *regular* people. Wouldn't they like a charity that offered classes on how government services actually work so they could get the most out of existing programs?"

I blinked and glanced at Bliss, who rolled her eyes.

She answered before I could even formulate a response. "Kait, you know that's only going to encourage them to game the system. That's how the country got in this mess in the first place. Honestly, it's like you don't hear a word I say."

Kait stared at the floor, and her back tensed while her shoulders slumped. Her face carefully wore no expression at all, which told me she'd suffered many a similar shutdown at Bliss's hands.

A flame of dislike flared inside my chest. "Which would you prefer, then?" I asked Bliss. "Services the government is paying for, which get underused because of bad PR, or no services at all, and it's every man for himself?"

Bliss slid her eyes to me then looked me full in the face, as if finally deciding I was worth talking to. She took a deep breath and gestured with her champagne glass. "Well, since you—"

"Ah, Pippa." Devereaux interrupted his daughter as if just realizing I was present. "May I call you Pippa? Pippa," he continued without waiting for my consent, "we're doing a straw poll." He indicated half a dozen people with his mostly empty champagne flute. "Tell us what you think."

He paused, and I decided I'd wait obediently until he spoke again—this time.

He smiled triumphantly. "What's your take on St. Augustine?"

Oh God, what's that supposed to mean? The saint? The city? To my surprise, Cam met my eyes from behind Devereaux's back and spun her finger as if she were stirring tea with a tight swirling motion. *Oh—the city, because of the Thanksgiving hurricane.* I scrambled to dredge up as much information as I could recall. "It's a tragedy."

He pursed his lips impatiently. "Yes, yes, but what do you feel should be done about saving them from their own failings? You *do* know the city has just filed for bankruptcy, don't you?"

"I had heard that—"

"All that mishandling of federal funds, the rampant corruption in their private sector." He shook his head, and most of his family followed suit, save for Lake, who thoughtfully tongued a molar and looked away. Devereaux continued, "We'd never allow such incompetence in our companies. What's your opinion on giving handouts to people who want everything handed to them instead of putting in an honest day's work?" He looked at me expectantly.

I hadn't heard a more biased question since Chloe offered me a "delightfully simple" glazed doughnut or the "overbaked, dried-out, lumpy bear claw" that she clearly wanted all for herself. I also took exception to his take on "ordinary" folks in seaside towns. Seacrest prided itself on its "do it yourself, or do it together, but get it done" attitude. No one I knew would take a handout without first putting in their best effort, unless the handout involved Tyleen's cooking at a public event on the Green. The previous summer, the Founding Day chowder line had stretched for a hundred yards.

I returned my focus to Devereaux. I'd need a little help handling him, but I knew just who to call on. *I am Morwen, the maverick fence with an eye for opportunity and a distaste for jerks.* "Surely you've already acted on the only obvious answer, Mr. Ivens."

My confidence seemed to throw him off. He glanced at Auda, who merely raised an eyebrow. To me, he offered a game smile. "Do enlighten us."

"You must run a tight and profitable ship, having companies that don't have to deal with corruption and waste. I bet you can get your hands on several key businesses in St. Augustine for bargain-basement prices now that the city's declared bankruptcy. Play your cards right—invest in basic city services, buy up repair industries, and put reliable managers in place—and you'll be the most trusted businessman in the city within what? A year? They could hail you as the savior of St. Augustine. What might that do for your future prospects?"

The group was silent.

I examined my manicure. "Or have all your competitors already bought up everything? Someone's going to make a killing. Might as well be you. Easy work, easy profit."

Again, silence. I figured that might be all the agreement I could hope for from a man who was hoping to embarrass or insult me.

But he finally spoke. "Easy? Hardly. I've worked hard all my life to get where I am. Nothing about my life came easily."

I stared straight into his mild blue eyes. "No one's life is really easy, Dev. May I call you Dev? Dev, let me offer a quick demonstration. I read it in a book this week, and I'm curious how it'll play out in real life."

"Knock yourself out," Bliss answered, wearing an expression of cool porcelain.

"Great. Let's pretend we're donating to a charity. You run some charities, right, Bliss? A charity for, say, the citizens of St. Augustine. How much can you give right this minute? You think you guys—the collective Ivens family—can conjure up five hundred dollars?" I asked, hoping my estimate wouldn't ruin the experiment.

Devereaux looked at me with consternation. "I don't just go handing my money to random people."

"Dad, it's just an experiment," Lake said. "Hand it over—I know you've got it. You'll get it back." He shot me a warm look, and I was relieved to finally recognize my boyfriend somewhere under all those airs he'd been putting on.

"Fine. As you wish." Devereaux pulled a money clip from inside his jacket and peeled off five crisp one-hundred-dollar bills. He didn't hand them over, though.

"About thirty seconds," I estimated. "Not too bad."

Paper rustled near my ear, and I turned. Bliss waved the same amount at me. The small smile at the corner of her mouth bragged silently.

I overwhelmed it with a dazzling smile of my own. "Great! Double the amount in half a minute. Now, wait here for just a bit." I descended the steps and darted through the crowd, dragging all my friends—Trudie, Gabe, Jordan, Sebastian, Tyleen, and even Mallory, though I knew she might skew the results—back onto the dais with me.

"What can I help you with?" Tyleen asked, giving her uniform tunic a tug. "Is the food all right? Would you like a special order?"

"Nothing like that," I assured her. "We're trying to raise another five hundred dollars for St. Augustine. Can you guys help out?" I dug my emergency twenty out of my clutch.

Though puzzled, everyone dug through their pockets and purses. Sebastian dropped a couple of twenties and had to crouch to retrieve them, and Gabe offered a handful of wrinkled singles.

"All I got," he said apologetically.

Jordan counted our cash with swift fingers. "Three hundred ninety-four dollars," she announced.

I checked the timer on my phone. "Just over five minutes." I turned to Devereaux again and offered a wry smile. "You alone came up with much more in much less time. It looks like 'easy' is relative." I turned to my friends. "Thanks, guys. You can take your money back now."

Tyleen didn't even look at the money Jordan held. Her troubled eyes studied mine. "You mean this wasn't real? We're not actually donating any cash for anything? But... it's Christmas."

I could've hugged her, but Devereaux was looking embarrassed and malcontent. And so was Lake. In fact, his whole family wore various shades of annoyance, and I felt a pang of guilt for my sass. I'd overstepped by challenging Devereaux in front of his guests. But I wasn't sure, looking back, that I'd have done anything differently.

Except to make the donations real. Because Tyleen was right: it was Christmas. I mentally drew a door number three and opened it. "Do you have a big empty can in the kitchen, Tyleen? Maybe we can make one of those old-fashioned donation tins and set it on the end of the hors d'oeuvres table."

Her face brightened. "Oh, I know just the one! I have some left-over gold foil, too, so it'll match the décor."

I turned my back to the Ivenses and walked down the dais steps with her, followed by my friends.

"It's hard to imagine that a whole city can go bankrupt, and no one will help them out."

I itched to turn and see if Devereaux had overheard Tyleen's remark, but I managed to keep facing forward. "That's a good point."

Tyleen whipped up a lovely donation container from an empty Number 10 can of peaches, some gold foil, and an extra invitation folded inside out, detailing the destination for the money. A few people gathered, hoping she was setting out new food, and that crowd drew more folks. Folded bills plunked through the slit in the gold foil, and I smiled so hard that I nearly teared up. Lake dropped in some money with a smile and a wink for me. But no one else in his family did. I did see Cam sliding in a folded bill, though.

It's Christmas, all right. God bless America!

"That was stupid, Winterbourne."

Aaand there goes my Christmas spirit. "I don't think the people who get that money will think so," I said lightly.

"I tried to warn you about the Ivenses. Maybe now you see what you're dealing with." Mallory looked down at her untouched glass of champagne. "I shouldn't have come. I don't like what I'm seeing."

"Were they always this way?"

"I'm not talking about them. I used to *be* them, remember? But now..."

Jordan sidled up to us, wearing an expression that told me she was there to rescue me from Mal if I needed it. "But now what?" she asked brightly, before I could shake my head at her not to.

I ended up giving her wide eyes that I hoped said, "Dude, bad timing."

But Mal accepted the question without prejudice. "Seacrest is changing me. Like it changed Lake. I didn't think it would. I thought..." She looked toward an open patch of floor. "I don't enjoy change."

"Me either. That's why I always pay with credit," Jordan said.

Despite her quip, I could've smacked her. To salvage the conversation, I said, "Change can be rough. Especially between a world like theirs and a world like Seacrest. But you knew Lake was coming here, and you chose to follow him." I stifled a stab of pain at the thought, even though I could understand her motive. "You were willing to trade your old environment for a new one, as long as it was the same one Lake was in, or else you'd never have come. This way, both of you will change together."

Jordan stared at me as if I'd grown a second head that had taken my romantic rival's side against me. I was a little surprised myself.

Mal registered no such shock, but she did meet my eyes. "That's a nice piece of logic, Winterbourne. Did it hurt?"

I matched her half smile with one of my own. "Stung a bit, yeah."

Her dark eyebrows briefly lowered as she nodded, and her smile was a quicksilver flash. Then she glanced back up at the dais, where Lake had remained with his parents and sister. They chatted to a new cluster of chosen few. "I don't like seeing Lake change back, though. Seacrest fits him a lot better than it fits me."

"I'm not a fan either," I muttered.

Mallory's eyes met mine, and a strange collaborative vibe bounced between us.

"Help! Someone, help! Is there a doctor in the house?" Wren's frantic voice rang out from the corner of the room over the general murmuring of the party.

We couldn't see Wren through the crowd, but Mallory stalked toward her anyway, abandoning the feminine walk she'd been using in favor of her standard powerful stride. *Cop mode activated.* I grabbed Jordan's hand and followed in Mallory's wake. Mallory pushed through the edge of a gathering crowd, and I wedged myself into the first row. Jordan clutched my arms and tucked her chin over my shoulder so she could see too.

Wren knelt at Mort's side, holding his hand, while he lay on his back, staring up at the ceiling as if he couldn't see it. His chest was barely moving, and he seemed to be trying to gesture with his free hand. Then it dropped to the ballroom floor with a thump that carried in the shocked silence.

I glanced around. Gabe and Tru stood with Sebastian and Tyleen, nearly opposite me in the circle. Their faces wore various versions of shock. Over on the dais, Lake's family stared with vague interest toward those of us forming a knot around Mort. Dev showed no sign of coming down, but Lake stepped around his father with a hand on his shoulder then headed toward us. Cam followed at a distance, as if to observe and report back.

Mallory hurried to Mort's other side and reached for his wrist. She loosened Mort's collar, listened at his mouth, then felt for a pulse. As she placed her hands on his chest to begin compressions, she looked right at me. "Call Doc Stevens, Winterbourne. She's with her brother and his family at their cabin just outside Summerpoint."

"Right." I pulled my phone from my clutch and dialed.

"Merry Christmas Eve!" Doc Stevens greeted me, sounding uncharacteristically cheery. I heard laughter in the background. "What can I do for you, Pippa?"

"There's been a... Someone's hurt, Doc. We're up at—" I suddenly blanked on the mansion's address.

Jordan leaned forward and recited it loudly. "Big mansion on the hill. Come quickly. Mort collapsed, and Mallory's doing CPR."

"You two." Doc Stevens's voice regained its usual tired cynicism. "I should've known. I'll be there in five." She hung up.

Mallory was still performing chest compressions, but Mort lay still under her ministrations. Wren had backed away to join the watching circle, her jaw tense and her eyes wide. Several people nearby were on their phones, probably calling 911.

Someone pushed their way into the circle beside me, and I felt the delicate kiss of old silk against my arm. In her black-and-silver gown, Geneva Laine took a long look at the scene before her, both hands resting atop her ivory-headed cane. Then she thumped it against the floor and barked a quick laugh. "Mort *est mort*! Never thought I'd live long enough to make that joke. Well, it serves him right." She thumped her cane again.

Jordan gasped in my ear, and I looked from her to Geneva with wide eyes. Seacrest's nonagenarian matriarch always followed every social protocol to the letter, and her steely glare of disapproval was widely known for its liberal use against those who talked at the theater or dyed their hair in "unnatural" shades. Even Jordan had suffered it since she dyed her hair bright pomegranate. Yet there Geneva was, making a French pun about a man's death—possibly even before he was truly dead.

"You!" Gabe growled. He jabbed a finger toward someone in the first row of the crowded circle around Mort. "I saw you. What did you do?"

11

"We're all just skin and egg timers, counting down until we're hard-boiled."
Raymond Moore, 1954

WREN DREW BACK FROM Gabe's accusing finger. "I didn't do anything!"

"You did too. You were trying to stay out of his reach just before he collapsed. What did you do to him?" Gabe surged forward, breaking free of Trudie's calming grip, and dragged Wren from the edge of the circle by her upper arms. "Did you stab him? Where's the weapon?" He began to shake her, and she cried out in alarm.

"Gabriel!" Mallory's voice was a whip crack.

I squeezed Jordan's hand and darted to Mallory's side. "I'll take over," I murmured, kneeling by Mort's chest.

Mallory nodded crisply and rose, gathering her cream skirt in one hand. As I focused on giving chest compressions to the unresponsive Mort, she said, "Let her go, Gabriel. What did you see?"

Gabe pointed toward the hors d'oeuvres tables. "He was walking toward her, and she kept backing away. Didn't look like he could stand up straight. I think she did something to him, and she was trying to get away from him before he died."

Ah, Seacrest, making everyone see murder everywhere. I took a close look at Mort as I leaned into his chest, trying to keep oxygen circulating in his blood. His muscles seemed tense, though he wasn't breathing on his own. *Look closely. What don't you see that should be here?*

"Gabe," I called. "I don't see any blood. I don't think Mort was stabbed."

"Ms. Lundin was standing near me for several minutes before he came along," a handsome older gentleman said gallantly, gesturing to her with his champagne class.

"I saw her too," the woman next to him said. "Mr. Roark just approached her, and after a few words, she tried to leave, but he followed her. Whatever's wrong with him, it's nothing to do with her."

Wren finally spoke, looking from Mallory to the rest of us. "It really isn't. I swear, I didn't stab him. He just came up to me. We've known each other for decades. We're old friends."

"Then why didn't you want to talk to him?" Gabe pushed.

Along with the burning in my shoulders from all the chest compressions I was doing, I felt a pang of vicarious embarrassment. Gabe had a reputation for taking things too far, not knowing when to stop. That was how he'd landed himself in jail for assault a few years back. *And it's why no one will sell him a house. But his question needs an answer.*

"All right, that's enough." Mallory's voice cut through the low murmurings, and for that, I was grateful. By their tone, the wealthy had collectively decided that Gabe was not acceptable.

"Chief Tavish?" Doc Stevens called from the ballroom door.

Mallory glanced over then looked at my sister. "Trudie, please escort Gabriel out to the foyer for the time being." To Doc, she called, "Over here."

Trudie eased a glowering but mildly repentant Gabe toward the doorway, and Doc Stevens hustled to my side as I worked on the unresponsive Mort. I was desperately glad to see her, but bright-red sequins caught my eye as she knelt opposite me, and I looked up in surprise. The sturdy, middle-aged doctor, who normally sported a khaki anorak and mom jeans, dazzled me in a form-fitting crimson gown with a high slit up one thigh. Her usually frizzy gray curls were moussed and coerced into a pair of saucy jelly rolls that gave her an extra two or three inches of height. But her footwear didn't match her glam look—she sported a muddy pair of boots.

I realized I was staring and that I'd stopped giving Mort chest compressions. I started again. "Sorry. I've never seen you looking so—"

"Everyone needs an alter ego, Pippa," Doc said. "Mine just happens to be Professor River Song from *Doctor Who*." She began checking Mort over.

Time seemed to elongate, marked only by my pressure on Mort's breastbone. *One... two... three... four... five... One... two... three...*

Doc's strong hands took mine and stilled them. "You can stop now, Pippa. He's gone."

My hands throbbed with the sudden lack of movement. A sudden hush rippled out from where we knelt, silencing all talk in the ballroom, and a single loud gasp made the room sound even more tomblike. I looked at Doc in her lovely dress and dark red lipstick. "Did I... Did I do something wrong?"

She squeezed my hands. "No, kiddo. It wasn't you. You did all you could. I'm not sure what happened here yet. I'll know more after the autopsy."

"Autopsy?" My gaze flicked to Mort and back to Doc. "It's not a heart attack or something?"

"It could be natural causes. As I said, I'll know more afterward. But I don't know of any natural causes that could lead to someone frothing green at the mouth."

I looked at Mort more closely. Green flecks of foam lined the corners of his mouth. I drew back, disturbed. *Poison?* I mouthed.

Doc lifted her penciled eyebrows in a dark-golden-brown *Maybe*. "Chest compressions can do that, poison or no."

She'd spoken too loudly. The word "poison" rippled through the crowd, and more than one person screamed. A man standing in my peripheral vision hurled his mini quiche to the ballroom floor so violently that it splattered. *So much for no one saying a bad word about Moore's quiche recipe.*

Lake reached my side and helped me stand. As he drew me back toward Jordan with a hand around my waist, Mallory switched to full-blown-investigation mode, ordering everyone to back away but not leave the room. She made several phone calls as she stood near Mort and Doc Stevens, but her eyes constantly swept the crowd, never singling anyone out.

Mal's standing in the doorway between two worlds—her past and her present. The law in cream silk. No... Mallory's not in the doorway. She is the doorway.

"Hey, look at me," Lake said for what I belatedly realized was about the fifth time.

I managed to focus on his handsome face. "Sorry. I'm here now." I folded my hands over his as they clasped my face.

Relief brought a smile to his lips. "You got lost there for a while. I'm sorry you had to see that. I know you talk about death all the time with your authors, but it's got to be scary to have someone die right under your hands."

I looked at my hands as if for the first time. *Was I keeping him alive at all? Or was he already gone by the time I knelt over him?*

Lake quickly clasped them with his. "I shouldn't have put it that way. I'm sorry."

Mallory's voice reached my ears. "No, no one is to enter the dining room."

"But our guests are hungry," Auda protested in a voice pitched to carry.

Mallory's response was cool but not without compassion. "Better hungry than poisoned."

I stared into Lake's eyes. He glanced over at the hors d'oeuvres table then back at me. I clutched his tuxedo lapels.

My stomach roiled. "What did you eat?"

"I-I don't remember. A quiche, I think. Lots of champagne." He held my elbows. "You?"

My stomach turned sour and cramped. "I've had some of everything."

"Quit waxing dramatic, guys." Jordan's levelheadedness cut through our drama. "You two were the first ones here. If you're not feeling ill by now, you're gonna live."

I thought back over the evening and realized Jordan was right. Reluctantly, I let go of Lake's lapels and tried to smooth out the wrinkles I'd made. "Fair point. I guess I'm just feeling upset about Mort. And hungry."

Lake's eyes widened as if he'd just gotten an idea. He eased my clutch from under my arm. "I'll bring this right back." Then he snatched my hand up and pressed his lips against my fingers before disappearing into the crowd.

Jordan swooped in beside me. "Since when did he start doing dramatic exits?"

"I think he's been rewatching *Sherlock*," I murmured, staring after him.

My BFF put an arm around my waist and hugged me. "God help us. One high-functioning sociopath is enough."

Jordan and I sat together on a padded bench at the edge of the ballroom, and the great engine of Mort's death investigation geared up around us. Officer Vic Nuncio arrived from Seacrest along with a few Summerpoint police officers, and they began interviewing every guest. Two of them bagged up all of Tyleen's hors d'oeuvres, while she and Sebastian looked on in dismay. A pair of EMTs arrived to assist Doc Stevens with the removal of Mort's body, and the property developer was wheeled out past us on a gurney, draped in a white sheet.

Lake's family presided over everything from their dais with an air of inconvenienced patience, mostly thanks to Cam running interference for them with the police and guests alike. I had to admire her ability to give the Ivenses the distance they wanted. She knew exactly what to say to everyone to protect her boss's interests.

I showed Jordan the photo I'd taken of Tyleen and Sebastian in the kitchen. "I thought I'd print it on a mug for Tyleen, to commemorate tonight. Now, I'm not sure she'll want any reminders."

Jordan squeezed my shoulders. "Nonsense. They're positively radiant. You practically owe it to them to put this picture on a mug so that they remember what a wonderful note the night started out on. I mean, it's not like they killed Mort."

Then Lake reappeared, holding two big bags of Jade Noodle takeout. "Fresh, hot Chinese food, definitely not poisoned."

My heart did a double flip and landed in a meadow of sweet affection.

Meanwhile, Jordan fixed her eyes on the bags. "You need to marry this man pronto, or I will." She pulled one bag from his hand then set it on the bench beside her and rummaged through its boxes.

Lake handed my clutch back with a grin as he sat beside me. He pulled one box from the bag he still carried and offered it to me, along with a pair of chopsticks. "Orange chicken. Your favorite." His smile was wide and a little smug.

"Thank you so much, Lake." I took the takeout box and snapped open my chopsticks. "How did you get this here? You weren't supposed to leave."

He flicked an eyebrow at me. "I didn't. I got one of the valets to do it for me. He'd been outside the whole time. Never entered the house, let alone the kitchen. He couldn't have tampered with any of the food."

I paused my chopsticks on their way to their first nugget of chicken. "A valet just decided to help you? Do you know him?"

"No, but he knows my friend Benjamin." Lake rubbed his fingers against his thumb and grinned like he'd just robbed a bank.

A slow realization dawned on me. "You bribed a valet to drive Sadie into town to get Jade Noodle takeout? You gave Sadie to a stranger? Lake, that car isn't mine to give, let alone yours. Sadie is Hilt's car."

His confident grin wilted a little. "But... how else was I supposed to help you? You were hungry."

I stared into his eyes as I stuffed two nuggets of orange chicken into my mouth and began chewing. "I am hungry. And thank you for the food." I looked to Jordan for support, but she was busy handing out chopsticks and takeout boxes to Trudie and Gabe, who didn't look conflicted in the least.

Lake slid back onto the bench beside me and cracked apart his own chopsticks. "You're welcome. Did you see the box of Mongolian duck anywhere in there, or is Jordan eating it?"

"I do not do duck," Jordan said through a mouthful of spicy vegetables. "I won't have you start such filthy rumors about me, Lakyn Ivens."

He chuckled. "Yes, ma'am."

I gave in to their banter and handed him his favorite from the bag. He propped one ankle across the other knee and unbuttoned his tuxedo jacket before digging in with his chopsticks. I couldn't help but stare at him. He was so relaxed and confident, looking so fine in his tux but eating the same takeout as the rest of us. *He's hot and* complicated. *God help me, but I love him.*

"So." Jordan nabbed a piece of my orange chicken with a not-sorry grin before her expression sobered. "Poison."

"Poison," I repeated.

We all stared out at the ballroom floor, which was empty except for yellow caution tape that had been strung through the backs of fancy chairs positioned around the spot where Mort had fallen. All the guests stood or sat around the edge of the room. No one spoke above a murmur. Mallory and Vic consulted near the caution tape, she in her cream gown and he in his long-sleeved blue uniform. *They look like they walked straight out of* Miss Fisher's Murder Mysteries. *I wonder if they've got any leads yet.*

I spotted Tyleen standing near the doors to the kitchen with wide, worried eyes. Sebastian stood with her, hugging her around the shoulders with one arm. She caught my eye and hurried toward us.

"Are you okay, Pippa? Are you all okay? None of you are feeling sick, are you?"

"No, Tyleen," I said. "We're all just fine. Are you hungry? Lake got plenty of takeout."

She waved my offer away. "I couldn't eat a bite. I'm far too worried. What if I did this?"

"What do you mean?" Tru asked.

Tyleen shifted her gaze to the floor. "What if I accidentally got some ingredients wrong? What'll happen to me? To Sebastian?"

I stood and put a hand on her shoulder. "Tyleen, you're the best cook in the state. There's no way you 'accidentally' got some ingredients wrong."

She clutched at my arm. "Oh, but don't you see? That's so much worse! If Mallory thinks like that, she could assume I killed Mort on purpose!"

I tried to laugh off her ridiculous suggestion. "That's absurd. Why would you want Mort dead?"

Tyleen's eyes darted off to the side, and the corner of her mouth quirked down.

I leaned over into her line of sight again. "Tyleen? Why *would* you want Mort dead?"

"Well, I did tell him to drop dead," she whispered. Her eyes wouldn't meet mine.

I clutched her hand and dragged her to the archway, away from our friends and as far as I could go while still remaining in the room. "Why? What happened?"

"It was after the mystery dinner at Moorehaven," she replied, adopting a dramatic stage whisper. Her eyes had found somewhere to look, and unfortunately for her, that somewhere was straight at Mallory. "He and Wren stepped into the kitchen to say their farewells, but he stayed a minute longer."

I looked from her to Mallory, who hadn't noticed her staring from fifty feet away. Tyleen's eyes were wide with alarm and maybe anger. When she spoke again, her voice had a tremor. "He patted me on the shoulder like some kind of peasant and said I'd had a fair shot and how brave it was of me to try to contribute to Seacrest's mystery ambience, but shouldn't I stick to serving food, where I belong."

My eye twitched, and I had a hard time keeping my voice down. "Where you *belong*? He didn't think you belonged in Moorehaven?"

"He meant the diner on the highway, 'with my own kind of people.' Look at me," she added before I could string together a coherent sentence in my fury. "I'm fifty years old. I dye my hair so I can look pretty. I get things wrong all the time. And I'm a single mom. Where else should I fit in except the diner on the highway?"

Aghast that my good friend might start thinking of herself the way the deceased Mort had, I held her shoulders and stared into her blue eyes. "No. No. Don't do that. That's not you." I swept her into a crushing hug that made her yelp, but she squeezed me back. "I mean, yes, you're fifty, and yes, you color your hair. Okay, I can't deny those things. But you belong everywhere, Tyleen. This is your town. Mort's low opinion of you shouldn't outlast his death. It's not worth holding on to. You make so much food, for so many people, so often. You've probably fed every single Seacrest resident a dozen times. *You* are worth holding on to, Tyleen." I added an extra squeeze. "Because you're amazing. And you're already pretty. And you're not a jumped-up toad in a fancy suit who's afraid he might feel less special if he has to acknowledge other people's skills."

"Toad in a fancy suit," Tyleen repeated. She let out a soft wail and sniffled into my shoulder. "That's it, Pippa. That's it."

I pulled back. "What's it?"

"I'm putting you in my will. You're just too kind to me." She pulled a handkerchief from her uniform pocket and blew her nose. Then she headed back to our friends, who were all busily stuffing their faces on the bench. "You all feel okay? No green foam or anything?" She clapped a hand on Jordan's forehead, feeling for a fever.

Tru examined her takeout box as if she might see a sign of green foam inside, but everyone else answered that they felt fine.

"And some of you had the mini quiches, right, but you feel fine?" she pressed.

"Yeah, Tyleen," Lake said, using his deep, serious voice. "We're okay, really."

Tyleen's shoulders relaxed, and she nodded. "I was so worried, you see, that the green foam was from the *quiches*. What was I thinking, serving those?"

The way she emphasized the menu item reminded me how she'd decided to serve quiches in the first place. "Don't worry, Tyleen. This isn't a case for Agatha Raisin. We're fine, all of us."

"Except for Mort." Jordan's voice was flat.

"Deadpanning. Nice." I gave her a Seacrestan nod of approval for her morbid humor.

"And extra points for that meta reference." She high-fived me.

Mallory strode toward our group, wearing her stoic-cop face, fully in job mode, with Vic plodding resolutely at her heels. "All right, Cool Kids, you're up. Vic, you interview Lake. Winterboune, with me. The rest of you, don't move."

I'd only taken a few steps in Mallory's wake when Wren approached her. "I don't mean to be a bother," the nursery owner began timidly, "but I really need to use the little girls' room. Please, Officer Tavish. If you like, I can have Odeon escort me. He's offered."

Behind her, Lake's uncle Odie nodded genially at Mallory.

Mallory pursed her lips. "Come right back. The Summerpoint officer on the door will know if you try to leave."

Wren breathed her thanks. She took Odie's arm, and together, they headed into the hallway.

"Now then, Winterbourne. Where were we?"

I gave Mallory details as best I could while she jotted notes in a precise hand, wearing her best ice-queen expression all the while. I couldn't help but tear up as I recited how I'd taken over the chest compressions, only to have Doc Stevens tell me Mort had died.

To my shock, Mallory squeezed my shoulder—a little too firmly, though, as if she were trying to startle me out of my grief rather than comfort me. "That's not your fault, Winterbourne. Whoever poisoned him—if indeed Doc's autopsy reveals poison—that's whose fault this is. Unless you actually did poison him. Then it would be your fault. And I'll absolutely catch you."

I blinked. "Uh... thanks, Mal. That makes me feel a lot better."

She offered me a lukewarm smile, which surprised me so much that a feather could've knocked me onto my bottom.

"Happy to help," she replied, not having picked up on my mild sarcasm. Over her shoulder, she called, "Next!"

During my friends' interviews, I split my time between watching Vic and Mallory and studying the rest of the room. Everyone looked just as they had an hour before though nervous and stressed by the evening's turn of events. "But one of these people is probably a poisoner."

Wren grasped me by my elbow as she returned from the restroom, looking so stricken that I worried she would faint.

I touched her forearm supportively. "I'm sorry. Thinking out loud like a Seacrestan. Are you feeling okay? Do you want to sit down?"

"It's just the shock of it all. I was video chatting with my dogs, trying to cheer myself up, you know?" She tapped her phone and showed me what looked like a security-footage feed about a foot off the floor in a nicely appointed living room. "I've known Mort for so long. It'll be so strange not having him next door anymore."

On the screen, three fluffy corgis crowded around the camera, seemingly staring at a screen just next to it. "Hi, babies," Wren cooed. Her sweet doggies whined eagerly and lolled their tongues. "I'll be home soon, okay?"

Seizing an opportunity, I asked, "Why didn't you want to talk to Mort just before he collapsed? You two seemed to get along well enough at dinner the other night."

A flash of irritation crossed Wren's face, followed by tearful remorse. "I was irritated with him because he was trying to talk about work during the party. I just wanted to relax and have a good evening. That's all. I feel so terrible. Did you know he proposed to me once? It feels like so long ago. And now he's gone."

I nodded and squeezed her arm supportively, and Wren moved away to tell Mallory she'd returned. Her lip had trembled as she mentioned Mort, who'd clearly been a complicated person. *Just like Lake.* I could definitely identify with her chaotic tumble of emotions.

Lake's parents stood with some disapproving folks I didn't know and frowned a lot, looking quite put out. I didn't blame them—their party was ruined. Cam had returned to her boss's side and was texting up a storm, wearing a look of intense concentration. Sebastian and Tyleen held hands nervously as they awaited their turn to be interviewed. I could see Tyleen's white knuckles from twelve feet away. Geneva spoke to Wren as if comforting her, and Wren hugged her clutch as if it were a stuffed animal, but Geneva kept shooting dark glances past Wren's hunched shoulders to where Mort had lain. Jordan had finally finished the whole box of spicy Mongolian vegetables, and she slumped back on the bench, looking dyspeptic and overfull. Lake's uncle Odie, who'd come in separately from Wren, seemed to be trying to rouse the guests to conversation again, without much luck—then he saw me looking at him.

He headed in my direction from across the ballroom, wearing a genial smile that would've fit on a benevolent king or a crafty villain about to let loose his master plan. I swallowed, bracing for yet another joust with one of Lake's relatives.

"Pippa, my girl." He raised his champagne glass and leaned close, as if toasting me on the down low.

Unsure what he wanted, I offered him my best hostess smile.

He gazed around before continuing. "Indulge an old man, and escort me out to see your sweet ride? I think I heard her name is Sadie." He looped his arm around my hand and began drawing me toward the hallway.

Startled, I let him pull me in his wake, even though no one had been dismissed from the ballroom. I didn't know the man at all, and he'd just commandeered me like Captain Jack Sparrow swiping the HMS *Interceptor* out from under Commodore Norrington's nose.

I scrambled for the words to bow out of the illegal excursion with some grace before the officer at the door had to tell that wealthy man "no" to his face—or worse, give in to his social rank and actually let him pass. "Actually, uh... I was just—"

"Coming with me to pester Mallory to let us head home," Lake finished, taking my other hand and tucking it into his elbow. He stopped, halting me, and Odie reluctantly turned away from the hallway.

"Are you sure you have to go so soon?" Odie wore an avuncular smile, but his tone carried just a hint of petulance.

"Yes, Uncle," Lake said.

"Then perhaps I can call on the classy lady later?" He folded his hands and smiled as if he'd already been told yes.

I stood straighter. "I'll have to check with the car's owner, of course. But if he's willing, I'm sure something can be arranged."

"Splendid, splendid. Then I bid you both a pleasant evening." He moved off, a plump, smiling nobleman, entirely comfortable among his own kind.

I put my other hand on Lake's arm. "Why do you both assume Mallory will just let us go? Is it because you're Ivenses?"

Lake's lopsided smile was brief. "No. It's because I'm the one who's asking. Watch: she'll let me leave, then she'll have to let everyone else leave so that it's fair."

He was right. Mallory studied her notepad while Lake asked if we could depart, then she gave a curt nod that made the soft curls at her neck bounce like springs. We hadn't even turned away before she raised her voice and informed the rest of the guests that everyone was free to go but not to leave town or check out of their hotels yet.

I glanced around. Gabe came back in to help Jordan gather the takeout boxes and used chopsticks, while Trudie held one of the big takeout bags as a trash bag. Gabe shook his head ruefully as he took my chopsticks and box. "I take back what I said earlier. I don't think you could pay me enough to live like the Ivenses, after all. And I'm not just talking about the dead guy killing the party mood. You really can't buy love, can you?"

I nodded and patted him on the shoulder in commiseration, hoping Lake was out of earshot.

Geneva Laine stood in statuesque fashion as guests filed past her, as if determined to be one of the last to depart Auda's presence. Sebastian and Tyleen started gathering the leftover hors d'oeuvres on the table, but they stopped when Vic approached them.

"I'm sorry, guys, but I need to ask you not to leave Seacrest and to make yourselves available if we have any further questions. Mallory's orders." Vic stuffed a chocolate cake pop into his mouth and withdrew its stick. "You're a great cook, Tyleen. I'm sure you have nothing to worry about."

"Thanks, Vic," Sebastian said.

Tyleen couldn't look at him, though, and her face had gone white.

I pursed my lips, frustrated that I couldn't help her more. Lake was leading me out, though, and I knew she had plenty of cleanup to do. *Focusing on my work takes my mind off my troubles. I hope Tyleen will get the same effect.*

Incredibly, Lake's family still stood on the dais at the far end of the ballroom, chatting with their select friends. If they'd descended after Mort's dramatic death to mix with us mere mortals, I hadn't noticed.

I spotted Wren among them. She seemed to feel the weight of my gaze as she stood silently between Auda and Bliss. Her face seemed to sag under the weight of Mort's death. She tucked her lower lip up and nodded a solemn farewell to me.

The valets were kept hopping as everyone requested their vehicles, and Lake and I slowly inched forward in line toward the front doors. After a good ten minutes, I heard yelling from somewhere up on the second floor. Nearly shrieking, in fact. I looked at Lake in alarm.

He just sighed. "My sister, taking out her frustrations on Kait. I've learned not to barge in anymore. She just yells at me instead."

"What could Kait possibly have done to warrant getting screamed at like that?" I asked, half-afraid of the answer. I clamped my arm on my clutch, making sure I didn't drop it. I was very ready to leave.

"Probably something horrible like not bringing Bliss's champagne fast enough or being too witty in front of some handsome guy." He tried to shift forward in line, but I jerked him to a stop.

"Seriously? You're being serious right now."

He nodded.

"Lake, your sister's a total—" I broke off, remembering I was still in earshot of half the party guests.

"You're probably right," he said mildly.

"Shallow, vapid Disney villain," I finished under my breath.

He chuckled. "You're definitely right."

We finally reached the front of the line, and I fished my ticket out of my cleavage and handed it to the available valet. He grinned and yelled to the other valet, who was pulling a nice Benz into the drop-off zone. "You owe me twenty, Duncan. I get Sadie!"

The few remaining guests laughed appreciatively, and Sadie soon glided in from the foggy darkness. "Dog check," Duncan murmured, and both valets took a moment to look through Sadie's windows.

"Something wrong?" I asked.

"We heard a dog barking in the lot earlier," Duncan said, tugging his red valet jacket straight. "But we couldn't find any. We worried someone had left a pet in the cold."

"Well, I only have cats, but thank you for keeping an eye out," I said.

Odie materialized from the shadows, clasping his hands in delight at the sight of Sadie. As I walked around to the driver's side, Odie reverently ran a hand along the side of her hood. "She's a classy dame," he told Lake.

"And the car's not half bad either," Lake replied with a grin. He offered me a hefty wink and tucked himself into Sadie's front passenger seat.

I slid in beside him, and as Lake waved good night to his uncle, I gunned Sadie's engine a couple of times. Odie laughed, clapped his hands once, then waved until I couldn't see him anymore in the fading gloom.

"Your uncle's an interesting guy," I said as I navigated the road down to the highway. "He's not much like your mom and dad."

Lake shifted on the leather seat. "I think that's on purpose. He's been married three times, but it never seems to stick. I think women expect to marry my dad's doppelganger, and for one reason or another, they're disappointed with what they do get. But I like Uncle Odie. He's less..."

While Lake searched for the right word, I cruised onto the highway. "Pretentious?"

"I was going to go with *Wolf of Wall Street*, but I see how you might think that."

His easy tone left me feeling defensive. "'Might'? You were the only member of your family to bother coming off the dais when Mort up and died in the middle of their party!" *And they were awful to me, but I'll let that go.*

"Yeah, but if everyone starts running around like chickens with their heads cut off, you've got chaos, and nothing gets done. Someone had to set the standard that kept everyone calm."

I hadn't thought about it like that. I shifted into fourth gear, mindful that the fog made driving extra hazardous on a dark, curving road at the edge of the sea. A big corner was coming up, and I had no intention of flying off into empty space.

"I know what you think now," Lake continued, "but you're one of the most open-minded people I've met. Stop thinking of them as the bad guys, and get to know them a little better, and you'll see—"

"I can't stop," I blurted. My knuckles went white on the steering wheel.

"Come on. They're really not that bad once you get to—"

"No, I mean I literally can't stop! The brakes aren't working!" I pumped the pedal hopelessly, willing more brake fluid into Sadie's lines. My rising panic triggered a flash of vicarious alarm—a scene from *The Diamond Charm*. Hilton Gray narrowly avoided death by cut brake lines in the very first chapter by downshifting and skidding out into a gravelly spot.

"Moore, you'd better be right about this!" I howled. I wrapped my fingers around the curly maple inlay on the stick shift then stomped on the clutch and shifted into third gear. Sadie protested with a loud growl. That big corner was right in front of me, but Sadie wouldn't slow down in time to turn safely. I stared wide-eyed into the oncoming fog. Its impenetrable darkness told me the other lane was empty... or that I was about to crash into some idiot driving with his headlights off.

I cranked down my window so I could see better into the fog and veered into the left lane as the tires protested with angry squeals. Lake grabbed Sadie's oh-crap handle and let out a long "whoa" as we arced through the damp night.

Sadie drifted back into the right lane as the long corner came to an end. Lake's "whoa" shifted seamlessly into an "oh God" as we pitched down a long incline toward a short bridge and its winter-filled creek.

I downshifted again, and Sadie protested more loudly. "Hilt is gonna kill me," I said through clenched teeth. My eyes were pinned to the foggy road and the bright-yellow dashed line that flew by far too fast. The brake pedal was still determinedly ignoring my demands to perform.

"I sure hope he gets the chance," Lake replied. He braced against the dash with his other hand.

"Better not do that," I said. "No airbags. If we crash, you'll break your arm."

Lake yanked his hand back as if it had been burned.

Emergency flashers. I scanned the dashboard, but I couldn't find a switch or a lever to turn them on. *Does this car even have emergency flashers?*

"Pippa, look out!"

I jerked my gaze back out the windshield and swerved to the right just in time to avoid an oncoming pickup truck whose driver laid on the horn. "Sorry!" I yelled to him, to Lake, to Sadie.

With Sadie's engine howling in protest, we sped toward the little concrete bridge at the bottom of the hill. The highway turned and rose on the other side of the bridge. The fog ahead lit up with oncoming headlights—a semitruck. There was no way I could make the corner past the bridge without using the other lane. Dread drained my mind of every other emotion. My chest went hollow, and my hands got damp.

"Lake, I can't do this!" I cried.

His left hand gripped my thigh. "I love you. Whether you can do this or not."

My girly wail morphed into a harpy screech as I tried to thread the needle between the oncoming semi and the bridge's near railing. Sadie's tires protested. Her engine whined. I overcorrected right, then left, then right again. We cleared the bridge without hitting anything, but I didn't have time to be thankful. Sadie had begun a slow spin to the right across the damp, icy pavement. "No, no!" I stomped on the useless brake pedal again.

The road curved up and to the right, but Sadie had other plans. As the road veered out from under us, we spun out to the left side of the road, just past the bridge, where the cliff gave way to scrappy vegetation. Sadie's headlights spun past a fallen boulder, some wind-sculpted pines, then foggy nothingness. We lurched forward into darkness and pain.

12

"There's nothing like the warm, purring weight of a cat to comfort you in your favorite chair after you've crashed your car again."

Raymond Moore, 1959

MY LEFT ARM BURNED as I frantically pumped my hands on Mort's chest. "Come on, breathe!" I gasped.

Mort's dark-chocolate eyes opened—the only part of him that moved. "It's no use, Pippa. I'm already dead."

Strobe lights flashed in my eyes. The ballroom's decorations gleamed way too brightly. Then someone called my name from far away.

"Winterbourne! Winterbourne! Wake up, you second-rate excuse for a budget-motel owner!"

Pain flared in several parts of my body, including my forehead and my left arm. Bright light illuminated Sadie's steering wheel. Steam hissed somewhere nearby. "Moorehaven's Yelp reviews are top-notch, I'll have you know," I mumbled.

Mallory's cool hand clasped my shoulder, and her steady voice was a rock I clung to in a churning sea of confusion. "I knew that'd bring you around. Are you badly hurt?"

I didn't think so.

"Lake!" I blurted. My hand flailed toward the passenger side and encountered Lake's arm. I gave it a squeeze.

"Ow," he said slowly, as if he'd already been building up to it before I touched him. "Seat belt bruise in three, two, one…"

Relieved beyond words to hear his humor intact, I blinked and looked around. Sadie had tipped over a gravel embankment with her front wheels, and her headlights shone down into the fog toward a shrouded creek. Mallory stood outside my window, holding a big Maglite. Lake braced his hands on Sadie's dashboard to relieve the pressure of the lap belt against his waist. His breathing told me he wasn't too hurt, aside from his seat belt bruise. Sadie steamed and groaned, as if she'd really wanted to see what lay at the bottom of the ravine that peeked through the foggy wisps in her headlights.

"Brakes. Our brakes weren't working."

"Help is on the way," Mallory said as if she hadn't heard me. She ripped open a sterile bandage and pinned it against my hairline.

The pressure stung, and I realized I'd been bleeding. "Thank you."

Lake gently rubbed my shoulder. "You okay?"

I nodded gingerly.

"How'd you find us?" he asked Mallory. "Black car, nighttime…"

Mallory pulled her phone from her pocket and showed us the screen. The little marker bubble read *Lakyn*. "GPS tracking."

The significance of her words didn't sink in because so much of me was shaken and sore, but Lake leaned over and stared up at her through my window. "We're going to have words later, you and I."

Mallory didn't even blink. "I expect so. Here's Doc Stevens now. Tow truck's five minutes out." She walked away, her shoes crunching on the gravel of the highway shoulder.

"You sure you're all right?" Lake held me lightly, and he leaned his forehead against my temple.

"Just bruised. You?"

"Same. That was some great driving. You can crash the car I'm riding in any time."

"Ha-ha—ow." I winced. "Maybe let's not. And I want to talk to Hilt about updating these seat belts and getting airbags. I might not have banged my head if I'd had—oh God."

"What?" Lake patted me over. "What happened?"

I grabbed one of his hands. "Hilt. I have to tell Hilt."

"He'll understand."

"Oh ho ho, *no*. Hilt is understanding about yea many things, Lake, but damage to Sadie is not one of them." Finally, tears filled the corners of my eyes. "He'll be so mad. I'll never get to drive her again."

"That won't happen," he assured me. "He'll be far too relieved that you're alive."

Mallory returned, leading Doc Stevens down the incline. Together, they escorted Lake and me back up to flat ground. The skirt of Doc's sequined red gown hung below the hem of her anorak. She examined me first, at Lake's insistence, and found nothing more than the bruises I already knew were there.

"Pupils equal and reactive, good. Your head just took a bump, Pippa. It should be fine tomorrow. Call me if it isn't."

I grasped her hand as she started to stand. She looked at me inquiringly.

"I just wanted to say, Doc. You look absolutely stunning."

She softened and gave me a friendly smile. But I heard her say to Lake as she approached him, "Careful with that one. I think she hit her head pretty hard after all."

The tow truck arrived, and its operator, a lanky twenty-something with limp ash-brown hair and a uniform with the name Yuri sewn on it, let out a groan of anguish at seeing Sadie's condition. "That's just not right, a beautiful girl like that."

"Take good care of her," I told him.

"Aw, I'd love to, but I ain't got the parts for a classy lady like this. Not sure who would. It'll take me some time to check around."

I pressed a hand to my throbbing forehead. "Okay, just tow her back to Moorehaven, then. It's the Victorian mansion on the cliff—"

"Oh, everyone knows Moorehaven. I'll put this lovely girl wherever you like."

"Thanks, Yuri. Let's get her home, then we'll figure something out for repairs. Hilt might want to do them himself."

"You got it, boss lady."

Doc Stevens said Lake and I were free to go then headed back north to her family's cabin, but I didn't want to leave until I knew Sadie was safely loaded. Yuri took his time strapping her down safely, turned off her headlights, and slowly headed into the fog. Sadie's forlorn silhouette stared back at me, and I nearly cried again.

"I'll see you both home," Mallory said.

Lake and I held each other in her back seat, bracing against the pain of our bruises as our police chief silently drove us back to Seacrest, which was nearly lost in impenetrable billows of fog.

"Lighthouse or Moorehaven?" Mallory asked as we turned off the highway.

"Moorehaven," Lake said. "I want to make sure Pippa's comfortable. I can walk home later."

"You'll fall into the river, the way this fog is going," Mallory countered. She drove slowly through the whiteness. "You said your brakes weren't working. Knowing you, I'm sure you suspect foul play."

The terror of that disastrous drive came flooding back, and my heart rate shot up. I had to lean my head back and stare at her cruiser's tan ceiling. "My brakes totally failed. If I hadn't read that chapter in *The Diamond Charm*, I would've been a lot more panicked, and we might not have made it."

"Gotta love how Moore reaches forward like that," Lake said.

"I do. Suspect foul play, that is. We had brakes, then we didn't. Someone tried to kill us, Mallory."

She hung a slow left onto the Cedar Street bridge. "Got any suspects?"

"No one comes to mind. And everyone does."

Lake said, "The curse of Seacrest."

I nodded before I remembered I'd bumped my head then winced at my painful stupidity. "Too dang many mystery novels. They get into our heads. You've been here long enough to feel it, right, Mal?"

"Who says I didn't already suspect everyone of everything? I'm a cop, remember?" We ambled past Seven Vistas, its ghostly height lost in the fog as if it rose forever. Emily's bake shop and Sebastian's pet-psychic business drifted past on the left, their structural lines dimmed to blurred suggestions of dark and light.

"All right, fair enough," I allowed. "But the real question is—"

"If your brakes *were* cut, does it have anything to do with Mort's death, or have you just annoyed someone so much with your very existence that they want to wipe you from the face of the earth?"

I blinked and hesitated before answering. Lake cleared his throat as if to remind her that he was right there.

"Yeah, thanks, Mal," I said. "Exactly how I would've worded it."

"Well," she continued, ignoring my sarcasm, "I can think of one person who fits that description."

Alarm shot through me at her serious tone. "What? Who?"

"You didn't notice, Winterbourne? She was watching you all evening. Even after Mort died. Some sleuth you are."

"Mal, who are you talking about? Mom? Bliss?" Lake's tone was deeply concerned.

"Cam Cooper, your father's assistant. Kept staring at your girlfriend over the top of her champagne glass."

I shook my head, baffled. "Why would she want to kill me, though? I don't even know her. I think she even helped me out once."

Mallory *tsk*ed. "Honestly, Winterbourne, you must've hit your head. *She* doesn't want you dead. But her boss might."

"That's not fair, Mal," Lake protested.

She straight-up admitted she was following me for him, though. I shuddered and rubbed my arms, wincing again as I pushed on a fresh bruise. "Come on. Would he really try to do that with Lake in the car too?"

Mallory eased into Moorehaven's parking lot and shifted into park. Yuri had already unloaded Sadie and left, and the classic car sat quietly in front of her garage. Through the fog, I couldn't even see any damage to her curves. *If only fog could heal. Then everyone would live here, and it would be way too crowded. Why does every silver lining have a cloud?*

Mallory turned in her seat and met my eyes. "He disowned Lake years ago. What's he got to lose from getting rid of the common little girl who's keeping his son from returning to the fold, except a boy who'd choose that sort of commoner over his own family? What kind of heir would he be, and what kind of heirs would he produce? Baby, bathwater, et cetera."

Her voice was cold and calculating. I couldn't tell if she was just expressing Devereaux's perspective or embracing it. I shuddered again. Lake pulled me against him as if comforting me against her words, but his somber silence seemed eerily like agreement.

"Well, I guess... I guess I'll have to watch how I interact with certain people from now on."

"Smart move. Rest well, Winterbourne. I'll be keeping an eye on Cam Cooper."

I opened the cruiser door then paused. "Who do you think killed Mort?"

"I don't guess," she replied. "But I'm sorry to say that the evidence does seem to point to something in the food as the source of the poison, and that means—"

"Tyleen." My heart sank.

"Or Sebastian, yes." Mallory reached for her gear shift then looked back at me with a soft, hesitant expression. "I know they're your friends. Your neighbors. And I know what you're like. Just *try* not to get in the way of the official investigation, Winterbourne. I'd consider it a favor."

Is she... is she being... nice *to me?* I almost couldn't grasp the concept. "I'll do my best. Thanks again for everything." I slid out into the damp air.

Lake followed me and held my hand. "Good night, Mallory."

As I clicked my way up the porch steps in my high heels, Mallory's headlights swung around, and she vanished back into the pale soup. "Your dad wouldn't really... Would he? I mean, Mallory's just being dramatic."

Lake kissed my temple. "Of course she is. She and my dad have their own issues. He's a teddy bear, really."

He opened Moorehaven's front door, and the familiar smells of books and food surrounded me. I leaned against the doorjamb to pull off my heels, feeling a million years old.

Hilt popped out of the side hall, looking chipper. "Back already, you two? How was the party? You survive?" His smile slipped as his eyes found the bandage on my forehead.

"You didn't hear the tow truck?" I blurted.

"Ain't heard much of anything. Been banging away at the heating system for a couple of hours. Why?"

The truth pulled at my cheeks until my face seemed to weigh five extra pounds. "Well, I did survive. But not everyone did. Mort died at the party. And Sadie's... Sadie's hurt." Tears welled in my eyes again, and I covered my mouth with a shaking hand.

"What?" Hilt swept in, arms outstretched, and Lake guided me toward him with a hand on my lower back. My uncle took me in his arms then looked me over closely. "*You're* hurt! All these scrapes... Pippa, Lake, what happened to you?"

"I'm so sorry," I began. "It's my fault. I was driving, and I couldn't keep her on the road..."

"Chloe!" Hilt's voice was taut. He guided me into the big parlor and parked me on the big red couch.

Lake followed, untying his bow tie with a scraped hand.

"Shh, Hilt, I just took Ruslan his nighttime hot cocoa." Chloe walked through the broad archway, took one look at us, and wheeled around. "Oh boy. I'm getting the usual," she called as her footsteps pounded down the hallway. In moments, she'd returned with what had become a Moorehaven fixture, the usual treatment for authors who got too carried away with their research trips. She set the plastic bin on the coffee table and removed its lid.

Hilt scooped out the first aid kit, but I waved him off. "Doc Stevens already looked us over."

"She ain't your uncle. I'm gonna Band-Aid you to within an inch of your life. Now, hold still."

I submitted to the lifelong-bachelor equivalent of tender ministrations while Chloe fished a big bar of chocolate and a little bottle of vodka from the box.

"No, not those. Go get the ice pack from the freezer, and hide that vodka while you're in there. Not taking any chances with that head jiggler of yours," Hilt added to me.

Chloe returned with a frozen gel pack wrapped in a kitchen towel. Hilt plumped a pillow for me, and Lake lifted my legs so that I could lie down on the couch. Chloe gingerly set the ice pack against my head. "How's that?"

"Mm-hmm," I murmured.

Lake squeezed my hand.

"Hilt, go check on Sadie. She's your baby."

Hilt patted his pockets as if he might be carrying a magical tool to repair his beloved Phantom 5, and his face tensed. "Right. Yeah. Okay. Glad you're safe, Whip."

As he double-timed it out to the parking lot, I sighed. "He called me Whip again. He's been doing that more often recently."

"No one should outlive their kids," Chloe said. "That's what my dad says, anyway. I guess that goes for cars that are younger than you too."

"Losing Sadie would make Hilt feel more alone," Lake added. "I hope she didn't get too damaged, for his sake."

"No wonder Hilt and Ruslan get along so well," I murmured. "A pair of old lions, those two, full of memory and myriad sunrises."

Chloe spotted the scrape on Lake's hand and dug into the first aid kit for more Band-Aids and some antibiotic cream. "Gimme," she insisted, holding out her hand for his.

"What? No, I'm fine."

Chloe dragged his hand out of mine and pressed it against her knee so that she could spread cream across the long scrape. Lake, confused and embarrassed, tried to pull it away, but she clamped down on it.

"Hold still, guinea pig. How'm I gonna get better at this sort of thing for our more adventurous guests unless I practice? And besides, I don't need to see blood all over the breakfast bowls tomorrow morning."

"What are you talking about? I'm not even bleeding."

"You wanna keep it that way? Hold still." Chloe brandished the tube of antibiotic cream like a cudgel.

I chuckled as Lake reluctantly let Chloe place a couple of bandages on his hand. She'd added so much cream to his cut that it oozed out the sides of the Band-Aids like they were overfilled burritos. "There. Good to go."

"Thanks. Looks awesome." Lake's smile was way too bright, and he held his hand stiffly as he pretended to admire her handiwork.

"You're a terrible liar," she said grumpily.

"What? *Nooo*." His exaggerated denial made me laugh, and I clutched my sore head.

Chloe shot him a look full of fake daggers. "Someday, you'll need my help, and you'll be glad I practiced on you."

"You know what? You're probably right, with the way our evening has been going." Lake lifted my feet, slid onto the couch, and rested my legs across his lap. I intertwined my fingers with his. My cats padded in, smelling adventure but having waited until our ruckus died down. Rex licked my cheek comfortingly, while Svetlana butted her head against Lake's shoulder. They settled onto the back of the red couch, purring. It felt good to relax with friends and family, and though my body still ached from Sadie's crash, my soul was refreshed, at least until I remembered that there could have been three dead bodies that night.

After checking Sadie over, Hilt returned, looking troubled and relieved at the same time, and reluctantly went to bed after Chloe promised to look after Lake and me. Soon after that, I heard Lake's breathing change, easing into a light sleep.

I considered reading further in *The Diamond Charm*, but then I remembered Aunt Felicity's journal. I managed to ease my legs off Lake's lap without waking him, but Chloe, who'd been reading an Old West thriller in a chair nearby, whispered that she would get whatever I needed. I gave her detailed instructions to the spot on my bookshelf where I'd hidden the journal.

She returned with it still tucked inside the birding book's dust cover. I pulled the cover off and sat beside my sleeping boyfriend to begin reading. I studied the cover for a moment, resting my fingertips on the same pressed linen that Aunt Felicity had touched. Then I smelled the pages, and decades of ink and secrets filled my mind. The history of my home, of its creator, awaited me within the pages I held. My fingers twitched with anticipation.

"Smell good?" Chloe asked quietly.

"Smells like a page-turner." I gently opened the journal and paged carefully to where I'd left off. "See?" I joked.

"Let me know if you learn anything juicy," Chloe demanded in a stage whisper.

I agreed. Felicity's deep-blue ink swirled and looped, carrying me to another time. Her words danced in my aching head, and I could almost hear her speak to me in a firm contralto laced with glints of amusement.

She wrote of the changing fashions, the new highway that was coming into town, various public events, and verbal jousting with other prominent members of Seacrest society, such as it was. Felicity seemed to delight in the challenge of living as loudly as possible while maintaining an impenetrable barrier of class.

Then thirty pages in, she confessed something I had never heard before, something that challenged everything I thought I knew about her.

You know the year of my birth, Raymond. After the Civil War ended—and there was nothing civil about it, according to my father and his fellow industrial tycoons—our shaken country took stock and realized it had lost over half a million of its young men to battle and war-related illness. A whole generation had been decimated. It fell to those who remained to repopulate, and thus I entered the world. I and a vast number of other children, products of a war already decided, born to step forward into the future.

And step forward, we did. My father indoctrinated me in my duty from a very young age. You can imagine his profound dismay—and my bafflement—when he learned that I was with child while still unmarried—and by a dockhand, no less!

I sat up straighter then regretted it and rubbed my aching head.

I had rather incorrectly assumed that the rules on such things were relaxing to the point of quiet acceptance. Imagine my shock when my father not only insisted that I never see my beloved Charles again but that

I lock myself away, give up the child, and never set foot in my father's home again, forfeiting all my claims on his vast fortune.

You can see that I failed to do one of those things, as you are standing in the product of much of my investment in real estate. I've never told you how I managed to keep my money, though.

The truth is, dear Raymond, that I did not keep it. Not exactly.

This was getting good.

I ran away and spent the rest of the year with Charles. We were happy—as happy as two destitute lovers can be. But the day I fled New York City to be with him, I visited my father's banker, Mr. Arndt, armed with my father's signature. I claimed to be on an errand for him, and the kindly old man, a longtime family friend, had no reason to doubt me. Twenty minutes later, I had transferred a large portion of my father's fortune into a separate bank account, and by lunchtime, that money had been moved through three different banks.

I wouldn't have pegged her as a money launderer, but stranger things had happened.

While Charles and I awaited the birth of our child in a tiny seaside town on the coast of Connecticut, I kept the money moving, knowing my father would be looking for it. He taught me well, and I had such plans for that money—my child would never know the struggles Charles had grown up with—but my father had resources I'd never known about. He sent Pinkertons after us, and they found us just a few weeks after I bore Charles a son. We named him James. I'm sure now that my father had sent them to search for a newborn child around the time I was due to give birth. They were very efficient—and very insistent.

I will never forget that day. Charles fought them off and told me to run—and I did. We had escape plans in place, meeting locations, and trains to catch. But with the baby to look out for, we couldn't both run. Charles insisted on staying behind with him, since it was me my father was most furious with. I waited at the train station for hours. My life had just burnt down, even if I hadn't been aflame myself.

My father had captured my lover and my baby. I had only one way to prevent him from ruining everything.

May God forgive me—I took the money and ran. I ran all the way across the country, to a place he'd never think to look—a tiny, foggy speck of coastline that didn't even have a town yet.

I never heard from my father, even though I always expected to. He died not long after I left. But I ached for Charles and James. I even sent the Pinkertons to look for them—turned my revenge inside out—but they were unsuccessful. How could they find Charles once but not twice? I feared the worst, and I still do. I failed them, Raymond. I abandoned my son out of fear of—and hatred for—my father. You were my second chance, and I hope you can say that I did a fair job of raising you after your parents died. Perhaps you will succeed where I have not and one day learn the fate of my darling boy.

I sniffed and wiped tears from the corners of my eyes. I'd always imagined Felicity jaunting westward on a sort of rollicking adventure quest, bright-eyed and hopeful. Her journey had instead been wracked with guilt and sorrow, and she'd lived with deep regret the rest of her life. The widow walk she'd built on Moorehaven's roof seemed even lonelier all of a sudden. *She lived by the sea the rest of her life, remembering their time together. She must've been so sad, so angry, when she got here. But she persevered. Gave herself a second chance with Raymond.* I wiped my eyes again and lay there in awe of the mighty woman Felicity Moore had been.

Lake still dozed, and Chloe was deep in her own book, so I read a few more pages on much lighter subjects. I came across a section that drew me back into the mystery surrounding those hidden newspapers Naoma had found.

I do not presume your ignorance of the rumors that tend to flock around me, as seabirds in migration will pause amid fertile wetlands for a time. I do try to keep the most boring of them from your ears, my dear Raymond, as they shan't inspire you in the least. Differences breed misunderstanding and resentment, and as every person on this earth is unique, there is bound to be constant jostling of feelings. It is no false claim to say that I am more unusual than most and thus naturally attract a larger portion of discontent and speculation. 'Tis my lot, and as long as it does not become my final plot, I am content with it.

My little jest in claiming my tea was poisoned was indeed false and only written for your mental digestion, but it did stem from my own speculation that perhaps one day, someone would indeed try to shuffle me off this mortal coil without my consent. With that in mind, be aware that I have made arrangements with a funeral home in Florence that will handle all the particulars after my death so as not to upset my dear friends in Seacrest—or delight my enemies.

You know more than everyone but Tilly regarding our numerous and dear house guests, and she would rather die than reveal what she knows—of that, I have no doubt. I pray you keep as many of their secrets as you know, though I shan't ask you to what extent your knowledge stretches. They lost much and left behind more, and those stories must never see the light of day.

For my part, I will take their secrets to my grave. I know your tendency to spin the truth, but I also trust in your sense of self-preservation. And if I may presume a step further, never use the following names in your novels: Chantilly Beechwood, Gayle Jones, Abigail Travers, Jane Smith, Rachel Donner.

If you have found the jewel vault, pray leave it be. No one expects those treasures to surface again, nor the tales attached to them—not in my lifetime nor in yours.

I stopped reading, my breath caught in my throat. *Criminy on a cracker!* Felicity's own words lent more legitimacy to the lost newspaper article's claims of grifting than I ever thought possible. *Stealing money from her dad is one thing, but a whole vault of jewels? Where did that come from? Did she work alone, or were her house guests in on her schemes? Did they steal from their families for her?* With a jolt, I recognized the name of the librarian, Abigail Travers, whom Naoma was researching. *Why does Felicity want to keep her name hidden? Was she a main accomplice or another victim?* "What's she hiding?" I muttered.

"Something juicy?" Chloe asked hopefully.

I really wanted to bring Chloe in on the secret, but the only person I'd told was Hilt. As much as I loved Chloe, she didn't have nearly as much invested in Moorehaven as we did. One wrong word spoken in confidence before Hilt, Naoma, and I got to the bottom of the mystery, and our lives could be ruined.

"I'm not sure yet," I said. "I'll tell you as soon as I can, but for now, I think the fewer people who know what's in this book, the better."

Chloe pouted. "You don't trust me? After all we've been through? Everyone she knew back then is long gone by now. What could her words possibly endanger now?"

I gave her my most serious look. "Everything."

13

"I used to build gingerbread houses every Christmas. Then I'd march my nutcracker through them and send in the gingerbread men to search for clues as to whodunit. I'd always eat the evidence before the case could be brought to trial, though. That's just the way the gingerbread house crumbles."

Raymond Moore, 1937

LAKE AND I SPENT THE night in my cozy bedroom behind the hidden pantry door, while Chloe reluctantly returned to the lighthouse. Her last words to me were "I'll be there before you get up, and I'll take care of breakfast, because you need to rest after that car crash. Let me take over, at least for the morning."

I was sore enough to agree.

We were too exhausted to do more than spoon, but I slept amazingly well in his arms and woke him with a passionate kiss, to which he eagerly responded. By the time we emerged from our secret hideaway, I smelled bacon, eggs, and applesauce-gingerbread muffins.

Hilt gave Lake the stink eye as we joined the others at the table, but Chloe slid full plates in front of us with a dazzling smile. "Good morning, lovebirds! I hope you slept well," she trilled.

I gave her a once-over. She'd pulled her black hair back and wore one of my bright Christmas aprons over the sleeveless silver blouse she called her "most grown-up top."

"It's like looking in a mirror," I said.

Chloe offered me a curtsey and headed back to the kitchen.

"I like her very much," Ruslan said. "She's lucky to have you and this place."

I dug in to my eggs while Lake inhaled several strips of bacon.

"We're lucky to have her too," I responded. "You never think you need an intern, then you end up with an assistant you can't live without."

"I'll remember that the next time I ask for a raise," Chloe said from the archway. "Coffee, boss?" She approached, picked up my coffee cup, and poured me a drink topped with decorative foam in the shape of holly leaves and berries.

"Wow," Lake said, leaning over my cup. "Can you make mine a wave? Not a tsunami, though. Had enough of those recently," he added, referencing last summer's murderous chaos.

"One perfectly safe little foam wave, coming up." Chloe popped back to the kitchen.

"Perks of hiring someone who worked as a barista along the highway for a summer," I said.

"She was telling me earlier," Ruslan said softly, "about her parents. It's been a long time since I was young, and I never had the luxury of growing up with my parents after the Blitz, but I feel she truly wants to make as much of her life as she can, with as much of her parents in it as possible. I think she has everything she needs—including you folks—to help her achieve that. You all are her family too." He raised his coffee cup in salute.

I raised mine too. "To family."

Chloe bustled back in with Lake's coffee and poured him a perfect foaming wave.

He clasped her hand under his and raised the cup for both of them. "To family."

Hilt gave us a wry smile and lifted his cup too. "Can't live with ya, can't kill ya off."

Our laughter broke up the serious side of the emotional high, and I returned to stuffing my face with Chloe's amazing breakfast, trying not to ponder that someone *had* just tried to kill me off. I pushed that aside, though, and focused on not moaning as I ate.

Hilt and Chloe begin to chant, "Quiz, quiz, quiz!"

I flicked my gaze to Ruslan, who fairly wriggled with anticipation in his seat. "I'm ready, Pippa. I've been preparing, you see."

I set my fork aside. "Oh, preparing, have you? Well then, Ruslan, you'll be able to tell me which of your characters would be most likely to return a library book on time and who would skip out on their fines."

Ruslan's eyes twinkled as he rubbed his sturdy hands together. "Let me see. Morwen, one of my fences, would return the book on time, because it's just good business to avoid those fines in the first place. Levi, the apprentice bounty hunter, isn't nearly as put together as he seems, so he'd forget to return the book then be too embarrassed to show his face to pay the fine. Old Gaye, though, she'd keep the book to test the librarian, act all surprised when she learned of the fine, then play the pity-an-old-woman card to see if she could get out of it. Probably claim one of her cats ate it, too, ha!"

We all laughed. "I have one," Chloe volunteered, her cheeks flushing with excitement. "Who would bake the best gingerbread?"

A ring of *ooh*s flew around the table, and Ruslan made a thoughtful pout. "Well," he said finally, "you'd think it would be Farina, my heroine. And she does have great skill with her father, Balian's, favorite gingerbread recipe. But the true king of all the gingerbread is actually Gregor, who has a not-so-secret love of pastries, as his girth will attest!"

Chloe lifted her muffin in salute to Ruslan's bounty hunter. "To Gregor, king of gingerbread!"

After cramming in one last applesauce-gingerbread muffin, I leaned back and sighed in utter contentment. But with my stomach full, my mind started spinning. We still needed to find out what lay beyond the wooden panel in the laundry chute, but a more pressing matter had overtaken me: I needed to find out who had a motive to kill Mort. And I knew just where to start.

"I need to go see someone," I said.

Everyone studied me.

"It's related to Mort's death, isn't it?" Chloe asked.

"Yes. Maybe. I hope not." I stood and collected my plate and silverware. "I need to speak to Geneva Laine."

Lake stood as well. "I should check on my parents and see how they're coping after a death at their party." He kissed me on the cheek. "Catch up with you later."

"I want to come," Chloe told me eagerly. "I never get to go investigating with you. Let me tag along this time."

Hilt shrugged amiably. "Ruslan and I can hold down the fort together. If Mallory calls with an update on Sadie's brakes, we'll let you know. And you call us if you learn anything."

"Yes!" Chloe darted down the hall. She returned with her coat on and mine in her hand before I'd even set my plate in the sink.

I put it on as we headed outside for our bikes. I paused to pull on my gloves after unlocking my retro bicycle. "Just remember, Ms. Laine is a few generations removed from yours. She's used to a whole different kind of politeness and social interaction."

My warning didn't even dent her incandescent smile. "Don't worry. I'll let you do the talking."

"Deal. I just need to make one stop first." We biked slowly through the fog, and after a quick detour to the mailing center to drop off my order for Tyleen's picture mug with Andy, the genial proprietor, we made our way across the river toward Laine Manor, which sat atop a small rise. The damp air was bitterly cold, biting through our clothing and turning my fingertips numb by the time we puffed our way through the stately iron gates and up the short drive to the historic house.

I slung my icicle of a leg off my bike and nudged my front wheel into the bike rack next to the manor's small white porch, gasping for breath. My lungs felt like they'd been lit on fire with icy blue flames.

Next to me, Chloe effortlessly rested her charcoal-themed touring bike next to my old clunker. "Great ride, right? Super refreshing. What's the plan? Is there gonna be good-cop-bad-cop stuff? Can I be bad cop?"

"That's not the genre I use when I investigate. I'm just going to talk to her. Come on."

Maude, Geneva's longtime secretary, let us in with a welcoming smile. Classy as always in an understated mint skirt suit, she reminded me of Perry Mason's secretary, Della Street. "Good morning, ladies of Moorehaven. Is Ms. Laine expecting you?"

I brandished my hostess smile. "We'd just like a quick word with her."

Maude deflected with a secretary smile of her own. "Regarding?"

Dang it. She wins this smile battle. I let my voice get complex with emotion. "Last night."

Maude's face softened, and she rested a hand on her chest. "Oh. Yes. Such a tragedy."

Geneva didn't seem to think so. "Is she up for talking about it, do you think?"

"I'll pop in and ask. Please wait here." Maude's purposeful waddle carried her down a white-carpeted hallway into the manor's interior.

"What *did* Geneva say at the party last night?" Chloe whispered.

"I'm more interested in why she said it out loud in front of so many peers."

Chloe took in the high foyer, with its ornate white paneling and clear windows—not a scrap of color to be seen. "They say people who live in glass houses shouldn't throw stones. I wonder what people in ivory towers shouldn't throw."

"Shade."

"Oh my God, is that what happened last night?"

Maude returned before I could answer. "Right this way, ladies. Ms. Laine will see you in the Burgundy Lounge."

We followed her down three hallways and through a broad white door to the left. It was decorated with delicate scrolling that matched the lintel bracing it. I felt like I was walking into Rivendell, the city from *The Lord of the Rings*.

Inside the lounge, however, the vibe was entirely retro Seacrest. Long, narrow windows dominated one wall and looked out toward the sea. Their high perspective made Seacrest seem like a green-and-gray carpet disappearing into the fog. Heavy burgundy drapery had been pulled back to showcase a full view of the fog, and various Heywood Wakefield chairs were clustered around the room. A matching trio of deep-red Kashmir carpets blanketed the mahogany floorboards nearly to the windows, and vibrant seascapes shone from several frames along the walls. None of the paintings had a wisp of fog. *This art is Laine Manor's answer to Moorehaven's stained glass. Nice.*

Geneva Laine sat on a jade velvet chaise, reading a slender book with a deep-blue cover. She wore a blue-gray blouse with a drop waist that evoked the sailor blouses of the twenties, over a long white skirt with soft draping. Her snow-white hair rested in a firm chignon, giving off an air of competence rather than romanticism. She studied us with as-sharp-as-ever cinnamon-hazel eyes as we entered the room, and a wry smile curved her lips.

"Pippa Winterbourne. I might have known. You've heard about the approaching storm?"

I assured her that I had.

"That'll be all, Maude."

Her secretary let herself back out and pulled the ornate wooden door shut behind her. Geneva indicated a pair of chairs across from her, and we sat.

The matriarch looked tired, but she slipped a bookmark into her book and gave me her full attention.

I reciprocated with a smile. "Good morning, Geneva. You know my assistant, Chloe, of course."

Geneva nodded. "Miss Braxton. Your father's well, I hope? Recovered from his temporary bout of insanity at the last town council meeting?"

Chloe's back stiffened, and her mouth drew tight. "I wouldn't know, Miss Laine. I moved out a few months ago. We don't talk much now."

Genuine concern claimed Geneva's features. "But, my dear, it's Christmas. Surely, you'll want to be with your family for the holiday."

"The only thing I want for Christmas is a time machine," Chloe replied.

A sad smile softened the firm lines on Geneva's face. "Ah," she murmured. "Yes, of course. I understand. All my favorite Christmases lie far in the past as well." She took a bracing breath and lifted her chin. "Now, Miss Winterbourne, may I assume you've come to delicately question me regarding my macabre delight at the untimely passing of Morton Roark? Perhaps with added curiosity as to whether I might have... How do they put it? 'Offed' him myself?" The grand old dame's smile was cheerfully predatory.

She's lived in Seacrest since even before it became Moore's world-famous, murder-centric hometown. Of course she knows why I'm here. "You'd be disappointed if I came on any other matter."

Geneva smiled triumphantly. "Indeed, I would. Ask me your questions. It's about time some of these secrets get aired."

"Ooh, secrets," Chloe whispered. Her eyes glinted with anticipation.

But Geneva had known Raymond Moore well. Whether from admiration or sheer peer pressure, she'd adopted his reluctant-witness attitude whenever anyone wanted information. I would have to earn my answers by asking exactly the right questions. I sat back and lobbed my first one at her. "Your outburst at the Ivenses' party tells me that you wanted everyone to see you acting delighted at Mort's demise. You knew something about him that, for whatever reason, not many others did. Showing your feelings is going to get people talking, and Mort's secret is going to get around, just as you intended. So what's the secret? What did you know about Mort, and was it really bad enough that you thought he should die over it?"

Geneva's warm eyes studied me, then Chloe, then me again. "And you've brought your protégé so *you* can show off *your* cleverness too. How delightful. It's always nice to see the next generation taking up our local traditions."

"Uh, I'm, like, ten years younger than Pippa. Hardly next generation," Chloe protested.

Geneva *tsk*ed, her eyes still on me. "Like, dude, your millennial is harshing my baby boomer vibe."

I quashed the grin that threatened to break the mood. "I'll have a word with her later."

"See that you do." Geneva broke her serious I and gave Chloe a saucy wink. "Now, to answer your question, I must first ask you a question. Are you familiar with the Hothouse?"

"Of course."

The Hothouse was a roadside market the size of a semi-truck—exactly the size, in fact, since it was housed in a modified shipping container. It sat in a wide spot south of town on a large curve in Highway 101 and attracted plenty of business with its hand-painted signs that featured sexy vegetable characters. Their produce was always fresh, either from local gardens or greenhouses, and the three sisters who ran it managed to sell plenty of food year-round. Lots of it ended up on Moorehaven's table too.

"Did you know Mort owned it?" Geneva continued.

"No, actually. I assumed Stella Benton did, either with her sisters or as sole proprietor."

The firm lines on Geneva's face returned in force. "And were you aware that the market also serves as a..." Her eyes darted to Chloe before she continued. "House of ill repute?"

I coughed in surprise. "I'm sorry, a what?"

Chloe said, "The Hothouse isn't a brothel."

"It's a cathouse, I tell you!" Geneva insisted, jabbing a finger toward the Kashmir carpet.

"The Hothouse is a whorehouse? But... where... I mean, there's literally no room in there for..."

Chloe cracked up, while Geneva managed to turn a delicate shade of pink.

"I have it on good authority," Geneva said finally, "that Stella and her sisters operate a bordello on the premises. I have no exact information on where."

I willed my face to be serious, since Geneva seemed earnest, but I honestly couldn't picture three middle-aged ladies getting jiggy right there with the peaches and eggplants. Stella resembled a scarlet bombshell, sure, and she had a great head for business. But Mina, the middle sister, who kept the books and organized deliveries, always struck me as someone who would fit in better at a museum, since she was half-desiccated already. And the youngest, Tonya, was so wholesome that she wore frilly gingham aprons and sold her homemade jams in matching cloth caps and ribbons. "Who's your authority, Geneva? Did someone see something?"

"Yes. *I* did. Just this past summer. And I took myself off right away to demand the full truth from Mort. And do you know what he did? He laughed in my face!"

That sobered me up. A rumor was one thing, but to dismiss the eyewitness account of the town matriarch by laughing at her was a step too far, even for Mort. His rudeness hardly seemed enough reason to kill him, though I could understand Geneva wanting him dead for the insult alone. "What did you do next?" I asked.

"I took the matter to the town council, naturally." Geneva nodded to Chloe. "And your father entirely lost his mind."

"Not a difficult task," Chloe replied.

"Apparently not," Geneva continued. "Your father managed to speak with such authority in defense of the Hothouse that I began to, er, have certain *concerns*." Geneva's tone seemed to hint at a very delicate accusation.

"Concerns?" I glanced at Chloe.

"That is... I mean to say," Geneva hedged, "Mercer Braxton doesn't seem overly enthralled with fruits and vegetables on their own merits."

Chloe's face tightened, and her lower lip flexed into a frown. "What you're *really* saying is he isn't acting in a very town-councilor kind of way because he doesn't agree with *you*."

Geneva's nostrils flared. "I have proof, and he wouldn't accept it. That says something to me. I'm disappointed it doesn't say anything to you."

I raised my hands in a pacifying gesture. "Ladies. Let's take a breath, shall we? Geneva, what proof did you see, exactly, and did it involve Mercer?"

Geneva shook her head. "I saw Tonya climbing down from a trucker's cab, gingham frills flapping in the breeze, as the truck idled in the wide spot behind the Hothouse. She gave the trucker a long kiss and dashed back into the market, and he drove away. It was near the end of the day, and no one else was around. I stayed in the car while Maude went in for some acorn squashes. No one witnessed Tonya's indiscretion but me. And no one will believe me!"

Her chignon fairly vibrated with geriatric outrage. "Do I seem even the slightest bit senile to you? I assure you I know what I saw."

I nodded. "Well, I know a way to help clear all this up. I can ask around—delicately—for any other solid proof of impropriety out at the Hothouse, including proof that Mort knew about it." The Gossips would be overjoyed to help confirm or deny such a juicy bit of gossip, especially since Geneva Laine was the source of the rumor.

"You think someone killed him over the Hothouse?" Chloe asked, seemingly jarred out of her indignation.

"I don't know. But someone killed him over something, and we'll all be safer once we figure out what it was. And, Chloe, you can help us out too."

"I get to be an honorary Gossip?"

Geneva frowned in mild disapproval, but I nodded. "Your mission, should you choose to accept it, is to talk to your father and see what he knows about the Hothouse, if anything."

Chloe's expression morphed into mulish resistance. "You're just saying that to get me to spend quality family time with him at Christmas."

I raised my chin and owned my subterfuge. "You don't have to wait that long. Are you in?"

Chloe studied the carpet then the foggy view. She glanced at Geneva and seemed to receive an invisible signal. With a sigh older than I was, Chloe turned to me and nodded. "Challenge accepted."

Geneva offered us a proud, gaunt grin. "Excellent. Such fine, investigative ladies you're turning into."

I couldn't help but swell with pride in the glow of Geneva Laine's approval. Chloe seemed to read my expression and sat up straighter too.

"It's just too bad that society can't shake itself of these filthy habits, isn't it?" Geneva continued. Then she gestured to me as if including me on her side of the issue. "Pulling oneself free of scandal is hard work, after all. It takes quite a bit of effort, which should by all rights be applied somewhere more useful."

She'd lost me, and my confused expression must've told her so. She clarified, "The Moorehaven sex scandal, of course."

A chill shot down my spine. Dismay clogged my belly like a shower drain that needed Drano. *Of all the terrible timing, Geneva. And what the heck, Naoma?*

Chloe sat bolt upright and stared at both of us. "The what now?"

The old woman's eyes darted between Chloe and me. "Surely you've told her, Pippa. She needs to know so that she can guard against such immorality in the future."

"I'm confused," Chloe said. "Are you warning me I'll become a hooker on top of my usual duties? Because I don't have time for lying down on the job I already have."

I couldn't have been prouder of my friend in that moment. Geneva usually had her head on straight, but she seemed pretty hung up on that one particular kind of immorality. *She knows about the rumors. Felicity, the grifting, the theft. And apparently quite a bit more. If she knows, who else does? Good Lord, what am I going to do?*

"Pippa?" Chloe looked at me.

Geneva had forced my hand. I had to bring Chloe in on the secret Naoma had found. "There's an old rumor that Felicity Moore was up to something more than her usual tricks. Ladies would stay with her, and jewelry would go missing—not hers—and people disappeared, never to be heard from again. People called Felicity a grifter, thought she was conning people. Or worse."

"Does this have anything to do with the laundry chutes?" Chloe asked.

I wasn't ready to bring Geneva in on that particular detail. "Not sure, but we need to find out one way or the other, and soon."

Geneva leaned forward. "That sounds ominous. Has someone else stumbled onto Moorehaven's secret, Miss Winterbourne?"

"Just a little piece of it. And you know how dangerous part of a secret can be." I gave the matriarch all my attention along with a half smile. Geneva Laine was a determinist who had spent several decades trying to will Seacrest into her perfect version of itself. She very well might kill to protect Seacrest. And despite her insistence that Mort hadn't been a threat to her beloved town, I wholeheartedly believed that she would lie to protect it. I had no reason to believe what she told me. "Are you sure you didn't kill Mort, Geneva? We both know you'd do anything to protect this town."

Geneva gave an unladylike snort and sat up straighter. "I most certainly would. But Morton Roark wasn't a threat to the town. And besides," she added, holding up her gnarled, liver-spotted hands, with long fingers and neat lavender nails, "I couldn't kill anyone with these hands. Not anymore."

I blinked. *Not anymore?*

Chloe let her black hair swoop down over one eye and gave Geneva a direct look with the other eye. "What about your staff, though? They're pretty loyal to you."

Geneva offered a small nod of appreciation. "I'll be sure to tell Maude you think she's capable of murder. She'll be so pleased. The poor woman literally couldn't hurt a fly. You should've seen her during the Great Housefly Debacle of 2009." She settled back with a satisfied smile. "It seems that my one comic weakness is the sight of a middle-aged secretary, who spends an hour each morning making sure every single hair on her head is in place, yelping and hi-yi-yi-ing her way down my halls at full speed, shaking her fingers through her hair and waving her arms over her head as if warding off the devil himself." Geneva let out a helpless cackle. "Ah, but you must never tell her how amusing I find her distress. She'd be terribly embarrassed, and I simply cannot live without her."

A knock came at the parlor door, and Maude poked her head through. "There's a package, Ms. Laine."

Geneva quickly composed herself. "I'll open it later, dear. You see I have guests."

"But, Ms. Laine, it has no postage, the return address is Laine Manor, and I don't recognize the handwriting."

"What? Bring it here."

Maude slipped inside and padded across the Kashmir carpet. Geneva took the small box and shook it gently. "Bring me a knife."

Maude left and returned with a small, sharp pocketknife. Geneva slit the packing tape and opened the little parcel. She stared down into it but didn't take out whatever was inside. "Maude, be a dear, and tell the police to pop over."

Maude dashed out of the parlor, and Chloe gasped.

I stood up, alarmed. *What's in there? A finger? A bomb? A venomous snake?* "Geneva, what is it?"

She gingerly turned the small cardboard box around. Nestled in the bottom, a jewel-encrusted bracelet winked up at me, sparking with rubies and diamonds. I stared at her, confused.

"It's not mine," she said. "Neither is the handwriting. No postage. I doubt this recipient address is legitimate either. You think I'm about to put my fingerprints on an obviously stolen piece of jewelry that someone mailed to me as a frame-up?"

"Good call," Chloe murmured.

"Are those stones real?" I asked.

Geneva obligingly took another look. "Yes, I believe so. This bracelet is worth several pretty pennies. You'll stay, naturally, and give statements to the chief." It wasn't a request.

Before I could answer her, my phone rang. "Excuse me, Geneva." I stood and walked to the far end of the parlor. "What's up, Wallis?"

"My dear, something very strange has happened. I believe I have a curiosity for the group." My florist friend's funereal tone was more sober than usual as she offered up something for the Glaze & Gossip ladies to investigate. "I've just gotten a package delivered—well, returned—to the flower shop. But I don't remember sending it out. This isn't even my handwriting. And you'll never guess what's inside."

Her Eeyore-ish tone made me envision the severed finger I'd worried about in Geneva's package, but I knew better. "Something sparkly and expensive."

"Oh, you did guess. How on earth did you know?"

"That's just another part of the curiosity. I'm calling a meeting. Let's all meet at Emily's in ten. Something very strange is afoot in Seacrest." I hung up and sent out a group text, mobilizing my fellow Glaze & Gossip ladies. "My deepest apologies, Geneva, but I'll have to leave Chloe here to corroborate your package story. Something urgent has come up." With a wicked smile and no further explanation, I left.

First, Felicity's accused of stealing jewelry. Now, it's turning up left and right. What's going on in this town?

14

"Quiche is just a poison vector moonlighting as an entrée. Get me a steak."
Raymond Moore, 1967

TWELVE MINUTES LATER, I dropped into a folding chair in Emily's kitchen, surrounded by almost all my Glaze & Gossip friends, although Tyleen had texted back and refused to show up. I guessed I didn't blame her.

The air in the kitchen smelled like heaven and Christmas rolled together. While we nabbed fresh, warm gingerbread muffins from the sunshine-yellow platter Emily had set in the middle of the table, I filled everyone in on the Hothouse situation with Geneva and how I'd conscripted Chloe to delicately investigate with her father.

"So, Geneva wanted Mort dead because she thinks he was some kind of greengrocer pimp." Naoma, as usual, got straight to the point.

"And Chloe's dad might have been a customer?" Wallis asked.

"Whatever Mercer's connection to the Hothouse, I'm very certain it's not that," I said.

"What's the deal with Tyleen?" Lori asked as she eased into a chair. "Is she really just sitting on a bench across from the police station?"

Jordan sipped a dark-roast coffee she'd made in the front of Emily's pastry shop before entering the kitchen. "That's one way to stay out of trouble."

"It's December. She'll freeze to death," Wallis protested.

Naoma tapped a fuchsia nail on the tabletop. "No, Sebastian's bringing her thermoses of soup and coffee."

"I should take her something," Emily said. "And maybe we should go sit with her as a sign of solidarity."

"She already refused my company," Lori replied. "Said I needed to share with you guys everything I learned from typing up Doc's notes on Mort's autopsy. As if I couldn't do that in a text."

"Texts don't come with free gingerbread muffins, though," I said then took a big bite of mine. "And I hate to say it, but how are we going to prove she and Sebastian are innocent of Mort's murder if we're all jammed onto a bench where Mallory and Vic can keep an eye on us?"

"That's a good point," Wallis said. "We should all be investigating, and Tyleen should just surrender herself so she can stay in a nice, warm cell."

Jordan and I exchanged amused glances. Wallis's suggestion was far from the worst idea she'd ever had and definitely a step up from the time she accidentally trapped herself in a coffin at the mortuary because she hoped to learn whether the dead actually felt peaceful.

Naoma thumped her muffin on the tabletop in a muffled attempt to call our meeting to order. "I know we all want to hear Lori's info on Mort's death, but let's start with Pippa's curiosity, since it's the reason she called this meeting."

Everyone turned to me. "As I said, I was just at Geneva Laine's house. As we were talking, Maude brought in a little package. Its return address was Laine Manor, but the handwriting was unfamiliar. It had no postage, and inside was a really expensive jeweled bracelet, so Geneva had Maude call the police. Then Wallis called me, saying she'd received a similar package."

Wallis opened her big, floppy purse and pulled out a small white box with its lid open. She set it next to the muffins in the center of the table, and we all stood to examine its sparkly contents. A set of enormous emerald teardrop earrings ringed with diamonds winked out at us.

"Ooh," Emily cooed, reaching for the box, her eyes nearly as sparkly as the emeralds.

Naoma firmly pressed Emily's hand to the table.

"Right, sorry," Emily said.

"They both arrived in today's mail," I continued. "I think we need to ask around to see if anyone else got an unexpected present in the mail today. Something weird is going on, and with Mort dead, I don't want to take any chances."

"You think the jewelry could be poisoned?" Wallis asked, staring at the glittering earrings.

"Did you touch them?" Jordan asked.

Wallis whimpered and balled up her right hand as if protecting her fingers.

"Congratulations. You get to get fingerprinted so they can eliminate you as a suspect," Lori told Wallis.

Wallis's eyes lit up. Deputy Vic was her boyfriend, after all. I tried really hard not to envision them playing around with arrest fantasies.

"We can ask all we like," Naoma said, "but what's to stop people from lying and saying they haven't received any incredibly valuable trinkets?"

Jordan snorted. "I wonder if that's the point—to scatter this jewelry far and wide, with no easy way to track it down."

My phone rang, and I stepped into the kitchen's back-door nook to answer Lake's call. "Hey, you."

Lake's voice was low and serious. "Pippa, something awful has happened."

"What's wrong? Has someone else been killed?"

"What? No, nothing like that. I'm at Seven Vistas. Someone broke into my parents' suite and stole every piece of jewelry my mother brought with her. It's all gone!"

My heart sank, but my mind rang like a bell. "Have you reported it to Mallory?"

"Of course we have. It's just so... Who would do a thing like this?"

"I don't know, sweetie. But I'll help you in any way I can."

"Thanks, Pippa. I need to go, but I'd appreciate your support on this one. My mother was robbed in our town. We can't let that stand. We're in room twelve-twenty-nine."

"You're absolutely right. I'll come over as soon as I can." We hung up, and I returned to my chair.

"Well," I began, "I think that telling folks that it's a felony to be caught in possession of stolen property should get them to open up about receiving mysterious packages in the mail."

A shocked silence ringed the room.

"Spill the deets, girl," Jordan demanded.

"The jewels are Auda Ivens's. She's been robbed. They don't know who or why yet. But maybe our questions can help the police solve the theft."

"Seven Vistas has had a robbery? I need to get back there! Fallon's going to want my help." Jordan stood abruptly.

"I'll see you there after we're done," I called after her. She waved a hand in acknowledgement as she vanished through the doorway. Though I was worried about the robbery, I was grateful I would be facing Lake's family with Jordan by my side again.

"You sure she needs every single piece back? She has so many," Emily murmured, her eyes locked on the earrings.

"They were mailed to me, and I will fight you." Wallis flexed her fingers into cute little claws.

"Skinny little florist like you? You got no chance," Emily teased.

Wallis's smile was creepy and bright. "Florist who's more comfortable with the dead than the living."

Emily gave her muffin top a hefty slap with both hands, grinning confidently and looking like a cross between the Pillsbury Doughboy and an MMA fighter. "Bring it on. I've got more than enough calories on these hips to sit on you until you surrender."

"Ladies, please, let's focus on the crimes already committed instead of committing new ones, okay?" Naoma held her hands out to separate Wallis and Emily then leaned protectively over the earrings.

Grudgingly, the pair settled back in their chairs.

"So, how *did* Mort die, Lori?" I asked, ready for a distraction. "Was it poison after all?"

Lori polished off the last bite of her muffin and reached for another. "Yes, it was. Mort died of water hemlock poisoning."

"Water hemlock? Isn't that what killed Socrates?" Wallis put a hand on her chest.

"That was just plain hemlock," Lori said.

I gave her a mental high five for rocking the historical reference.

She added, "Water hemlock is a poisonous plant that grows in marshes and such around here and in lots of places. They call it cowbane, too, because cattle sometimes eat it and die." Her phone beeped, and she took a quick look at it. Her blank expression told me she was hiding her reaction to a bad-news text.

"Oh, cowbane!" Wallis exclaimed. "Was it in the quiche after all?"

I picked up on her reference to Marion Chesney's novel *Agatha Raisin and the Quiche of Death*. "It couldn't have been. I had about five of those mini quiches, and I was fine."

Lori said, "Mort didn't eat any quiche at all. In fact, his stomach contents were entirely green."

The memory of green foam at his lips resurfaced, and I set my gingerbread muffin down. "So the green foam wasn't the poison?"

"Just his last meal taking an encore after all those chest compressions." Lori's explanation was matter-of-fact, but it didn't make me feel any better.

"What did he eat, then?" Naoma asked.

"Looks like a smoothie packed with green ingredients. Doc Stevens found spinach, kale, avocado, apple, banana, jicama, pear, some flax and matcha powder, almond milk, and a whole lot of water hemlock."

Wallis hummed happily. "Is it creepy that I kind of want to try it? Minus the death leaves, of course."

Emily nudged my foot under the kitchen table. "Looks like Moore's quiches are off the hook."

My sigh of relief lasted until Naoma spoke.

"But maybe Tyleen and Sebastian aren't." Naoma's sharp investigative-reporter gaze mesmerized me. "Could Mort have drunk that smoothie before he even got to the party, Lori?"

I stared at Lori, heart in my throat, hoping she would give us a window of time that proved our friends couldn't have poisoned Mort.

The nurse spread her hands helplessly. "I'm so sorry, guys. Water hemlock does have a variable window of effect, but Mort drank so much of it that it killed him within half an hour of ingestion. He definitely drank that deadly smoothie at the Christmas party."

"Oh no. Poor Tyleen." I pressed a hand to my mouth.

"I'm afraid it gets worse," Lori continued. Her eyes offered a heartfelt apology. "Doc Stevens had to report these findings to Mallory. Doc just texted me a minute ago. Sebastian's fingerprints were found on a blender in the mansion kitchen. It still had smoothie residue inside. Mallory's headed out to arrest him now."

15

"Blood is just a good place to keep my scotch. Family is what you make it."
Raymond Moore, 1942

AS OUR MEETING BROKE up, I swiped the earrings Wallis had received and tucked them into my pocket. She gave me the stink eye but said nothing. I wasn't super excited about seeing Auda again, but maybe returning her valuables to her would give me a leg up.

I touched Naoma's arm. "Any word from your Portland friend yet?"

She shook her head. "Benji's in a play that performs on weekends, but he texted me back and said he'll search the database first thing Monday morning. Oh, wait, I guess I do have news. You'll never believe it. Remember how I said Cecelia Front moved to Portland and never came back to Seacrest? Well, the reason Benji's so eager to look into these old mysteries with us is because Cecelia Front was his great-grandmother."

I clamped my hand onto her arm. "Is that bad? What if he withholds something from us?"

"No, I'm not worried. Benji never knew her or his grandfather—her son. And besides, he 'prefers data to actual humans,' as he puts it. The man's as unbiased as any I've met. Trust me. Now, I've got to go. I'm going to spend some time on the bench with Tyleen."

Part of me wanted to bail on supporting Lake and his mom through a robbery in favor of supporting my neighbor through the arrest of her son for murder. But I knew Tyleen wouldn't be alone, and I wanted to see Lake.

We exited Emily's warm, cozy pastry shop into a bitterly cold wind laden with icy droplets. "I'd wait five minutes for the weather to change, but I'm only walking across the street," I muttered.

My friends chuckled supportively.

As Naoma and I parted ways on the sidewalk, I zipped up my heavy waterproof jacket and told her, "I'll be over to see Tyleen as soon as I can. She'll be so upset. I'm glad you're able to go now."

Naoma gave me a pragmatic smile. "She's a good friend. And this is a good story. I'll tell her you're coming later."

I pulled my hood up to block most of the stinging drizzle and strode across the street to the Seven Vistas lobby. Jordan's bright-pomegranate hair was nowhere to be seen, but I'd visited her at work tons of times during inclement weather and knew where she hung her coat. I left mine next to hers in a back alcove behind the front desk, waved to Marcy, the concierge on duty, then jumped into the first available elevator. I smoothed my clothes and checked my hair in the mirrored elevator wall. *Time to look like I've got my act together.* I would have no trouble figuring out which suite belonged to the Ivenses if they were bleating about a robbery.

Sure enough, I heard voices down the hallway as I stepped out of the elevator. The hallway was broad and opulently decorated with re-claimed wood panels painted in subtle blues, and the door on the far right was open. Fallon, Jordan, Lake, and Auda stood talking in the doorway. Though Lake looked comfy in jeans and a long-sleeved ma-roon shirt, everyone else looked like they'd walked off the set of *Suits.* Fallon even wore a pocket watch on a chain clipped to the vest of his three-piece suit. *Maybe he came from* Tombstone *instead of* Suits, *then.*

I trotted up and clasped Lake's hand, and he flashed me a grateful look.

I dug out the emerald earrings and offered them to Auda with a perky smile. "Mrs. Ivens, I believe these are yours."

Lake studied them in surprise. "Where did you get—"

Auda raked the earrings from my hand, leaving pink scrapes on my palm, and grabbed a fistful of my coat collar. "You filthy thief! How dare you saunter back in here like the cat that got the cream? Did you think you could throw me off with this paltry—"

"Mom!" Lake yanked his mother's hand off me, and I stumbled back in shock.

Fallon looked on, clearly embarrassed, but Jordan stepped between Lake's mom and me. Her eyes tightened like they did whenever she wanted to smack the antagonist in one of our favorite rom-com movies.

"I'm okay," I said, mostly to calm her down, though I rubbed surreptitiously at my sore neck. Indignant adrenaline shot into my veins as I addressed the other three. "I just came from meeting some friends, and one of them received the earrings in the mail today. I knew they were your mom's, Lake, after you called, so I figured I'd bring them right over." Finally, I spared Auda a glance. "Silly me, expecting her to show gratitude for her returned property."

"Someone mailed a friend of yours my earrings? Preposterous." Auda's voice was arctic. "Where's the rest, then?"

"Yes, Winterbourne, I'm interested in your answer too."

Mallory came to the door from inside the suite, leaving Devereaux standing alone in the middle of a lavishly appointed foyer of seafoam green with sunset accents. Lake's dad seemed annoyed that he had to set eyes on me again, but Mallory wore her usual ice-queen expression—with just a hint of a smile around her eyes. *Is she still my ally?*

I glanced at Lake, half expecting him to jump in and help me and half knowing that he wouldn't. "I paid a visit to Geneva this morning," I told her, shamelessly name-dropping for Auda's benefit.

"While I was there, she received a package containing jewelry that didn't belong to her. Neither she nor her secretary recognized the handwriting on the package. Then I met up with my friends, one of whom had also received a package with jewelry. And both packages had no postage, so they were 'returned' to addresses that hadn't actually mailed them. It seems the jewelry thief has gone postal."

A split second of silence greeted my last statement before Jordan let out a suppressed groan. "That was physically painful. How dare you make me hear that terrible pun with my own ears."

I flashed her a *sorry-not-sorry* expression before returning my attention to Mallory.

"I've already spoken to Geneva—in fact, I just came from Laine Manor—but I'll need to verify with your friend."

"If you don't catch Wallis at Callendine Floral, she'll probably be consoling Tyleen." I kept my tone mild—it wasn't Mallory's fault she had to follow the evidence and have Vic arrest Sebastian. But I was absolutely going to keep reminding her that I was working to prove him innocent.

"Very well. I think I have all I need here."

"Thanks, Mal," Lake said. "I appreciate your helping my family more than you know."

My boyfriend's voice was warmer than I thought was absolutely necessary, but Mallory didn't seem to hear it. She nodded a crisp farewell and strode toward the elevators.

"I'm terribly sorry for this inconvenience," Fallon Vanderveer said to Auda. "We'll work with the police—and apparently the post office—to track down all your jewelry and return it to you as soon as possible. Jordan, I'm putting you in charge of that coordination."

"Very good, Mr. Vanderveer. I'll contact the Seacrest postmaster immediately." Jordan whipped out her phone and scrolled through her contacts.

"And of course," Fallon continued, "we'll be reviewing our security and making all our video available to the authorities in order to further the capture of this despicable thief."

Auda glared at me.

Fallon rested a comforting hand on her forearm. "You have my word. We'll do everything we can to get you through this and return your belongings to you. And it goes without saying that your suite and all charges made during your stay will be comped, as the first step in our heartfelt apology."

"Yes, thank you." Auda's reply was dismissive, and she reentered her suite. "Lake, come in, darling. That'll be all, Fallon."

Fallon's shoulders slumped a little, and he touched Jordan on the elbow to draw her back toward the elevators. As she followed her boss, she paused to squeeze my free hand. "Meet me for coffee when you're done up here. I'll be at my desk."

I squeezed back, grateful for her support.

An unreadable Lake let me enter the suite first and closed the door tightly behind us. I'd never been in one of Seven Vistas's fanciest suites before, so I took a moment to drink it all in. Past the foyer, a large main room opened toward the corner of the hotel building, littered with elegant burgundy wingback chairs and draped with long sunset-hued swag curtains. Misty daylight lit the room with a cool glow. A grand piano sat against the far wall. As we walked into the large parlor, I spotted a wet bar occupying one corner. Plush cream carpet made me feel like I was walking on a cloud. To the right, a broad space that appeared more like an anteroom than a hallway presumably led to individual guest rooms. A wide glass-walled room reminiscent of a screened-in porch lined the left side of the parlor, allowing the Ivenses to stand at the edge of the hotel and gaze across the Pacific from twelve stories up, perfectly protected from the elements.

Auda picked a wineglass off the piano and sat with an undignified flop on the padded piano bench. Then she saw me as if for the first time, and her spine straightened as if reluctant to resume its formal parade march, and she offered me a sour smile before sipping her white wine. "Pippa, dear, how desperately loyal you are to my son. Do join me on the balcony." She gestured with her glass toward the glass-walled viewing room.

Just before she entered the enclosed balcony, Auda picked up a fluffy angora shawl and draped it over a shoulder with her free hand. I followed her toward the chilly glass room, suddenly regretting abandoning my coat downstairs. So I detoured just a little and swiped a decorative wool table runner from underneath a miniature driftwood spar carved into a Spanish galleon. *Ooh, Fallon got Gabe to carve that ship in commemoration of last summer's crazy treasure hunt!*

I wrapped the table runner around my shoulders and stepped through the double-paned glass door after Auda. She tightened her eyes disapprovingly at my decision not to freeze like an undeserving peasant in her presence, but she didn't mention it. She stepped right up to the glass wall at the edge of the hotel, offering me her stiff spine as part of my view. Like her husband at the party, she'd invited me over then made me wait for her to speak.

Ugh, this controlling stuff is getting old. I ambled toward the far end of the room, turning my back on Auda, and gazed down and to the north, where the Silver River's mouth foamed and fought with the Pacific Ocean in an endless estuarine battle for dominance. Right then, the ocean was winning. *Funny how it looks like a battle between salt water and fresh water, but it's actually a battle between moon and Earth. Ha! I understand the gravity of the situation. Boy, do I.* I took a deep breath and straightened my shoulders.

"Life is harder for women than it is for men." Auda's tone was firm and high, and the words sounded rehearsed.

I let her soft lob drop into the silence between us. She would get to her point faster if I didn't interrupt.

"We have harder choices," she continued, "and the allies we surround ourselves with are vital to our successes, both large and small."

I couldn't disagree, but my smirk, reflected in the rain-spattered glass, was cynical. She was about to spin that solid statement so fast that it could probably power Seacrest until spring.

"But on the other hand," Auda inevitably continued, "allies need to be careful where they lend their energies. Surely, you have endlessly needy people here in your little town, people who always ask and never give, people who never greet you without holding out their hand. People with much to offer need to protect themselves from giving too much to just one person. It minimizes their usefulness. Surely, you can see that."

I was committed to my silence. I gritted my teeth and didn't reply, even though my skin fairly itched with eagerness.

Auda wasn't used to being ignored. In the chilly glass, her reflection turned toward me, her chin high and her lips pursed. "Let me be plain, Pippa."

Yes, please do. Because I totally couldn't tell what you were implying before now.

"I have a lot to offer. To my friends, to my country, to commercially minded people everywhere. But no one acts alone. I chose my closest ally very carefully. I made my bed in Devereaux's bedroom, and I've lain in it without regret ever since. No matter what. Because we are an even match. And we all need to choose an evenly matched bed to lie in, don't we?"

I was almost surprised that the glass walls didn't explode from trying to contain so much smug condescension.

I took a deep breath to get my indignation under control and finally turned to face her, my hostess smile riveted in place. "I didn't climb into Lake's bed. He climbed into mine. Repeatedly. Now, if you'll excuse me, I'm late for a meeting downstairs." I swanned out of the balcony with my heartbeat pounding in my ears, clutching the wool table runner angrily.

Lake stepped toward me with concern on his face, but I wasn't about to let anyone know Auda had gotten to me. I folded the runner neatly and draped it over the back of a chair. Then I smoothed my expression into an easy smile and kissed Lake on the cheek. "Gotta go, hon. Big meeting. See you later." I left before he could reply.

I was still steaming like a latte five minutes later, when I slipped into a chair across from Jordan at Coffee Breezes. The hotel coffee shop had giant windows facing the sea, reminding me of the balcony where I'd just been insulted, so I picked a chair facing the hotel hallway instead.

Jordan slid me a peppermint mochaccino. "Ooh, that bad, huh? Did you win or lose?"

I took a sip of the holiday coffee and let its sharp heat warm my throat. "Well, she didn't make me cry, and I didn't hurl her through the balcony window to her watery doom, so more of a draw."

"She has no idea how lucky she is," Jordan said. "You could kill her six ways from Sunday, and no one would be the wiser."

I let out a dark little chuckle. "I could. But she does know how lucky she is. She just assumes she deserves it. And that I don't deserve Lake."

Jordan squeezed my hand tightly. "Well, she's dead wrong and a total idiot to boot if she can't see how Lake's life is better with you in it. He's always happy around you. And I don't know if you've noticed, but he hasn't been super cheerful since his family arrived, so who's actually good for Lake, after all? Hint: it's you."

I hadn't realized how much I needed to hear that until she said it. I squeezed her hand back. "You're the best friend ever. Maybe it's you I don't deserve."

Jordan went quiet, and she studied the whipped cream atop her coffee.

"What is it?" I asked. "Did I say something lame? Was my grammar confusing? Are you dying of some weird rare disease? Are you Batman, the hero I actually *do* deserve?"

Jordan's solemn expression cracked into a breathy laugh. "Is it gonna be super cheesy if I jump on the Christmas-season-emotional-sharing bandwagon and tell you something mushy I've never said before?"

"Absolutely not," I replied stoutly. "All those Christmas movies can't be wrong."

Jordan let out a sigh that seemed part relief, part sadness. "I guess I thought Lake's family must be perfect just because they're rich, but now that I've met them, they... They don't seem to be what I think of as 'family,' although I don't always think of my own family as 'family' either.

"I hated being an only child. All my friends at school had brothers and sisters. I wrote Santa every year from the time I could spell, asking for a baby sister. And when I realized he wasn't real, I asked my parents. My mom had a really difficult pregnancy with me, though, so she shot that down.

"My whole life, I've been looking for a bigger family than the one I was born into. Somewhere that feels perfect. I had so many friends in high school, but none of them really felt like family. I try to be centered and professional here at work, but when I go home at night, it's just me. Some nights, I sit in the dark, and I kind of get crushed by these waves of loneliness." She finally looked up from her coffee. "And I don't call you and tell you about it, because I don't want to bring you down. I don't want to interrupt your busy life."

I stood and hugged her as she sat in her chair. "How dare you assume you're interrupting, you noodle. You absolutely call me the next time you're feeling alone."

Jordan sighed into my shoulder. "I mean, we see each other most days, anyway, so I didn't want to bother you even more."

I met her eyes. "You've never bothered me one time in the seven years I've known you. I bet it's physically impossible."

A tentative smile played around her lips. "Is this how you are with Trudie?"

"Where I'm the bossy one, and you have to try to prove me wrong? Basically."

"All right, cool. Can I change my last name to Winterbourne?" she teased.

I squinted one eye. "Legally, yes. Practically, I wouldn't recommend it. My family is a bag of cats."

"Are we talking Gucci handbags or forty-year-old gym bags with small-town high school sports logos that get donated to Goodwill?"

"Oh, ye of little faith. We're absolutely a forty-year-old gym bag tucked inside a Gucci handbag."

"You, Trudie, and Hilt would have plenty of room in a Gucci handbag, though."

"Actually, I mean my whole family. Stepdad, stepsiblings, and all that baggage."

"The 'Albany Winterbournes' are actually from the suburb of Bag-of-Catsville?" Jordan asked.

"Ha, we *so* are. They have a small-town high school there *and* a Gucci outlet."

Jordan's teasing expression turned wistful. "You think you're poking fun, but you honestly make your family sound so interesting."

"The curse of the Winterbournes. We're always interesting." I held out my arms helplessly.

"And that's why Fallon Vanderveer keeps hanging around you and Trudie," Jordan reminded me. "One of these days, he's going to make a move on at least one of you, and I really hope for Gabe's and Lake's sakes that you're ready for it."

"I can handle Fallon Vanderveer," I proclaimed. Then, worried I was jinxing myself, I glanced past Jordan to the hotel hallway, just in case the hotelier was passing by. Thankful that he wasn't, I focused on Jordan again. "Next time I head back to Bag-of-Catsville, you're invited. If you dare."

Jordan sipped her coffee then said, "Oh, honey, I dare."

I had no plans to return to the house I'd grown up in any time soon, but I admired Jordan's devil-may-care courage in pursuit of her dreams. "I can't believe Sebastian's been arrested. No offense, but he's the last person in this town I'd suspect of murder."

"Oh, none taken. Like most perfectly normal people, I have a short list of things I'd literally kill for, including a great hair day, the perfect coffee order, and to avenge my BFF's hurt feelings."

"You're the best friend ever."

"And you have shovels in your shed and a mental map of all the best places to bury bodies. You had to drive Al Daulton around for two days to identify them last year. Mallory got so irritated with you guys!"

I laughed in recollection of the guest most dedicated to "authentic" research I'd ever had. "Good times." I gestured to the broad windows behind me, where low clouds scudded across the gray sea. "So, are you ready for the storm?"

Jordan nodded. "Fallon had the seals along the lobby's glass wall redone in September. If Mother Nature wants to come in, she'll have to use the door like everyone else."

"As she should. I hate to drink and run, but I need to pick up something for Tyleen. I hope it'll cheer her up," I said.

Jordan and I air-kissed like wealthy divas, and I walked her back to the concierge desk, where Marcy was low-key waiting for her return. "Got a minute to show me what I did wrong here, Jordan?" she asked.

"Don't I always?"

I left the concierges to discuss the issue of a misapplied charge from Andy's shop, Charon's Dead Letter Service, as I retrieved my coat from down the hallway behind the desk. I waved to Jordan as I headed out, but she and Marcy had their heads bent over a computer screen.

"Oh, that's the Ivenses' room," my friend muttered. "Because of course it is. Just apply the charge to the account. They won't quibble over it."

Wanna bet? I left Jordan to her work and stepped out into the frigid Oregon air.

I grumbled about the four blocks I had to walk to reach my destination and debated whether it would be worth it to head back to Moorehaven for my bicycle. But I reluctantly decided that walking would keep me warmer, and I wouldn't stay any drier by riding in the drizzle. I shoved my hands deep into my raincoat's warm pockets and hustled up the block.

16

"A grifting dame will steal your wallet—and your heart, if you're not paying attention—but God help you if you anger a mother."

Raymond Moore, 1928

TEN MINUTES LATER, I stepped under the hard awning in front of Charon's Dead Letter Service, Seacrest's all-around stationery store and mailing center, and shook myself off like a puppy before stepping inside. An antique bell jingled over my head as I pushed the old glass-fronted door open.

"Ah, Pippa," Andy called from behind the counter. Far from resembling an Egyptian ferryman for the dead, the slightly built, russet-haired man looked like a cross between Sebastian and Sheriff Kettleman and had more than a passing resemblance to Tim Robbins. Naturally, half the town called him Dufresne after Robbins's character, Andy Dufresne, in *The Shawshank Redemption*. I wasn't one of them, though.

"Morning again, Andy. Is my order ready?"

"You betcha. Follow me to the printing counter," Andy said, taking an exaggerated step to his left. "Ah, here we are." He reached under the counter and lifted a pale-blue mug. "Look okay?"

I examined the mug and the picture I'd asked Andy to print on it, the shot I'd taken of Tyleen and Sebastian wearing their catering uniforms in the kitchen at the fateful Christmas party. They'd been so thrilled to be asked to cater the event. My smile slipped. Sebastian was getting arrested for poisoning Mort to death.

Andy fixed me with a compassionate look. "Naoma stopped in to mail photos from her latest fog series to the editor who makes those nice nature calendars. She told me the news about Sebastian. You ask me, I think Tyleen needs that mug—happier times and some hope to get back to them."

I clasped the mug to my chest and gave him a grateful smile. "Look at you, all full of homey wisdom today."

He waved off my compliment with a deprecating grin. "I'm just trying to get you to buy the mug you already ordered is all."

"Sure, that's all it was." I paid for the mug and let Andy wrap it in a pretty blue box for me.

"That's the last blue one I have, and I'm happy it's going to Tyleen. Note to self—reorder boxes." As he handed it over, he added, "You figure out who really poisoned Mort, okay? We all know Sebastian could never do that. He's the gentlest soul I've ever met."

I straightened as if reporting for duty. "I'm doing everything I can. He's my neighbor and my friend, and I'm not going to sit by and let the real killer get away with murder. Not in my town."

"You're a treasure, Pippa. You take care, now."

Tyleen had said she was going to sit outside the police station, but with Sebastian's arrest and the rain, I knew she'd have gone inside, demanding to see him. Maybe she was still there. I texted her as I stood under the shop's awning, avoiding the rain: *I have something for you. Still at the police station?*

No. I'm home, looking for a cake pan big enough to bake a file into.

Her reply made me chuckle, but there was never any way to tell whether Tyleen was serious about her crazy ideas. *Mallory will probably check for that.*

She won't if she's been poisoned too.

I rolled my eyes. *Tyleen, you know texts count as evidence.*

They do?

Yes. I'm coming over with a present for you. I hope you like it.

New phone, who dis?

I gave up with an amused sigh and stuffed my phone into my pocket. Cradling the blue box under my coat, I hoofed it back toward Moorehaven. One street early, I hung a right and knocked on Tyleen's front door.

Cold, salty air swirled around me as I huddled in the porch nook. I leaned my head back next to Tyleen's soup-tureen porch light and breathed deeply, feeling cleansed. A strong gust buffeted my shoulder like a big, friendly dog saying hello, and my worries relaxed their grip. *Just me and the coast. This is where I belong.*

Tyleen's front door opened, and I offered up the blue box.

"It looks too small to hold a file," she said as she turned the box over. She nodded toward the warm, inviting interior, and I followed her in.

"Don't worry. We'll get Sebastian out, no matter what it takes."

Tyleen led me to her kitchen, which was decorated in reds and yellows, and set the gift box on the island. "It's not really a file, is it?" She clutched at the box as if it offered her one last hope, despite her disappointed pout.

I leaned against the island's sunny-yellow tile top. "It's more like a memory combined with a promise. Things will be better again, like they were before."

"You and your pretty words." Tyleen shook her head, but she was smiling. She opened the box and lifted the mug. A wide smile pushed away her sadness, and she gently brushed her thumb along her son's printed cheek. "Such a good boy. Thank you, Pippa. I'll treasure this. You're a good friend, and I know you're helping all you can."

"I am. Tell me absolutely everything you can remember about that night. Did Sebastian actually make Mort's smoothie for him?"

Tyleen clasped the mug in both hands and stared at it as if it would play a movie of her memories. "He did. But Mort delivered us a gallon Ziploc bag with all the greenery rinsed and cut. All Sebastian had to do was chop everything a bit and blend it with almond milk. You were there for that part."

I remembered the collection of green ingredients Sebastian had been working on. "Okay, that's good. Maybe the water hemlock got into his smoothie bag before it even got to the kitchen."

"Mallory would know about that. She's good with details. You should check with her," Tyleen said.

Strangely, the idea of asking Mallory how her murder investigation was going didn't immediately fill me with revulsion. "Was there any time when the smoothie ingredients bag was left unattended?"

"I'm afraid so. Mort brought the bag in early and asked that we wait until eight to make it. Sebastian put the bag in the fridge to keep everything chilled until then."

I let out a sigh. "I know Mallory's investigating all the catering assistants, but you hired them all yourself, right?"

"I did. They're all locals, great people."

I hesitated a moment before clarifying. "Locals who regularly read murder-mystery books and know a dozen ways to poison someone's food?"

"Er. Yes." Tyleen rallied and added, "But I don't know anyone among them who had trouble with Mort. And they'd never let Sebastian take the blame for something they did. They call me to make sure I'm okay, offer to help out, even bring me really good food. Not to toot my own horn, dear, but do you think you could cook well enough to impress me if you were struggling with guilt over murdering someone while my son took the rap for it?"

I blinked. "That's a fair point. Does Sebastian have any enemies? Maybe someone tried to frame—"

"No. Of course he doesn't." She looked affronted.

I smiled. "You know I have to ask."

I murmured a follow-up apology as she pretended to pick at the bottom of the mug.

"So... did any guests come into the kitchen before Mort received his smoothie?"

She set the mug down and nodded. "Oh, at least a couple dozen people. It was a madhouse back there. So many people wanting specialty orders, hotter food, colder food, another fork."

"Can you remember who they were?"

"I can remember their requests. If I work backward, I can get a list for you."

"Great! You'll probably need it for Mallory, too, so it's good to have it."

Tyleen grabbed a notepad decorated with strawberries and blueberries in the margins and began jotting notes. I made us each a cup of hot chai while I waited, trying to work quietly in the background of her kitchen so as not to interrupt her efforts to remember.

Ten minutes later, Tyleen ripped off the top sheet of paper and handed it to me triumphantly. "There. That's everyone who talked to me in the kitchen."

I took the paper and folded it carefully. "I'm on it, Tyleen. I'll get Glaze & Gossip to check out every one of these people." I tucked the page into my coat pocket and patted it. "You're welcome to help investigate, if it'll help distract you by giving you something to do."

Tyleen hovered on the edge of accepting then settled back onto her heels. "No, no. I shouldn't. Sebastian needs me to visit him and keep him apprised. And I won't have him eating that jail food. It's mostly vending machine chips! So unhealthy." She glanced around her kitchen. "And it seems I need to steal a cake pan to smuggle a file to him."

"Steal? *Tyleen!*"

She shrugged. "If I buy one, there will be a paper trail."

I waved away her concern. "No, just drive up the coast a ways and pay cash. That way, there's no information on your credit card statement. Wait, what am I saying? Do *not* bake a file into a cake for Sebastian. We're on this. Just be patient, please."

Tyleen stood tall and fixed me with a bright-blue stare. "I am not patient, Pippa. My only child, my only family in this world, is in jail for a murder he didn't commit. I'm sorry that I can't help you search for the real killer right now, but as I just said: *I am not patient.* What would happen if I talked to someone on the list in your pocket, and they were the real killer, the person who's sitting by and letting my son be accused, letting his reputation suffer? What would happen... to *them*?" Without glancing over, she grasped a bright-purple silicone serving spoon from a utensil holder and brandished it between us.

My eyes widened. I'd never felt intimidated by Tyleen's presence before. She was everyone's goofy aunt who cooked amazing food and saw too many fictional details in the real world from all the mystery novels she read. But at that moment, her maternal anger filled the kitchen and sucked out all the air. I felt like Bilbo in the presence of Smaug the dragon as he protected his gold hoard. Hilt had once said of Tyleen, "She's like a hen with one chick," and now I understood the other side of that doting coin.

I swallowed and straightened my shoulders. "You're right, Tyleen. The best use of your energy is helping to keep Sebastian's spirits up. You can tell him all the things we learn. And if Mallory overhears them while you're there, so much the better."

Her mood shifted, and suddenly, she was all sunshine and purpose again. "Yes! I'll make sure to talk loudly while I'm there."

I hid a smirk as I imagined Mallory's irritation. "You do that. I'm going to get this information to everyone right away. Don't worry, Tyleen. Glaze & Gossip is on the case!"

17

"Is Raquel based on my great-aunt Felicity? You came all the way from Portland to ask me that? Sir, can I interest you in some scotch?"

Raymond Moore, 1932

THE RAIN HAD STRENGTHENED to a pounding deluge by the time I slipped out Tyleen's back door. I hunched over and bolted for the gate to Moorehaven's backyard. The gate's black iron handle slipped in my grip, and I thumped my shoulder against the stained wood in futility, muttering curses against the rain gods and their penchant for vacationing along the Oregon Coast. My second attempt was successful, and I dashed to the sliding glass door on my back porch, sheltered from the worst of the weather. Chloe heard me thud against the glass, peeked curiously from the kitchen, then hurried to let me in.

I let her fuss over me a little, and I ended up with my feet propped on an ottoman in the small parlor and a cup of hot cocoa garnished with a candy cane. I took a sip and let the minty goodness spread through me. "You sure you don't need me right now?" I asked.

"It's all good," Chloe replied, seemingly unfazed by my leaving her with Geneva earlier.

I briefly filled Chloe in about all that had happened and considered asking whether anything interesting had occurred after I left the older woman's manor, but she beat me to the punch.

"Ruslan has been writing steadily for hours, and Hilt's poring over that old journal of Felicity's, looking for more clues. It's super quiet right now. You should enjoy this moment."

Her idea sounded good. "I think I'll do that. Thanks."

She nodded at me as if I were an obedient daughter who'd agreed with her wisdom, and I barely managed to keep a straight face. As soon as she'd left, I studied Tyleen's list of possible suspects. Then I texted it to the Glaze & Gossip ladies, asking for any information they could find that related any of them to Mort and possible motives for wanting him dead. Done with that, I fetched *The Diamond Charm* from the library, intending to read another chapter or two.

I read through the part in which Raquel fled from Hilton Gray, assuming he was another thug her father had sent after her. She wasn't wrong. But Gray, the clever protagonist, saw more than just a bunch of men sent to bring Raquel back to New York with all the jewels she'd stolen, and he began to doubt the story he'd been fed.

I read through Gray leading Raquel through the underbelly of Los Angeles in order to outrun the goons on her tail. The part in which she broke down in the rainy alley behind the Chinese restaurant and confessed everything to Gray always made me tear up. But the way the plot played out, devoted Moore readers endlessly debated whether her "confession" was just a show and if Gray was finally getting played by a dame smarter than he was—Moore's answer to the Woman Doyle had crafted for Sherlock Holmes and a fitting tribute to Felicity herself.

I read through the climactic part in which Raquel's father strode into the kitchen of a farmhouse surrounded by an orange grove outside Hollywood, told his daughter he'd personally shot her lover dead, and tossed Lucky's gold-nugget ring onto the butcher-block table as proof. Everyone with a soul hated Raquel's father after that scene.

Since I'd read so far, I couldn't stop just a couple of chapters shy of the end. I breathlessly read about Raquel kissing her lover's ring, sliding it onto her index finger, and threatening to blow the whole farmhouse up unless her father let her keep the jewels and let her disappear.

The first time I read *The Diamond Charm*, I'd thought Raquel was bluffing. But her impassioned speech about how she'd used her stolen funds to purchase a dozen properties along her escape route and paid men to follow her exact instructions—how she hated that she was turning into her father in order to save herself from him—was no less a joy on my twentieth rereading than it had been the first time.

In the end, Raquel got what she wanted, and she blew out of Hilton Gray's life much as she'd blown into it, in a glittering whirlwind of danger and charm. Gray, in typical hardboiled fashion, simply poured a scotch and downed it, counting himself lucky to be alive after encountering such a determined and dangerous woman. He never did find out whether or not she'd stolen the jewels, but he figured that either way, she'd earned them. He pragmatically decided that the highest tribute he could pay Raquel was to let her have her way, let her escape, especially since so few in her life had ever paid her that particular kindness.

Hours later, I jerked awake. I'd read the evening away then dozed off in my comfy green chair. With alarm, I bolted out into the hall, thinking I'd missed something. But all was quiet and calm, and Moorehaven was in night mode, with most of the lights off. I hurried to the kitchen, and my tummy rumbled. Svetlana sat up in her windowsill perch when she saw me. Her demanding meow told me she was also assuming that a treat would appear. "We'll see, Svetta. Give me a minute." That was not the right answer, however, and a more strident meow told me so in no uncertain terms.

A note from Chloe was taped to the fridge. *Hilt and I ate with Ruslan. There's a plate in the fridge if you want. I was going to wake you, but Ruslan didn't want to disturb your sleep. See you for breakfast!*

I sat in the kitchen nook and ate my cranberry steak and mashed potatoes cold, occasionally dropping a tidbit onto a napkin on the tabletop for Svetlana. We dined surrounded by the constant, gusty spatter of chilly rain against Moorehaven's solid, comforting walls. I had rarely felt so cozy.

"Honestly," I said to my cat through a mouthful of mashed potatoes, "you could read the book and think that Moore made it all up, or you could read it and assume he knew every one of Aunt Felicity's secrets. It works either way."

Svetlana twitched one ear and held it in a bent position as she stared at me.

"You disagree?"

Svetlana straightened her ear.

I took a big bite of steak, and she watched it intently all the way to my mouth. "Well, I mean..." I chewed, frowning. "But, Svetta, the lamp. Are you really trying to tell me..."

Svetlana solemnly blinked her mismatched eyes at me as if I were a slow kitten, only just discovering the obvious.

"Of course you'd say that. And maybe you're right. You're the smartest cat in the world." I stood and dropped a kiss between her ears. "Shh. Don't tell Rex I said that."

She purred and rubbed her head against my chin, a promise to keep my secret.

I tucked myself into bed, and my cats joined me, snuggling around my feet. I gave Rex extra pets and snuggles to make up for my earlier favoritism, and Svetlana turned her back on me and began bathing a back foot. I slept, dreaming of Raquel and exploding orange orchards.

My phone rang at six the next morning. I blearily glanced out the windows, which occupied three sides of my octagonal room. Sure enough, it was barely light out. I fumbled for my phone and answered it.

"Pippa, I have a theory." Naoma's voice was aggravatingly chipper for such an early hour. But maybe she had some good news.

"Is there word about any of the people who talked to Tyleen in the kitchen at the party?" I ground my palm into my left eye, trying to wake up enough to sound coherent.

"Nothing suspicious, but we're only halfway through the list. But that's not why I'm calling. I have a theory about Felicity."

AAAnd I'm awake. My spine stiffened, and I took a deep breath. "What is it?"

"Have you finished *The Diamond Charm*?"

"Just last night, in fact."

"Oh, perfect. Remember the reference Raquel makes to 'being stuck in a waiting room' and how it seems to be a metaphor for her waiting for her life to begin again?"

I scooted to the edge of the bed and stuffed my feet into my bunny slippers. "Yes. Waiting between two worlds seemed to be a big theme. She'd run away, but she couldn't have a new life until she really escaped."

"Exactly. Now, the ladies in my book club think it could mean many other things. The waiting room and all the storm references are kind of the same metaphor. There's that one storm that forces Raquel and Gray to take shelter in the lobby of a run-down hotel in LA. But Raquel tells Gray that she's running from a storm, too, meaning her past. When everyone started wondering if the storm was a storm of justice, because Raquel had actually committed the crimes she was accused of, I couldn't help but think about the"—Naoma lowered her voice to a whisper—"grifting."

Svetlana began licking my cheek. "Yeah, my cat tried convincing me of that last night."

Naoma took that in stride. "Oh? Which one?"

"The smart one."

"Good girl, Svetlana."

I chuckled. "It wouldn't be the first time Moore disguised actual truths in a novel of his."

"And we all know it, which makes this so much harder to pin down. Was Felicity running? Was she being chased by some kind of storm? What was she hiding? Herself? Something else? A secret?"

Naoma was on a roll, and there would be no stopping her investigative mind until she got to the truth. And I wasn't sure I should stop her. Perhaps Felicity's journal and Naoma's investigation into the grifting rumors had been leading us toward the same truth. "Naoma, come over for breakfast. There's something you need to see. Something we all need to see."

I got up, woke Hilt, texted Chloe, and laid out my plan. Hilt insisted on including Ruslan, since he'd helped us with the "brick" search in the library. Luckily for us, he was an early riser. He came downstairs in a faded denim shirt and old jeans, his halo of white hair brushed to orderly fluffiness.

"Private Penley reporting for duty, ma'am," he said by way of greeting.

Hilt escorted him to the dining room and popped back into the kitchen to help Chloe with breakfast.

Naoma knocked on my door at seven sharp, and I ushered her into the dining room. "Naoma Jassley, meet my guest, Ruslan Penley. Ruslan writes historical mysteries."

"How lovely to meet you," Naoma said. She shook Ruslan's big hand and took a seat opposite him.

I addressed them both. "We're serving pancakes this morning. I know it's on the simple side of our usual fare, but we'll have plenty of toppings to dress them up however you like."

"In a hurry to check out the next clue?" Ruslan asked with a good-natured smile.

Naoma's head whipped around. "He knows?"

Oof. Juggling secrets is hard work! "He knows some. Enough." I crossed to the kitchen and grabbed the syrup and sprinkle caddies. On my heels, Chloe brought out two platters of pancakes.

"Blueberry on the green platter and gingerbread on the red," she announced, setting them within easy reach. "The buttermilk-and-chai-spice pancakes will be out in a few minutes."

Soon, all of us were clustered around the table, stuffing our faces with fresh, hot pancakes. I couldn't choose just one kind, so I made a short stack with one of each flavor, with the gingerbread on the bottom and the chai spice on top. I drizzled maple syrup on them, dropped a handful of Hothouse raspberries on top, and added a couple of shakes of powdered sugar. I paused with my first bite stabbed on my fork and admired the pancake layers as a drop of syrup abandoned them for the plate below. *I love my job so hard right now.*

By the time we were eating seconds—or in Hilt's case, thirds—the conversation had shifted to Ruslan's reminiscing about his childhood in England during the Blitz. Everyone listened raptly, and Hilt and Naoma were particularly entranced.

"I've always loved Christmas," Ruslan mused. "My favorite memory of my childhood was a perfect Christmas Day in London, with everyone in my family gathered around. Dozens of people smiling, happy, singing and laughing. I like to imagine that C. S. Lewis was invited as well—one of my uncles knew him, you see—though he probably wasn't. My name is a version of 'Aslan.' It means 'lion' in Turkish. My whole family emigrated from Turkey to England before I was born. And I just wonder if my uncle didn't mention my name to Mr. Lewis one day, and it inspired him during the creation of his Narnia series." He winked at me. "I've no proof it *didn't* happen that way."

"Ruslan's the opposite side of my coin," Hilt said. "I'm named after one of Moore's characters, and Lewis's Aslan is named for Ruslan. I like it."

Naoma chuckled as she swirled her last bite of pancake through a puddle of cinnamon-marmalade syrup on her plate. "And rumor becomes truth."

"Two sources were good enough for Woodward and Bernstein, Naoma," Hilt said mulishly.

"But Richard Nixon wasn't one of them, was he?" she teased back.

"Ruslan comes over from Boston every Christmas," I said, steering the conversation back on track, "and we let him decorate Moorehaven as much as he likes. We'll never be as amazing as that one perfect London Christmas, but we can be a collection of pretty good Christmases. Now, let's clear this table and get downstairs. We have a mystery to solve!"

A flurry of activity cleared the table in less than two minutes, and soon we were staring through the laundry room's open door. Hilt balanced a ladder against his shoulder. "You ready?" he asked me.

"What are we doing with the laundry chute exactly?" Naoma asked.

Hilt filled her in, and she nodded.

I'd tried to lobby for Chloe to take the first look past the old wooden barrier that blocked off the laundry chute—I thought she would enjoy being more involved—but she'd insisted that the right belonged to me, since Moorehaven was mine.

I eyed the wide gap in the chute. "You're sure the panel is loose enough for me to squeeze by?"

"Loose? It's detached and leaning against the wall down here." Hilt pointed with his free hand. The whole panel had indeed been pulled out of the laundry chute. "Took it down earlier. Didn't look past it. Would've had to climb in, and my knees weren't feeling that spry."

"Whip to the rescue," I murmured, using Hilt's pet name for me when he was feeling his years.

"Go get 'em."

Naoma handed me a small flashlight, and Ruslan helped Hilt set up the ladder right underneath the open chute.

I took a deep breath to steady my nerves. "Here goes nothing."

I climbed the ladder and eased into the old chute on my hands and knees. The floor of the chute angled up just a little, and a metal lip marked the spot where the old wood had blocked it off. My light illuminated a few feet of chute then a wooden ceiling made of old planks.

As my body thrummed with anticipation, I crawled forward. My knees thudded on the chute. "Subtle, this ain't," I quipped. I eased my shoulders past the metal lip and played my light around on what lay beyond. "Oh... my... syrup-drenched *pancake stack*, this is *amazing*!"

"What?" everyone chorused behind me, loudly enough to echo in the chute.

I had to drink it all in before I could reply. A broad grin nearly split my face as I looked down on the secret room lurking quietly in my bed-and-breakfast. Only six or so feet square, the room held a small table with one chair, both dusty with age. A delicate teacup and saucer sat on the table. From my high vantage point, I could even see dark dregs in the bottom of the cup. Another table, tiny and round, rested in the far-right corner, bearing a small book and an old, thick pen next to a rough wooden box the size of a loaf of bread. A couple of old silk scarves had been hung on nails like poor-women's tapestries, adding softness and charm to the tiny space. One nail also sported an old bonnet. Its dark ribbons trailed down the wall like rain shadows.

I didn't immediately spot a door, but I did see a dumbwaiter shaft on the right wall. Several squares of pale glass high on the wall opposite me caught my eye, too—Moorehaven's south-facing outer wall. A row of dusty wooden rungs led down the right wall next to my chute. *Holy butternut squash soup. I know what this is!*

My heart hammering, I backed through the chute with an awkward banging of knees and elbows until I could climb down the ladder and into the laundry room. Several impatient faces awaited me.

"Well?" Naoma asked, pen poised over her notebook.

I wiped the back of my wrist across my forehead. "Felicity had a safe room."

That realization brought a dozen more questions to all our minds—most prominently, who Felicity intended the safe room for—but none of us had any answers. There was nothing for it but to go back in. Chloe followed me without asking permission, and Hilt stationed himself alongside the blank wall past the laundry room, in case we located a door.

I eased down the safe room's old wooden rungs with care, and none of them popped off the wall. Chloe hopped straight down from the chute's mouth, showing off her teenage agility. Jealous, I focused on videoing the room so that Hilt and the others could see what it looked like. After a slow pan around the room, I tucked my phone away and used the flashlight again. Chloe headed straight for the book as I examined the teacup.

As she began turning the little book's pages, she asked, "What's with the glass in the wall up there?"

"It's an old-fashioned way to let light in for underground rooms." I gave the old teacup a sniff, but it smelled only of dust. "If you've ever seen clear or purple glass squares set in a sidewalk, that's basically old-timey skylighting. The siding is blocking the light now, but before it was installed, this room was relatively well lit for having no windows. Well enough to read by," I added, spotting a different book under the chair. I dusted its cover off. "*A Study in Scarlet.* How about that? Felicity was into mysteries even before Moore started writing them."

"That's probably *why* he started writing them. This book looks like some kind of register. It's just pages of people's names. Check out this super-old pen too." She held up a fountain pen with a swirling red-and-black casing and gave it a gentle shake. "Probably all dried out."

I shifted the bright flashlight beam from the pen to examine the teacup's floral pattern. "I think the rest of this tea set is in storage in the attic. Hilt mentioned that he packed it away because it was missing one cup and saucer. To think it was sitting down here all this time. Wait, names? Anyone you recognize?"

"Not yet. It's all Adelia and Josephine and Abigail."

"Abigail? Abigail what?"

Chloe angled her light for better visibility. "Travers. Why? You know her?"

"I don't. But someone did." *Cecelia Front, busybody extraordinaire, certainly did. Was Seacrest's librarian hiding in Moorehaven's secret room?*

"She wrote a note by her name," Chloe added. "'Ruth 1:16.' You think it's significant that these are all women's names? Even that Bible book is named for a woman."

I made a note to look up that text. "Maybe there's a lot more to this story than we realize."

Chloe opened the lid on the plain wooden box. "It sure looks like there is."

I leaned over and stared down into the box. It was lined with lace handkerchiefs, lengths of loose lace, cheap pendants on string, a few impressive necklaces, and a rattling collection of rings both simple and ornate. My heart sank. *Chalk up one more point in the grifter column.*

"Does that dumbwaiter go anywhere?" Chloe asked.

"I'm sure it used to. Let's see. Where are we?" I studied the ceiling, imagining the floor above. "I think we're under my office. It used to be the pantry before Moore remodeled it."

I looked at the dumbwaiter for a second, but then Hilt knocked on the wall, making us both jump.

"Any door handles in there?" he called. "There's no sign of an opening out here. From the aging of this wood, I think Moore put this wall right up against whatever door there might be."

I explored the wall with my fingers, hoping to feel an edge or a release panel, but after several minutes, I'd found nothing. "Either there isn't one, or I'm just bad at locating secret panels."

"Maybe Felicity meant for people to crawl back out the way they got in." Hilt's voice was muffled through the wall.

"Seems pretty dead-end-ish for a safe room," Chloe muttered. She climbed up the old wooden rungs and slithered into the laundry chute near the ceiling.

A shiver of foreboding licked down my spine at her words. I put a hand on a rung but then reached back for the register and the old wooden box, adding them to the copy of Doyle's Sherlock Holmes novel.

Once in the laundry room, I showed everyone the video I'd taken, to intense interest. Then Naoma lifted out the box's contents, one item at a time.

"What's all this?" Ruslan peered over her shoulder.

Naoma and I shared significant looks, and I gathered everyone in.

"I think it's time," I said to Hilt.

He nodded.

"Time for what?" Ruslan asked.

"Time to tell you all everything we know and time to figure out exactly what Felicity's journal has to do with this safe room and with all those dusty old rumors about her. Follow me."

18

"Sherlock Holmes's first case existed because no one treated Lucy Ferrier like a real person. That's the real crime."
Raymond Moore, 1979

HILT TOOK POSSESSION of Felicity's journal at one end of the library table, and I sat next to him with a Bible open to the book of Ruth, scanning the text: "Don't urge me to leave you or to turn back from you. Where you go, I will go, and where you stay, I will stay."

Chloe sat across from me, holding the register book reverently. Naoma was by me, holding the old wooden box, and Ruslan rested a hand on the old copy of *A Study in Scarlet* and took the seat by Chloe. I summed up everything I knew so far, from the damning newspapers Naoma had found in the wall of her rental duplex to Felicity's letter to Raymond Moore we'd found in the lamp to the hints she had given in her journal about the secret room's existence, if not its purpose.

"Is this where someone asks, 'What does it all mean?'" Chloe asked.

Hilt chuckled. "Apparently so. Seems Felicity left that secret note because she didn't want to tell Ray about the safe room in person." He flipped to the first page. "It's dated 1930, the year she died. Maybe she couldn't bring herself to tell him about it while she was alive, so she wrote it down when she knew she was dying."

"What did Miss Moore die of?" Ruslan asked.

Hilt sat back and stared toward the far wall. "If I recollect right, her death certificate listed an unspecified illness. Back then, doctors weren't always too sure what killed someone unless it had a knife stickin' out of the body's chest. I always figured it was something like cancer or heart failure. Can't remember which day she died, exactly, but I do remember her funeral was on the last day of the year."

Naoma frowned and fished a ring from inside the little treasure box. "Was she confessing, do you think? To stealing all this?"

Chloe studied the ring Naoma held. "Some of that stuff is valuable, but..."

Naoma lifted out a cheap tin bracelet.

Chloe continued, "Why would Felicity Moore need something like that? She was rich."

"Some people steal because they can," Ruslan said. "I had a cousin like that, back in London. He was seven years older than me. He liked how smoothly his hands could slip into pockets and lift things from store shelves. Made him feel powerful, in a way. I never told on him because he nicked sweets for me and bought my silence. Cheeky fellow. Died because of a mine."

"He was a miner?" Chloe asked.

"No, he tried to nick a sea mine that washed ashore long after the war was over. He was going to sell it to a collector, no doubt. But the thing was still active. Left a crater in the rock when he tried to tow it away with his stolen motorcycle. They named the crater after him, so there's that." Ruslan shrugged.

"Wow, that's some cousin. So, maybe Felicity grifted the ladies on this list because she felt compelled to." I was initially doubtful, since I'd been building another theory entirely. But then I remembered something. "Moore could be offering support for that theory too. Remember how Raquel stole things throughout *The Diamond Charm*? She started off by taking her father's diamonds, but she also stole things to spite people, like when she took that crooked preacher's carpet bag with all his supplies because he told that prostitute she was going to hell as he was coming out of the cathouse himself? He so deserved that," I added.

"That part always makes me laugh. The outrage on his face! Classic Moore." Hilt chuckled with a fond smile. "But don't forget, now—she finds his pocket watch in that bag, and she sells it and gives the money to an orphanage. Coulda kept that. Didn't."

"So is Aunt Felicity Robin Hood? Or is she just a common criminal?" Chloe asked.

I pointed at her while tapping my nose. "Moore left the question open too. If there's good to be found in Felicity's actions, I think we can do it here. We have her journal and what I suspect is a register of women who hid in the room."

"And I have pictures of the lost article about the scandal." Naoma held up her phone.

"Perfect. So I have a theory."

Everyone leaned forward.

Chloe was literally bouncing in her seat. "This is the best part!" she stage-whispered.

"What if the crooked preacher and the Mafia don in Moore's book are one and the same real person?" I began. "Not in their actions but in their attitudes. And what if the orphanage that Raquel takes the pocket watch money to is Moorehaven itself? And what if the little orphans she helps are these women in the register? What if," I added, leaning my elbows on the table, "Felicity was helping women run away, just like she had?"

"From whom?" Ruslan asked.

"What about the lace and jewels, then?" Chloe asked at nearly the same moment.

"Well, that would explain the string of Moorehaven's mysterious female visitors who were never seen in Seacrest," Naoma said.

"But the jewels," Chloe repeated.

Naoma shrugged. "Maybe they were actually gifts from Felicity. And the ladies refused to take them."

I pursed my lips. "Why was the registry in the safe room? Was it always there, or did someone put it there?"

"You think Felicity made all the ladies try out the escape chute?" Hilt asked.

"Then sign in at the bottom? Seems extreme," Naoma said.

"Maybe she left it down there to hide it," I guessed. "Or to be discovered one day, long after she was gone. Chloe, read the last entry in the register."

Chloe flipped the old, thick pages and read, "'Chastity Hanneran, September 4, 1930. May God bless you, Miss Moore, for your kindness.'"

"She doesn't sound like she's being cheated of anything," Hilt muttered.

"A good grifter will get away with the con intact, though," Ruslan said. "If they're found out, the whole thing falls apart. I had a nephew who ran investment cons—that same cousin's son, actually. He kept getting outed every few months, and he had to relocate to a new city, rent a new 'office,' and start over. Felicity wouldn't risk starting over, would she?"

"Not if she was runnin' herself," Hilt acknowledged.

I tapped the text in front of me. "The verse from the register is quoting Ruth when she tells Naomi that she's going to give up her old life and stay with her for the rest of her days. What if one of them—one Abigail Travers—decided to stay on and help? For good or ill, she threw her lot in with Felicity's." My mind dredged up a faint detail, and I jumped tracks. "Wait, the last entry is in September? How far apart are the other entries?"

Chloe flipped through the pages. "September has two entries. August has four. July, just one, but three in June." She met my eyes.

"What does it all mean?" She chuckled and added, "Chloe asked unironically."

"I don't know, but it seems like Felicity's house guests stopped coming as regularly a month or so before she died. There must've been a reason. If she was healthy enough to travel out of town just before she died, it probably wasn't because she was feeling poorly."

"Oh! Oh, I see! I understand now!" Ruslan suddenly cried. His big hands gripped the slender copy of Arthur Conan Doyle's book. "Pippa, I think you were right about Felicity's secret. I've been holding this book for ten minutes, and it's just now occurring to me. Oh, I *am* getting old."

"What is it, Ruslan?" I asked.

He propped the book on the table for us to see, channeling LeVar Burton from *Reading Rainbow*. "*A Study in Scarlet* is, at its heart, a revenge story. Men force a woman into a life that kills her, and so her beloved avenges her death. Er, spoilers?"

"No, we've all read it," I assured him.

"So," he continued, "Felicity put this book in the safe room because her guests would identify with its theme. Women who run away from their lives have very good reasons for doing so. Miss Moore would have wanted them to know she understood their struggle."

"If the rumors about Felicity from *The Diamond Charm* are true, then she did understand." I gave Naoma a sober look. "But still... something must've happened in or after September of 1930 that made Felicity stop taking female guests. Did her secret get out, despite the hidden newspaper issues Naoma found? Did she just get too ill? Did the women stop trusting her? Did they realize she was stealing from them all along? We need to find these answers. Maybe they're in the journal, Uncle Hilt." My chest cramped with worry.

Hilt closed the journal. "The answer isn't in here." He rested his hand on its cover and wore a serious expression. "It's out there." He tilted his head to the left.

"But there's so much history that's been lost outside these walls," Naoma began. "How could we ever hope to track down something with enough definitive proof to be sure of what the records said? Even here in town, record keeping isn't what it should be, and I should know."

Naoma rambled on in distress, but Hilt kept his eyes on me. A small smile lurked at the corner of his mouth. He tilted his head to the left again.

What happened in 1930? What changed in 1930? My mind raced. "The highway!" I crowed. "You guys, Highway 101 reached Seacrest in 1930!" I pointed to Hilt's left, where he'd been trying to direct my attention. "When the highway came to town, women didn't need to stop and hide in Moorehaven anymore. They had a direct route out of the area."

Chloe pressed her hands onto the tabletop. "So she *was* helping them escape. If she'd been tricking them into staying, she wouldn't have stopped because of Highway 101."

"That's good thinking," Naoma said. "And, Hilt, correct me if I'm wrong on this, but wasn't Felicity one of the strongest proponents for creating a coastal highway in the first place?"

"That, she was."

"Her and Abigail Travers," Naoma added.

"Apparently," Hilt continued, "she pestered the highway commission with handwritten letters on a weekly basis. She wanted to be certain they knew of the writing successes of her grand-nephew, A. Raymond Moore, and how the world would beat a path to his door with or without the commission's help. And she absolutely offered them signed copies of his novels as bribes. The woman was a force to be reckoned with."

I pointed at the journal under Hilt's hand. "As we're still learning. Naoma, I bet you're going to want some independent confirmation of this highway theory."

"Please, oh please, yes, can I go a-hunting?" Naoma's dark eyes gleamed. "I should hear back from my Portland contact in the morning on Abigail too."

I glanced at Hilt, who nodded. My shoulders relaxed in relief. "Yes. Take the names from the register and see if you can find anyone out there who can corroborate our theory that Felicity was helping women, not grifting them. Especially any details that can confirm that this jewelry and lace and stuff was freely given."

"Maybe donated to the cause?" Chloe offered.

Naoma pointed a finger at her. "Yes, I like it. Let me get some pictures of all the names and dates in the book, Chloe." She pulled out her phone and began snapping images.

I let out a sigh. "This means paparazzi at Moorehaven. Again."

Hilt nodded in resigned agreement. "Par for the course, though. We'll be fine."

"Truitt Volavola will have a coronary, though," I added. "We should send him some pfeffernuesse."

Ruslan sat back in amazement. "I'm not sure I've ever seen this much excitement here before. Is it usually like this, and I'm just missing it?"

"It varies from week to week," I said.

"I admit I was not expecting to be so touched by the actions of a woman I never met." Ruslan leaned forward and gave me an earnest smile. "But she truly did create a haven, then she shared it with those who needed shelter. As a child of the London Blitz, I find myself deeply moved by her giving spirit."

Moorehaven. Moore's Haven. I ran my fingers along the edge of the old library table. "It really did live up to its name, didn't it?"

19

"No, popping the question *is* saying your vows. You've already chosen. No matter her answer, no matter your fate—once upon a time, you decided to love someone forever."
Raymond Moore, 1978

BY MIDMORNING, GLAZE & Gossip had investigated all the names on Tyleen's list, and everyone checked out. Lori had spoken to the kitchen staff member who'd received Mort's green smoothie ingredients—already washed and bagged. No one could remember seeing anyone suspicious in the kitchen.

"But are wealthy guests really 'suspicious'?" Wallis's tone implied that the question was rhetorical. "Speaking of suspicious, I wonder how long it would take Sebastian to succumb to frostbite in Mallory's cell if the power randomly went out on Christmas Day when no one was there to check on him."

"Tyleen would never let that happen, Wallis," I told her. "She has a file cake with that cell's name on it. Now, go spend some time with your boyfriend, and let Vic's warm, fuzzy heart melt your icy soul, okay?"

"You're such a romantic, Pippa," Wallis said mournfully. "I've always loved that about you."

Half an hour later, the front door burst open and let in a quarrel. I hurried out to the hallway, worried I was being beset by Lake's family again. But it was Chloe, and she was dragging her father by the arm, thoroughly ignoring his protests.

205

"Really, Chloe, this isn't—I mean, I don't think you should be... Perhaps now isn't the best time for—"

"Pippa. My dad has something to say. If he ever gets around to finishing a sentence, that is." Chloe finally stopped halfway down the hallway.

Behind her, Mercer turned and held still as if he could become invisible.

"Something to say about what?" I kept my eyes on Chloe, which gave Mercer a chance to compose himself—or to believe he'd actually gone invisible.

"The Hothouse and why he defended it so insistently against all the questions about it being... you know."

I looked expectantly at Mercer. The silence stretched.

Finally, Mercer broke. "All right, all right. I confess!"

I shot an alarmed look at Chloe, but she shook her head with a dismissive smile. "Wait for it. There's a lot. I finally got it out of him."

Her father's shoulders slumped. "I was at the courthouse one day, just routine work, when Tonya Benton came in, all white gingham and bows, with a bearded fellow in a really nice suit. They were eloping, and they needed a witness. So I volunteered."

"Tonya's husband is a long-haul trucker!" Chloe said gleefully. "She's stealing away from the Hothouse to see him when he drives past on his route. I think it's pretty romantic."

I frowned. "So Geneva Laine was wrong about the Hothouse selling anything other than fruits and vegetables?"

"Yep," Chloe said. "But tell her the rest, Dad. It's important."

Mercer shuffled his feet and looked like a shy schoolboy. "Mort and I got into an argument after a city council meeting one day because he was buying the Hothouse out from under the sisters. The sisters were sure it was a good business maneuver and didn't want to sue him, but I let him know that I'd be keeping an eye on him in future."

"Were you interested because of something you witnessed at Tonya's wedding?"

"No, this was before," Chloe said. She nudged her dad when he didn't immediately speak.

"Those, um, suggestive vegetables... the ones on the sign?" he began. "Variety painted them." His cheeks flushed slightly.

What? Chloe's mom? "For the Benton sisters?" I asked.

Chloe shook her head almost violently. "No. For *Mort.* The signs got people to stop and buy, but the sisters got hassled now and again, as you might imagine. Mort stepped in like a white knight and offered to buy them out so they could say the sign was all the owner's idea. Which was true. And it did take pressure off them. But it was all according to his plan. Mom didn't know she was painting part of a scheme to take over the sisters' business. Dad figured it out pretty quickly, though."

Understanding rose like the sun above a fog bank. "That's very sweet of you, Mercer."

Mercer's usual vapid-politician expression faded as a shy smile tugged at the corner of his mouth.

I laid a hand on his arm. "Thank you for coming forward and helping us clear the air. I can see why you were upset by his actions, but now that Mort is dead, I hope they can regain possession of their business again."

Mercer straightened his shoulders. "I'll make sure they get the best chance at it."

I turned to Chloe. "You know, you do have your own place this Christmas." I paused to give Chloe the opportunity to reach the same conclusion I had and decide for herself.

She squinted at me like an author trying to puzzle through a plot twist, then her expression cleared. "Oh, hey. Great idea. Hey, Dad. Why don't you bring all that cooking you always do over to my place? You and Mom can eat with me."

Her dad's politely baffled look was back in place. "I... What?"

"Christmas dinner. You can use the lighthouse kitchen and cook everything there. My roommate's gonna be out." She winked at me. "That way, you can teach me all your little tricks, and I'll even be interested in learning them this time. And you and Mom can stop fighting over who gets me on Christmas. Because I'll get *you* this year." She shot me a smile, her chin high. "I'll be the hostess, and you'll be my guests."

Mercer hemmed and hawed for a minute. "I-I'd like that, I think. Yes, that might be very nice."

Chloe's face lit up. "Thanks, Dad." She tucked her arm through his. "And to make sure you don't 'accidentally' forget, let's go right now and work on that menu." She herded him back toward the front door and shot me another wink over her shoulder. They stepped out into the watery light of morning, murmuring about their traditional chicken parm and homemade cranberry sauce recipes.

I sent Jordan a text to contact Tonya and verify any details she could from Mercer's story, and she said she would get right on it. The middle of my day was relatively quiet, but near sunset, I got a text from Jordan saying she'd confirmed with Tonya the story of her elopement and the sisters' belief that Mort had been doing them a favor by buying them out. Mercer had already been in touch with them, too, offering guidance on regaining control of the Hothouse. A weight rose from my shoulders, and I texted her my thanks.

We're getting closer to finding out whodunit, Jordan. I just know it. Maybe by Christmas, we can all safely chill and stuff ourselves.

I sure hope so. I think I'm gonna spend New Year's with my good friends Ben and Jerry, though.

I hesitated at her code for loneliness. *Am I invited?*

Girl, you're never not invited.

As the sun set, the fog moved in. The western-facing windows filled with a glorious, diffuse glow that shifted from pale gold to cool orange to greenish blue before settling on a thirsty gray that soaked up all the remaining light in the sky. Its shadowy, drifting mass was held at bay only by the warm light blazing from Moorehaven's windows. Tyleen brought over a Crock-Pot of clam chowder, and Ruslan, Hilt, Chloe, and I joined her for a hearty supper, safe and warm in a haven that shut out the cold and the dark.

"You really don't need to cook for us, Tyleen," Hilt said.

"I do, though. I need to keep busy. And not to toot my own horn, but I know my way around a kitchen. Since I'm trusting my friends to help Sebastian, I can at least make sure they're fueled up and ready to go. You want seconds?" Tyleen held up a full ladle.

"Yes, ma'am." Hilt eagerly lifted his bowl. At his feet, Rex seconded the sentiment with an insistent meow.

Halfway through the meal, I got a text from Lake. *I need to see you. Meet me on the beach across the street. It's important.*

"Something wrong?" Hilt studied my face.

I glanced up at him and around the table at my friends' interested expressions. "I need to pop out for a second. I should be back soon."

I grabbed my raincoat from the coat rack and zipped it all the way up before I stepped into the thick fog. I tucked my hair behind my ears and adjusted my hood as far forward as it would go. The damp air brushed my cheeks, and I filled my lungs with salty breaths as I crossed the street to the beach stairs. I rested a hand on the wet wooden banister. Those stairs had led to my first meeting with Lake last April. *Where would I be without that man?* I glanced back at Moorehaven's welcoming light, dimmed by a thick roil of fog. *In the same place I've always been yet so very far away from where I am now.*

I pattered down the wooden steps and across the sand. Its gentle gray-gold colors were muted to a concrete gray by darkness and damp, and with mist settling on it, the sand had become firm even above the high-tide line. The beach was short, shorn off after a hundred feet by the current that pushed into the little bay just south of

Moorehaven's cliff. But I couldn't see anyone else through the dense misty billows. "Lake?" The fog swallowed my voice almost immediately.

A figure finally resolved ahead of me, darker than the fog, striding toward me at an angle from the water's edge. But as it approached, I knew something was wrong. The person walking in my direction was several inches too short to be Lake. I halted in alarm and glanced around, worried I was being ambushed or something. My heartbeat pounded in my ears. *Gregor would have three weapons ready to use by now. Solomon would already have shot into the fog.* I clenched my phone inside my pocket, though I wasn't sure whether I would be better off calling for help or using it as a blunt weapon. But no one else stepped out of the gloom.

"Who are you?" I called in my most confident voice.

"It's me, Cam Cooper." Devereaux's personal assistant came into clear focus only a few feet from me and stopped, her hands casually resting in the pockets of a fitted lime-green windbreaker. A thick, dark braid rested across her shoulder. "I'm the one who texted you."

Though her voice was casual, her body language was practically shouting at me—she was on alert too. Even though I didn't really feel threatened by her, my instincts wouldn't let me lower my guard. "Then where's Lake? Maybe I should just call him and ask what's going on." I pulled out my phone.

Cam's hand halted my wrist. "Don't do that. He'll only get angry. Trust me."

"I don't trust you, though. You're being very mysterious. And while I'm pretty good with mysteries, I don't usually enjoy the process of figuring out what's really going on. So how about you just tell me the whole story?" *Like that ever works.*

Cam took her hand off my arm, and I put my phone away for the moment. She eased her head to one side and considered me with a thoughtful expression. "Dev sent me."

Holy Hannah's handbasket, it did *work!* "Why? And what does that have to do with stealing Lake's phone?"

"Dev sent me to 'encourage' you to break it off with his son. He doesn't consider you a worthy match. And I didn't steal Lake's phone. I cloned it."

Emotions rocketed through me, and my eyes grew wide with outrage. I grabbed the lapels of her lime-green jacket and yanked her close to me. She was an inch or so taller than me, but I glared up at her. "Where is Lake? Have you hurt him? You can tell Devereaux Ivens that he can go jump off a cliff! If he's not sure how to pick a *worthy* cliff, I have several I can recommend."

Cam stood stock-still in my grip but with the coiled tension of a martial artist. I suddenly worried I'd made a terrible mistake, but she said, "Lake is perfectly safe. He has no clue I'm talking to you. That's all I want to do. Talk."

My teeth hurt from clenching them so hard, but I pulled myself together and let go of her coat. *Farina wouldn't show fear, not when family's at stake.* "Usually, when someone confesses to a series of shady acts and claims they just want to talk, it's because they're about to dispose of the witness. Are you planning to dump my body in the ocean, Cam?"

To my surprise, Cam chuckled. "I knew I'd like you, whether I wanted to or not. And honestly, I wasn't sure I'd want to. Which is why I suggested that Dev send me instead of anyone else."

I scanned her face closely. Her cheekbones carried a strong Southeast Asian influence, though they were surrounded by European features, and her wide, confident eyes carried flecks of blue and hazel. "I'm not following."

"I needed to know." Her voice carried a hint of vulnerability.

The serious timbre of her voice struck a chord, and suddenly I wasn't sure we were talking about the same things at all. "What do you want to know? What do you want from me? Who are you?"

Cam stepped back and smoothed her crumpled lapels. A soft laugh escaped her lips. "That's the question, isn't it?" she murmured almost to herself. "Who is Cam Cooper? A girl from the streets of Bakersfield? A fixer with all the right connections? A woman with no past, no family, no culture? All I know is Cam Cooper is a woman in search of who she really is. Which is why I'm here in Seacrest."

I studied her face, and despite the dim shadows that wreathed her, I found no lie, though I did wonder why she was being so melodramatic. "You're not here because of the Ivenses' Christmas party, are you?"

Cam sighed through her nose, an apologetic breath. "A means to an end. I've been watching someone in town for a long time, but it's not you. You're also just a means to an end."

The woman standing in the fog with me fairly vibrated with tension but not the threatening kind. She didn't seem quite capable of speaking her true purpose, as if it were a secret she'd carried far too long to simply expose to a stranger. But she'd texted me and drawn me out there. *She may not want to share her secret, but I think she needs to.*

I rested a hand on her arm and held on tightly. "Tell me."

Her eyes locked onto mine. "It's Hilt. I'm following Hilt MacKellar. I found out where he lived early this year, but I couldn't just... I needed a plan, and my plan ended up bringing the Ivenses to Seacrest so that I could hitch a ride. I didn't know at first that you were Lake's girlfriend, but that made everything much easier." The words poured out of her like a torrent of snowmelt in the first warmth of spring. "And I thought, 'Christmas is a perfect excuse to get everyone to Seacrest, then I can finally learn the truth about Hilt MacKellar. Then I'll finally know.'"

"Know what?" My voice sounded faint. Cam's arm was an iron rod under my hand. Whatever she said next, I sensed it would change my life.

"What kind of man my grandfather really is."

The fog around me suddenly seemed to move too quickly. I felt transported to an alternate universe, where the damp sand didn't feel quite the same under my shaky legs, and the salt in the air somehow got sharper. "Say that again?" I whispered.

Cam reached into her pocket and offered me an old photograph. She clicked a tiny key light on her keychain and illuminated it for me. The black-and-white image showed a willowy Vietnamese woman leaning against a young Uncle Hilt in an army uniform. His face was unlined, his forehead broad, his hair a proud wave. And his smile was a mile wide—it looked exactly the same as the last time he'd smiled at me. I flipped the paper over. Faded ink read Hilton and Tuyen, 1970 in a hand that seemed unfamiliar with the English alphabet.

Cam said, "My grandmother and your great-uncle."

"While he was in Vietnam." I couldn't tear my eyes from Hilt's face. It was definitely him, so young and dashing. His arm drew the woman close against his side, and she was absolutely leaning in. They loved each other, and the picture proclaimed it in far fewer than a thousand words. "Oh my God. Did he know?"

"About my father? No. Grandma Tuyen didn't even know she was pregnant when Hilton was transferred. She managed to escape to America when Duc—my father—was four years old, in the last months of the war. She settled in Los Angeles, but she always looked for Hilton, everywhere she went. She never stopped searching for him." She tucked the photo away.

"You grew up in Bakersfield, then?" I asked, remembering her earlier comment.

"My father started spelling his name like John Wayne's nickname, Duke. He married a dancer. She was beautiful—Irish, Colombian, Thai—but she died when I was three. He was heartbroken, and I basically raised myself after that. The streets of Bakersfield weren't known for their kindness. But I picked up some skills. I got by. Grandma Tuyen would write and tell me stories about Vietnam, about Hilton. I didn't realize how much I clung to those, but..."

"You felt adrift, and they anchored you," I supplied.

"They did. And I wanted more. When I was sixteen, I spent a summer with my grandma, and I pestered her to tell me all her stories. Now, I realize that not every story she told me about her and Hilton was the truth. The one about saving a whole village by himself, using just a bamboo pole, seems a little iffy. Or his catching three fish at once in the river behind her house. But I don't know for sure. Which is why I'm here. I never connected with Vietnam, where all my cousins and aunts and uncles lived. And I never had siblings or cousins in America. My mother's family was scattered back east and across the globe." She shrugged. "I was pretty deeply alone, and I hated it. So I promised myself I'd find Hilton or die trying."

I winced. "Ooh, careful. That sort of promise has a tendency to get nasty around here. We already have one death from the Christmas party."

Cam blinked, pulled out of her story. "Right. Sorry. I didn't mean literally."

"Well, let's keep it that way." I took a deep breath and let it out into the foggy air. "So, when I saw you in your exterminator outfit, you were checking me out as a way to get to Hilt? Why didn't you just show up at Moorehaven?"

"I was. I didn't just show up because something about it felt off." She looked away. "I saw you in action at the party, too, trying to save Mort's life. That was brave."

"Someone had to help Mallory."

"And you decided to do it, even though you have a complex history with her. That says a lot too. I mean it, Pippa. I really do like you."

"Well, that's good," I began, about to try the feel of a brand-new concept on my tongue. "Because we're family. You're my second cousin."

With the way Cam's eyes flickered, she hadn't made that connection before.

"And I'd like to welcome you to the family. Is it okay if I give you a hug?" I held out my arms. "I haven't seen any of my cousins in years."

Cam's hands twitched, and her face stilled in a failed attempt to hide a sudden rush of emotion. "Me neither." Her voice was rough and tight, and she opened her arms to let me hug her. I squeezed her tightly, and after a moment, she returned the hug.

The fog moved around us. Gentle waves tickled the beach in the darkness. I had a new cousin. I had full cousins twenty years older than I was, who had only begrudgingly played with me when I was a child because my aunt bribed them with cold hard cash, and I had step-cousins embroiled in family politics, none of whom had spoken to anyone in my parents' immediate family for a decade. My head knew full well that finding a sudden family member on a beach was no guarantee of a close bond or even trust. But my heart had already decided I liked her.

We walked along the wet sand, surrounded by fog, lost in a world that didn't yet have to be real. "How do you want me to tell Hilt about you?" I asked. "Or has this gone so well that you just want to run up to the house?" I had no idea how he would react.

Cam picked up a few smooth, wet stones and stared at the waves splashing nearly to her shoes. She tossed one rock into the foamy dregs of a wave, and it disappeared with a plop. "I want to run up there. And I want to hide. And everything in between."

Cam's emotions were too intense for me to relate to, but I respected her quandary. I understood creative indecision—I'd seen it plenty in my authors. But this was real life. This was our lives. "Let me know the minute you need me. I'll help you with whatever I can. Or I'll get out of the way. Whatever you need."

Cam nodded, and the muted rhythms of the fogbound sea enveloped us. We walked in silence, neither ready to give up our new-found bond.

"Can you tell me about your grandmother?" I asked. "I've heard lots of Hilt's stories over and over. But he's never told me about her. And you know more of it than he does."

Cam threw another rock, farther this time. It sank into the top of a small, curling wave about twenty feet out, where I could barely make out any detail. "Sure. It'll be good practice, anyway." She took a breath, but she didn't speak for a few more steps. "Grandma Tuyen met Hilt in 1970, when he was stationed near her village toward the end of his tour. She worked on the army base. Food-waste disposal."

"Throwing away kitchen scraps?"

"Yeah. She managed to find plenty of leftovers and unused pieces to sneak home and feed her family. It was a good job, and she was glad for it. Then she met Hilt, and they fell in love pretty quickly. You can guess what his friends thought of her, but Tuyen's family was cautiously optimistic that having a GI looking out for her would extend a little protection to all of them. She got pregnant just before his tour was up. He went home without ever knowing about my father."

"That must've been hard on her family."

"It was, but they were far from alone in that situation. Duc was born, and Grandma Tuyen decided she wanted to go to America, after Hilt. She even gave my dad the last name of Makela."

"Like MacKellar. But your last name is Cooper now."

Cam gave a faint snort. "Two divorces later. I kept the last one because I like alliteration. But," she said, returning to her topic, "it took the end of the war and all the chaos it brought for Grandma to find passage to America for herself and Duc. He was four by then, and they landed in LA with no idea where Hilt lived."

"He never told her?"

Cam glanced over. "I bet he did. But she only knew he lived at the seaside, and the US is huge compared to Vietnam. She told me once that she used to think the US was like a mirror image of Vietnam, except maybe twice as big. Then she got here and finally understood how enormous it is. I think she had these romantic notions about heading out into the unknown and somehow managing to find her true love. But once she landed here, once she really understood what she was up against, especially with the language barrier, she kinda gave up. It was all too intimidating."

"I'm so sorry. So, your dad grew up in LA?"

"Yeah, he fit right in. Made his own way. Then he met my mom, a dancer who grew up in Texas and was visiting from Bakersfield, and he fell hard. He moved up there, and I was born a year later. They were so happy until my mom died." Cam went quiet and threw another stone.

"I'm glad you got to know how much they loved each other."

"I guess."

I let the silence stretch. Cam threw her last rock. It slipped below the waves without a sound.

"I was lost," she said. "Vietnam was a story my grandmother told me. And I had no story of my own. I started getting into trouble as a young teenager, and my father sent me to my grandmother to sort me out. She told me all the stories she knew—or at least, she told me what she wanted me to believe. Oh, she would swear like a sailor too! Or actually, like an army soldier."

Her tone gave me all the subtext I needed. "Wait, she learned to swear from Hilt?"

Cam laughed. "Oh yes. The potty-mouthiest grandma on the block. Why is that strange?"

"Oh, it's just that... Hilt doesn't swear at all now. Only Sunday slang since the day we met. And I know he's not doing it for my sake. Sorry, go on."

"Well, Grandma's stories helped me decide that I wanted to write my own story. The story of how I found my long-lost grandfather. It took years for me to realize that my quest began that summer. But she planted that seed in my heart, and it took root. Grandma died two years ago, and I didn't find Hilt until early this year. But after all that time, I couldn't just jump right in. I don't work that way."

"What do you mean?"

"I've learned that helping things along for others is the best way to get what I want too. Conflict is never profitable, unless you're an arms dealer, which I'm not. So I got a job for Devereaux, because he's a powerful man, and I knew his son was estranged. Then I hacked Lake's phone and sent him a text, supposedly from a beach-bum friend of his, suggesting Seacrest as a town he could easily get lost in."

Her casual confession caught me off guard. "What? You're saying you sent Lake here because Hilt lived here?"

Her nod was crisp even in the foggy air. "Yes. Then I'd arrange a family reunion—which I have—and I'd just happen to run into Hilt. If things went well during our initial conversation, I'd show him the picture and confess everything."

"So why didn't you do that?"

"Well, for one, I couldn't actually convince Devereaux to invite Hilt to the party. Then the murder threw my concentration off, and now, I can't help but feel like that little lost teenager again. I don't have a backup plan here."

A worm of suspicion squirmed in my mind. "Did you have anything to do with Lake and me falling in love?"

Cam laughed, a sudden bright flash in the gloom. "Of course not. I'm not that good."

Only partly reassured, I asked, "Does it help or hurt your cause that I'm dating him?"

She hesitated before replying, "I don't know yet, but it's certainly a fun complication. Don't worry. I don't have any plans to disrupt your relationship, no matter what Devereaux says. I only worked for him to get to Seacrest. And here I am."

Would she try to break us up if I weren't related to Hilt, though? I dared not ask. She was a canny woman, clear in her goals and decisive in her actions. I was glad she was family. But I didn't care to pit myself against her.

She sighed and gazed out at the fog. "I just wish I'd been able to find him before she died."

"I'd have loved to meet her. She's basically my great-aunt, after all."

Cam looked at me with surprise. "Oh, hey, I never even... You're right."

I clasped her hand and pulled her to a stop. "You're out of rocks. Have you decided what to do next?" I tipped my head toward Moorehaven.

Cam's gaze shifted to the fogbound cliff above us, and she took a deep breath. "Almost."

"If you think food will help—and it definitely will on Hilt's side of things—I make a mean brunch. Or a warm, inviting brunch. Whichever you want."

Cam blinked a few times before meeting my eyes. "A sit-down meal with family? It's been so long that I've forgotten what that's like. I mean, I can get a bánh mì and a pho and feel like I'm sitting back in my grandma's kitchen. But I haven't had a real family since I was a kid—all my dad does is work. And I wouldn't want to impose on your business."

I glanced toward Moorehaven, which was lost in the fog, with us and beyond us at the same time. "Family is my business. I'll make it work. Is tomorrow too soon?"

Cam's lips twitched as if she was going to speak. She pressed them together with a calculating expression then said, "With everything else happening around here, I think tomorrow is better than waiting."

I hopped with glee in the sand. "Ten thirty?"

"Deal. I'll make whatever excuses I need to get away from the Ivenses." Suddenly, she squeezed my fingers hard. "And I hate to sound cliché, but beware of Devereaux. He has no good intentions toward you and Lake. He wants everyone to think he has a warm, romantic soul deep beneath his hard exterior—well, he doesn't." Her eyes glinted in the pale gloom, and I got a feeling of foreboding deep in my tummy.

"Did he send you to cut my brake lines after the party?" I blurted.

"What? No!" The muscles around Cam's eyes twitched in alarm. "You're okay, though?"

"Lake and I are fine, but the car—Sadie—she's Hilt's, and she's pretty busted up."

A thoughtful smile came over Cam's face. "Well, then, I think I know just the guy to fix it up for you. And I'll look into those brakes myself. If it is Devereaux, I want to know sooner rather than later."

"So do I... cousin."

We returned to the boardwalk, chatting as if we'd known each other for years, and parted ways in the fog. A warm buoyancy carried me back into Moorehaven's sanctuary from the elements, but I could still feel a bond with my newest cousin and ally. *She's not alone, and neither am I. Maybe Lake and I can finally find some peace. I hope Cam and Hilt can too.*

20

"Anchors aren't meant to last forever. If they were, they'd be made of art."
Raymond Moore, 1936

AFTER I MADE CHLOE and Ruslan some breakfast, I did my best to plan a brunch menu for Hilt and Cam's first meeting. I changed the entrée four times before circling back to my first choice. With a sigh, I underlined *sausage and eggs*, Hilt's favorite, so that I wouldn't fifth-guess myself. *And some gingerbread muffins. Okay, let's do something else before I overthink this some more.*

My phone beeped with a text from Cam.

"Please don't be canceling," I muttered.

But her message wasn't about brunch—she had news about Sadie's brakes.

I called her immediately. "That was fast. How'd you do that?"

"I work for the Ivenses."

"Tell me everything."

"I don't have 'everything' yet. But I do know this: the valets stayed outside the mansion during the party Saturday night, and one of them, Duncan—who avoided talking to Mallory because he's had some minor charges here and there—said he thought he heard a dog barking. He worried someone had locked their pet in one of the cars, out in the cold. He checked all the cars with a flashlight and didn't find any dogs. But when he headed back to the foyer to get warm, he thought he saw a figure scurrying for the side entrance."

"Where does that lead?" *It could have been the murderer. Scurrying is never good.*

"Let me see. Utility rooms and kitchen."

"Did this Duncan have any idea who the person was?"

"He did. But he said it was more than his life was worth to tell me. And that means only one thing."

Cold shot up my spine, and I shivered. "An Ivens. Oh God, maybe Mallory was right."

"If I can learn more, I'll tell you, but this is where the rubber hits the road."

"Don't risk yourself for me, Cam. It's not worth it. The Ivenses could destroy you."

"Pippa, you're family. It *is* worth it. Besides, do you think I took this job without protecting myself first? I gotta go, but Odie's coming over to look at Sadie this morning, like I said. I think you can trust him, and he's really great with vintage cars, but that's no reason not to be careful."

I hung up and stared at my phone, trying to picture each of the Ivenses cutting Sadie's brakes. I could see each of them doing it, except possibly Uncle Odie. *I should tell Mallory, but let's see what plays out first.*

I couldn't dwell in a state of paranoid suspicion all day. I shook off my worries and set myself the task of repairing the hole Bliss's shoe had made in my bright-red couch cushion. Svetlana set herself the task of closely monitoring my progress, complete with interrupting me every two stitches for some petting.

Before I could tie off my thread, the doorbell rang. I glanced through a clear pane in the parlor's stained-glass window and saw Odie on my porch.

I pasted my professional smile in place and opened the door, hoping Cam hadn't overstepped and gotten herself renditioned to

Outer Sokovia for trying to help me. "Good morning, Odie. What can I do for you today?"

The man's dark pompadour bobbed, and his smile seemed genuine above the white patch in the center of his short beard. "Actually, I'm here about what I can do for you. Cam tells me your car had a little accident, and I know a thing or two about old cars."

Accident, my foot. But at least that's all he's here for. "We were a little banged up, but at least Lake and I will heal."

"Lake was there too?" The news was clearly a surprise to him, with the way his eyebrows shot up. "Dear me. She didn't mention."

I wasn't surprised, but Odie's demeanor made me think he was sorry for the chasm between Lake and the rest of his family. "It's nothing, really," I said, putting on a brave front. His surprise also made me suspicious—maybe whoever cut the lines wouldn't have done so if they knew Lake would be in the car.

"Well, I'm no doctor, but I am particularly fond of classic cars. If you'll allow it, might I see the patient? I have a friend who might be able to help fix her up."

"I'll have to ask the owner. Come wait in the parlor while I check on that, won't you?" My hostess smile got a little wicked around the edges as he accepted. I showed him toward the bright-red couch, and he stopped abruptly at the sight of my mid-patch-job curved needle and its scarlet thread. His stiff posture and drooping shoulders told me he remembered Bliss's faux pas as well as I did. "Be careful not to sit on the middle cushion there," I said. "It's got a bite to it today."

"Er. Yes." After giving a chair a side-eye check, he settled gingerly in it, and I went in search of Hilt.

We returned soon enough, since Hilt was eager to hear Odie's offer of repairs, and the men shook hands with the firm grip and solid eye contact of their generation.

Hilt and I led Odie to the garage. The weather was surprisingly mild, and my skin was half-convinced it was March. Inside, I flicked on the lights, and Odie immediately stepped to Sadie's side and pressed a gentle hand on her hood.

"Oh, you poor thing," he murmured. "I hate to see you like this."

"Aside from the damage you see, Sadie will also need new brake lines. We crashed because they were cut." I kept my tone crisp.

Hilt looked as though I'd grown three heads.

Oh, right... I never told him what caused the accident. I smiled and squeezed his shoulder.

Odie didn't seem to notice. "Golly, that's terrible." He sounded like Beaver Cleaver, chipper because his audience expected it. He squatted with some difficulty and examined the damage to Sadie's front end. But as Hilt lifted Sadie's hood so that they could take a look underneath, Odie surprised me. "Dev and I were flying back from Hong Kong about twenty years ago, and our plane's fuel gauge started beeping. Turned out a business rival had created a slow leak, trying to force us to ditch in the Pacific."

Surprised, I forgot to be suspicious for a second. "What happened?"

"Oh." He waved a hand casually. "The leak wasn't as slow as they'd intended. We pulled a one-eighty and glided back down to the airport. Landed right on the numbers too. It was pretty exciting for a few minutes, but the only damage was to the fuel line." Clearly comfortable with the outcome of his two-decades-old brush with death, he checked under her hood, wiggling hoses and poking at various parts. Finally, he nodded to Hilt in satisfaction. "I'd like to help, and I hope you'll accept it, if only as an apology."

My spine stiffened.

"After all," he continued, "you were on your way home from a party we threw for your boyfriend. Let me call my guy."

I am the daughter of a pawn shop owner but no one's pawn. I can hear the ring of truth behind any story, whether sappy or cheery. "You were itching to get your hands on Sadie in the early hours of the party Saturday night. When we headed home, though, you'd lost your eagerness. And just now, you said that you hate to see Sadie like *this*... as if you've seen her up close and undamaged. You sneaked out at the party, didn't you? You couldn't wait for permission to check her out."

Odie tried to look innocent, but his shoulders got twitchy when I kept staring at him. His face fell into a Beaver Cleaver mope. "I didn't break in or anything. I just wanted to see her. And I certainly didn't damage her in any way, let alone cut her brakes!"

The tilt of his eyebrows convinced me he was telling the truth—that, and he'd had a protective hand on Sadie's chassis for the past three minutes. "I believe you, Odie. But tell me, did you see anyone else out there? Or any... dogs?" I added, recalling the valet's comment.

Odie looked flustered, and his eyes darted to the side. "I can't imagine... That is, of course I saw no one suspicious."

I pursed my lips. *Wallis was right about certain people not seeming suspicious.*

He continued, "I would have reported it immediately if I had. Surely, you believe I have Sadie's best interests at heart."

"That, I believe," Hilt said. "Not sure 'bout anything else just yet." He seemed cranky.

I put my hand on his arm. Odie's intricate phrasing seemed to dance around a secret he didn't want to reveal yet. He might as well have been playing Tyleen's murder-mystery game. And I stood no chance of persuading a wealthy, influential man of spilling secrets he didn't want to reveal. "My uncle's not going to let this car travel out of state for repairs."

"She's probably right." Hilt's voice left some wiggle room, though.

Odie's casual smile brushed away my concerns. "No problem. My friend used to work for Jay Leno, but he retired a couple years back.

Lives less than two hours from here." He held up his phone, silently asking Hilt for permission to make the call.

I raised my eyebrows encouragingly at my uncle. *It would be a win for me if I could get one Ivens to repair another's damage.*

Hilt's shoulders relaxed as he gazed at Sadie. "Knock yourself out, then."

"Excellent!"

I added, "And thank you. I appreciate this. I wish it were this easy to get along with the other members of your family." *Oops. Mouth, I did not want you to give that last part away!*

But Odie only chuckled. "It's not the first time I've heard that sentiment. But they're all family, and we can't help who we love, can we? Or who we are." He dialed his mechanic, leaving me to stew over both sides of his statement.

I couldn't help loving Lake, and Odie couldn't help loving his brother. *What a tangle. Maybe it's not the sort of knot that can be untied.*

Odie hung up and beamed at Hilt and me. "Good news. Dale's up for the challenge. He'll be here in a couple of hours to pick Sadie up, and he says he can have her as good as new in a few days. I can loop you in on the repair progress if you give me your phone number."

Hilt immediately rattled off his digits. I was glad Odie hadn't asked me for my number. *Although if the Ivenses really wanted it, they would probably already have it.*

Odie departed jauntily, as if doing a good deed had lifted his spirits and put a spring in his step. Hoping with all my heart that Odie's definition of a good deed was the same as mine, I polished off my patching job and got to work on brunch. I'd taken a chance and invited Trudie over as well. Chloe knew something was up when I asked her to give us some space for an hour and see to any of Ruslan's needs, but she didn't pry. We both knew she'd get the truth out of me later.

I set the table with muffins, gingerbread loaf, scrambled eggs, and sausage. As I was debating whether to put the syrup caddies on the table just in case, I got a call from Naoma, who was out of breath with excitement.

"I found her, Pippa. I found Abigail Travers. Her real name was Jane Smith, and she lived in Seattle."

"Jane Smith? That was one of the names Felicity told Moore never to use for a character. The name right above Abigail's in the safe room register. They're the same person? Why would she have written herself into the register twice?"

"Yep. Looks like she wanted a whole new identity, and I don't blame her. She married into a troubled but insanely wealthy family. Her sister-in-law died under mysterious circumstances in 1909, and Jane went missing later that year—the same year 'Abigail' arrived in Seacrest. Rumors flew for years that they'd both been murdered by their twin husbands. But it looks like Jane made a clean getaway. If I had to guess, I'd say she found an ally in Felicity Moore and stayed to help others get to safety too."

"That's why she got a job at the library," I said. "She received copies of the local paper before everyone else. She could search for articles about runaways—it's possible they printed coded messages from other safe houses." I leaned back against the counter and smiled, envisioning Felicity and Jane teaming up to make the world a better place, right under everyone's noses.

"My Portland contact has a few names from the journal besides Jane's now. We'll move slowly, since this is a sensitive issue, but if I can track down living descendants who will allow me to publish their grandmothers' stories of escape through Moorehaven, this is gonna be the story that keeps on giving."

"It's a story that needs to be heard." *And it'll help, not hurt, business.*

Naoma agreed and hung up to resume her research.

While I figured out where I'd been in my breakfast routine, Tru let herself in the front door and strolled into the dining room. She gave me a squeeze. "Morning! Can I help with anything? A mystery brunch makes me want to prowl around and look for clues."

I hoped she would be as enthusiastic when Cam's secret was revealed. I wanted to tell her, but it wasn't my information to share. "Go see if Hilt's ready. He's probably trying to pick between two equally hideous ties. You know what to do."

Tru skipped back into the hallway. "Burn them both!"

"You know it."

Trudie pulled Hilt into the dining room as he grumbled about wearing a button-front shirt with no tie as if it were as bad as forgetting to put on pants.

"Wait," he said, spotting the fourth place setting. "Who else is joining us for this 'family' brunch? Is Lake popping the question?"

"Omigod, squee!" Tru cried. "Is that it? Is it?" She hopped up and down, inadvertently tugging Hilt with her.

"No, it's not that." The doorbell rang again. Cam was right on time. I hurried to let her in.

She stood on the porch in a fuzzy salmon-colored sweater and jeans, holding a covered carafe of juice. "Mango-papaya OJ. I wasn't sure what to bring."

I took her offering with a smile. "It's perfect. Come on in. I'm glad you're here."

I led her toward the dining room, and the cats followed us, seeming to give her their feline approval by rubbing on her legs and chirping. As we walked down the hall, she whispered, "Have you told them anything?"

"Just that this is a family brunch." We rounded the corner into the dining room.

Hilt and Tru stared at Cam in surprise.

Then Hilt's eyebrows lowered. "Ain't this the fixer what works for Lake's dad?" he asked with a dangerous growl.

I stepped forward. "Yes, but mostly no. Relax. She comes in peace and with juice. And the cats like her, see? I invited her because she has something very important to tell you."

Hilt and Trudie sat on the same side of the table, and I invited Cam to sit on my right, across from them. The cats weaved past her ankles, marking her with their kitty scents.

"Not sure I'm particularly interested in any messages she's brought." Hilt chose a blueberry muffin from the muffin tower.

Cam took a deep breath. "I don't bring any messages from the Ivenses. I'm here of my own accord." She slipped a small piece of paper from her pocket and fiddled with it. "I know it seems like I'm the bad guy. Or one of the bad guys. And I'm really sorry for that. I didn't really understand what this would all mean when I started out. It's funny how you can lose perspective when something's been so close to your heart for so long."

Tru looked from Cam to me. "I'm not sure I understand. What's going on?"

Hilt crossed his arms and aimed one of his signature glares of disapproval across the table. I knew how harmless they were, but Cam couldn't have.

The last of her resolve melted. She dropped the little paper on the table and stood abruptly, sending Rex under my chair with a disappointed *mrrw*. "I'm sorry. I don't think I can do this after all." She hurried through the back door into the library, then her voice drifted back to us. "God, how do I get out of here? This place is a maze." We heard her thump her way up the Oubliette room's stairs.

Hilt turned his hairy eyeball on me. "What in tarnation is going on?"

Hoo boy. Like when we played Tyleen's mystery dinner game, I gotta be careful about what information to explain and what to protect. Stay on topic, Pippa. I picked up the paper, turned it over, and slid it toward him. "If you don't go after her, Hilt, I will. But she wants you to. She *needs* you to."

His bushy eyebrows rose halfway up his forehead. "What? Why me?"

I tapped the picture. "Because she's Tuyen's granddaughter. She's *your* granddaughter. Now go after her."

Poleaxed, Hilt froze, staring at the old black-and-white image. His younger self peered up at him with a smooth forehead and a confident smile. With a delicate reverence I'd seen only when he held Moore's first editions, my uncle lifted the photo and studied it more closely. "Tuyen." His whisper was more like a prayer, and tears welled in his blue eyes—blue eyes with hazel flecks, like Cam's. His eyes flicked to mine then returned to the photo. His lips trembled as if he were trying to speak again, but he couldn't quite manage it. He scraped a work-roughened palm across his mouth, trying to control all those sudden emotions and bottle them inside. But he couldn't.

He bolted from the table, running after his granddaughter. "Wait! Wait, please!" His voice cracked, and his heavy tread thudded up the Oubliette's staircase as if his work boots bore wings.

I pressed my hands to my cheeks and sucked in a shaky breath, happy, sad, giddy from the mere ripples of Hilt's geyser of emotion.

Trudie, who I'd kind of forgotten was there, startled me by swearing in astonishment and asking, "Is this for real? She's our cousin or something? This isn't some cruel trick?"

I dabbed at my eyes. "Well, I'm convinced. She has the picture and a really good story."

"She could be lying for the Ivenses, though."

"Yes, but her job is to make their lives easier. And by telling us this story, she's making it harder. If it's true, then her loyalty is to us, and they've lost their fixer. She proved it last night by telling me what she was instructed to do to me—then not doing it. And even if it's not true, it would show their hand and put us—well, me—on the defensive."

Tru sat back. "What was she instructed to do?"

I took a deep breath. "Devereaux told her to warn me off Lake. They're not here just to exchange Christmas gifts. They want Lake back in the family fold, and since I'm not worthy, that means he needs to leave me behind. And that'll be a lot easier for him to do if I'm the one who pulls away." *Although it's seemed lately like their plan is working—he's been distant.*

Tru stared at me. "You know you're talking like a psycho villain right now, don't you? And it's creepy, so if you could stop, that would be great."

I belatedly realized I'd been talking in an emotionless monotone. "Sorry. I'm just seeing things from their perspective."

"Well, knock it off. You have to be on your own side, not theirs."

But it's part of my job to embrace different perspectives. It's what I do! I wanted to say. However, she had a point. I wasn't sure if any of Lake's family would see my side, let alone take it, so I needed to stand up for myself. Especially where my love life was concerned. "You're right." I glanced up as if I could see through two stories of Moorehaven to where Hilt and Cam were, I hoped, having a deep and meaningful conversation up in the Oubliette. "They could be a while. I suppose we should eat."

"You don't have to tell me twice." Tru stuffed a forkful of scrambled eggs into her mouth.

I joined her, relishing the warm comfort of home-cooked food. Rex and Svetlana took up stations by our chairs, hoping for yummies. But I only managed to enjoy three eggy bites in blissful silence before my sister spoke through a huge mouthful of gingerbread loaf. "Remember that thing at the Christmas party?"

I glanced up from the rim of the mango-papaya OJ Cam had brought. "You mean Mort's murder?"

"No, not that. The thing where I decided to look into interim property management as a career."

I squinted at her, lost. "I'm not sure you said that part out loud. And if you did, I was probably distracted by Lake's horrible family or the dead man on the floor." My sister looked abashed, but I could tell it was important to her. "So tell me again."

She plunked her elbows on the table, and her hands entered full-animation mode. "Okay, so, I've been learning all these skills from Tyleen, right? Cooking, organizing, cleaning... Mostly cleaning. Who knew there were so many different cleaning products out there?"

I subtly raised my eyebrows, but Tru was at full tilt and didn't notice.

"And sure, it would be great to be able to keep a house of our own clean and neat. It's the American dream, isn't it? A house with a picket fence. And a dog and two-point-four kids. But see..." Her brown curls seemed to droop along with her shoulders. "I'm just not sure I'm cut out for the American dream, after all." Sadness dragged at her apple-bright cheeks.

I leaned forward. "What do you mean? Everyone deserves to be happy, Tru, and that definitely includes you."

"No, I know. I'm just not sure that a picket fence will make me happy. You see, I think I might need more than one picket fence."

"You're saying you don't want to settle down?"

"No, I do! I absolutely do. I want to settle down with Gabe, more than anything. But I don't want to, y'know, *settle*."

I stabbed a few sausages and set them on my plate before drizzling them with maple syrup. "I'm not sure I'm following. Just tell me what you want to say."

Tru ran her fingers through her wild curls. "Argh, I don't know what I'm trying to say. I just want... I mean, I'm a nomad. I don't *want* a house. I just want Gabe. In lots of houses."

"Whoa, TMI Tuesday is tomorrow," I teased, trying to shut that image out of my mind.

"Shut up." She smiled.

"Okay, so let me get this straight. You want to move from house to house with Gabe and find some way to make a living off it?"

Tru slapped the tabletop. "Yes! Yes, exactly. If I'm an interim property manager, I can still clean and stuff, but I'll always have somewhere else to travel to, and nothing will get so familiar that it becomes boring."

I took a second to envision Tru sashaying from house to house in a tunnel-vision montage, wearing a chocolate-sequined ball gown and waving a caramel-hued feather duster at endless rooms filled with fancy décor. "I gotta say, I think that suits you down to your toes."

"Right?" Tru's incandescent smile faded. "It's just..." She pushed her fork around on her plate. "Gabe's so set on giving me that picket fence."

I picked a blueberry out of its bowl and flicked it down the table, where it bumped against her hand. "Gabe doesn't want to give you a picket fence, Tru. He wants to give you whatever you want most. And right now, I bet he thinks you want that picket fence. I mean, have you told him otherwise, maybe in one of those talks I've seen you having?"

"It's kind of all we've been talking about since summer ended. I think he's the one who really wants the picket fence. After all the chaos in his family history and all, you know."

I knew. Gabe's grandma had spent more than fifty years in an unhealthy state of mind after her brother's sudden disappearance, and the small part I'd played in bringing that story to an end the previous summer had offered a first step toward closure for Gabe and his family. But wherever his road took him, its first steps had been nurtured by an angry, grieving grandmother. I could see why Trudie believed that Gabe wanted nothing more than a perfect, stable family.

But he'd fallen in love with my sister, who was far from perfect and only mostly stable. *Doesn't that say something about what he really wants in life?* I remembered what he'd said after Mort's death at the Christmas party, that money couldn't buy love. "Trudie, listen. I think you need to be honest with Gabe about what you really want. You might be surprised to learn that his perfect life aligns more closely with yours than you thought."

Tru sat up straight. "Are you serious? What did he say to you?"

"He didn't say anything. I'm just—you know—reading the clues. It's kinda my thing."

Her eyes were a mile wide. "You'd better not be messing with me right now. This is my life. It's not some cute little mystery to be solved in forty-two minutes before the late news comes on."

You're so all-or-nothing, Tru. "Trust me. And trust Gabe. Talk to him, okay?"

Her eyes went soft, as if she were envisioning that conversation going exactly the way she wanted. Then a goofy smile overtook her face. "Omigod, can you imagine? Gabe and I hooking our trailer up and just... going? We'd drive everywhere, never staying too long, seeing all the sights. I'd have so much inspiration for my art I think I'd die of the overload!"

I blinked. Only at that moment did I realize what Tru achieving her dream would mean for me. *She'd leave Seacrest. It's only been half a year, and she's burrowed into my world, my one connection with my childhood and our whole family mess. She's the best part of it all. And she'll be gone.* I imagined a perfect round fruit with a giant bite taken out of it, never to be whole again, and it made me want to bake a pie to cheer myself up.

"What a life," Tru breathed.

What a life, I silently echoed.

Then in a very Trudie-esque mercurial shift, she asked, "Can I look at Felicity's journal?"

"Sure but not near the food. Come into the library."

I fetched the old journal from my room and took it to the big library table, leaving the remains of brunch to the whims of fate, aka my cats. Tru and I sat on opposite sides of the table, and I leaned onto my elbows for a closer look. "Whatcha lookin' for?"

She carefully turned the journal's pages. "I love this aesthetic. The old ink, the flowing lines. These pages would make a lovely contact paper or even wallpaper."

I shot my hand out protectively. "Don't you dare."

Tru's brown eyes met mine. "Relax. I'm not gonna rip them out. You're so touchy." She flipped through the pages faster. "I suppose scanning them wouldn't work, since it would put all her secrets on display. Maybe I can just copy her handwriting, though. Wouldn't that be cool?"

"The word for that isn't 'cool.' It's 'forgery.'"

Tru let another saucy epithet slip past her lips.

I smirked. "Now who's touchy?"

"No, look at this." Tru gripped my wrist like a steel vise. "You didn't notice this before, or you'd have said." She carefully pressed the journal's first page flat. "Look, Pips. Really look."

I shivered with delight at the idea of finding a new clue in Felicity's hidden journal. My gaze fell to the first written page. I read it over three times but divined nothing new. Then I got the bright idea to search for hidden text, faint shadows from dry pen marks, watermarks, anything. I lifted the book and tilted the page in the light, but

I couldn't spot a single thing that hadn't been there before. "Tru, I'm not seeing it, whatever it is."

My little sister took the journal from me. "No, silly. Not *that* side." She tipped her head and widened her eyes with comic exaggeration, indicating the inside cover.

I felt my face scrunch up in confusion. "But there's nothing there either. Just the publisher's imprint—which now I have to read because you're making squinty eyes at me. Okay. Gimme."

Tru spun the book around and slid it to me, and I read every single word. At the very bottom, the journal's print date caught my eye.

"But..." I couldn't finish my sentence. My brain was too busy having an out-of-body experience.

"You told me," Tru said, "that Felicity's funeral took place on December 31, 1930. Last day of the year." Her tone was rich with triumph, and she deserved it.

"That's what Hilt told me, yeah. But then how," I added in my best musing-sleuth voice, "did Felicity Moore write *anything* in a journal that wasn't even made until *January of 1931*?"

"She wasn't dead!" Tru cried exultantly.

My voice was still in sleuth mode. "She wasn't dead. Why all the clues for Moore to find? Was this just another game? What really happened to her? Was she just, I don't know, running away again?"

Trudie's face became contemplative. "I run away a lot. I never thought I'd have that in common with Felicity Moore."

"Why do you run, Tru?" My voice was soft.

She offered me a helpless shrug. "It's hard to stay in one place. You need a good reason. An anchor. Like you and Lake. You anchor each other here."

"We kinda do. And Raymond, he was Felicity's anchor. He needed her, so she stayed for him. And for her girls. But then the highway came to town, and Raymond Moore became a bestselling author."

"They didn't need her, and she knew it was time to move on," Tru supplied.

"But to what?" I wasn't just being rhetorical. "Maybe she went to go look for her child."

She took my hands and shook her head. "To her next great adventure. She crossed the entire continent in 1891 as a single woman. She built Moorehaven and created Seacrest with the force of her will. She took in an orphan and turned him into one of the world's most prolific and renowned mystery authors. She'd have to work pretty hard to top that. But she left that note in the lamp for Moore because she wouldn't want"—she took my face in her hands—"she wouldn't want those she left behind to worry about her."

Tears welled in my eyes, and I framed her face with my hands too. "You're going away with Gabe. You've decided. You're anchored to Gabe but not to Seacrest."

Her eyes were damp. "I go where my heart leads. Just like you and just like Felicity."

We hugged for a long time, and in Trudie's tight, sisterly embrace, the final step to understanding Felicity's message to Raymond Moore unfolded in my mind. "*I'll take their secrets to my grave.*" *And you did, didn't you?* When Hilt and Cam came downstairs a few minutes later, they stepped into the library holding hands. I smiled, relieved and thrilled for them both.

"Hey, girls. Whatcha been doin'?" Hilt asked.

I stood up and leaned one hand on the table, pointing with my other hand at the clue in the journal. "I hate to be all melodramatic, but we need to dig up Aunt Felicity's grave."

21

"Diamonds may be a girl's best friend, but they're no friends of mine. They're glimmery little gossips who don't know when to shut up. Never trust a stone you can see through."
Raymond Moore, 1941

I'D ONLY GOTTEN TWO sentences into my explanation of Felicity's secret clue—and Hilt still wore a poleaxed expression, for which I didn't blame him—when Chloe tapped on the library door and poked her head in. "I'm really sorry to interrupt, Pippa, but Tyleen's having an emergency. She's on the phone. Can you come?"

I took a deep breath and ran my tongue over a wisdom tooth while I rearranged my plans for the next few minutes. "Yes, I'll be right there. Tru, can you fill Hilt and Cam in?" At Trudie's questioning look, I nodded firmly. "She's family. And she's pretty capable, from what I've seen. I'll be back in a jiffy, guys." I slipped out through the small parlor and took the phone from Chloe at the L-shaped hostess station. "Tyleen, has something happened with Sebastian?"

I was relieved to hear her say, "No, no, he's safe and sound. Thank God." But her voice was strained.

"Why didn't you just come over? You know I'm always here for you."

"I think I need to stay right here. Mallory's coming here, you see." A distant thread in her voice told me that something was really distracting her.

"To your house? Why? She's not arresting you, too, is she?"

She ignored my question. "And I'd like you to be here before then. See, my kitchen is just a mess, and I need your help. I need you to stop me from cleaning it up."

Baffled, I asked, "I know you love a clean house, Tyleen, but why do you need me to stop you from cleaning your kitchen?"

"Well, see, it's a crime scene."

I froze. Tyleen had a reputation for exaggeration and another for misrepresentation of details. How she managed to remain the head of our local neighborhood watch association was still a mystery to me. But exaggerated or not, the "crime scene" in Tyleen's kitchen had spooked her. "Don't move. I'll be there in twenty seconds."

I hung up and dashed outside into the chilly morning without my coat. "I'll be back as soon as I can!" I called to Chloe, who kindly slid the glass door shut behind me. With my breath huffing in big white puffs, I dashed through the gate and across Tyleen's backyard, which lay beneath a scarlet blanket of damp maple leaves. At her back door, I rapped on the old wavy glass until she let me in.

She looked despondent in a wrinkled yellow shirt and jeans, her usually lost glasses riding atop her head.

I hugged her. "Tell me what's happening."

When she pulled back, I read tension in her lips and the subtle crow's-feet in the corners of her eyes. "Come with me," she said.

I followed her up the short staircase, which led to a tiny landing between her pantry and her kitchen. I stood beside her in the doorway and studied the scene.

Tyleen's kitchen had been ransacked. Her fridge door hung open. Two of the fridge shelves had been toppled, their contents spilled to the floor. All but one of her cupboard doors hung open like a swarm of wooden butterflies that had come to rest near her crockery, their wings askew. Plastic containers lay scattered across the floor, mixed with an impressive array of handheld kitchen utensils, spilled flours, a broken bottle of grapeseed oil, and three kinds of dry beans.

Her counters were strewn with flatware and broken ramekins, and her recipe books had been ransacked. Pages lay limp where they had fallen. An entire rack laden with cooking and baking pans had been tipped over in the corner, scattering porcelain and metal across Tyleen's little breakfast table, her two chairs, and the surrounding floor.

"Ow, ow, Pippa."

Tyleen was wiggling my hand. I looked down. I'd been squeezing hers painfully without realizing it. I twitched my hand away and rubbed hers in apology. "This is a travesty. Who would do this to you?"

"Well. The killer. I presume." Her voice was matter-of-fact.

"Possibly. But why? If they're getting away with murder because Mallory's arrested Sebastian, why draw attention to themselves by attacking your poor kitchen? What did it ever do to them?"

"You think it's something else, then?" The idea seemed new to her, but I didn't blame her. If one of my family members had been arrested for murder, I would have thought of nothing else.

"I don't know. But I'll stay with you until Mallory gets here. Maybe there's some evidence that will tell her who did this. So let's go wait in the front room for her to get here, then you won't have to stare at this room and resist the urge to clean it up, okay? Try not to touch anything." I gently herded Tyleen down the hallway to her living room and parked her on a pale-lemon couch with apricot trim. I squeezed her hand as I sat next to her. "It's going to be okay. Once we're clear, I'll help you clean everything up. We'll have this place spic-and-span in no time."

Tyleen took a deep breath and nodded with pursed lips to buck herself up. "You're such a dear, Pippa."

A minute later, Mallory's cruiser pulled up at the curb outside Tyleen's large front window. Mallory walked to the porch through a sudden spattering of raindrops and clouds of her own breath, wearing blue latex gloves and carrying an awkward collection of items. I opened the door for her before she could knock, and she stepped inside with a nod of thanks and the smell of fresh rain.

My eyes fell to what she carried—a glass of juice, a baggie of ice cubes, and a few empty evidence bags. "What on earth…?"

"You would not believe what just happened." Mallory headed into the living room and set the glass down on a small wooden table that held Tyleen's Christmas cactus. As she opened one of the evidence bags, she continued, "It sounds like something out of one of your guests' books, Winterbourne. But I trust that if I tell you, I won't end up reading it in print next year?"

She actually wants to tell me this story. Who is this, and what has she done with Mallory Tavish? "Sure thing."

Mallory carefully poured the reddish juice—*cranberry?*—into one evidence bag, and a tiny clear stone plinked into the bag with it. "I don't mean to be callous, Tyleen. I take your call seriously. But you did have excellent timing, and I was happy to leave my new neighbor's house, evidence literally in hand. I didn't have time to bag it up before I got here."

"You have a new neighbor?" Tyleen asked.

I was surprised too. Naoma hadn't been able to rent the other half of Mallory's duplex out for love or money. But apparently, something else had sufficed.

Mallory sealed the bag of juice, opened another, and inserted the glass itself. "They moved in yesterday. A husband and wife. He's working at the sporting goods store on the highway. She hasn't found employment yet. But she did think it was important to say hello to me for some reason. So she invited me over for a quick drink."

"And how did that go?" I asked.

Mallory emptied the ice cubes into the last evidence bag and sealed it. Then she began writing on it with a Sharpie. "Well, it did seem to throw her off when I showed up in uniform. I informed her that I was on duty and couldn't have a beer with her, but she insisted that I come in anyway. She poured me a glass of cranberry juice—which I didn't ask for—and decided it would be fancier if she dropped in a few ice cubes. In the middle of winter."

"She's just trying to be neighborly," Tyleen said.

"I'll have to file 'acting neighborly' under 'things that look suspicious to a cop,' then. She chattered on and on, and she didn't even notice that I wasn't drinking the juice I didn't ask for. Then I heard a *clink* inside my glass." Mallory held up the juice-filled evidence bag. "A loose diamond. Part of the stolen jewelry collection. Apparently, Auda was in the middle of having a necklace custom designed, and she happened to be storing the loose gems with the rest of her jewelry."

My eyes widened. "Oh my God. Was it her? Is your neighbor the thief?"

"Judging by the way her eyes nearly popped out of her head and how she started cursing her husband, I'd say no. According to her, he checked the mailbox yesterday when they moved in, and there was a package he wouldn't show her."

"A package of diamonds?" Tyleen asked.

"Yes, and he allegedly froze them in the ice cube tray so his wife wouldn't find them. Except she had a house guest whom she tried to impress with fancy chilled cranberry juice."

"Are you going to arrest him for withholding evidence?" I asked.

Mallory's lips twitched into a brief grin. "We'll see. I had to walk out with this evidence in hand when I got Tyleen's call, but Officer Nuncio will be stopping by the sporting goods store to have a chat with him. Let me lock this evidence in my car, then we'll check out your kitchen, Tyleen." Mallory gave her a crisp nod.

Two minutes later, the three of us stood in the kitchen doorway. "You say this happened overnight, but you didn't hear a thing?" Mallory asked, notepad in hand.

"I've been taking sleeping pills since I got hired for the Ivenses' party. When Sebastian got arrested, I decided I still needed them." She shot a mildly accusing glance at Mallory. "A herd of elephants could've been tenderizing meat and cracking walnuts in here, and I wouldn't have heard them."

Mallory pulled out her phone and began easing her way around the pillaged kitchen, snapping photos. "I'll have to dust for prints, so I'll need yours, Tyleen." Her eyes settled on me. "And yours, too, Winterbourne." A tiny evil smile graced her lips for a second.

"I didn't touch anything," I protested.

"That's what they all say." Mallory turned her back and snapped another set of photos near the fridge.

A cluster of blue porcelain fragments near her left boot caught my eye, and I recognized a smooth curve among them as the handle of a mug. "Oh, no, Tyleen, is that the mug I gave you?"

Tyleen squinted toward the floor, though her glasses were nestled in her hair. "Probably. I had tea in it last night. I left it on the counter." She sighed heavily.

I squeezed her forearm. "Don't worry. I can have Andy make a new one for you."

Mallory finished in the kitchen and took our fingerprints with a portable print scanner in the living room. "Winterbourne, if you could entertain Tyleen at your place until I'm through here?"

"Sure thing. Come on over, Tyleen."

"Wait. Mallory, what if the real killer did this? What if this break-in means that Sebastian is innocent?" Tyleen clasped her hands together like an orphaned waif.

Mallory's dark eyes shifted from Tyleen to me. I raised my eyebrows at her, indicating that I'd wondered the same thing.

"I don't believe in coincidence," Mallory said. "But I'll need to see some hard evidence that this break-in and Mort's murder are connected before I can chase that rabbit." Her eyes lingered on me.

Is she giving me permission to investigate? I thought I knew Mallory, but she's been so helpful lately that I barely recognize her. "Understood," I said, not really understanding. "You like pfeffernuesse, Mallory?"

"Why?"

"Because you're a lot like them: crusty on the outside, soft and squishy on the inside."

Mallory stared, nonplussed. "I am not a cookie, Winterbourne."

Half of my mouth drew up in a smile. "If you say so." I led Tyleen through the damp to Moorehaven, and we slipped in through the sliding glass door.

Chloe, Hilt, Ruslan, and Cam sat at the dining room table, enjoying some leftover muffins and tea. Hilt genially invited us to join them all. I glanced at Tyleen, gauging her mood.

She swiped at a strand of brassy blond hair that had escaped her updo. "Sitting down sounds great. Muffins and tea sounds even better." She seated herself across from Cam. "So, I just got burgled. What are you all up to today?"

A chorus of "What?" ringed the table, except for Uncle Hilt, who replied laconically, "We're going to dig up Aunt Felicity's grave."

"*What?*" Tyleen exclaimed.

I couldn't help it. Giggles overtook me, and I had to lean on the back of a chair for support. *Oh my God. This day. I just can't.*

Then my phone rang with Lake's ringtone, "Under the Sea." I stepped into the kitchen to answer it.

"Can you come to lunch with me today?" Lake asked.

I melted at the idea of getting away from all of the chaos for an hour with my boyfriend. "Absolutely. Just tell me when and where."

"Great. Meet me at To Dine For at one."

I checked the kitchen clock. *Just under an hour to get ready.* "I will be there with *all* the proverbial bells on." My voice got all breathy of its own accord, and I didn't try to stop it.

"Well, that, I gotta see. See you there, hon."

I made arrangements with Hilt to let Tyleen stay for lunch and informed everyone that I would be out on a date. Their whoops and whistles as I headed to my room to get ready lifted my mood. While trying to decide what outfit to wear, I texted the Glaze & Gossip girls to let them know about Tyleen's break-in. Their swift responses of sympathy and commiseration warmed my heart even as I stood barefoot in front of my closet. Every one of them promised to stop by to see her or to bring her something yummy. And they all agreed with me that the real killer might have been behind the burglary.

I thought about Tyleen sitting at my table, surrounded by friends but caught in a maelstrom of crime and upset. I texted the group: *Coordinate with Tyleen's neighborhood-watch contacts. Maybe someone saw something. They won't be thrilled that someone burgled their leader. We've got to catch this guy.*

I pulled a sequined cream top out of my closet and held it in front of my reflection in the mirror. "Look out, killer. We're coming for you. You don't mess with Glaze & Gossip."

22

"Grind anyone into the dirt far enough, and they'll have the world at their back."
Raymond Moore, 1955

I STRODE DOWN MOOREHAVEN'S hallway in my cream top, a navy maxi skirt, and some warm, stylish boots, wearing my hair up and feeling like a million bucks with a side of butter sauce.

Cam spotted me from the parlor entry and ended her phone call with a brusque "I gotta go."

"What's up?" I reached for my coat.

"I did some digging while you were back there with your fairy godmother—you're gonna kill Lake with that look, by the way."

"Thanks! Anything new?"

"Yes. I managed to get ahold of that valet, Duncan, again. He and Odie saw something in the parking lot the night Sadie's brakes were cut. Odie's still not talking, so I tried to winkle some more info out of Duncan instead. He reiterated that he never found the dog in the parking lot. But he did recall something a little strange. While he was searching near Sadie's parking space, the barking abruptly ended, like, mid-bark."

I paused, my fingers on my coat zipper. "Why didn't he mention that before? And what does that mean?"

Cam tipped her head and shrugged. "I think it means there was never actually a dog in that parking lot. You go enjoy your date."

That didn't make any sense, but I didn't have time to think about it. I smiled and said goodbye.

The storm was definitely on its way. The western horizon was nearly black with clouds, but the sun blazed overhead. I was glad I'd left when I did, because I would definitely make it to the restaurant before it broke. Feeling daring, I let the intense wind push me up the slope from the sea until I reached To Dine For. As I walked, I pulled on a few threads surrounding the car crash, still unsure what my attacker's motive was. Something was nagging at me, and I could practically feel my why-didn't-I-solve-this-sooner moment zooming closer, preparing to ambush me with a massive facepalm.

I needed to focus on my love life, though. Inside the posh dining establishment, the maître d' took my coat, offered me a wide smile, and showed me to Lake's table. When I spotted Lake, my elation deflated a little. He rose to his feet and kissed my hand, but he moved slowly, as if exhausted, and two little lines had taken up residence between his dark eyebrows.

"You okay?" I asked. "You look like you just went ten rounds with Poseidon and lost."

"I'll be fine." His reply was dismissive, but he gamely smiled down at me. "How are things at the Big Mystery House?"

I squeezed his hand on the tabletop. "Oh, geez, there's so much going on that I don't even know where to start." Hours' worth of pent-up secrets gathered behind my lips, eager to spill out.

"Ooh, am I missing the small-town gossip?" Bliss interrupted. She dragged a chair over and sat by Lake's elbow. Kait followed suit, sitting as close to Bliss as she could, as if trying to stay as far from me as possible.

I stopped myself from rolling my eyes but only just. It was supposed to be a date, Lake was acting weird, and I wasn't too keen on hanging out with his family.

"You're not missing much," Lake said as if attempting to placate his sister. But his words hurt my feelings, even though he couldn't have known how wrong he was.

Bliss shot him a fake smile. "Oh, I'm not really interested. But one has to say something when one interrupts. It's just creepy otherwise."

"You could try not interrupting at all," I sniped.

Bliss needed half a second to process that, and Lake spoke into the silence. "What do you want, sis? I'm on a date."

Bliss turned her cold blue eyes on me. "Are you, though?" She wrinkled her nose delicately. "I heard that Pippa has something to say to you."

As Lake turned inquiring eyes on me, I remembered Cam's mission from the previous night. *Was it only last night that Lake's dad sent her to break Lake and me up? Gosh.* "Maybe you should listen to small-town gossip more often, Bliss, because your information's wrong."

Bliss's supermodel face froze in surprise. Then her expression morphed into something like wicked glee. "Oh my God. You blew off his offer! I cannot *wait* to see what happens next. I take it all back, Pippa. You're not boring at all. I'm going to *enjoy* sitting back and watching you light yourself on fire."

I set my jaw and scrambled for something more erudite than "bring it on," but Kait spoke first. "Seriously, Bliss. You're foaming at the mouth over this tiny little mess. Take a breath, and let it go already."

Bliss huffed and looked at her perfectly manicured fingernails.

"I'm sorry," Lake interjected. "Am I the mess in this situation?"

"No," both women chorused.

Lake looked confused when he turned to me. A mirthless laugh escaped from between my teeth.

Kait continued, "Bliss is just bitchy because Daddy told her to break up with this one guy, and she did it because she still thinks Daddy knows best. But she was in love with him, just like you're in love with Pippa, and for all her pretending to stand strong with the fam, she can't. Your dad betrayed you, Bliss."

Bliss turned huge, furious eyes on Kait, who stared back as if she were no more threatening than a mouse wielding a toothpick. I couldn't help but be impressed by her.

"What are you doing?" Bliss finally muttered.

Kait offered her a slow blink. "Your monolithic I got boring. And you only came here because you wanted to see the look on Pippa's face when she broke up with Lake because your father paid her off. It's sick."

Lake froze.

I held still, too, feeling adrenaline pounding through my veins. "Except he didn't, and I'm not." I met Lake's eyes. "Not for any price."

Lake seemed to reinflate a bit.

Bliss shot me a calculating look. "Cam texted and said it was done. Maybe your little girlfriend is just lying to you, Lake. Trying to cover her ample behind."

I took a deep breath. "Cam Cooper? My long-lost second cousin, who pulled dozens of strings to get your whole family to Seacrest so that she could meet her grandfather for the first time? Whose every move and motivation escaped the notice of your entire family? That Cam? Nah, she must've left that part out during our epic family reunion." I shrugged casually.

Kait clapped a hand over her mouth and uttered a muffled "Oh, snap!"

Lake and Bliss eyed each other before looking at me.

"My dad's assistant is your cousin? For real?" Lake asked.

"Really, really." My grin was a mile wide.

"Well, she's not Dev's assistant anymore. She called to say she'd quit half an hour ago," Kait said.

"What?" Bliss's head turned so quickly that her hair actually got disheveled for once.

I pressed my nails into my palms to keep from cheering.

"You didn't tell me?" she asked.

"I know you think otherwise, but you don't actually own me. Oh, you thought I'd forgotten that comment?"

While Bliss sputtered, Lake asked, "And you were in on this, this... plot to get rid of my girlfriend?"

Kait waved him off, but Bliss answered with some of the bile she clearly would have preferred to unleash on Kait. "She's no one, and you deserve better. We're all thinking it. Daddy just took steps to ensure the outcome he wanted, like he always does. He should've seen Cam's betrayal coming. I never liked that Asian mongrel—"

My lip curled. "You gonna finish that sentence, or shall I finish it for you?" My heartbeat thudded in my ears, and I could actually taste my desire—spicy and salty—to climb across the table and smack her in the face. My hands were already flat on the table, and I leaned forward, breathing heavily through my nose.

Kait clamped a warning hand on Bliss's arm. Lake rested his on mine.

I ignored it. "Retcon your feelings all you like, but you're the one whose affections your father has bought off. Not me and not Lake."

Lake's hand spasmed, and I looked over.

His back had gone ramrod straight, and he stared down at his sister. "He was never going to give me the boat, was he?"

Bliss's reply was a bitter, twisted smile that flashed briefly like a shark fin and was gone.

"Son of a..." Lake squeezed my arm in apology. "I need to speak to my father. Let's get out of here. We can catch up another time."

Bliss glared at Lake's proposed sudden departure. But something in Kait's eyes flickered like relief and settled into satisfaction. I had a brainwave, remembering the mess Jordan had been sorting out at the concierge desk.

No one would send mail to an empty house. "You go ahead, hon," I told Lake. "I need to have a word with Kait."

Lake's eyes darted to Kait then Bliss. "Okay," he said doubtfully. "Text me if you need anything."

"Ditto." I let him kiss me goodbye on the cheek.

After he walked away, I put my elbows on the table and pinned Kait to her chair with my gaze. "Bliss wouldn't take them," I began conversationally. "She's clearly still drinking the Ivens Kool-Aid. Auda gains nothing good from faking a robbery. Dev wouldn't invite the bad press of having his family embarrassed. Odie? I don't think he really dislikes anyone in his family, despite being so different from them. So that leaves you, Kait."

"Leaves me what?"

"As my only suspect. You stole Auda's jewels."

Kait's face stilled.

"I'm not psychic or anything, though. You had your plan. You had access to the jewels. You had time while everyone else was getting ready for the party. No one pays any attention to you, do they? But you forgot one critical thing. Mailing boxes."

"What is she going on about?" Bliss's tone was casually oblivious.

Kait's eyes were locked onto mine.

"You ordered them from the local stationery store, and you had one of the hotel concierges add the charges to the room. It had to be an inside job. It was just a matter of figuring out who had the right motive. And that turned out to be you, getting revenge on them for some reason."

Kait's lower lip trembled, then she forced a sneer onto her pretty features. "I thought I'd be long gone before anyone figured that out."

Bliss actually wrinkled her perfect brow. I was momentarily cheered by the knowledge that Lake's sister could appear perfectly ordinary.

Kait continued, "My going-away present. Maybe a wake-up call for you, Bliss. If you want one."

"Waking me up for what?" Bliss asked faintly.

"The realization that your parents are scrambling for the entire local police force to hunt down handfuls of little rocks, but they didn't care one bit when your sweet, adorable Killian got a flat on his way to pick you up for a secret weekend. In fact, they hid the news from you so you'd feel stood up. Then Daddy bought you off with hotel shares in Cabo, and you agreed to dump the man you loved. You told yourself it was the right move. I heard you, actually talking to yourself in the mirror. You said it over and over while you stared into your own crying eyes. So maybe redistributing a little of your parents' wealth here and there will hold up another kind of mirror for you. A little Robin Hood goes a long way. And so am I."

"You're leaving?" Bliss repeated, ignoring everything else Kait had said. "What do you mean?"

"I'm moving to Vail."

"But we don't have any property in Vail." Bliss's voice was high and thin.

Kait sighed. "Exactly. I'm leaving all of you. You're so close to one another—and to no one else—that it's toxic. I don't want to turn out like your parents. And I can't stand by and watch you turn into them either. It hurts too much."

I reluctantly broke the awkward silence that followed. "You might not get to move to Vail for a while. The jewelry you stole was worth a lot."

The gravity of her actions seemed to sink in, and Kait's eyes widened.

"No, no, it was just a prank," Bliss said, clasping Kait's wrist. "Just a joke. No harm done. I'll speak to the judge."

"Let's start with an arresting officer, shall we?" I said, pulling out my phone.

"No. Please." Bliss's voice had never sounded so soft, so hurt. I looked past my phone at her, waiting. "She's my friend. Like a sister. You can't."

Kait finally blinked.

"She's a thief," I pressed, though I kept my voice gentle. "Would you choose her over your mom? Over your dad?" *She should. They're both horrible, and Kait seems all right.*

Bliss and Kait stared at each other so long and so intently that I suddenly felt like I was intruding. I couldn't read the textbook of their history, but I felt the weight of it against my chest.

"I'll give you until tomorrow to decide. Merry Christmas." I stood and headed for the restaurant doors just as the waiter approached with a wine list.

<h1 style="text-align:center">23</h1>

"The only things you should keep track of with friends are how many times you've saved each other's lives and who bought the last round of drinks. And everyone lies about that last one."

Raymond Moore, 1981

I STEPPED OUT OF THE restaurant into a sudden gust of gale-force wind. My breath got sucked away, and my eyeballs nearly froze in their sockets. I threw myself behind a sturdy brick pillar and pressed my back against it. "Well, I guess the storm's here." The smell of rain swirled around me, promising a deluge.

Since I'd extricated myself from Bliss and Kait, I worried for Lake—he'd seemed almost fragile. I wished I'd bothered to get my tangerine hatchback out of the Moorehaven garage, but I'd had that sudden craving for the childlike wonder of feeling Mother Nature blowing me along the sidewalk, so I had to trudge through her fury. Seven Vistas was only a few blocks away.

I pulled my knit cap from my coat pocket and tugged it over my ears then strode full into the wind, feeling like Rose at the prow of the *Titanic*. Rose and Jack's fate wouldn't be Lake's and mine. *Ain't nothin' gonna sink this ship.*

Soon, I heard the massive booming of storm-driven waves against the cliff. Giant sprays of foamy sea flew into the air above the cliff-top boardwalk. The huge waves stretched across the street and splattered heavily across Seven Vistas' seaside patio. I pulled up short,

254

not wanting a soaking, and dashed inside just as the first raindrops began to fall.

Jordan looked up from her concierge station, read my face, and waved me over like a really obvious 1930s spy. It didn't hurt my imagination that her mahogany hair was upswept and matched her killer skirt suit. "You want me to come with?" she stage-whispered. "Lake's face was as stormy as..." She aimed a thumb toward the lobby's glass I.

I am Farina, avenger of wrongs, and I never do dangerous things alone when I can drag a friend into danger with me. "Yes. I'm invoking the girl code."

Jordan's eyelids lowered just a hair over her caramel eyes, and she flashed a smile.

I followed her to the elevators, trying to copy her badass hip swagger. *Even if I owned a killer skirt suit like that, I couldn't make it look that good. I can practically hear her superhero theme song from here.*

Then we had to stand still in the elevator, listening to tinny music and staring at the numbers as they lit up one by one.

"This is the part they always leave out of action movies," I said.

Jordan nodded diffidently and rocked onto her toes. "Not actiony."

The elevator doors opened on the top floor. Lake's voice carried down the hall from his family's suite.

I winced. "Oof."

"Looks like a rescue mission." Jordan touched my shoulder. "It'll be okay. I've got this."

My hopes rose as I followed her to the suite door. She pushed me to the side, out of sight against the wall, and rapped loudly. All the voices inside ceased. A red-faced Devereaux opened the door and stared out at her.

"I've had a noise complaint, sir." Jordan's voice was perfectly professional. "Is there some way I can be of assistance?"

"We're fine. Get out." Devereaux started to shut the door.

Hot rage flared inside my chest. With an Amazonian war cry, I darted past Jordan, put my foot on the door, and shoved it open with all my might. It slammed against the doorstop with a huge thump. I stepped inside and brought my foot down in a wide-legged pose, fists clenched.

Devereaux, Auda, Odie, and Lake all stared at me as though I'd turned into the Hulk. "Okay, that may have been a bit much," I conceded, adopting a more natural pose.

Lake looked at me pleadingly. "Pippa, what—"

"I said get out." Devereaux gestured imperiously. "This doesn't concern you."

Be cool. Be cool. What would Becka do? She'd bluff and act like she belonged. I snickered, and it morphed into a belly laugh. "Yes, say it loudly and angrily," I told him. "*That'll* make it true." I strode over to Lake and held out my hand in dramatic fashion.

"Let me guess. I should come with you if I want to live?" Lake's expression was a shifting skirmish between exasperation and amusement.

I slid my gaze to Devereaux without moving. His glare could've sliced the planet in half. Our silent war had reached its final conflict. One of us would win Lake, and the other would lose.

"Just to be perfectly clear, then, Dad." Lake's voice was light and conversational. "You never intended to buy a boat for me, no matter how I tried to fit back into your mold. Yes?"

Devereaux sneered. "Your track record doesn't inspire confidence. It never has."

Aude and Odie stood stock-still in the corner.

Lake's eyes lingered on his father's face. Something subtle shifted in his cheeks. His mouth fell open, but no words came out. My boyfriend had just broken before my eyes. My heart nearly cracked in two.

I lunged for his hand and clasped it. My other hand turned his cheek so that he would meet my eyes. "No, don't dwell on him. You made your decision years ago. Don't forget why." I didn't even know if my words made sense, but they gushed out of me like a spring.

Lake hugged me with one arm as if bereft and soaked from an inner storm. A flashback from the moment we met struck me—I'd pulled Lake to safety from the midst of a stormy disaster.

A powerful gust of wind rattled the glass windows on the enclosed balcony, and the sharp sound of splintering glass startled us all. The shrill whistle of wind drew everyone's gaze toward the balcony.

Holy handbell choir! The ivory tower just cracked.

"Oh, that's gonna be expensive," Jordan muttered.

"I'm not paying for it." Devereaux turned his frustration on her.

Jordan smiled sweetly and crossed her arms. "Oh, I wouldn't think of charging you for it, not when you have so many more important things you're paying for." She gestured subtly to Lake.

"Get me outta here," Lake muttered into my hair.

Without a word, I led him into the hall. I didn't even think about looking back. Stepping through the doorway was like portaling out of a war and landing in a sunny meadow. Lake's whole body shivered with what I thought was relief, and he leaned against the wall next to the elevators as if he'd run a marathon.

From behind us came Jordan's parting words to Lake's family. "For the sake of our other guests, please keep the noise level to a bare minimum. Thank you for your understanding."

She joined us at the elevators just as one set of doors opened. As we stepped inside, Jordan gave Lake a once-over. "You all right?"

Lake ran a hand over his face and groaned. "Not really, no. But it's nothing a hot shower, a drink, and some time with my best girl couldn't fix."

I snuggled against his chest and wrapped my arms around him, drinking in his warm presence, and he draped himself over me.

"Well, let's see, where are we with the rescue count?" Jordan mused. "Pippa saved you. You saved her. You both saved me. You saved that guy by jumping off a cliff. Then Pippa saved you again, because you're such a delicate flower."

With zero hesitation, Lake said, "It's true. I am very delicate. You know how much moisturizing I do every morning?"

"It's a lot," I supplied.

Jordan ignored us. "And now she and I have saved you. So I'm on the scoreboard." She played up her smirk, trying to cheer Lake up.

It worked. "Hey, now," Lake protested. "No one in that room was trying to murder me. It doesn't count."

"Weren't they, though?" I murmured.

Lake leaned on my shoulder. "Yeah, in a way. Fine, Jordan. You get a point too."

Jordan accepted her credit with a wink, and I gave her a fist bump.

In the lobby, guests had gathered in front of the glass I to take pictures of the massive waves that sprayed foam all the way to the top of the windows. The marble floor seemed to shudder with every wave that struck the cliff.

Jordan pulled Lake and me to an alcove containing a giant potted plant. "I think you two can take it from here. Now, if you'll excuse me, I need to let Fallon know he's about to get a huge complaint from his 'good friends' upstairs." With another smile, she pivoted and sauntered off.

Lake stared after her. "Your BFF is so awesome. Are you sure she doesn't need a boyfriend? I bet I could find her a really cool one."

"Well, if you know someone good—wait, no. Jordan is just perfect as she is, thank you very much. If you're so impressed with her, buy her a big, pretty bouquet from Wallis."

"That wouldn't weird you out?" he asked.

"Dude, I was just upstairs with you guys. *I'm* gonna buy her a big, pretty bouquet from Wallis."

Lake managed a low chuckle. "Let's pick one together, then. Just maybe not right this second. How about this: I'll head home and shower. Then I'll go over to Moorehaven, and we can have that drink."

My heart soared. "Deal! And I have so much to tell you that it isn't even funny." I glanced at the intimidating weather. Vats of rain vied with the enormous waves trying to wash the promenade away. "You gonna come over in your scuba gear or your submarine?"

Lake followed my glance. "This? This is nothing. I'll barely get my rain gear wet in this."

"Whatever, Aquaman. I'll have a stack of warm, dry towels waiting for you."

A broad smile broke out across his handsome face. "Deal. Give me half an hour."

I headed for the lobby's side door. "I'll time you."

"Ha-ha, good." Lake darted past me, out into the sluicing rain, then ran up the block toward the Cedar Street bridge.

I was bracing myself to step back outside into the deluge when Chloe texted me: *Time to fly my kite and let the wind dance. Wish me luck!*

A light, happy feeling flooded my chest at the thought of Chloe stepping up and having a holiday dinner with her estranged mother. My thumbs flew across the screen. *Good luck! Don't eat too much dessert. I'm headed back now. Hilt knows you're going?*

Hilt and Ruslan are at On the Rocks. And Tyleen's with Lori and Wallis.

I chuckled. *An empty Moorehaven. Horrors.*

I know, right? Better get in there, boss.

I stared out the rain-drenched lobby doors. *Empty Moorehaven. Empty. Like a mug with no coffee, it's just not right. Oh, I should order Tyleen a new mug to replace that poor broken one. It's not much, but it'll cheer her up.*

I pulled up the photo gallery on my phone and smiled at the sight of Sebastian and Tyleen beaming proudly in their blue aprons in the middle of the kitchen at the Ivenses' party. "God, everything was so much better back then," I muttered to no one in particular. "Mort hadn't been murdered. Sebastian hadn't been arrested for it. How was this only a few days ago? It feels like months."

Something shiny in the photo's background caught my eye, and I zoomed in. I couldn't quite make it out, so I adjusted my screen brightness all the way up and tried various zooms. "What *is* that thing?"

The faintest flash of recognition tugged at my memory. I cast my mind back to the night of that fateful party. *Lake checked my wrap. I took this picture. Mort keeled over in the ballroom. Geneva made that terrible French pun. Mallory activated cop mode and crushed it. Gabe thought Mort had been stabbed, but there wasn't any blood. The green foam told Doc Stevens he'd been poisoned. We ate Chinese food.*

Wait. Go back, I told myself. I zoomed in on the photo one more time, but my mind's eye was seeing a different scene.

The blood that wasn't there when Mort died. That wasn't all that was missing! The dog that wasn't in the parking lot... With a flash of recognition, I understood what the glitzy gold-and-blue object was in the background of my photo. *Tyleen's robbery wasn't a robbery after all! Holy habaneros! Everything makes sense!*

"Pippa? How funny to run into you here. I just stopped by Moorehaven, and Chloe said she didn't know where you were."

Startled out of my realization, I stared into Wren Lundin's serious gaze. Her stylish lavender slicker protectively framed her face, but a few damp curls of dark-blond hair waved in the breeze from the open lobby door she was holding. Her other hand was tucked protectively in her pocket. Too many concerns flicked through my head, and I couldn't pick anything to say, so the awkward silence dragged out until I finally held up my phone and blurted, "You forgot your clutch in the kitchen."

Wren's penciled eyebrows settled, and her mouth tensed. "I really wish you hadn't said that." Her hand moved abruptly inside her pocket.

All I could think about was that she had a gun in there. I had no intention of waiting around for her to threaten me. My adrenaline spiked, and the pencil sketches of a plan formed in my mind.

Those sketches must've shown on my face, though. "Uh-uh," Wren chided. "No funny business. You come with me now, and no one else gets hur—"

I grabbed a handful of my maxi skirt and bolted across the lobby toward the storm-soaked western doors. Terror and excitement blended with relief that I'd worn practical footwear. "Jordan, I really should've been hitting the gym!" I hollered as I hurdled an ottoman.

To her credit, Wren reacted quickly, crying, "What's wrong, Pippa? Don't worry, Jordan. I'll go after her."

Well, this'll be a hoot. I shoved open the heavy glass door and sprinted into the storm. Fat raindrops pelted my face as I caromed toward the boardwalk that edged the cliff. I'd only made it halfway there when the next enormous wave landed on me. The water drops had separated after slamming into the cliff face, but I still felt like I'd stepped into the Green Giant's shower stall by accident. I covered my face with an arm and kept running.

"Pippa, wait!" Wren yelled.

Not interested in being murdered, I reached the broad wooden planks of the boardwalk and hung a left, automatically dashing toward Moorehaven instead of doing something smarter like going to the cops.

Wren's feet thudded on the boardwalk behind me. I risked a backward glance. She was only thirty feet behind me.

The next wave slammed into the cliff directly to my right, and it was a doozy. I had time to shout half of a frantic epithet before a wall of green water leaped into my mouth and washed me into the street. My world spun and tumbled. Everything was saltwater, mist, and asphalt. I ragdolled against the curb next to Sebastian's pet-psychic shop with a painful thump to my shoulder. Icy seawater tangled my skirt around my legs and dragged my hair toward the storm drain. Coughing and choking on brine, I pushed myself up so that I could breathe.

My eyes and scrapes stinging with salt, I desperately wiped my face with a sopping sleeve and searched for Wren. A lavender shadow detached from a parked car just up the street from Sebastian's shop. I staggered to my feet. Water cascaded out of my clothing and sucked at my waterlogged boots, and I nearly fell over again.

Wren claimed the corner of the sidewalk with a braced pose that told me she'd gotten bruised by the wave too. "Pippa, wait. I can explain."

I bared my teeth. "No, you can't." Doggedly, I wadded the hem of my skirt in my fist, shuffled into a jog, and made for Moorehaven's porch.

"Pippa!" Wren's voice faded into the storm.

Another wave attacked the cliff, and I hugged the fence post at the edge of the strip mall to anchor me. Behind me, Wren cried out. I spun to see her clinging to the giant red lobster on the strip mall's decorative outer wall. An angry burst of seawater savaged us both, but I kept my feet, huddling against the fence post like a limpet until it passed.

As soon as the wave began swirling in the street, I gritted my teeth and dashed pell-mell for home. I cut across Moorehaven's parking lot and the lawn and took the porch steps two at a time, clinging to the handrail. I yanked open the front door just as the next wave struck behind me, but I didn't look back.

Skidding on wet hands and knees on the hardwood floor, I gasped and coughed. The warmth inside Moorehaven brought on a severe case of the shivers. *I could really use one of those warm towels I promised Lake.*

I scrambled toward the front door and cranked the rarely used dead bolt into place. Relief settled over my shoulders like a warm cloak. I drew my knees up and hugged them tightly.

Rex hopped out of a chair in the big parlor and trotted out to see me, his tail high. He paused uncertainly at the smell of seawater, though.

"Hey, boy, it's okay." I held my chilly hand out to him, and he sniffed my fingers interestedly before giving them a thorough licking.

Heavy thudding on the door made me jerk forward with a cry, startling Rex. Something in my side twinged painfully. My cat folded his ears back and stalked off indignantly toward the library. He would be safer there, and I would make it up to him later. *If I have a "later."*

"Pippa!"

I scrambled away from the door and stared at it like a terrified teenager in a horror movie.

Crack! The beautiful stained-glass window in the front door shattered, and tiny red and gold shards pattered onto the floor before me. Wren's sopping figure glared at me through the hole, more terrifying for being only partially visible.

I uttered a wordless cry, torn between terror for myself and outrage for my window.

Wren slammed something against the glass again, and more fragments spilled across the floor. I could clearly see a handgun in her grip, but she was too focused on reaching the dead bolt and hadn't realized she could just shoot me. Or maybe she wasn't quite ready to commit murder again.

Either way, I had only a few seconds to save myself. A few seconds to catch a murderer. A few seconds to live like there was no tomorrow. *Because there might not be.*

And there it was, my fully formed plan. I grinned like a triumphant maniac for two rushed heartbeats, then the fear kicked back in. "If this doesn't work, I'm toast. Come on, Pippa. Get it together."

I forced my sopping, bruised body upright again and staggered for the stairs, wringing my skirt out onto the hardwood floor. Seawater and rain left an obvious trail behind me. My skirt had torn along a side seam, so I went with the design suggestion and tore it halfway up. I tied the ends around my waist so that I could run better. Wary of slipping in my rumpled and agitated state, I scrambled up the stairs on all fours.

I'd achieved a perfect view down the hallway toward the front door, about two-thirds of the way up the stairs, when the door flew open, and Wren staggered in with the storm at her back. Her eyes found me immediately. I froze, caught, and hunkered against the steps. A storm wave boomed against the cliff just before the door shut, and it gave Wren's entrance a dramatic, ominous tone.

She smiled with the gun dangling at her side. "Let's be reasonable, Pippa. You want to be reasonable, don't you? See, Mort, he wasn't reasonable." She approached slowly, as if trying to send a signal of harmlessness.

I didn't buy it, but as I slumped on the stairs to catch my breath, I realized my side had started to hurt every time I inhaled. I pressed a hand to the spot, scrambled up, and dashed for the second floor.

"No! Pippa!" Wren thudded down the hallway toward me.

I hooked a hand onto the second-floor railing and swung around, caroming toward the next flight of stairs. My head was full of a refrain I'd picked up after watching way too many action-adventure movies: *You'll be trapped if you flee upstairs! Do you have a helicopter waiting on the roof? No, you don't!*

I yanked myself around again at the staircase, and hot pain bloomed in my side, causing me to cry out. Behind me, Wren's head and shoulders popped into view as she gained the second floor.

She tilted her head mockingly. "Oh dear. Did that wave do some damage? I'd tell you to put some ice on it, but it won't matter in a few minutes." She stalked toward me as I clung to the banister.

Every breath hurt, and tears came to my eyes, blurring my vision. *Aylin fought off Becka's killer even after he broke her arm. I can do this!* I huddled against the banister until Wren was close enough to grab me. Then I leaned out of reach, cocked my leg up, and kicked in the direction of her stomach. I caught her thigh instead, at an angle that made her knee bend, and she tumbled to the floor with a drum solo of thudding elbows and hips.

I four-legged it up the stairs again, muttering angry curses at my ribs for distracting me with all that pain. Bracing my arm against my sore side, I hurried to Aunt Felicity's old bedroom and let myself in. My chest heaved painfully as I listened to Wren's screech of rage.

I leaned on the door and locked it, and the Diamond Room enveloped me in sweet sanctuary. *Please, Felicity, let me be as clever as you were. She's not gonna stop. But I need time!* I felt for my phone, but I must have dropped it in the milieu.

I glanced around the octagonal turret room. Beaded white pillows transformed the bed into a sugar-encrusted marshmallow pile.

Crystal bead curtains in rose and gold hid the small closet and winked in the light from the three windows facing the sea. Vertically striped wallpaper ringed the rest of the room with a subtle white-on-white pattern that evoked muslin prison bars.

Then I spotted the clear glass discs that dangled from the white-rose-themed shade on the Tiffany lamp beside the bed.

"I'm so sorry, Aunt Felicity." I yanked a dozen or so off the lamp and shoved them one by one into the narrow, hinge-side crack between the door and its jamb. My poor-woman's penny-jam might buy me a little more time.

Not two seconds later, Wren threw herself against the door as if she'd expected it to be unlocked. Then, to my surprise, she knocked.

Politest killer ever? "I'm sorry," I called as I leaned on the wall for support, "but Moorehaven is closed. I'll have to ask you to exit the building for your own safety, as there is a mad killer on the loose."

Wren's response was soft, hurt, and angry. "He killed my dogs."

Despite my fear and pain, I was rooted by her words. "Mort? On purpose?"

"He poisoned them. Two years ago. He denied it, of course. But the previous month, he'd been hassling me about the attention I gave them. Said it was unbalanced of me, that I should get over them. Asked me to my face what I'd do without them."

My heart shook. Rex and Svetlana were like family. *What would I do to someone who maliciously poisoned them?* "That's terrible."

"I told you how important my dogs are to me. You understood. But Mort, he's a beast. He's got to be right about everything, and everyone else is weak or stupid—they deserve to be cheated and controlled. But I had no proof, you see. I couldn't do anything about it. And the Venn diagram of his business clients and mine is nearly a circle. Thank God one of my babies lived. If Parsnip had died with the others, I don't think I could've stood it. But she didn't eat as much of the poisoned meat, and she pulled through. My little hero."

"I'm glad your dog is okay," I said lamely. *I'm comforting the woman who's trying to kill me. What?*

"This past summer, Mort bought a plot of land from me, next to where I live. He said he'd give me time to transfer my doggy cemetery somewhere safe before he started developing the land for vacation rentals. Instead, he dug it up first, without warning me. That's when I decided to kill him."

Aghast at Mort's dark side, I needed a moment to gather my thoughts. "And Sadie? Why did you cut her brakes? Why did you try to kill me? I didn't know anything about Mort's death yet. All you did was make me angry."

Wren's voice shook. "I'm sorry about that. I hadn't expected you to be invited to the party. It's not really your circle, after all. But there you were, and you were already starting to piece things together, and Mort wasn't even cold yet. Your reputation precedes you. I panicked."

Irritated by her assumptions and flattered by her backhanded compliment, I needed a second to shake myself out of the spell Wren had cast. *What am I doing? I need to get out of here.* I eased to the floor and scooted toward my escape route. But as I lifted the ornate metal grate on the laundry chute, the hinges gave an alarming yowl.

"Pippa? Pippa!" Her fist slammed against the door, followed by what sounded like a Mack truck. Two of the glass discs I'd jammed the door with shattered.

My heart hammering agonizingly against my sore ribs, I eased my legs into the chute. Wren body-slammed the door again. A few more glass pieces rained onto the floor.

With Wren's increasingly frantic attacks making the floor shake, I slithered farther into the laundry chute. My damp skirt stuck to the chute floor. Lying nearly flat while holding my head up was agonizing. I was almost all the way in when the door burst open, ripping part of the jamb apart.

I shoved myself under the metal grate just as Wren lunged for my head, her fingers outstretched like an eagle's talons.

"Sorry to accuse and run, but I'm finally grasping the gravity of the situation!" I yelled as I slid out of her sight.

Her frustrated yell echoed after me like a banshee wail. I clutched my left arm against my ribs again as I zoomed into darkness. *This next part is gonna hurt like crap—*

The grate hinges squealed again, and my eyes sprang open in the dimness, darkened further by a shadow of pursuit.

On a cracker!

The dull thuds of Wren's descent haunted me like a *Pac-Man* screen full of ghosts. I lifted my feet higher, hoping for more speed, but it hurt too much, and my heavy, wet boot snagged against the corner of the narrow space, painfully jerking me to a stop. I yanked my foot back, but my momentum had been used up. Slowly, I slid toward the laundry room and its drop. My life depended on what happened in the next minute.

When the chute leveled out near the drop hole, I rolled onto my stomach and backed across the gap, using my right arm to hold on to the handles in the side of the chute. Feet first, I shoved myself up the other side, past the drop gap into the laundry cart. I flailed for the ladder on the left side of the safe room's wall and clung to it with both hands, stifling my moans of pain. *Shh, shh, it's okay,* I told my aching body. *I'm sorry I got mad at you earlier. Look at what you did. You got me in here in one piece. We might get through this after all!*

The next few seconds stretched to an eternity as I listened for Wren. She growled her way down the laundry chute like a nervous, angry dog. I squeezed the ladder rungs until my hands ached. Then she yelped in surprise, and a rattling crash emanated from the laundry room.

Relief flooded through me so strongly that I had to drop off the ladder and slide down against the wall. I'd done it. I'd saved myself. *Well, Felicity Moore helped too.*

"Nice try, Pippa. But I know you're down here somewhere."

The laundry cart rattled threateningly, and I imagined Wren flailing her way out of it. *Oh, pfeffernuesse! It was full of towels!* My heart rate skyrocketed, and I suddenly felt anything but safe, trapped in a room with only one way out.

Then Wren cried out as if she'd hurt herself, and a series of thuds, clatters, and muffled shouts followed. I shrank into the far corner of the room, clutching the old red-and-black fountain pen that Felicity's guests had used to sign the register.

The pen is mightier. The pen is mightier.

Who am I kidding? It's not mighty. But I'll certainly have the element of surprise.

The noise from the laundry room reached a fever pitch, and I bared my teeth at the high chute entrance. I couldn't tear my eyes away from it, but the waiting was as agonizing as my side.

"Come on! What are you waiting for?" I yelled.

"Calm your tatas, woman. I've never done this before. It's really uncomfortable in here."

My jaw dropped. "*Jordan?*"

My best friend's dazzling smile and bright-red hair emerged from the chute, and she illuminated me with her phone's flashlight. "Miss Winterbourne, I presume?"

"I—uh—what?"

"I believe what you're trying to say is 'Wow, Jordan, your amazing rescue totally makes us even now! You're definitely my personal hero, now and forever.'"

I worked some moisture back into my mouth. "Yes. That's exactly what I was trying to say."

"I knew it. Now, are you all right?" She swung in and climbed down the wall ladder. As she came closer, I realized she was sopping wet. A few grains of sand decorated her hairline.

"I think I might've cracked a rib when a giant wave hit me while I was running for my life along the boardwalk."

Jordan paused halfway to my side. "That's why I ran along the *inland* side of the street."

"What? No points for trying to get Mother Nature to take out the killer for me?"

She *tsk*ed. "Since it didn't work, no. Here, let me help you up."

Jordan gave me a boost into the chute, and I gingerly eased toward the gap over the laundry room, wondering how I was going to get down safely with her behind me.

Lake gazed up at me from the laundry room, wearing a brilliant smile. One hand steadied a ladder for me while he toweled his hair dry with the other. "You said I could have towels," he reminded me.

Relief flooded me with warmth and chased away my shivers. As I pivoted and put my feet down on the ladder, I scanned the rest of the laundry room. Mallory had bent Wren over my folding table and was handcuffing her as she recited her Miranda rights.

I nearly fell into Lake's arms, but he carefully balanced me until I reached the floor. Then he folded me into a warm, wet hug.

"Ow."

Lake drew back. "Did she hurt you?" The low rumble in his voice was deliciously dangerous.

"No, no. I tried outrunning Mother Nature."

Lake pulled me back against him, bracing my sore ribs with his big, warm hand. I leaned into his support as much as I could. I was really safe. And my friends had come to my rescue just when I needed them the most. Then a horrible realization struck me. "Oh no."

"What? What is it?" Lake looked down at me in concern.

Jordan stuck her head out of the chute gap over my head. Mallory even looked over from where she was collaring her perp.

"I just realized that the three of you teaming up to rescue me actually puts *Mallory* in the rescue-count lead!"

Lake kissed my hair and snorted quietly. His "I love you" was nearly lost in Jordan's shriek of laughter.

"Guess we'll have to rescue you next, Mallory," Jordan said.

Mallory's smile was cool as she marched a dejected-looking Wren to the laundry room door. "I assure you that will not be necessary." To me, she said, "I'm glad we weren't too late, Winterbourne."

"Me too. Thanks, Mallory."

She gave me a crisp nod—and a tiny smile—and took Wren away.

I leaned into Lake's warmth and felt my muscles trembling. The terror of being chased in my own home wasn't going to fade anytime soon. *Will I ever look at the Silver Room the same way again? What if I can never break free of this feeling—*

"Hey, you two." Jordan's voice held wicked amusement. "We need to stalk Mallory and start saving her from literally everything. Like, strong winds. Litter. Overly hot coffee."

And just like that, my mind was drawn from its downward spiral and into a world of humor. Without moving anything else, I blindly raised a loose fist toward Jordan, who was still hanging out up in the laundry chute.

She pressed her knuckles to mine in a fist bump and left them there for several moments. "Girl code."

"Girl code," I repeated.

"Girl code," Lake added seriously.

Jordan cackled again and began to descend the ladder, and I let out a sudden *ha* that turned into a groan. "I've already been almost murdered once today. Please, have mercy."

Jordan kissed my cheek with a loud, cheesy smack. "Just this once. Because you're hurt, and we love you."

"You guys are the best."

24

"I once bought an entire treehouse, one plank at a time, by telling stories to the lumberyard owner's son. I wrote them down and gave them to him that Christmas—my very first book. The look in his eyes as he held it told me I was onto something big, and I've never looked back."

Raymond Moore, 1966

"I CAN'T BELIEVE IT'S Christmas Day already." Tru stared dreamily out my kitchen window, not noticing how unevenly she'd been chopping the celery.

"I can," Chloe responded. She pulled my formal plates down from the top cupboard shelf two at a time. "My dad spent all day yesterday bringing ingredients and crockery down into the lighthouse kitchen. I only got away for half an hour to help you guys set up because I needed a breath of fresh sanity. Thank Lake again for me, will you, for putting up with my crazy family's invasion."

"Pretty sure your 'crazy' family is a breath of fresh sanity for Lake," Tru snarked.

I couldn't disagree. "I'm glad you're having Christmas on your own terms, Chloe. We'll miss you here, but it's important to be with those you love most." I shared a big grin with my newest cousin, Cam, who did her best to balance the plates as Chloe unseeingly stacked them atop the growing pile.

"I hope you have a good time today," Cam told Chloe. Her smile was as firm as always, but her eyes were clearer than I'd ever seen them.

"I hope you don't bust a gut!" Tyleen added over her shoulder. She'd stationed herself at the stove, overseeing four different side dishes steaming merrily from under their lids. "You're still growing, so you're probably gonna be fine, but just in case, take some—"

"Mom, enough with the indigestion treatments." Sebastian paused in his potato mashing to help Chloe count out the right number of forks.

He handed her a bunch as if they were a bouquet, and she pretended to smell them. "I'm a sucker for stabby bouquets," she said.

Sebastian grinned. "Someone should tell Wallis to start stocking them."

Cam looked at me with the starry-eyed wonder of someone who wasn't sure she should believe what she was seeing. "This family is so weird."

I smiled. "Thank you."

Ruslan stuck his head around the corner of the doorway. His ring of white hair, brushed to fluffy perfection, glowed like a halo, and his eyes twinkled like a five-year-old's. "Can I help?"

"Yep." Hilt's hand came down on his shoulder from behind, and he pulled Ruslan toward the dining room. "Help me pick a table-cloth. You like green or red better?"

I looked past them to where Gabe stood on a stool to reach the fancy candlesticks on the top shelf of the dining room cupboard. *So much family. I think I'm gonna cry. No, wait—that's the onions.*

The doorbell rang as I scraped the onions into a sauté pan. I tried to calm my burst of adrenaline as I hurried down the hall to greet my final two guests.

The storm had blown itself out overnight, and the western sky hung thick and quiet behind Lake and Mallory. My boyfriend looked amazing in a wine-red shirt and black slacks under his thick coat. Mallory had recreated the loose-knot hairdo she'd worn at the Ivenses' Christmas party, and a long royal-blue skirt draped prettily past the bottom of her puffy baby blue jacket.

"Welcome! Get in here. It's freezing outside." I waved them in and took their coats. Lake kissed me warmly on the cheek, and I gave him a fierce hug. "Listen, before we go in, I need to say something."

Lake kept his gaze on me, but Mallory twisted her fingers in an uncharacteristic gesture of nerves.

"We're an odd trio. I don't expect we'll ever get past all of our issues with one another. But I'd like to think that no matter what, we'll *try* to. Thank you again, both of you, for saving my life." I squeezed Lake's hand then reached for Mallory's. She glanced at Lake's clasped hand then reached out and took mine. I inhaled slowly, basking in the pinnacle of interpersonal triumph. How long had it taken me to warm up to Mallory? Or more importantly, her to me? Yet there we stood, bonded in friendship on Christmas Day.

"We going to eat anytime soon, Winterbourne, or are we just going to stand in the hallway and sing 'Kumbaya'?"

I sighed and let go of her hand. "Yeah. Moment's over. Let's eat."

I organized a revolving line of food carriers while Tyleen and I pulled the cherry-glazed ham from the oven and settled each dish in its own pretty bowl or platter.

Chloe tossed her apron onto a chair in the kitchen nook. "Drinks are poured. I'm off. Enjoy yourselves, everyone!"

"You too. Thanks for helping, Chloe," I said. "Now, go have a good time."

"Yes, boss." With a flick of her black hair and a confident smile, she strode toward a future of her own making.

I blinked back proud tears. "That's my girl."

In minutes, everyone had taken a seat in the dining room. I couldn't see a single inch of tablecloth past all the entrees, side dishes, platters, and various support crockery. Hilt stood right back up and began a speech that wasn't quite a prayer, but I heard the depth of emotion in his words.

"We give thanks today for our loved ones, for our friends and family." His gaze took in all of us, and I felt warm and fuzzy inside. "For those who never leave our side." He looked at me fondly. "And for those who come running when we call." His eyes landed on Mallory, and he nodded and gulped before continuing. "And for new family, who we look forward to getting to know." He smiled warmly at Cam. "We give thanks for what we have. We don't ask for much, and we value what's given. We could have less, but instead, we have more. We have each other. And that's more than enough." He picked up his glass, and we all joined him. "Here's to us, our Moorehaven family."

I drank past the lump in my throat. *How am I gonna fit all this food in my tummy when my heart already feels so full?*

Tru dabbed the corners of her eyes with her fingertips. "Ah, Uncle Hilt, too many onions in your speech there."

Everyone chuckled, and Lake kissed my fingers.

Gabe reached for the basket of rolls and set one on his plate. "Which way are we passing?"

At the same moment, Mallory, Cam, Lake, and I said, "Counterclockwise."

A frisson of energy rippled between Mallory and me, and our eyes locked.

She managed a superior smile and added, "Obviously. It's the optimal choice."

I smiled back. "Hilt, you're on ham duty, unless you want to defer. Ruslan, get those orange-glazed carrots started. Tru, don't make me take one of those three bánh mì from you."

Hilt tackled the ham and offered delectable slices over the slow "Be Our Guest"-esque dance of entrees and vegetables that ringed the table.

I was determined to get at least one bite of every dish—especially the marshmallow-topped sweet potatoes—so I crammed about three meals' worth of food onto my plate in a glorious kaleidoscopic overkill. I tried a dozen dishes in as many bites, and I was in heaven. *Friends, family, and food. There's nothing better in the world!*

"This is so much better than the last big meal we had in here." Tru spoke through a mouthful of sweet potatoes. "Can you believe we were eating with a murderer?"

"She hadn't killed Mort yet, though," Ruslan pointed out.

"She had planned it out, though, and that in itself is a crime," Mallory said.

"You found proof?" I asked.

Mallory nodded and sipped her wine. "I shouldn't talk about this, but since you're... well, since you're *you*, in her confession, she admitted to interesting Mort in a green-smoothie regimen. She told him it was for health and energy. But she chose its ingredients carefully to mask the taste of the water hemlock."

"How horrible," Tyleen said.

Sebastian squeezed his mom's hand. "Did she say why she chose to kill him at the party?"

"I'm not sure she knew, herself," Mallory said. "She rambled about her feelings and her memories for a long time. I tried to bring her back to the question, but she didn't want to go there. It's possible that she's held on to her grief and rage for so long that it's altered her mind. Such things do happen."

"That's awful," I murmured. Once again, I imagined what I would do if someone took my cats from me. *You can bet I wouldn't wait to act, though.*

Ruslan put down his fork with thoughtful slowness. "Unlike water hemlock, grief can be a slow-acting poison."

My mind cleared of its dark ideas with the simple truth of Ruslan's statement. "That's why you write your family into your books."

The octogenarian's smile was gentle. "I've done my grieving. Now, I wish to celebrate their memory."

Inspired, I raised my glass. "To celebrating memory." Everyone joined me, and we had a second toast.

"Sometimes, you just have to let things go and move forward," Lake said. "I just learned that the hard way. Again."

Across from us, Cam raised her glass, saluting Lake. The two of them knew firsthand what chaos the Ivenses could enact. I squeezed his hand and clinked my glass against his. Then a worm of worry started squirming in my tummy, and it had nothing to do with the salmon puffs I'd scarfed. Lake was breaking ties with his family all over again, walking away from those who tried to control him, just as he'd walked away from Mallory when she tried to fit him into a mold.

Water doesn't compress.

Lake is the sea. He cannot be contained. I need to make sure I never try to control him, either, or he'll just leave me too. A beat later, a rock landed in the pool of my lost hopes and sank into the depths—a rock I didn't realize I'd been holding on to until it had left my hand. *I guess marriage is not in my future, then.*

The rock landed in my belly and weighed me down. For a moment, Christmas dinner seemed surreal and distant.

"Did you hear about Naoma trying out headlines for this story, Pippa?" Tyleen's question dragged me back into the bright, cheery present. "She's feeling a little foolish for being friends with a scheming murderer, and she's trying to make up for it with as savage a headline as she can concoct."

"Oh dear. What did she come up with?"

"'Deranged Nursery Owner Cultivates Murder Weapon in Own Backyard.'"

"Wow. Naoma has outdone herself."

Gabe murmured something to Tru, and her face changed. She took a deep breath and tried on a giant, brave smile. Raising her voice, she said, "Guys, I have an announcement. Gabe and I are leaving town next week."

A chorus of shock ringed the table. I hugged myself tightly. When Lake leaned in and asked if I'd known about her news, I merely nodded.

Trudie continued, "We're interim property managers now. See, I had business cards made and everything." She held up a card showing attractive cartoon figures with crossed arms smiling widely in front of a nice big house. "We've got a job down in Crescent City for two weeks. I don't even know how word got around so fast!"

Gabe said, "Well, Lake's uncle stopped to talk to me at the party, and he called me yesterday too. I told him we'd decided to make a change. Then today, boom. Job offer. Your family might be a little crazy, Lake, but your uncle's okay in my book."

Lake grinned. "You could be right."

"And don't worry," Tru said, fixing her eyes on me. "We'll be back in town whenever we can. You guys are family, after all."

"Even me?" Ruslan asked with a chuckle.

Tru got up and hugged him from behind, planting a big kiss on his weathered cheek. "Even you, Ruslan!"

"Well, well." The old fellow dabbed at his eyes with his napkin. "Well, that's all right, then."

After seconds—and in some cases, thirds—I started swapping dishes and platters for dessert pans and trays. Cookies, pies, and puddings flooded the tabletop, including a figgy pudding Ruslan had helped me make. Everyone groaned about where they would find room for such rich desserts.

I grabbed a pfeffernuss and took a big, chewy bite that left powdered sugar on my lips. "Don't worry. We have all day to find room."

The doorbell rang. Curious, I took my cookie to see who it was. Bliss stood on my porch. She looked down at me with a subdued expression. Regret seemed to flicker around her eyes. "Can I see my brother?"

She'd actually asked instead of demanding. "Come in out of the cold. I'll see where he's at." *Mentally if not physically.*

I shunted Bliss into the small parlor then went to tap Lake's shoulder in the dining room. "Bliss is here. She wants to talk to you. Are you up for that right now?"

Lake shoved another bite of apple pie into his mouth and nodded. "I've got enough good vibes to ride on. She probably just wants to say goodbye." He took my hand. "You want to come with?"

I balked. "I... I'm not sure I should."

Lake stopped pulling me after him and looked me in the eye. "I'm sorry. I'm assuming things again. It really upsets me how easily I fell back into my old habits. I feel like a fraud and a liar, and those are two things I don't want to be with you. Can I ask for your help to get me back into shape as the adorable boyfriend you deserve?"

I threw my arms around him. "You can ask. But the answer is already yes."

Lake squeezed me back, and I felt tension draining from his lean body. "Thank you. I don't deserve you."

I pulled back and studied his bright-blue eyes. "I'm sorry you feel that way. But I'm happy to let you start earning me again."

"Ooh. Yes, please." He planted a warm kiss on my lips.

My heart turned into bubbles and floated away. "All right, I give in. I'll go see Bliss with you."

We left the comfortable babble of the dining room behind and slipped into the small parlor. Bliss stood behind one of my green wingback chairs, clutching it with both hands. Her eyes flicked to me and back to Lake. "Hey. I needed to tell you something."

Lake sat in a chair, and I sat next to him. He sat crookedly in his, a cross between the Elvenking Thranduil and Captain Jack Sparrow. *Holy cats, he's even hot when he sits in chairs.*

"I'm all ears," he told her.

Bliss came around her chair and joined us. "I've been thinking about what you've said and what you've done. And what's happened to you." She glanced at me again. "And maybe you're right. Maybe Kait's right. And maybe... Maybe Dad's wrong. I mean, we all know no one's perfect," she added. Her tone sounded rehearsed.

Lake cleared his throat in a disbelieving way.

"No, you're right. It's more than that. I know," Bliss said. "I just don't want to lose Kait. Not like this."

"Like what?" I asked.

Bliss pursed her perfect lips. "She's trying to tell me something that's very important to her. I want to listen. And if I listen, that means certain things will have to change."

"Like what?" Lake echoed my question.

Bliss went so still that she seemed to be trying to mask all kinds of agitation. Then she raised her chin and met her brother's eyes. "I want to buy you your boat. With my own money. I'll put it on my insurance. Dad can't stop me from doing that."

Lake shifted abruptly, leaning forward and clutching the chair arms with his long fingers. "Are you sure?"

Bliss's eyes tightened, and a challenging smile crossed her face.

"You got any rules you want to impose on me along with this generous offer?" he asked.

"You can't name it *Mazu III*," she replied.

"I concur," I blurted. "Listen when the universe is telling you stuff."

Bliss moved her gaze to me. I gave her a shrug that said, *When you're right, you're right.*

Lake shifted uncomfortably, no longer the rebel king slouching on his throne. "I don't know, Bliss. Everything's up in the air right now. I don't want to take advantage of you being upset over Kait."

Though I was almost literally wriggling with excitement over Bliss's generous offer, I could see Lake's point too. *I am Old Gaye, full of personal examples and gifted with good timing.* "Did I ever tell you about how I earned my college tuition?" I asked him. "Well, I say 'earned,' but it was more like I paid it back in a way that had nothing to do with money."

Bliss stared at me as though I'd just proclaimed my love for frogs in clown suits, but Lake knew me well enough to smile patiently and wait for me to make a relevant connection.

I continued, "See, my stepdad gave me a full ride to the college of my choice. He'd done the same for all my stepsiblings, and he figured it was only fair to offer me the same thing. But my mom had raised us to pay back favors, whether directly or indirectly. There was no way I could literally pay him back for four years of college tuition, so I started emailing him stories about my college life.

"My stepdad was a lot older than my mom, and he really enjoyed reading about how college was going for me... even when I lost my car keys in Saguaro National Park, and my friends and I had to hike for hours until we found this abandoned farmhouse with a pantry stocked with the best canned peaches I've ever eaten. I think it helped him feel young again, and it definitely brought us closer. In fact, it's one of the best things about our relationship." *One of the few good things, really.* "So." I gestured to Bliss and Lake. "Maybe Lake can keep you informed on how your boat is doing. He always tells me great stories about tourists and their adventures." Another idea struck, and I turned toward Lake. "And you should name the boat after your sister."

Lake's eyes widened with inspiration.

"You are not calling it *Chambliss*," Bliss warned.

"Oh, no, it's so much worse than that." He chuckled and pointed at her with a grin. "I'm calling it *Burgundy Bliss*."

"Like Geneva Laine's lounge?" I asked, confused.

The Ivens siblings' blue eyes settled on me.

"My first name is Burgundy," Bliss explained in a flat tone that disapproved of her brother's choice.

I wasn't sure why I felt surprise over her name. "Your name is Burgundy Chambliss Ivens? My sympathies."

Bliss's lips twitched, and she couldn't quite stifle a snort of amusement. "Thank you."

"Big-fish stories." Lake reclaimed his sassy-king pose.

"What?" Bliss asked.

"I'll pay for my boat in big-fish stories. You know, stories that exaggerate—"

"I know what big-fish stories are, Captain Ahab."

Bliss shot Lake a smirk, and he pretended to clutch a harpoon embedded in his chest.

"Ooh, sunk!" I teased.

Bliss rested her hands on the arms of her chair. "Listen, I should get back. Kait's waiting for me to talk to Mom." She studied me. "We won't need an arresting officer if no one's pressing charges." She rose.

I stood too. "For what it's worth, I hope you can stay friends with Kait. Is she still planning on leaving?"

Bliss took a deep breath. "Yes. And I'm actually considering..." But she couldn't seem to finish the sentence.

Lake stood as well and gave her a brotherly one-armed hug. "I hope you figure it out."

"Thank you. I'm sorry for everything. You were happy. I hope we haven't ruined that. I hope *I* haven't ruined it."

Lake clasped my hand. Bliss smiled sadly and nodded.

"On your way out, you can apologize for your words regarding my cousin," I remarked mildly.

Bliss hesitated then nodded. "You're right. I'm sorry."

I shook my head and gestured with my thumb toward the dining room. "Not to me. We both know that wasn't the only rude thing you said about her."

Bliss's shoulders slumped, and she rubbed the bridge of her nose. "*God*. Being wrong sucks." But she dutifully hung a left toward the dining room.

The tension in the room left with her, and Lake enveloped me in a giant warm hug. "I'm sorry too. I couldn't see what I was doing to you. I was too distracted. I just wanted to do the right thing, but the right thing has been here all along."

I nuzzled into his chest and tucked my hands into his back pockets. "Open your eyes, then, and see what you're doing to me now." I offered him a smile that was brilliant with forgiveness and love.

A knock on the door interrupted our long, soft kiss. I pulled Lake down by his collar for one final smooch before I answered it.

Hilt nodded toward the front porch. "We got a caroler."

"Oh!" I grabbed Lake's hand and pulled him down the hallway. Everyone else had already gathered in the foyer, and the front door was propped open, letting in the chill. Lake and I slipped in between Cam and Hilt to listen to our annual Christmas guest.

On my porch, Mozzie the sandwich maker stood in a dramatic pose that wouldn't have been out of place on an operatic stage. He was dressed in thick black wool with a brightly patterned fur-trimmed cape and holding a walking cane. A few gray curls escaped his thick deerstalker cap. I couldn't help but applaud, and everyone else joined in. Mozzie gave us a deep bow and launched into his first song, "Gloria in Excelsis Deo."

We were all transported as Mozzie's rich baritone rippled up and down the chorus. Our caroler graced us with four more songs, belting his heart out and making mine soar with joy. I clung to Lake's arm and let Mozzie's voice carry me away.

I insisted that he take a cup of coffee and a slice of pie as payment, and he graciously accepted.

Ruslan insisted on having another piece of pie alongside the singer. "My second cousin was a vocal artist," I heard him say as I carried the rest of the pie back to its place on the kitchen table.

When I stepped back out, Sebastian stood in the hallway, his hands in his pockets. Mallory lurked in the background, staring toward the front door.

Sebastian said, "I have some new friends who need a ride. I wondered, Pippa, if you'd like to join me." Beneath his cinnamon freckles, his face was as sober as I'd ever seen it. My gaze dropped to his right pocket, where three brightly colored leashes peeked out.

When I realized what he was planning, a lump formed in my throat. "I'd be happy to."

Mallory touched Sebastian on the shoulder. "I'll see you there." She strode out, nabbing her coat from the rack.

"You can stay until I get back?" I asked Lake as I followed her lead.

"I'll be here." His voice was low with promise.

"We all will," Cam added.

Sebastian and I stepped into the nippy Christmas weather, but with my heart so warm, I barely felt it.

25

"I like my characters like I like my friends—with a thick skin. They can stand my company, and every now and again, I get a glimpse of their soft side. My soft side? It sticks out over my belt."
Raymond Moore, 1971

SEBASTIAN PARKED IN front of a sprawling pale-yellow house a few miles outside of town. Its landscaping was gorgeous, even in winter, with bright-red leaves and berries adding emphatic punctuation to a spreading evergreen ground cover. We dashed to the front door through a light misting, and Sebastian let himself in with a key.

Three corgis leaped off their doggy couches in the living room and happily barked their way toward us. Sebastian knelt and held out treats for each of the dogs, and they were obviously in love with him, as all pets were. "Hello, Parsnip. Hello, Pacifica, you gorgeous girls," he murmured. "And Legolas, my brave boy. Want to go for a trip with me?"

Fluffy tails wagged, and poofy bottoms wriggled with excitement. While Sebastian leashed the dogs, I found their bowls, food, and some toys in a utility room off the kitchen and tucked them all into a big sack. Sebastian let the dogs lead him around the first floor of the house a few times while I loaded the car with the supplies and added their doggy beds to the back seat. Three eager pooches trailed Sebastian out to the car and hopped into the back, where he secured them safely.

I sat in the passenger seat, hugging a bunny pillow one of the dogs slept with. "This is kind of breaking my heart, Sebastian. It's not their fault their mistress killed someone."

"I know. But it'll be okay. I promise."

He drove us to the police station through an intermittent mist. The world seemed to be holding its breath, cold, moist, and full of trepidation, not daring to breathe until the last part of Wren's fate was resolved.

My heart hung heavily in my chest as we unloaded the dogs onto the old gray sidewalk outside the police station. Mallory opened the door for us herself, and the corgis trotted inside curiously.

"I don't remember ordering a trio of K-9 officers." A little smirk tugged at the corner of her mouth. "Will it make you feel better to hold my gun during this next part?"

Surprised by her concern for my mental state, I begged off. "No, but I'm glad you're here. You won't hesitate to shoot *anything*."

Mallory's gaze fell to the cuteness overload that trotted in happy circles on her floor, smelling desks, trash cans, and hallway corners. "*Almost* anything." She unlocked the metal door and led us back to the cell where Wren sat.

The prisoner rose from her narrow cot at the sight of her dogs and pressed her hands over her face. "I'm so sorry, babies. I'm so sorry. I did it for you, I swear! Please, please forgive me." She knelt at the edge of her cell, and her dogs threw themselves at her hands with eager abandon.

My tummy swirled with a mix of anger, frustration, and sorrow. I leaned against the pale-blue brick wall opposite Wren's cell while Sebastian knelt with the corgis and murmured to Wren.

Mallory joined me. "I suppose I should say I'm glad you're alive, Winterbourne."

"Because you're a cop, and it's your job to protect your citizens?"

She tilted her chin up, and a smile flickered over her face. "Because it's true, and I figured you'd want to know I felt that way."

I didn't know what to say.

"Can you imagine what a mess Lake would be if you died?" she continued blithely. "He'd never get over it, and I don't need that kind of negativity in my life."

That sounded more like the Mallory I knew. "Glad I could oblige, then. Far be it from me to die and help you with your plans to steal my boyfriend."

Mallory patted my shoulder consolingly. "It's so cute when you try to understand me."

"Oh, I'll learn every tooth on every gear that makes you tick. See if I don't." I offered her a smug grin and a chin flick of respect.

"I..." Mallory faltered, uncharacteristically vulnerable for just a second or two. "You're welcome to try, Winterbourne." Her tone sounded strangely like permission.

We would never be BFFs. I still didn't trust her with my boyfriend. But I did trust her with my life. And that counted for a lot. *Maybe I really will try, then.* "What's the word on the Ice Cube Smuggler?"

Mallory gave her head half a shake. "Seems I'm out of neighbors once again. I caught up with Mr. Cool Customer and had a chat about reporting suspicious packages and possible crimes. Next time I saw him, he was frantically shoving an easy chair into the back of his pickup while his wife strapped down their suitcases with a bright-yellow bungee cord. She hurried over to say goodbye. He wouldn't even look at me. She said she knew they should've moved to Walla Walla instead, and maybe he'll see sense from now on. But she didn't hold out much hope."

I suppressed a chuckle. "Well, good luck to them both."

On the floor by the cell, Sebastian said, "I'll keep them until I find a good home that will take all three of them together."

Wren sat back and wiped her tears. "You're too good, Sebastian. After what I put you through, I don't deserve this."

Sebastian's voice was no less gentle than it always was. "I'm not doing it for you."

"I know. Can you make sure they get to Corgi Day in Cannon Beach next summer? It's important to them. They love to go in costume."

"I think we can manage that."

Legolas pressed his head against Wren's arm, comforting her.

Sebastian added, "I'm thinking of training Legolas to be a therapy dog. He's got the temperament for it, and he can help me at work."

Wren nodded tearfully. "That's lovely. I think he'd enjoy that."

Sebastian met her eyes. "We can't change what you've done. But together, I think he and I can start to balance it out."

His soft words seemed to cut deeper than any outrage he might've hurled at her. She slumped in on herself and went quiet. "Thank you, Chief Tavish. I think I'm done here."

Mallory waved us out to the front room again and locked the barred door. Wren didn't look up as we left.

I wasn't sure whose punishment was worse: Mort's death for his attack on Wren's dogs or Wren having to give them up for killing him. "I'll walk home from here, Sebastian. You go ahead with the dogs. Are you really going to keep them until they can be adopted?"

He gathered their leashes, and they gazed up at him expectantly. "Honestly, Pippa, I think I might keep them forever."

Thrilled, I threw my arms around him. The corgis milled excitedly around my ankles. "The world does not deserve you, Sebastian."

"But these dogs do, I think. We can all move forward together. Right, guys?" he asked them. Their fluffy corgi butts waggled madly. "I'll see you around, okay? Thanks, Mallory. Merry Christmas, guys."

I leaned against the door, not quite ready to leave. My heart still ached over Wren's actions and their consequences. "She really did love them so much. This shouldn't have happened."

"We make our own fate, Winterbourne. Some would say that Mort got exactly what he deserved. Maybe for what he did to Wren's dogs. Maybe for what he did to everyone else."

"Mallory, are you *sure* you're not a pfeffernuss?"

The Seacrest police chief leaned against a desk, her uniform impeccable, her arms crossed, and frowned at me. She had let the man she'd wrongfully arrested for murder bring the real killer's dogs in to see her on Christmas Day. "I'm not made of gingerbread, Winterbourne."

"Yes, you are. Your crusty exterior hides the fact that deep down, you're just warm and sweet. Really, *really* deep down."

Mallory stared at me. I didn't budge.

Then she softened, relaxing, as if tired of being crusty. "Merry Christmas, Pippa."

She used my first name! My heart nearly burst. "Merry Christmas, Mallory."

26

"There are more secrets in my novels than you'll ever know. But some secrets are so sacred they're a privilege to take to the grave."

Raymond Moore, 1958

TWO DAYS AFTER CHRISTMAS, Ruslan finished his manuscript and packed for his return trip to Boston. We threw him a goodbye-breakfast bash, and I packed him a tin of pfeffernuesse for the trip home.

"I'll see you again next year," I murmured as I hugged him farewell.

"I look forward to it already."

That afternoon, Lake's uncle Odie brought Sadie back to Moorehaven in perfect condition. As Hilt prowled around under her hood, Odie told me, "I also got your girl here a free yearly maintenance checkup from my Oregon guy." He handed me a business card. "Dale does house calls."

"Thank you so much. It's great knowing that you love Sadie as much as we do."

Odie rocked onto his toes then settled back on his heels. "I know I can't make up for certain things you've had to deal with..."

I offered him my best smile, canny and sharp. "You can't. But I'm not asking you to."

I offered my hand, and instead of shaking it, he pressed a quick, dry kiss to my knuckles.

"Lake is a lucky man. Luckier, perhaps, than all of us. I wish you well."

Odie's blue eyes shone with sincerity, and I flushed, caught off guard.

He left Seacrest with his family half an hour later. They didn't say goodbye to anyone, not even Lake.

Cam checked out of Seven Vistas that same morning and came to say goodbye. After exchanging tight hugs with Hilt and me, she pressed a page of Seven Vistas stationery into my hand. "My grandma's bánh mì recipe and my favorite pho too. That's how you bond here at Moorehaven, isn't it? With food?"

I squeezed her again. "It sure is. When will we see you again?"

Cam's eyes twinkled with mischief, just like her grandfather's. "Oh, I have some prospects in Portland. You might see me in just a couple of months."

"We'd better." Hilt's voice was gruff with emotion. "Text me with updates, all right?"

"Yes, *ông nội.*"

He smiled. "That's my girl."

We waved goodbye from the corner until Cam drove out of sight.

The chill winter wind brought more leave-takings the next day, when my sister and Gabe loaded up their Airstream and piled into his old gray truck, headed for their next great adventure.

The end of the year seemed to weigh too heavily on me with fewer pillars to share the load, and I clung to my sister and cried. "Do you have to go, Spunky Spork?" I murmured into her hair.

"Yes, Goofy Noodle." Her hug nearly squeezed me in two. "But don't worry. I'm starting a whole new Instagram to record our adventures. I'll be almost as obnoxious as in real life."

I giggled, took out my phone, and became her new Insta's first follower.

The last few days of the year passed in relative quiet. With Sebastian home safely, all charges dropped, Tyleen finally made the finishing touches on her murder-mystery game and submitted it to a game company the Moorehaven Trust had been in touch with. Then she teamed up with Emily, and together, they cooked and baked enough food to feed us all through the new year. My fridge was bursting with leftovers, and my cats haunted the kitchen, guarding it.

Lake spent much of his free time at Moorehaven, helping Hilt with the odd repair and lending his height to dusting and repair projects. As the days passed, he melted back into his old self, and his self-deprecating half smile reappeared. My boyfriend was back. I didn't think twice about catching him up on all the Aunt Felicity drama that had gone on—he was family too.

The phone rang late in the afternoon of the thirty-first. Lake and I were still straightening the dining room chairs after an early supper of herbed rolls and chowder. Chloe passed the phone to Hilt, who listened briefly then yelled loudly enough to bring the house down around us.

"Cam did it! The order's come through! Get to the graveyard!"

Lake, Chloe, and I piled into Sadie while Hilt slid into the driver's seat, and we drove through a blustery wind to the site of Seacrest's original graveyard, beside its oldest church, Seacrest Methodist. The exhumation crew was already there, wearing jeans and flannel shirts, carefully excavating the rich, dark soil of Felicity's grave.

"That looks so weird," Lake commented as we all walked closer across the damp, uneven grass. "Like a reverse funeral."

Hilt had a few words with the man in charge then rejoined us. "Won't be long. Brace yourselves, kids. This is as literal as digging up the truth gets."

"What was it Felicity said again? 'I'll take their secrets to my grave'?" Lake asked.

"They must've been some pretty powerful secrets," Chloe commented.

"Hilt?" I gripped my phone tightly. "We should tell Naoma. She's the one who got this whole thing started."

I could practically read Hilt's objections as they scrolled through his mind, but eventually he nodded. "It's only fair. And I suppose if what we find is just too terrible to print, we can stuff her into the casket and bury it again."

Already texting Naoma, I glanced up. "You think that's funny, but all you're really asking is for Glaze & Gossip to hunt you down. You know that, right?"

"'Spose I do."

Naoma arrived twenty minutes later, just in time to snap a few shots in the orange light of sunset as the crew excavated the casket from its soil mausoleum. She stood by me in a cream-colored duster that flapped in the strong breeze, a notepad in her hands, and her camera around her neck. "This is big," she murmured.

"Not so big that we can't handle it together," I said.

The workmen wrestled the muddy casket onto a plywood board, and the foreman waved us over. With my heart in my stomach, I clutched Lake's hand. He tightened his arm around my shoulders.

We followed Hilt to the casket, and the foreman offered him a crowbar. He took it but hesitated, his knuckles white.

I stepped forward and put a hand on his forearm. "It's okay, Hilt. We're all doing this together. She led us here, remember?"

He nodded and straightened his shoulders. Fitting the crowbar into the tight seam along the casket lid, he said, "Beggin' your pardon, ma'am," and threw his weight against the tool.

The lid released its tight seal with a creaky pop, and he eased the crowbar along the gap, widening it evenly. I stood by one end, my fingers gripping the muddy wood, waiting until he reached the far end.

Hilt took hold of the other end of the casket lid, and we raised it together. A gust of wind howled through the graveyard trees. A shiver rippled up my spine. All of us, even the exhumation crew, leaned forward to see what lay within.

The casket was empty.

Well, not *completely* empty.

But Aunt Felicity was most assuredly not at home.

"Where is she?" Chloe blurted. She shined the flashlight from her phone around the inside of the casket.

A dozen beautifully decorated jewelry boxes of various sizes sat atop a series of flat lead weights. Dozens of slender journals rested in a wooden box, their spines up. An envelope had been pinned to the shirred satin that decorated the underside of the lid.

Nothing else lay inside. I kept blinking, thinking I'd missed something really obvious—*like an entire body, maybe?*—but no matter how many times I looked, Aunt Felicity's body continued not to be inside its casket.

Hilt began to chuckle.

"This what you were expecting to find?" The foreman scratched his head.

"Not exactly," Lake replied.

I reached for one of the jewelry boxes, a lovely black lacquered one with Asian designs, and gingerly lifted it. Soft shifting noises came from inside. "It's not empty."

Chloe opened the top drawer, and we peered inside. Even in the dying light of the last day of the year, the jewels winked brilliantly. Chloe and I stared wide-eyed at each other then checked the rest of the drawers. Each one contained gem-laden jewelry.

Naoma started snapping pictures over my shoulder. Hilt and Lake began checking the other boxes, where they found more of the same as well as plenty of old American currency. The slender journals were full of personal stories written by the women who had stayed at Moorehaven before moving on to new lives.

But the envelope was calling my name. The diamond tie pin holding it in place seemed vaguely familiar. I unpinned it carefully and slid a folded message out then tilted the crisp page toward the light to read Felicity's curling words.

> *Well done, Raymond. You've come this far, and I expected no less. Here, you see the scattered remains of my wading through the world—my father's money, my ladies' gifts, my own stolen cash. I never could mince like a proper lady. I strode like a man. I made a mess like a man. But I will not brag like one. I will take my leave on my own terms. And you will let me. Because you, Raymond, are a man, and a good one at that. I have taken pains to raise you as such, and I expect my lessons to stick.*
>
> *Do what you will with these footprints of mine. I don't need any of them anymore.*
>
> *I look forward to spotting your upcoming books in bookstore windows soon. Don't you dare kill off Hilton Gray. He's my favorite.*
>
> *With all the love I ever had for you, I remain*
>
> *Your dear aunt Felicity Moore*

With tears in my eyes, I read the entire note two more times. I hadn't thought it possible that the legend of Felicity Moore could grow any larger than life, but it just had.

I handed the letter to Hilt, who read it. He hugged me tightly, and I hugged him back.

"What does this mean for us?" I asked. "For Moorehaven, for Seacrest?"

"It means," Naoma said, "that you're in the clear. Moorehaven's star is rising. And I've got a killer article to write! Oh, I need a really good headline, because this is going to go national."

My knees went weak with relief, and I sat heavily on the windswept grass. Lake crouched by my side.

"Look at this woman," I said. "She was willing to risk tarnishing her reputation to protect all these other women. She didn't need their jewelry. Or her own. She didn't need anything. But she never told a soul, not even to protect herself. She let people think she was a grifter rather than exposing vulnerable women to the public eye. I can't imagine how hard that was, being the only person with a secret that large. She didn't tell anyone, not even Moore himself."

Lake sat behind me in the grass and snaked his arms around me for a warm hug. "She told the women she helped. And at least one of them stayed and helped her. That librarian, Abigail Travers. She protected Felicity because she understood exactly what Felicity was doing. Felicity wasn't alone. She had all the allies she needed."

Hilt sank to his knees, bracing a hand on the edge of the casket. His face carried intense joy and relief, and he started to laugh all over again. "I can't believe I gave up swearing for fear of angering this woman's ghost," he said through his laughter. "She's more of a badass than I ever was, and I went to war!" Gales of laughter consumed him, and he doubled over, holding his stomach.

"We should get these things out of the weather," Naoma cautioned. "It's looking like rain."

The western horizon was swiftly darkening, and charcoal clouds ate the remnants of golden light that streamed across the gray-green sea. Chloe reluctantly put back the journal she was reading, and Lake picked up the small wooden box that held them.

As we loaded Sadie's trunk with our unexpected treasure, Chloe commented, "The lady whose story I was reading talked about traveling all the way from Phoenix to get to safety. It's like Felicity was part of, you know, a petticoat railroad or something."

Naoma froze in the act of putting one of the jewelry boxes into Sadie's trunk. A glorious smile overtook her lips. "God bless you, Chloe. There's my headline."

We got everything inside Moorehaven as the sun dipped below the horizon, just before the rain broke. Chloe and Naoma threw themselves into reading the stack of journals, but I had a different mission. I racked my brain for clues about that tie pin in the casket.

I dashed up to the Raymond Moore Gallery on the third floor and unlocked the room where the extra documents and photos were stored when not on display. I rummaged through an album of publicity photos, muttering. Then at long last, I found what I wanted. "Gotcha."

I hefted the album and took the stairs two at a time, all the way back down to the library. Dashing in, I set the photo album in the middle of the table, where everyone sat surrounded by old journals and dazzling antique jewelry. Pausing at the dramatic sight, I said, "We should decorate like this more often. But, guys, look. Look!"

Hilt leaned over and studied the photo where my index finger rested. "Ray at the book signing for *Diamond Charm*."

"Yep. Now look at these." I flipped back to publicity photos for his previous book releases. "Notice anything different?" During the pause in which no one answered, I flipped back and forth between two photos: Moore's *Diamond Charm* signing and the signing he'd done for the previous novel. "Look closely."

Lake stabbed his finger at the picture. "The tie pin. All these signings, he's wearing that diamond tie pin. Then for *Diamond Charm*, he's not."

I looked around the table. "For the book he based on Felicity's life, for the book he named after her, he *doesn't* wear the tie pin that so closely fits with the theme?"

Hilt's expression cleared. "You're saying..."

"I'm saying Moore wasn't wearing his diamond release-day tie pin because he'd already tucked it into Felicity's coffin." I pulled the tie pin from my pocket and set it atop the photo. It was a perfect match. "He did find the clues Felicity left for him. In her letter, she told him to do with this treasure whatever he wanted. And he did: he did nothing at all. He kept her secrets, like she had."

"He learned she was out in the world, and he let her walk away?" Lake asked.

"It's what she wanted," Hilt said. "He respected her too much to search for her, no matter how much it hurt to let her go."

We all sat silently, absorbing that latest bombshell.

"How can you live, knowing someone you love is out there somewhere and not want to be with them?" Lake asked.

Chloe's face transformed into a wise smile older than she was. "Sometimes, just knowing that someone you love exists and that they know and love you is enough. Sometimes, the line that binds you to them knows no limit in time or in space. Right, Hilt?"

Hilt squeezed her hand.

Chloe's complex relationship with her parents brought tears to my eyes.

Beside me, Lake nodded slowly. He took my face in his hands and pressed his forehead to mine. "I love you, Pippa. You are my safe harbor, and I'll always find my way to you."

I placed my hands over his then kissed his fingertips. Lake's words addressed my unspoken fears. "Good, because I wasn't planning on going anywhere." With the lifting of my worry, which had enveloped me like an endless fog, I caught sight of a good deed glimmering in the distance, just waiting to be performed. "So if I find my way to Jordan's house for New Year's Eve to surprise her so she's not alone, you'll...?"

"Carry the champagne?" he finished.

I gave him a firm, quick kiss. "I knew there was a reason I liked you. Come on, everybody! Grab something to eat or drink, and let's crash Jordan's house!"

"Ooh, I'm down." Chloe jogged toward the kitchen, presumably to raid my fridge for goodies.

Hilt gave me an assessing look and an approving smile. "I'm also what the cool kids call 'down.' And no offense, but I'll drive Sadie this time."

I laughed and pulled Lake up beside me. "Deal."

We all piled into Sadie, and Naoma and I texted the rest of Glaze & Gossip during the few-block drive to Jordan's house. I dashed through the rain with the others close behind me then stood on my best friend's old concrete doorstep and rang her bell incessantly until she answered.

She pulled open the door and stood there staring at me, her vivid red hair in a simple ponytail and the rest of her clad in a stretchy Wonder Woman shirt and yoga pants. Her eyes fell to the giant tin of popcorn in my arms. A moment of surprise stretched out in the early-evening drizzle. "One of the flavors in your tin had better be caramel," she said.

I *tsk*ed through a smile. "Girl."

She sighed dramatically, though her eyes were dancing. "You all get in here before you get soaked. And I'm not changing out of my comfy clothes just because you got lost on the way to some cool party."

As she stepped back and let us dash out of the rain, Chloe said, "Oh, no, we brought the cool party with us."

Jordan closed the door behind Hilt, who was the last to enter, and let out a string of tinkling-bell laughter. "Well, then, I'm *definitely* not changing."

I headed through Jordan's front room and took a left into her alleyway kitchen. As I set the popcorn tin on her gray-speckled countertop, I spotted a pint of Ben & Jerry's on the counter, its lid still in place and a giant spoon resting beside it.

"You're not gonna let me eat my loneliness tonight, huh?" Jordan murmured. She'd followed me into the kitchen, probably in hopes of hiding her ice cream in the freezer before I saw it.

I handed it to her. "Oh, you won't have any loneliness tonight. If you have room after all the food we brought, have some ice cream. But you'll definitely be too full for loneliness."

Jordan tossed the ice cream back into her freezer and eyed me speculatively. "It's unnerving how well you know me."

"Don't worry. I only use my powers for good. Now, grab a bowl that I can overfill with caramel corn."

As I filled Jordan's bright-blue porcelain bowl with popcorn, her doorbell chimed again. Naoma answered it and let in half of Glaze & Gossip. They were bearing everything from candy-sprinkled caramel apples to individual champagne bottles.

Jordan held her popcorn bowl absentmindedly and stared into her rapidly filling front room. "What did you do?" she asked breathily.

I gave her a fierce hug and planted a loud smack on her cheek. "Used my powers. We're gonna party this whole year away then ring in the next one, and you will never forget it."

Jordan grabbed another blue bowl, spooned out some popcorn from the kettle-corn section, and handed it to me. Then she raised hers for a toast.

I clinked my bowl against hers. "Cheers, Jordan. Happy New Year's Eve."

The doorbell rang again, and I heard Jordan's parents talking loudly outside the door with Tyleen and Sebastian, who all poured into the room, followed by Mozzie. The sandwich maker's gray curls were spangled with raindrops, and he carried a huge wicker basket covered with heavy cloth napkins.

"I brought sandwiches! Who's hungry?" he announced in his booming Italian voice.

"I wonder if he brought anything with smoked Gouda in it," Jordan said. "I suddenly have a hankering." She stuffed her mouth with caramel popcorn and gave me a giant popcorny grin on her way to see Mozzie's sandwich selection.

Over the next half hour, Jordan's house was filled to bursting with what seemed like half the residents of Seacrest. Someone began streaming upbeat music over Jordan's Bluetooth speakers. Food rested on nearly every surface, including the bookshelves. My friend stood in the middle of a packed front room and laughed with a cluster of a dozen friends, her bright hair shimmering.

Lake pulled me close. "You're amazing. Look what you did for her. For all of us."

I leaned against the firm warmth of his chest. "She deserves it. We all do. The year may be dying, but life goes on. And so do we."

Lake's warm arms snaked around my waist, and he kissed my hair. For a minute, we stood in silent unity as the party swirled around Jordan—eating, singing off-key, laughing uproariously.

"Do you think we'll ever learn what really happened to Aunt Felicity?" he murmured.

I took a deep breath. A smile tugged at my lips, and I imagined Felicity striding through the world, bending its chaos to her will, challenging those around her to be better, stronger, and cleverer, and leaving everything—everyone—better than she found them. I felt her eyes on me across the decades, challenging me to do the same, to be worthy of Moorehaven's legacy. "I hope not. She's not the kind of person who lets herself be limited by facts. Felicity Moore is a legend."

Acknowledgments

My effusive thanks to Becca, Dilsey, Bob, and Karen for pointing out all the ways in which my third draft stank. I'd like to thank Linda Ivy and my mom, Jeanie Reed, for their patience and/or enthusiasm as they accompanied me on a research trip. Thanks to everyone at the Gilbert Inn in Seaside, Oregon, for their accommodations, delicious food, and expertise. Thanks to Dr. Justin Olswanger for sharing his medical knowledge. Lastly but definitely not least, my eternal gratitude to my editing team at Red Adept Publishing for making my story as presentable as possible. As usual, any mistakes are mine.

Sweet and Spicy Gingerbread Pancakes

Pancakes
2 cups flour
3 tablespoons brown sugar
1 ½ teaspoons baking powder
½ teaspoon baking soda
½ teaspoon salt
1 teaspoon ground ginger
2 teaspoons ground cinnamon
½ teaspoon ground cloves
½ teaspoon ground nutmeg
1 cup buttermilk
2 eggs
2 tablespoons molasses
1 teaspoon vanilla extract
¾ cup water

Syrup
2 cups maple syrup
1 teaspoon cinnamon
¼ teaspoon nutmeg
optional: powdered sugar for sprinkling

Directions
Heat griddle to medium-high or 350 degrees.

Whisk the flour, baking powder, baking soda, salt, ginger, cinnamon, cloves, and nutmeg in a bowl; set aside. Beat the egg in a separate mixing bowl with the vanilla and molasses until smooth. Whisk in the water until completely incorporated. Stir the flour mixture into the molasses mixture until just combined.

Drop batter by large spoonfuls onto the griddle, and cook until bubbles form and the edges are dry. Flip, and cook until browned on the other side. Repeat with remaining batter. Serve hot and drizzle generously with cinnamon-nutmeg syrup. Sprinkle with powdered sugar if desired.

Light & Sweet Hazelnut Applesauce Gingerbread Loaf

L<u>oaf</u>

1 ½ cups all-purpose flour, sifted

1 teaspoon baking soda

1 teaspoon salt

2 teaspoons cinnamon

1 ½ teaspoons ginger

½ teaspoon cloves

¼ teaspoon nutmeg

1/8 teaspoon white pepper

¾ cup sugar

½ cup butter (1 stick), softened

1 cup unsweetened applesauce

1 teaspoon vanilla extract

1 large egg

<u>Icing</u>

1 ¼ cups powdered sugar, sifted

1 tablespoon hazelnut coffee creamer

<u>Directions</u>

Preheat the oven to 350 degrees. Grease and flour a 9x5 loaf pan.

In a large mixing bowl, combine the flour, baking soda, cinnamon, ginger, cloves, nutmeg, white pepper, and salt.

In a separate bowl, cream together the sugar and butter. Add the applesauce and vanilla and stir. Add the egg and mix well.

Pour flour mixture atop the sugar mixture, stirring just until blended.

Spoon the batter into 9x5 pan and bake at 350 degrees for 45-55 minutes.

Allow cake to cool in pan for 10 minutes, then turn out onto cooling rack to finish cooling.

In small bowl, whisk together powdered sugar and creamer. Drizzle over cooled loaf.

<u>Notes</u>

To make gingerbread muffins, divide batter equally among 12 prepared muffin cups. Bake for 20-22 minutes. Cool before drizzling with icing.

Dark & Spicy Gingerbread Loaf

L oaf
2 cups all-purpose flour, sifted

1 teaspoon baking soda

¾ cup sugar

½ teaspoon salt

2 teaspoons cinnamon

2 teaspoons ginger

½ teaspoon cloves

¼ teaspoon nutmeg

1/8 teaspoon white pepper

2 eggs

½ cup butter (1 stick), softened

1 teaspoon vanilla extract

1/3 cup molasses

1 cup buttermilk

Frosting

4 oz cream cheese, room temperature

1 teaspoon vanilla extract

1 teaspoon orange-flavored white balsamic vinegar

2 tablespoons milk

2 cups powdered sugar, sifted

Directions

Preheat the oven to 350 degrees. Grease and flour a 9x5 loaf pan.

In a large mixing bowl, combine the flour, baking soda, cinnamon, ginger, cloves, nutmeg, white pepper, and salt.

In another bowl, cream together the sugar and butter. Add the molasses and vanilla and mix well. Add the eggs and combine thoroughly.

Add the buttermilk and the sugar mixture to the flour mixture and mix until just blended.

Spoon the batter into your 9x5 inch loaf pan and bake at 350 degrees for 40-50 minutes.

Allow cake to cool in pan for 10 minutes, then turn out onto cooling rack to finish cooling.

In a medium bowl, beat together vanilla, orange vinegar, and milk until creamy. Add cream cheese and mix well. Add powdered sugar and blend until smooth and creamy. Spread over cooled gingerbread loaf.

<u>Notes</u>

To make gingerbread muffins, divide batter equally among 12 prepared muffin cups. Bake for 18-20 minutes. Cool before frosting.

Mutti's Pfeffernuesse

5 cups flour
   1 cup corn syrup
1 cup molasses
½ cup shortening
½ cup brown sugar, packed
1 teaspoon baking soda
1 teaspoon cinnamon
½ teaspoon ground cloves
Powdered sugar for sprinkling

<u>Directions</u>

Preheat oven to 325 degrees.

In a large bowl, mix all ingredients thoroughly. Dough will be stiff. (If you're using a handheld mixer, you might need to two-hand it.)

Form balls with teaspoons (the spoon, not the measure) full of dough. Place balls on baking sheet an inch and a half apart. Flatten tops just a little with a flat surface, to create pretty cracks around the edges of the baked cookies. Bake 13-14 minutes. Do not over-bake. Sprinkle with powdered sugar while just warm. Cool on cooling rack.

Makes several dozen cookies!

<u>Notes</u>

Dough may be chilled for easier ball formation.

These cookies are small but dense and chewy. They're great for snacking on while watching movies or playing games.

This is my German great-grandmother's cookie recipe. She immigrated to America in 1900. They're a sweet and spicy part of my childhood Christmases, and now I'm sharing them with you! Enjoy!

About the Author

USA Today Bestselling Author Morgan Talbot is an outdoorsy girl with a deep and abiding love for the natural sciences. Her degrees involve English and jujitsu. She enjoys hiking, camping, and wandering in the woods looking for the trail to the car, but there isn't enough chocolate on the planet to bribe her into rock climbing.

When she's not writing, she can be found making puzzles, getting lost on the way to geocaches, reading stories to her children, or taking far too many pictures of the same tree or rock.

Morgan is a member of Sisters in Crime and Mystery Writers of America and served as a panelist at Left Coast Crime 2015: Crimelandia. She lives in Eastern Washington with her family.

About the Publisher

Dear Reader,

We hope you enjoyed this book. Please consider leaving a review on your favorite book site.

Visit https://RedAdeptPublishing.com to see our entire catalogue.

Check out our app for short stories, articles, and interviews. You'll also be notified of future releases and special sales.